THE STRIX

The Strix

Katalina Leon

Author's note: This is the second edition of *The Strix*. This book was originally published with Loose Id Publishing in 2012. The current version has been revised, re-edited, and expanded by over 37K of new material.

Copyright November 2012, May 2016.
ISBN: 978-0-9981620-3-4
Cover design: Andy Atkins
Supervising editor: Becky Johnson, Hot Tree Editing
Content editor: Liv Ventura, Hot Tree Editing
Proofreader: Kristin Scearce, Hot Tree Editing
Critique and additional edits, Chelle Olson, Literally Addicted to Detail

RED JAGUAR

The Strix
Katalina Leon

"Welcome to Villa Lupus Unguis, the house of the wolf fang."
While getting her fortune told in a Wiccan shop in Salem,
Massachusetts, Arcona's reality has a screaming meltdown.
She discovers she'd been a bad girl in a past life and now her
long-ago deeds as a vengeful Celtic witch have come back to
bite her.

In a parallel realm, Arcona is flung headfirst into blood rites
on a sacred island, captured by Romans, and sold in the
markets of Pompeii as a pleasure slave to the sadistic owner of
a gladiatorial school. Seeking revenge against Rome, Arcona
lures a lonely Dacian gladiator into her bed and uses dark
magic to turn him into an immortal blood-craving "Slayer," a
warlike vampire to be set loose on the Empire.

Two millennia and an exploding Mount Vesuvius later, Tyr is
still pissed off about being forced to spend eternity as a
Vampiric mercenary. Desperate to break the Slayer curse, he
kidnaps Arcona, intent on learning the secrets carried in her
blood. But they're in for a surprise. Once these two damaged
souls share their stories, the possibility of redemption — even
love — is offered. When another Slayer tries to claim Arcona as
his blood slave, Tyr has to be her hero one last time.

This is an epic tale of witchcraft, vampires, reincarnation, and
a healing act of love. The story plays out in the past and the
present.

*Note to my readers: The Strix is not a straightforward romance. It's
dark paranormal with romantic elements.*
*The heroine's personality exists on two time frames. She is virtually
two different women, sharing the same experiences and evolving
from them.*

This story contains Upir Likhyi or warrior vampires, graphic violence and sex scenes, blood sports in the arena, and past-life mayhem messing up the present.

Table of Contents

Dedication

I dedicate *The Strix* to my dear friend Arcona, who taught me so many great things in life, and even after her death visited me with the germ of this story. Thank you, my friend, for holding the door between worlds open just a crack.

Prologue
Germania, the land of the Teutoni. 78 AD

The sacred island of trials sat in the center of a bowed river. A tumult of white water powered downstream and made crossing precarious. Isolated from the everyday comforts of village life, the setting was stark and lonely, as it was meant to be.

Arcona shivered in front of the failing campfire. An icy northern breeze combined with damp clothing made this a rotten day on which to plead favors from the gods. Most of the meager supply of firewood she'd brought to the island had long burned to ash, and the slender green branches she'd scrounged from the wet undergrowth refused to ignite past a smolder.

Chilled to the bone, she drew her knees to her chest, teeth chattering, and clutched the deerskin shawl closer. The spring snowmelt left the dense forest of the island soggy and surrounded by rushing water painful to bathe in, yet she'd already braved the frigid river twice to perform the ritual cleansing of her body and soul.

The wind punished her failing campfire. Ash gusted into the air and stung her sleep-deprived eyes. She turned away, drawing the shawl over her head. This was the third day of fasting, intense prayer, and focused intent. Allowing herself only water, she chanted until her ears no longer heard the sacred words, all in the hope that the goddess Nerthus would grant a seers' vision of days to come.

All rituals had been performed with exacting precision, yet her doubts lingered. No matter how sincere her appeal, a vision from Nerthus might be denied. It often happened. Many initiates returned from a quest discouraged and empty-handed.

The mother goddess chose only a select few to take into her confidence to whisper or shout her inscrutable secrets. Arcona's teachers had impressed an ominous warning that a vision from the goddess always came with oppressive responsibilities.

Blue wisps of smoke snaked above the fire, looking to her tired eyes like a pair of feathery wings. She stared in fascination as the apparition of an eagle in flight took shape and dissipated.

Three anxious days had passed, and the ephemeral silhouette of the raptor was the most interesting thing she had witnessed. Worry mounted. Perhaps she wasn't ready, worthy, or as adept in the ways of a priestess as she'd believed?

Few were. The station demanded ruthless resolve. Sacrifice was required; as a seer, there would be no marriage or family for her. Even if the handsome young warrior, Hedron, insisted on it, he would be denied. Personal feelings would not be accommodated.

A priestess served her people in chastity. But could she bear to watch others marry and rear beautiful children who looked like miniatures of themselves? She knew it would be difficult to stand apart while her peers shared their lives with lovers and made emotional connections she'd never have.

Serving as a priestess of Nerthus had some consolations. In a very real sense, the tribe's children would be her children, too. She'd help bring them into the world, bless and teach them, soothe their fevers. But she'd not birth them, and she'd never have the pleasure of lying beneath a man's strong body and feeling his warm weight pressing down on her, though she thought about it constantly.

These were disturbing times. Her plans were austere but necessary. The Teutoni were under assault. As a child, she'd lost both parents to a forest raid led by Romans. In pity, a priestess had adopted her. Without reservation, she'd embraced her training to become a wise woman. For years, the path had been clearly marked. This journey alone on the island of trial signaled the first profound fork in the road. What happened today would shape her future, and only the goddess had the final say in its outcome.

While staring at the struggling fire, the same question rose again and again: Was donning the amber amulet of a priestess and taking vows the absolute right thing to do? Could she serve her people well, or would she perish a bitter old fool without ever accomplishing all she sensed she was capable of? These days, harnessing the powers of the gods was all-important. A great danger to the Teutoni had arrived, one far more serious than the bleakest winter. The Romans had built yet another fort in a neighboring tribe's heartland. It would not be long before their heavily armored expeditions marched north. Every day, the melting snow drew the threat nearer. Her earliest training as a priestess had been focused on the healing arts and common perils of toothaches, wounds, and difficulties in childbirth, which were always present. She'd studied and used every medicinal root and herb in the river valley and knew its proper dose and preparation. Through several years of consistent practice, she'd become a trusted keeper of the tribe's secrets and could produce all basic brews and decoctions with predictable results.

With discerning eyes, she studied the night sky and knew how to track the seasons with accuracy. She'd mastered the first level of mystery teachings and could recite with ease the many incantations and enchantments of the gods and goddesses of the woodlands. She was ready to conquer more complicated spellcraft.

To make her training complete, she'd gone above and beyond all the other initiates in the valley by adeptly learning a little of the Roman tongue from an old man who had once acted as a scout to the Roman legions.

Speaking the tongue of the enemy was an unsavory but necessary burden. If the Romans marched onto Teutoni land, which they eventually would, she could step forward and negotiate for her people.

Her greatest hope was that a peaceful compromise could be reached with the legions. The Teutoni clung to the possibility that the Romans might pass through the valley looking for whatever they sought, not find it, and leave. There seemed to be little there the Romans would desire.

A whispered rumor was that deep snow and dense woods terrified the Romans, who marched ten men abreast and needed the intense heat of the sun to warm their shields and power their might. The cold northern woodlands were no place for such men.

Arcona leaned toward the fire, blew on it, and stirred the thick layer of gray ash with a knife blade. She gazed at the orange embers crackling with energy. After much effort, several branches lit and offered a little heat.

Could she become the leader she longed to be? Did she deserve to wield divine power?

Her thoughts wandered back to a vivid dream she'd had as a newly orphaned child. Within a nightmarish hailstorm of fire and ash, the gods of war had handed her a thunderbolt drenched in blood and asked her to ignite the world.

Of course, the bombastic dream had frightened her, but she often reflected on its possible meaning. Was she special in the eyes of the gods? Had she been marked as one of their own? If so, did that mean her life had a deeper purpose? She applied intense focus to every new skill she mastered, all to become a better instrument of the gods.

She shook those thoughts from her mind. Such assumptions were not becoming of a humble initiate hoping to pass her first great test in the realm of higher mystery with grace. If the gods wanted her service, she could not demand they accept her. They would have to step forward of their own volition and show her the way.

Lifting a wooden bowl to her lips, she sipped cold water. Her empty stomach cramped. The memory of her last meal made her heart ache with a sharper sort of pain.

It all came rushing back. Hedron had surprised her near her cottage. He didn't dare approach the tiny initiate's hut she'd been assigned to by the high priestess. To do so was strictly forbidden. Instead, he loitered nearby until she noticed him standing beside a tree.

A single glowing sunbeam filtered through the dense foliage above and bathed him in a circle of golden light.

Unintentional on Hedron's part, the effect was breathtaking. He wore a hunter's simple leggings and leather tunic, but he looked as beautiful as any god with his blond hair brushed away from his face. Even the downy hairs on his jaw and forearms glowed golden in the sunlight.

Once he was certain he had her attention, his warm gaze locked on her. "Come here." His voice was low. "I have something for you."

Her initiation on Nerthus's island was only hours away. After years of study and preparation, at sunset she would be rowed across the river and left to the will of the goddess. She knew this was not the time to provoke the ire or doubts of the high priestess with flirting.

She looked at Hedron and shook her head in silence, hoping he'd take the hint and leave.

"Please." Hedron coaxed her near. He reached into a hunter's sack and withdrew a succulent roasted rabbit with crispy brown skin. "I hunted and cooked this for you." He offered it with pride shimmering in his gray eyes. "I know the next few days will be hungry ones. Eat it before your fast begins."

Her mouth watered at the sight of the delicious roasted meat. Hedron often did kind things for her. It broke her heart that fate pushed her to choose against him. The inner calling to be a priestess was strong as iron, so why did the gods continue to torment her with temptation? It wasn't fair.

"What's wrong? You look worried." Hedron leaned closer and brushed his lips against the crown of her head. "You'll get the answers you need on the island. Don't you believe the goddess knows what's best for us?"

He reached for Arcona with his free hand, brought her hand to his chest, and held it over his heart. "I couldn't ask until now, but you know how I feel." He tensed. "I'll be twenty-one this summer and old enough to claim my own parcel of hunting land. I can have a home and—"

"Shush." Arcona held a finger to his lips. "I'm going to the island, and I'm going to pray for a vision. Beyond that, I have no future except the one the goddess guides me toward."

Hurt burned in Hedron's eyes. "Can I at least send you to your fate with a full stomach?" With a worried smile, he handed Arcona the rabbit. "Remember, I can take care of you, and I want to."

"We shouldn't be talking. They'll come for me soon." Her voice cracked. "You'd better leave."

"Arcona, I won't give up. You were meant to be with me. I'll be waiting on the riverbank when you return." Pivoting on his heel, he walked into the shadowy woods and disappeared from view.

For far too long, she remained frozen with the rabbit dangling from her hand. The smallest movements, even blinking or swallowing, hurt, and her eyes stung from holding back unshed tears. Watching Hedron walk away was more painful than she dare admit. Staring in the direction he had gone, she waited for something decisive to happen, anything, but couldn't say what she expected or hoped for. She sensed they'd never be lovers, not even illicit ones. She gazed at the rabbit; the cooking fire had charred its delicate feet to the bone. Like the rabbit, she too would never run free again.

A burning branch in the campfire made a loud pop and spit a burst of red sparks high into the air. The green branches had finally dried and lit. The flames came to life and were now so hot Arcona moved back. The dusk sky was a cold shade of violet. Night would bring a fine layer of frost to anything damp. She banked the fire with new green branches to dry them and keep the fire burning through the night.

Hunger became a constant. She remembered every juicy bite of Hedron's perfectly cooked rabbit and her empty stomach growled. With the heel of her palm, she rubbed her eyes. No grand vision had come, not even a hint of one.

Was no answer an answer?

Perhaps silence was the goddess's way of saying that she should go to Hedron's bed and be his woman? Could it be that simple? Could she have been so wrong in wanting to be shown a path to greater power?

Exhaustion from going without sleep drove her to the ground. She lay on her side huddled beneath the shawl, watching the flames ripple back and forth across the charred bark like ecstatic dancers. She stared at the fire for so long, even when she closed her eyes the graceful outlines of flickering flames remained.

All personal thoughts and petty worries exited her mind. An indifferent calm took their place.

In a heartbeat, her sense of inner tranquility was shattered. The gentle flames she saw behind her closed eyes became explosive and roared toward the heavens in a blast of fire. A vision came to her with the shocking force of a skull-cracking blow to the back of the head. Her world fell away and an image of utter horror and immolation unfolded.

The Romans were on the march, the cadence of their precisely measured strides pounding in her chest like drumbeats. The vision was so vivid she saw the leader's hawklike black eyes and broken nose with the same chilling clarity as if he stood before her. The man's personality came across as focused and determined. He mapped and recorded everything he saw with the acquisitive diligence of a master already in possession of the land.

Confrontation brewed. She sensed the Romans' seething terror of this mist-laden, densely wooded valley with its wild people and unpredictable gods. The Romans wished to empty the valley of all threat. They wanted a fort on the Rhijin River, and there would be no negotiation with the Teutoni, not this time. There would be only punishment for those who resisted their will.

They were almost here.

Arcona bolted upright with a piercing scream. "No!"

Perspiration beaded her brow. The breath heaved in her chest, and nothing could soothe it. Even with her eyes wide open, the horrible vision flickered on and on. Only now, it took on the hideous tones of a waking nightmare.

Death settled over the valley like a veil of the blackest soot. It came with grasping skeletal hands not just to the warriors but women and children, too. She saw that death would snatch anyone within arm's reach and wring their necks without mercy.

The Romans would sweep through the valley, seeking Teutoni warriors to slaughter and women to enslave while hunting the woods barren of game to feed the legion. Her people would be systematically butchered, sold into slavery, or starved. Rome would offer no fourth option.

The dreadful truth left Arcona's limbs shaking. Rome had to be stopped. That the Empire should even attempt such an offense was a vicious blight on her ancestors' souls.

In that moment of terror, it became clear what had to be done. Dark powers unlike any the Teutoni had ever befriended or dared to worship must be summoned from the twilight world and led forth into the light to wreak revenge. No matter the cost, the harsher gods of war and strife, with their dank love of bloodshed, must be appealed to and won to the Teutoni cause.

"Use me as your weapon!" she shouted at the serene night sky sparkling with stars that would have been lovely on any other occasion, but not now. "I give myself to the cause, my life, blood, and soul. I take full responsibility for what must be done. I call on Tyr, god of single combat, to give me the strength to fight as many. Let me prevail with my mind, skills, and wits. May the Romans have all the violence and wrath they toss at others thrown back in their ugly faces!"

A booming chorus of furious voices that seemed to speak as one echoed in her mind. *"We want blood!"* the voices shouted with authority. *"Prove your sincerity. We want blood!"*

The first violent action that needed to be taken flashed in her thoughts. She scrambled on hands and knees wildly, searching for her slender bone-handled knife. When she found it, she held the blade toward the fire with trembling hands.

"We want blood. We want sacrifice," the enraged voices demanded.

"Then you shall have it!" Arcona drew the blade across her wrist and cut a skinny gash that trickled crimson.

"More!" the voices roared.

She slashed the other wrist. The shallow cut stung as she watched the blood well to the surface. This was wonderful! The tide would turn. A dark enchantment overtook her. The gods drew her near to mingle their blood with hers. After tonight, she would never be the same. She'd become a living weapon to aim at the heart of Rome.

"We want blood!"

"Yes." She sliced herself again.

"You will walk among them, killing with indiscretion. In time, we will blow a mountain of molten fire from beneath the enemies' feet. Where you walk, Rome is doomed, and when your victorious work is done, we will reclaim you by fire."

Listening to the internal voices made her shudder with joy. This was what she'd been waiting all her life to hear. Long-held suspicions were now confirmed. The gods had made their choice known. Her time had come as their newest weapon.

She used the blade to slash her arm again. The blood flowed and its powerful release brought a giddy sense of hysteria.

"Take me," she pleaded.

Beyond the presence of familiar warlike gods, she also sensed demons from the deepest levels of the great abyss empowering this act. The pact with darkness was a dangerous one, yet she willingly invited all vengeful spirits into her soul. The risk had to be taken. Formidable enemies called for new and powerful avengers.

"This is my sacred obligation," she mumbled, "which I offer without regret. My soul is yours." The sight of trickling blood on her pale skin became hypnotic. She used the knife to make a dozen quick slashes in her forearm, bleeding her arms over the fire as she shouted skyward, "Make me strong, the greatest of priestesses. Lend me your authority to persecute and punish Rome!"

"What is your sacrifice? Give us something of value."

"Love!" Arcona blurted. "Take love from my heart. I won't need it for this task. I don't want to feel it anymore. Love is a burden I can't afford."

Thoughts of Hedron and the always-dependable look of warmth in his eyes whenever he glanced her way, threatened to suffocate her resolve. She gulped a bracing breath and continued. "Let me be cold and single-minded. I beg of you to make it so!"

Without love to dilute dark power, her actions would be more potent. This painful offering was necessary. Her throat tightened as if strangled by invisible hands. She barely croaked the last words. "Out of duty for my people, I sacrifice love!"

Blood dripped down her arms and sizzled to smoke as it struck the flames of the fire. In the next moment, the image of Hedron's beautiful but somber face faded from her mind and heart. A flinty, ambitious desire for vengeance filled the void he left behind.

Gulping a ragged breath, she screamed into the black of night, "This is the power I was born to wield! I will take the sacred vows. I will wear the goddess's amber. Use me to strike the enemy harder than they have ever been struck. Use me as your thunderbolt of fire!"

Chapter One
Salem, Massachusetts. November 2, All Souls Day. Present day

Nestled between clapboard Federation-era buildings, the Salem Witch Museum loomed tall like a gothic castle from a dark fairytale. In the fading light of a short autumn day, the brown stone turrets lent the imposing structure an enchanting gingerbread quality.

Devon slicked her palm through her windblown head of wavy dark hair and pointed to the front door. "The museum's still open. Shall we take one more peek before they close?"

A cutting breeze off the harbor left Arcona shivering. By Massachusetts' standards, this was mild weather, yet her skin pebbled. She clutched her lapels closed. Bringing a lightweight, travel-friendly West Coast trench coat on this trip had been a poor choice when she really needed a sturdy East Coast parka, like the one Devon wore. "Haven't we seen enough witch persecutions for one day?"

Earlier, they'd viewed the museum displays of life-sized wax figures depicting the appalling atrocities of the witch trials of 1692. "Those images are already seared into my brain and sure to give me nightmares for weeks."

"What?" With mouth agape, Devon stared. "You're not enjoying this? Why did we spend all afternoon doing the witch tours? I thought you were fascinated with witchcraft?"

"No." She laughed. "I have a phobia of witchcraft, not a fascination. You're the one who loves anything spooky. Not me."

"Holy crap!" Devon giggled. "I did the tour for you." Aiming her camera upward, she clicked photos of the museum's elegant window encased in gothic iron filigree and lit an ominous shade of crimson. "I would have said something but I thought the side trip to Salem was part of your historical research."

Too reluctant to mention that her nightmares about witches had been on the rise in past weeks and that she was determined to understand why, Arcona offered a vague answer instead. "This sort of was research...." She stalled. "But a little goes a long way. It's time for me to tap out." Devon's eyes filled with concern. "Okay. I think I get it. This is like the time you bolted out of Professor Morris's lecture on Joan of Arc after he went into lurid detail about burning a girl at the stake. I remember, you ran into the hallway and threw up."

"Yep." Patting her belly, she groaned. "I'm feeling the same way now."

"So why torment yourself? We could have gone shopping."

"I couldn't be this close to Salem and not steal a peek." How could she explain how repulsed yet drawn she'd been to Salem, a city devoted to the memory of witches? Since she was a kid, she'd believed some astonishing revelation or act of fate was waiting here, yet she'd been too timid to step foot within city limits until today. "I'd like to be free of this fear. It's so irrational."

Devon beamed a winning smile with just the slightest hint of an overbite. "I'm flattered you picked me to join you. I enjoyed today!"

"Thank you for meeting me here." Arcona's friend since college, Devon was always the adventurous one up for anything, and the perfect companion to face her fears with. She squeezed Devon's hand. "Promise you'll visit me in Los Angeles. I have a guest bed."

"Or you could visit me in the Bay Area. Fair warning, I have an apartment the size of most people's entryways, but I've got a comfortable couch. I can't believe we both live in the same state but have to visit Massachusetts to see each other."

Knowing Devon had just come off a hard, lonely year flying between coasts to see her mother through chemo, she lowered her voice. "How is your mom doing?"

"Better." Devon sighed. "Hopefully, she'll get a break." She steered Arcona toward a large wooden sign. "Let's get a picture of us in front of the museum and celebrate the day. The past couple of years have been hard, but we're both going to be okay."

Smoothing her wind-rumpled hair, Arcona asked, "Do I look like a witch?"

"Not at all." Typical Devon, always ready to lift a friend up. Her bubbly personality made her the one everybody wanted to dance with at parties. "Smile. You look like a hot tamale."

Arcona was pretty sure she didn't but it was kind of Devon to say so. The divorce had caused her to lose her mojo and gain a couple of dozen extra pounds and deeper frown lines as semi-permanent souvenirs from the split. She forced a smile.

Devon held her camera to her eye and clicked. "That's a smile? Come on, you can do better."

She thought about the seminar at Boston University and her gut lurched.

Lowering the camera, Devon frowned. "Now you look ill. What's wrong?"

A thousand petty things were wrong. She was only thirty-two and already worried life might hop in the car, hit the gas, and drive off without her. "I forgot to tell you something." She stalled. "Truthfully, I wasn't ready to mention it. You've already heard enough complaints."

"Tell me. I insist."

Arcona thrust her hands deep into the coat's pockets, her fingers clenched into fists. "Can you believe Mario's new research assistant had the courage—or the gall, I don't know which—to approach me yesterday at the seminar and introduce herself?"

Devon glanced at her sideways with soulful brown eyes that invited trust. "Wow. What did you say to her?"

With her emotions whirring, she started walking, and Devon followed. "We talked for a few minutes. After all, the divorce wasn't her fault. Mario wasn't going to change."

Slipping her camera into her purse, Devon strode at Arcona's side. "Was Mario there?"

"No. Thank God I was spared that humiliation. He's working on some big restoration project in Capri."

"Maybe he'll fall off a cliff."

Quiet laughter slipped past her lips. "Mario wasn't that bad. Just selfish."

Devon wrinkled her nose. "Mario thought he was the sun and the universe revolved around him. What was she like?"

"What do you think?" she answered with a joyless snicker that betrayed how hurt she still was. "Mario's so predictable. Like a moth to the flame, he picks the same woman again and again. Her name's Helga. The poor thing wears sensible shoes. She has auburn hair like mine and his first wife's." She patted her sides. "Same big hips. She's several years younger than me. I'm guessing late twenties. Ultra-serious about her work. Just wait until Mario claims some of her research as his own."

Arcona paused to stare at a gray, featureless sky. "I don't want to talk about him anymore. Do we have time to get an early dinner or a glass of wine?"

Devon glanced at her phone. "I promised my mother I'd have dinner with her before I caught the red-eye home."

"How about a glass of wine?"

"I've got another forty-five minutes before I have to leave. Why not?"

She squeezed Devon's hand. "I loved being with you today."

"I love our long phone calls but we need to get together in person more often."

They turned the corner and walked along a row of shops geared toward tourists. Passing the many signs and posters featuring witches being punished for some trumped-up crime gnawed at her.

Devon took hold of her hand and gave it a squeeze. "Are you okay? You look pale. Did mentioning Mario's new girlfriend bring you down? If it were me, I'm pretty sure I couldn't have been as polite as you were."

They stopped in front of an engaging storefront with a large carved sign that read Silver Moon Scrying Shoppe in purple letters.

Arcona pointed to an ornate tableau in the shop window and shuddered. "Uh, look at that."

Someone had meticulously carved and painted a horrific miniature scene of a woman standing on a ladder with a noose around her neck. Blindfolded, the mannequin's hands were bound in chains and her flowing petticoats were secured around her ankles. She was about to be pushed by a somber man in a black frock coat. "This stuff is starting to really bother me. I know it was all in the past but those poor women. It's so ugly and unjust."

Her gaze wandered to a painted ceramic figurine of another woman tied to the stake, scarlet flames licking up her skirt. "Who would want that in their home?"

Devon gestured toward a stunning African mask. The mask was a large dragon with two faces. Every millimeter of the mask's surface was covered in thousands of tiny rainbow-hued beads, each carefully placed. "Look at that! I love it. If I could afford it, I'd buy that in a second."

Arcona peered at the window display through cupped hands. "Witches being dunked, witches in the stocks.... This place is a house of horrors."

"Oh look." Devon pointed out an authentic-looking blade with a bronze hilt. "Something for you. Isn't that big dagger the sort of thing you identify and catalogue every day?"

"Yep." Arcona's gazed fixed on the blade. "That's not a dagger. It's a *gladius hispaniensis*, or Spanish short sword, the kind the Roman legions carried, and gladiators fought with in the arena. Easy to wield at close quarters, the steel blade was lethal and dependable. Unlike barbarian iron or bronze, Roman steel didn't shatter in battle. That simple weapon was the deciding factor between who conquered an empire and who perished. I can't tell behind glass, but that looks genuine, or else it's a fabulous reproduction."

"It's genuine." A lady with wavy, silver hair and brilliant blue eyes poked her head outside the shop door. "I was closing shop for the day, but you're welcome to come inside."

"No, thank you." Arcona shook her head. "We were just looking."

The woman persisted. "Pardon me, but I overheard a stray thread of your conversation. You seem knowledgeable about ancient world antiquities."

She nodded. "I practice forensic archaeology at UCLA's historical research department. Mostly authenticating and cataloging items."

"How enthralling!" With clipped New England tones, the woman' s speech rushed. "I must hear more about it. Come inside. No arguments. It will only take a minute."

Feeling wary, she glanced at Devon. "What will only take a minute?"

The lady's eyes twinkled. "To cast a fortune for you and show you something special I have in my storeroom. I would relish your opinion."

Gesturing toward Devon, she shrugged. "I'm sorry, we'd love to, but she has to catch a train."

"Nonsense! There's always another train. Just wait long enough and everything comes full circle again." The lady held the door wide. "Don't just stand there. It's getting chilly. We have a fireplace and hot cider."

Geez, this woman wasn't shy about making a hard sell that could put most used-car salesman to shame.

Devon looked hopeful. "What sort of fortunes do you cast?"

The woman's eyes narrowed, lending her the slightly smug look of a spoiled cat that had just lured a small bird within batting range. "Highly accurate ones tailored especially to you. For instance, you're dying to know what the future holds for your personal life, aren't you? I can tell you right now you're headed for a double serving of love."

With a squeal of joy, Devon grabbed hold of Arcona's hand. "I gotta know more! Let's do it."

Bringing her lips to Devon's ear, Arcona whispered, "She probably says the same thing to everybody."

"Who cares? It will be fun." Devon's goal in life was to try anything fun or interesting at least once. "How much does it cost?"

Brushing a strand of silvery hair from her brow, the woman tucked it neatly behind her ear. "Only your time and your effort to follow through on my advice."

Arcona bit her lip. "You won't need a credit card?"

"Certainly not. I work pro bono." She extended her delicate hand, embellished with a large moonstone. "Let's discuss this in private. By the way, my name is Dame Bishop. No matter what others might claim, I am the true preeminent witch of Salem."

Good God, another witch, just what she didn't need. She glanced at Devon, who was brimming with more enthusiasm than a second-grader being offered a pony ride. It seemed cruel to deprive her of something she wanted so much.

Stepping through the front door, Arcona gestured for Devon to accompany her. "Here we go."

Once inside the eccentric shop, the tourist-friendly exterior gave way to a somber vibe. The walls were paneled in dark wood and lined with leather tomes. The place felt more like a museum of the occult, with moldering things packed into every corner. Suspended from the ceiling by sturdy fishing line, twig brooms, two giant paper dragons, herbs, crystal-tipped scepters, and even a large copper caldron swayed overhead.

While looking up at the many magical objects, Arcona's boot crunched on a tiny pebble of something soft and crushed it. She glanced downward. Her foot had landed on a lump of chalk and turned it to powder. Just inside the entryway on the floor, someone had sketched a large circle in chalk with a pentagram inside it. Afraid she might scuff the drawing further, she lifted her foot and stepped back. "I'm sorry. I didn't mean to ruin it."

A slight smile curled Dame Bishop's lips. "You didn't. This circle of fate was cast expressly for you. You've always been meant to cross the threshold of my shop and break the circle. It's preordained."

"Always?" The intricate drawing had taken a considerable amount of time. "Wouldn't anyone who walked through the door break the circle?"

Standing at attention, Dame Bishop appeared ready for duty. "Not just anyone can pass through that doorway, at least not now. You're an exception."

"What do you mean? People can't just walk into your shop? That's got to be hard on business. And why would you draw a chalk circle for me? I didn't even know I was coming into your shop until a minute ago."

"True. But the potential of you coming into my shop and stepping into the circle has existed for years. Earlier this afternoon, the likelihood became so strong I decided to wait by the window for you."

Whatever. Arcona fought rolling her eyes. With luck this conversation wouldn't turn into a New Age version of probability theory. "You're making the claim that you knew I was coming and drew the circle?"

"Yes. To be clear, I'm not the only one who's been waiting for your arrival. There are other interested parties who are now alerted to your presence in Salem."

A shiver tickled her spine. Maybe she'd been wise to avoid Salem all these years? This town was treating her weirdly. "Why Salem?"

"Some meetings can only happen at specific places and certain points of time. This is the City of Witches, and today is All Souls' Day." Dame Bishop smiled with pride. "A potent combination."

Tell me something I don't know – that makes sense. "Why would any of this apply to me? I'm not a witch."

"But you're an old soul. Other souls you've interacted with in the past would like to meet you again. You smeared the chalk. Now they can find you within Salem."

Oh, man, this lady sounded wacko. "Scuffing the circle set off a sort of cosmic security alarm?"

"Something like that, but far more subtle. It's more like plucking a single thread on a spider's web and making the entire web vibrate."

"Or summoning the spider." She laughed, and Dame Bishop frowned. What was up with this sourpuss? "So, you're saying I sent the Bat-signal into the etheric realms? Who are these interested parties?"

Dame Bishop's eyes flashed. "We can discuss that in a moment."

Rubbing her hands together, Devon crowded past, being careful not to step on any chalked lines. "I'm loving this place and I want to stand closer to that stove." She hooked her arm through Arcona's and drew her deeper into the shop. "Come on. Have fun with it."

Maybe Devon was right. This was a tourist shop likely run by a wannabe actress. Time to chill and let Devon have some pleasure…but just below the inviting scent of cinnamon and apples, an acrid odor, like long-boiled herbs, drifted on the air. Something about the shop set off internal alarm bells, and she wished she could immediately turn around and leave.

Devon approached Dame Bishop, her eyes glittering with excitement. "I can't wait to hear my fortune. Do you read tarot cards?"

Dame Bishop lifted her square chin. "I certainly do not, but Witch Casey does. Your reading will be with her and quite unique. In the ways of divination, she is an expert without equal."

An attractive, middle-aged woman with red hair and piercing blue eyes peered from behind a curtain. "Hello." She stepped into the main room. "I'm Witch Casey. When the two of you entered the shop, I sensed a tremendous energy shift. Highly unusual." Her attention focused on Devon. A sly smile lifted the corners of her mouth. "I want to talk to you first, dear. You have such an interesting aura."

Aura? Seriously? Arcona regretted walking inside. They could be sitting somewhere more pleasant, buzzed on wine and sharing a good laugh. What a ridiculous waste of the last minutes she and Devon had together before they had to go their separate ways.

Witch Casey held up a small velvet brocade bag and gave it a shake. "We shall start with a wish stone. You'll each choose a stone from the bag, and based on your choice, I'll be able to divine your most likely fate. Now, who wants to know about their future love life?"

"I do!" Devon cheered.

Witch Casey's eyes twinkled as she offered Devon the bag. "I knew you'd go first. You're the daring one, aren't you?"

The atmosphere of the funky little Wiccan store was charged with a strange excitement as Devon thrust her hand into the bag.

"Let your fingers do the work." Witch Casey leaned closer to better see Devon's actions. "Don't think about it. Let your heart guide the choice."

Devon continued to stir the clattering stones between her fingers without sign of stopping.

"Wow, you're being so picky," Arcona teased. Their chance to get a glass of wine slipped farther away. "Just choose a stone, already!"

"Don't rush me." Devon laughed. "This is important. I want to choose the right one."

"You're going to choose just *one*?" Arcona scoffed. In college, Devon had been notorious for juggling several boyfriends at a time. "That doesn't sound like you."

"Why are you picking on me?" Devon giggled. "There's nothing wrong with being choosy and having a plan B and a plan C... especially where love is concerned." Refocusing her attention on the wish bag, she dug her hand deeper. "I need help. My love life has done a vanishing act."

Finally, Devon pulled a stone from the bag with a victorious flourish. "Here it is. I found it!"

Arcona gazed at the rock lying in Devon's palm. It looked like two very different minerals melted together. The egg-shaped stone was opaque on one side and a translucent purplish color on the other. The purple reminded her of an amethyst, while the other was a mottled shade of dusty rose. "Wow, that is an odd-looking stone." She reached for Devon's hand to tip the sparkling stone toward the light. "It's beautiful when things you'd never think would fuse together mix." She stared at the stone in wonder. "The world is full of unexpected things, isn't it?"

Devon looked from the two-sided stone to her friend. "It is different." She glanced at Witch Casey to see if she had an opinion as to why she'd chosen such a stone.

"Interesting, but not surprising." Witch Casey shook her head with her lips pinched together.

Arcona couldn't read the woman's eccentric gesture.

"A dual stone is often attracted to an undecided person." Witch Casey's words were terse.

"Undecided?" Devon stiffened and crossed her arms in a defensive manner. "What do you mean by undecided?"

Arcona knew where this was going. Devon had shown hesitance in choosing a stone, and the die was cast. Witch Casey would now deliver a trite and predictable forecast about Devon's future love life. She braced for the safe little clichés she knew were headed their way.

Witch Casey arced her hands through the air in a dramatic gesture. "Your heart is always in two places at once and refuses to choose a lasting home. Am I right?"

That statement actually did apply to Devon. For years, she'd watched Devon rush toward one goal while not so secretly desiring another. She'd say that she longed for a stable relationship, even a family, but then a rogue part of her would announce that she wanted to ditch all responsibilities, pick up a camera, and flee to the exotic wilds of Africa to fulfill her creative dreams. The same went for men. She could never make up her mind. She might as well tattoo *variety is the spice of life* on her forehead.

"There might be some truth in what you're saying," Devon sheepishly answered Witch Casey.

Witch Casey's eyes flew wide. "Might?"

Arcona leaned close to Devon's ear. "I remember our Amherst days. You were always dating at least two guys at once and trying to keep it a secret. It never stayed secret."

"Why can't a woman have more than one man and not be judged for it?" Devon rolled the stone in her palm. "I'll make my wish right now. Have my male harem bathed and brought to my tent." She handed the brocade bag to Arcona. "Your turn. Let's see what you choose."

Arcona took hold of the bag and thrust her hand inside. The stones were smooth and cool to the touch. One of them felt lighter than the others. Without further fuss, she pulled it free. An oval piece of amber the size of a nickel glistened like congealed honey in her palm. When she held the amber to the light, it glowed like flame-warmed cognac.

Witch Casey leaned closer to Arcona to examine her choice. "Blood amber; the blood of trees. Technically, it's not a stone but a mineralized fossil that carries an electric charge and an enhanced memory of its past." She wagged a finger. "Powerful stuff and not to be taken lightly."

It seemed doubtful to her that a fossilized bit of anything had much of a *memory*. To look at, the amber was cheerful as a campfire, yet cradling it in her palm had the same unsettling effect as holding a tarantula. Her first impulse was to toss it back into the bag.

"One rule about the wish stones." Witch Casey took hold of Devon's wrist. "Handle them with care, make a wish, and then return the stones to nature where they can be recharged. Will you both agree to do that?"

Arcona nodded. Lonely and bored with life, she was the one who needed to be recharged, not a fricking stone.

Witch Casey led Devon toward a curtained room. "I'm looking forward to telling your fortune. I think you're in for a double surprise."

Dame Bishop made a slight move as if ready to claim Arcona's hand. "Shall we?"

This was too much. She may have overdosed on Salem. Did she really want to be here listening to a self-proclaimed witch say crazy things? "Wait," she called to Devon. "I'm feeling a little ill. I think I'd better go back to the hotel."

Devon turned, concern obliterating her joyful grin. "I'll go with you."

"No. Stay and get your fortune told. It's just a headache," she lied. "Walking a few blocks in fresh air will do me good."

"If you're sure." Devon looked in Witch Casey's direction with longing.

Taking quick steps, she closed the distance between them, wrapped her arms around Devon, and gave her a hug. Once again they were saying good-bye and going their separate ways, and it stung. "We need to get together more."

"We will." Devon returned the embrace. "Call me after you get home, okay?"

Witch Casey stood too close, coral lips pulled tight and appearing impatient.

"I'd better let you go." With a light kiss on the cheek, Arcona released her hold on Devon.

"Bye." Devon smiled but she seemed sad.

"Go on." Arcona playfully shooed Devon away.

Devon gave Arcona one last glance that seemed to shout *don't be a killjoy*, before she followed Witch Casey behind a purple curtain and disappeared from view.

No doubt Devon was disappointed that Arcona couldn't relax long enough to enjoy something as silly and fun as having their fortunes told, but her sour mood thickened. She turned and headed toward the door.

With a wink, Dame Bishop called after her, "Are you sure you don't want to know your fortune?"

She shook her head. "Another time."

A slender grin curled Dame Bishop's mouth. "If it's meant to be, you'll be back."

Arcona doubted it. She could think of no compelling reason why she would need to return to Salem or The Silver Moon Scrying Shoppe again. "Thank you. Do I owe you anything for the wish stone?"

"Don't worry. I'll take care of it!" Devon called from behind the curtain.

"Thanks." She exited the shop as quickly as polite behavior would allow and stepped onto the street. Clutching her coat close, she strode past the decorative seaside storefronts, bracing against the cold ocean breeze swirling its way under her clothing. One thing was for certain: Salem was not her town. The chill witch vibe repelled her.

Arcona strolled beside the harbor, lost in troubling thoughts as she toyed with a translucent piece of amber. She'd chosen to walk along the promenade to enjoy the ocean view at sunset, but didn't do much looking. The green ocean beyond the barrier was picturesque, but she found herself staring at the glossy chunk of amber instead, wondering why something so lovely caused such a strong sense of unease.

Turning the stone over and over in her palm, she tried to figure out the mystery. It brought up bad feelings of self-doubt and guilt—but of what? She couldn't connect amber to anything negative in her life.

It's just harmless tree resin.

A tense breath whistled past her lips. Who was she kidding? The tiny piece of amber deviled her, and the reason remained elusive, like a disturbing dream that immediately faded upon waking.

Why not make a wish? That part was easy. *How about a hot, sexy bad boy to break the drought?* A new man in her life would be perfect. She wanted an unfussy, tough-guy type, who needed a good fuck as much as she did.

Lately, she lived like a nun. She should be enjoying her freedom, but she seldom met new people outside her tiny circle of boring coworkers. The few men she'd dated in the university's research department were less than thrilling. Her thoughts often wandered toward some idealized, fearless, blood-and-brawn hero from the past; a man who would treat a woman like a prize and every sexual act like his last. That was the sort of man she desired, but the modern world didn't seem to be producing many of those types anymore. At least none who were single and interested in quiet academic women carrying a few extra pounds.

Gazing toward a darkening sky, she wondered if she should make a wish and toss the amber into the turbulent harbor, but thought better of it. The piece of amber almost clung to her palm, as if it were loath to be parted from her.

The wind blew off the sea. She bundled her coat around her as she walked. Every shop and restaurant she passed still displayed Halloween decorations. Tiny orange lights sparkled in every window on the block. Occasionally, her boots crunched windblown candy wrappers and flecks of glitter on the pavement. Collapsing jack-o'-lanterns sat on front porches as evidence of a cheerful Halloween season.

Arcona turned the corner and walked a few short blocks onto what looked like a village street closed to automobile traffic. Hidden between an old-fashioned colonial pub and a cute bed-and-breakfast was the Wiccan shop where she had pulled the piece of red amber from the wish bag.

Stopping dead in her tracks, she stared in befuddlement. "What the hell?"

The shop should be many blocks behind her in another part of the neighborhood; what was it doing here? She looked closer; perhaps it was a sister shop to the one she and Devon had visited?

She scanned every item in the window display, paying careful attention to detail. Every ornament in the window case was exactly the same as the store on the other side of Salem. The same bead-embellished African mask of a two-headed dragon, the same Roman sword, and at the center of the display, the same disturbing ceramic figurine of a screaming woman writhing in the agonizing flames of a pyre. She shuddered. Had she merely walked in a large circle?

"You came back," a woman with a sweet voice called out to her through an open door. "I guess it was meant to be." Arcona glanced up. Dame Bishop looked at her with bright eyes.

"By any chance, do you have two shops in Salem?" Arcona asked.

"No. Just the one." She pointed to the rustic sign that read Silver Moon Scrying Shoppe. "It's getting nippy." She motioned toward a pile of dry leaves whipped to a tiny tempest by a brisk breeze. "Come inside. I'd like to show you something I think you'll find interesting."

"Is my friend Devon still here?"

"No. She left a few minutes ago. That young lady seemed quite pleased with her fortune. By the way, how is the headache? I have something that might help."

"It's better." She'd been certain she'd been moving forward, away from the shop. How was this possible? Why had she come back? She stared into the cozy shop with a fire burning in the stone hearth. The thought of warming up before restarting her journey was tempting. "I really can't stay."

"Where are you going?" Dame Bishop's tone was polite.

"Back to my hotel." She stalled. "If I can find it. I thought I was almost there. I suppose I've somehow been walking in a big circuit."

"Don't worry about it, dear. Salem is a lovely place to lose yourself. You're never far from where you need to be. I can guarantee it."

A whiff of spiced cider attracted her attention. She glanced inside the store and saw a steaming pot on a side counter warming over a hot plate. Her stomach growled embarrassingly loud.

Pointing a finger at Arcona's heart, Dame Bishop leaned close. "You're a historian, am I right? Studying the past is also a hobby of mine. I have quite a few friends in the academic world. Sometimes they loan me artifacts, wanting to know more about their magical or folkloric backgrounds. When you were with Witch Casey pulling a wish stone from the bag, I wanted to show you something special I have in my possession, but you left before I could show it to you."

Maybe her first impression was wrong? On second meeting, the lady seemed so pleasant, almost a colleague. Arcona's curiosity grew. "I'm not really in a rush. What would you like to show me?"

Dame Bishop's eyes twinkled. "Come in for a minute. I'm going to lock the front door. My business is finished for the day."

Arcona stepped inside the shop, relishing the warmth radiating from the hearth.

Latching the door on the inside, Dame Bishop drew a dark velvet curtain across the front of the shop. She turned and took hold of her gorgeous head of thick silver hair, twisted it into a neat chignon, and drove a carved hairpin through the center of it. The action instantly transformed her appearance from Wiccan hippie to Parisian chic. "Would you like some spiced cider?"

Arcona nodded. "Yes, please." But the little voice in her head protested. What was she doing? Why was she here drinking cider with a complete stranger instead of getting back to the hotel and confirming her flight home? This was crazy.

Knitting her fingers together in a prim gesture, Dame Bishop riveted her gaze on Arcona. "Like Witch Casey, I read auras, too."

Oh, no. The good impression didn't last. *Here we go, one express ticket back to Kookytown.* "I have never been clear about what exactly an aura is, or why I should care about it." God help her, she sounded like such a snob.

"An aura is the personal energy signature that surrounds us all. I watched your exchange with Witch Casey, and I couldn't help but observe that you have an exceptional aura. It's old, complex, and full of contradictions. I'm not sure what to make of it."

A jolt of alarm rocked her. "What do you mean?"

"I mean it's intense, heavy, and carries the complete history of all your past lives."

"Is that good or bad?"

"Neither. You're just different. Most people's auras only display fleeting glimpses of their past. An aura reading for them is like skimming through a skinny pamphlet, where you are a hardback Webster's dictionary. I seldom encounter anything like what I'm seeing with you."

"I'm a dictionary?"

"You're a tome! Based on merit, your soul has been granted complete disclosure." In a dramatic fashion, Dame Bishop drew a deep breath. "I believe this is your redemption lifetime. Redemption cycles are rare, difficult, and seldom come along, but a soul can make great progress if redemption is confronted with the proper attitude. I must warn you, this lifetime could turn into a wild roller-coaster ride of unpredictable surprises. My guess is, in the near future, you could use my help."

She wanted to groan in disbelief. Her life was so uneventful, isolated, and dull she had no idea where these allegations were coming from. Devon was a better candidate for exciting and weird adventures. "Are you sure you have the right person? Perhaps it was my friend?"

"I'm certain it's you. Even as we speak, your aura is roiling like a pot at full boil." Dame Bishop dipped a ladle into an electric slow cooker and filled two rustic earthenware mugs with warm cider, then handed one to Arcona. "I've had a lot of experience in these matters. I've been one of the most active witches on the Salem scene since '92, and I'm proud of pioneering the new spirit of tolerance for the earth-based religions." She paused to sip her cider. "What is your name, dear?"

"Arcona."

"Arcona?" Dame Bishop beamed. "The name has its roots in the ancient tribes of Northern Europe. I believe it belongs to the Germani. I haven't met an Arcona in such a long while. It's a lovely name. Of course you know what it means, don't you?"

She'd never been enthusiastic about her name and often wondered what the hell her parents had been thinking. "It means 'secret,'" she answered sheepishly.

"It certainly does." Dame Bishop became animated, eager to burst onto the topic. "It also means hidden knowledge, often *deeply* hidden knowledge, so much so that sometimes the keeper of those secrets doesn't even realize they harbor something valuable within." She smiled. "Isn't it funny how the universe can hide a broader truth in plain sight?"

Bringing the mug to her lips, Arcona paused. "I'm sorry, but I'm not following you." But that was a lie. A tingle of recognition provoked her. She'd always sensed something was different about her but had never guessed what. Dame Bishop was the first person to broach the subject in the open, and on some level she knew she needed to listen carefully.

"What is it about me that's hidden in plain sight?" Arcona sipped the cider, surprised by the unconventional flavor of several exotic spices she couldn't name that were far more potent than the usual cinnamon stick. She took another sip, concluding it was a pleasant drink. "What is the floral fragrance?"

"It's called *rosa lacrimae*, 'rose tears.' It's very rare and said to have originated in Antioch. There are other herbs in my cider, as well. I included them for their regenerative properties. No one wants to be anemic." Dame Bishop tilted her head as her gaze sharpened. "About your name, have you ever asked yourself the obvious question: what's my secret?"

"No, I haven't." Arcona laughed; the cider made her giddy, almost as if she'd consumed a bottle of champagne, but she'd only taken a couple of sips. "I never took my name literally."

"Maybe you should." Dame Bishop leaned close. "I sense you're hiding a secret that you've carefully concealed from everyone, including yourself."

"How would I do that?"

"We all do it to some degree, dear, but in your case, you've hidden the truth so deeply, we'd have to hold your feet to the fire and face the flames before you'd confess."

She recoiled in disgust at the image Dame Bishop's words conjured. "Why did you say that? I'm not concealing anything maniacal from anyone. I'm a researcher. I devote my days to cataloging historical objects, not hiding them."

In a single nervous gulp, she finished the cider. The warm liquid filled her with a vague sense of excitement, impossible to describe. She felt both dreamy and highly alert as she handed the mug back to Dame Bishop. "Thank you. This was delicious, but it's getting late. I should go."

"Very well." A gracious smile lit her face. "I'm glad you dropped by."

Arcona walked toward the front door, intent on leaving, but stopped. "Didn't you have something you wanted to show me?"

"I did." Dame Bishop looked serene. "But it's not important now. I don't want you to get caught after dark in a strange city."

Her hostess had been so welcoming, she felt she owed the lady the courtesy of a look. "I have a minute to spare. Show me."

Dame Bishop's cheeks flushed pink. For a fleeting moment, the middle-aged woman appeared youthful. "Come with me." She walked to the back of the shop, lifted a heavy purple curtain aside, and motioned for Arcona to follow her into a dimly lit storage room.

She followed. The storage room looked like a natural history museum's sorting tables. Ceiling-high shelves and a broad countertop were covered with a thick layer of dust as well as bleached bones, tattered books, seashells, bits of driftwood, murky jars filled with suspicious-looking dried things, and a stuffed goat propped against the far wall. A live black cat stretched across the back of the stuffed goat and blinked its yellow eyes.

Dame Bishop bustled toward a locked cabinet shoved next to an emergency exit. "Ignore the countertops. That stuff is just for tourists." Using a brass key she wore pinned to her hip, she unlocked the cabinet. "Here we are." She pulled a narrow wooden box from the cabinet with care. The polished lid had an ornate inlaid pattern of twisted Celtic knots. She opened the box and displayed the contents with ceremony. "You drew a piece of red amber from the wish bag, didn't you?"

Arcona nodded. "Yes." All of sudden, it became difficult to breathe. She needed to sit or run, but she couldn't decide which.

The box was presented to Arcona. "Look closely."

She gazed into the box, feeling a wave of unease. It contained a large piece of polished red amber as wide as her fist, fixed into an intimidating bronze setting and embellished with bony birds of prey that looked like they belonged in a Gothic nightmare.

The entire thing dangled from a leather thong, designed to be worn as a talisman. Without doubt, she was looking at ancient craftsmanship, but in all her years of European cultural research, she'd never seen anything like it.

Dame Bishop grinned like a child being offered ice cream. "Take a careful look and tell me what comes to mind. I'd like to hear about any feelings that might arise, or your intuition about the amulet."

Arcona leaned closer, noticing most everything about the piece was unusual. "I'm going to take a wild guess. Of course, the leather thong is contemporary, but the bronzework looks Roman. Without the proper tools, it's impossible to say, but it was likely made with a lost wax-casting technique. The bird motifs are odd. The owl skull looks almost Scythian in design. Or even medieval. I'm sorry, but I don't recognize it."

Her heart pounded with anxiety and she struggled to focus. "The red amber could be Siberian, perhaps lower Baltic in origin. It's hard to say; amber is lightweight and, once it's exposed at the surface, easily washes downstream. The bronze setting looks ancient, possibly first-century Common Era. Have you sought an expert's assessment?"

Dame Bishop interrupted with a gentle hand placed on Arcona's shoulder. "Perhaps I didn't make myself clear. I know the origins of the amulet. It was unearthed in Pompeii within the ruins of a gladiatorial school." Drawing a deep breath, well timed for its dramatic value, she waited a beat. "I asked how the amulet made you feel."

Arcona paused in confusion. "What does it matter how I feel about it?"

"I thought you'd be interested in something so old and rare. This is one of history's lost great treasures. It's said to be incredibly powerful and beyond price. Too powerful, in fact, to allow just anyone to view or touch it."

Something wasn't adding up. "May I ask why something so old and rare is sitting around in the back of your shop? You're a block from the ocean. Salt air is corrosive. It should be persevered in a climate-controlled vault or display case. Where did you get this?"

Dame Bishop leaned closer. Her voice dropped to hushed tones. "That information is proprietary. I'm not at liberty to say. I received the amulet on loan from a private collector, who shall not be named. People often entrust me with valuable things. I have an outstanding reputation for getting…how shall I say it…difficult items into the right hands. After all, we are simply custodians passing through time. Nothing really belongs to any of us."

Arcona held her tongue. That rambling explanation sure didn't sound kosher. If genuine, the amulet was worthy of a starring spot in a museum. The prospect that she was being used leapt to mind. "My biggest concern is the possibility that this is a black market item. What is it doing in the back of a Wiccan shop? Just so you know, I don't curate stolen antiquities, I report them."

Dame Bishop grabbed a folded letter from the box and waved it in Arcona's face. "I came across the amulet through legitimate channels. Here is the paperwork. I've been charged with documenting the possible folkloric background of this object. The Silver Moon Scrying Shoppe is the next-to-last stop on the amulet's journey to the Smithsonian, where it will be properly examined and preserved." She unfolded the letter and thrust it in front of Arcona's nose. "See. There's the Smithsonian's letterhead." Another piece of paper was flicked in her face. "And this is an invoice for arrangements for an armored car to pick up the amulet tomorrow morning at this shop and transport it to the Smithsonian. So you see, I take the security of antiquities and lawfulness seriously."

It all looked on the level. "Considering my line of work, I'm sure you understand my concern."

"Yes, I certainly do. But I would also respect your opinion about the amulet."

"I couldn't even pin point what I was looking at. My opinion shouldn't carry much weight."

"Are you sure?" Dame Bishop slid the box closer. "Look again. Pick it up if you like."

Arcona's hand hovered above the amulet. An odd hum rose in her ears, as if the pressure in the room had undergone a rapid change. When she reached for it, the amber shot a single, stinging green spark at her hand. She winced and drew back. "Wow, it shocked me!"

"There's a lot of static in the air. Amber can do that. Remember, it was once alive."

She took hold of the leather thong and lifted the amulet from the box with care. Even for its bold size it felt far heavier than expected as she placed it on her palm and tipped it into the light for closer inspection. In the dimly lit room, the amber looked bloodred. "It's funny; the amber seems vibrantly alive, yet the bronze birds surrounding it are cadaverous. From an aesthetic standpoint, it's an odd mix of elements."

"Are you familiar with the legend of the Strix?"

"No." Arcona shook her head, noting the amulet had warmed almost too quickly in her cool palm.

"You won't find this myth in many books. These days, few know or speak of the Strix. The Strix was a compilation of all ancient Rome's guilty fears about the so-called barbarians they punished, enslaved, and brought under their own roofs to be used as domestics, lovers, or discarded as lethal entertainment in the arena. The Strix combined fearful barbarian lore and Roman superstitions into a single horrific creature that traveled the night as a grotesque bird of prey, sucking the blood from unsuspecting men and turning them against Rome."

"Sounds ghastly."

"I'm sure it was. The Strix might have started life as a worshipper of Hecate, the goddess of witchcraft and necromancy. She could have been born Roman or Celtic and worked as a healer, witch, or midwife, but somewhere along the way, hatred and the need for revenge against the oppressor corrupted the witch's capacity for doing good. Rage and destruction took the place of healing acts. Witches gone astray made bargains with dark forces in exchange for the power to grant invincibility in battle to others, who in turn walked the earth in violent wrath."

Arcona grimaced. "The Strix sounds repulsive."

"She wasn't. Isn't. And by the way, the Strix is always a *she*. The essence of Venus imbued the Strix with the power to beguile and sexually torment any man she approached. The Strix sought out strong, battle-worthy men to do her bidding, and her victims were powerless to refuse. She would seduce them and at the climax of the sexual act, she'd bite their throats, drink their blood, and send them into a violent rage. During these unnatural couplings, sometimes a male Upir Likhyi was created."

Arcona was afraid to ask but had to. "What the hell is a vam-pir-lee-kie?" She struggled to pronounce the unwieldy words.

"It's a pagan Baltic term for vampire. An Upir Likhyi is a revenant, or undead soul, that seeks the thrill of blood sport and warfare. In ancient times, many were recruited to secretly serve the gods of war."

A shiver tickled Arcona's spine. "We certainly don't need any more of those violent bloodsucking sorts hanging around, that's for sure." Her sarcasm was evident and she laughed with self-conscious abandon until Dame Bishop's serious face brought her dismissive attitude to a halt.

Composing herself, she continued. "I don't mean to sound disrespectful because I love mythology, too. Folklore has had a huge influence over human history, but myths are just a way to explain human desires and behavior. I'm puzzled, though. You're talking about the Strix as if it's a real entity."

Dame Bishop blanched. "It *is* a real entity. Make no mistake; every myth carries a grain of truth. There are realms loosely tethered to this one, far stranger than anything you can imagine. To say these realms are less real than ours is to profess that Earth is flat; a statement only the ignorant dare to speak freely."

"I'm sorry." Damn, she'd really put her foot in it. She lowered the amulet back into its box. "Thank you for sharing this with me. It's fascinating."

Gazing at the skeletal bronze birds and strange craftsmanship one last time, she blurted, "How exactly did you come across this? A rare artifact of this age seems like it should already be safely stashed in a museum."

"I agree. And it will be, soon enough." Dame Bishop's expression brightened. "But for the time being, it's here. Some associates of mine at the *Universita di Roma* know of my expertise in such things and they insisted I examine the amulet first."

A witch needed to examine this? Really? That story didn't sound wholly professional. Things weren't adding up. After she left, it might be a good idea to call someone in the antiquities department of the Smithsonian and the *Universita di Roma,* and see if anyone knew anything about the damn amulet. *Meanwhile, play along.* "What a coincidence. I'm familiar with the University of Rome! My ex-husband once taught there. Who are your contacts? Perhaps I know them."

"Highly doubtful." Dame Bishop's mouth drew tense. "My colleagues are reclusive people." Her gaze dropped toward the amulet. "Tomorrow, the amulet leaves my hands, headed to the Smithsonian. I just wanted to share it with one last soul before it continued on its journey to lie locked away in some sterile vault until the curators can figure out what to do with it."

She gazed around the dusty storeroom. "If it merits a ride in an armored car, aren't you worried about security? You can't expect the stuffed goat to protect it."

"This shop is under my strongest security enchantment. The amulet is perfectly safe." A heightened gleam shone in Dame Bishop's eyes as she lifted the amulet from the box and held it toward Arcona. "Why don't you try it on? Just to see what it feels like." A sly smile flickered on her lips. "It's a bit of living history. You may never get an opportunity like this again." Something about the amber riveted Arcona's attention. The center of the amulet was translucent and glowed like a fiery ember. Against her better judgment about the careless handling of antiquities and possibly ill-gotten property, she reached for the leather thong and looped it around her neck. The amulet hung heavy and prominent atop her breasts. Arcona glanced downward at the big, bold piece of ornamentation, obviously meant to identify its wearer as a witch who had wandered over to the dark side.

A loud knock pounded on the front door of the shop. Arcona started.

"Excuse me." Dame Bishop pulled the curtain to the back room aside. "Let me see who's at the door."

Left alone, Arcona gazed at the amulet and decided that in spite of the somewhat disturbing motifs, it was quite beautiful in its starkness and must have made a strong impression in its day.

The warm, subtle scent of amber resin reached her nose. She sniffed again in disbelief, knowing there was no way this ancient piece of fossilized amber could still be emitting a scent.

She inhaled the mystery fragrance, and sure enough, the rich scent of earthy Baltic amber filled the air. Curious if there was anything near that could possibly be the source of the aroma, she glanced around but saw nothing she could hold to account.

The curtain moved. What was Dame Bishop up to? She didn't hear anything going on in the front of the shop. All was silent.

Should she take a picture of the amulet with her phone and contact the Smithsonian? Yes, of course she should. But maybe she could find a spot with better lighting than this dim back room. Where was her purse? Taking hold of the thong, she pulled it to her chin to remove it and her knees buckled. A moment of extreme dizziness knocked her off balance and sent her flailing across the dusty countertop in a scrambling attempt to keep from falling to the floor.

She made a second attempt to remove the amulet. As she lifted it over her head, a scorching sensation made her wince. It was so painful, she dropped the amulet back into place. For the third time, she tried to remove the amulet. Again, the pain of lifting the thong past her chin brought her to a halt. Drawing a bracing breath, she attempted to remove the amulet a fourth time. It heated so quickly in her touch she couldn't drop it fast enough. She staggered toward the back door, hoping to reach fresh air.

She yanked the thong to her nose and it scorched her. What was going on? Blinking in shock at the amount of pain the amulet could produce, she doubled over. God, it was warm in the room. Her skin felt burning hot.

Was the cider alcoholic? She'd not thought so, but something wasn't right. Gasping, she tugged her coat away from her body, but it didn't help. A terrifying sensation of thousands of vicious needle jabs prickled the tender soles of her feet and spread upward. She tried to kick her feet free of her tall leather boots but couldn't. The burning sensation licked higher up her legs.

Gulping air, she fought a rising sense of panic. The pain escalated until it became unendurable. "Help!"

The curtain of the back room was thrown open, and Dame Bishop appeared. "What's wrong, dear?"

Arcona pulled herself upright. As swiftly as the horrid burning sensations had arrived, suddenly, nothing was wrong. The only thing amiss was that the sleeves of her trench coat were covered in dust up to the elbows from her writhing against the countertop. "Dear God, that was weird. For a moment, it felt like I was on fire."

"Really?" Dame Bishop didn't look surprised.

"Really." Nausea and a vague sense of guilt warred for her full attention. "Something's wrong. I think this amulet is cursed. Wearing it feels awful, and it won't let me take it off."

"Cursed?" Dame Bishop frowned. "I thought you were a skeptic?"

"I'm still a skeptic, but I'm telling you, there is something unwholesome about this piece of jewelry. Perhaps it should be kept in a sterile museum vault."

"Hold on a minute. Don't be so quick to judge." Dame Bishop wagged an admonishing finger in the air. "You were the one who felt like you were on fire. Maybe we should concentrate on that."

"Are you implying that what just happened to me was my fault? I put the amulet on and immediately had the experience of being burned alive. That's never happened to me. Does that sort of thing happen to you? It's kind of weird. I think I'm entitled to blame the amulet." She cringed at the childish tone of her argument.

Arcona took hold of the leather thong and tried to yank the amulet over her head, but it tangled in her long, auburn hair. Grasping the bronze setting, she tried to untangle the thong. The setting hooked on to her sweater and clung like a bur.

"Look at this thing!" She tugged at the amulet in exasperation. "It's like an octopus grabbing me."

"Leave it alone." Dame Bishop was terse. "Don't provoke it."

"What?" Arcona balked. "I want it off."

"It's not coming off, at least not until it's ready."

"No way." Arcona grabbed the thong and gave it a sharp upward yank. A hellish burning sensation racked her, making her skin feel blistered. "Holy shit!" she wailed.

She let go of the amulet and the pain stopped.

Dame Bishop's brow creased.

"You didn't know this would happen, did you?" Arcona fought down a rising wave of anxiety. "Please take it off. I don't want it near me, and I'm afraid to touch it."

"I wouldn't dare." Dame Bishop took a cautious step backward. "I can't take it off you. You're the only one who can free yourself."

"There must be something we can do? It hurts too much if I try to remove it, and I can't walk around wearing something the Smithsonian is waiting to receive. In a few hours, I'm supposed to be at the airport boarding a red-eye. What can I do?"

"You're not leaving Salem with the amulet. That would be unacceptable and cannot happen."

Dismay washed over her. "I don't want your amulet! I'd love to take it off and hand it back to you. Please just tell me how to do it without getting burned alive."

"It's not my amulet. I'm just a temporary caretaker." Despite a calm tone, Dame Bishop's gaze pierced her. "You're the only one who knows how to break the curse. I'm not the Strix — you are."

"Whoa, wait a minute, this is nonsense. This is a Halloween joke, right?" Arcona glanced around. "Am I being filmed for a reality show? Are you having fun jerking a tourist around, because I'm not enjoying it. Whatever you've rigged to this amulet causes real pain. If this is a prank, it's gotten abusive."

"I'm abusive? You're the one entering a redemption cycle. You'll find out." Dame Bishop shook her head. "I'm not doing anything to exploit or harm you; I swear it. It hurts because you're in the process of remembering your most regretful deeds. Take note that you came to me. I saw you were in need, but I let you go, and you quickly returned to the shop of your own will."

"I was lost!"

"Yes, you were, but a clear path has opened to you, and I heartily encourage you to use this brief opportunity on All Souls' Day to walk the path and set your wrongdoings right. It's the hand of fate at work."

"Regretful deeds? Punishing amulets?" Arcona's temper flared. "It's all bullshit! I don't know what you're talking about. What is it exactly that you think I've done? I know I'm not perfect, but my misdeeds in this life have been petty, stupid stuff. I have no idea how you would know any of this, but if you're talking about the potato I shoved in Principal Ross's tailpipe in middle school, I apologized profusely for that. I had no idea a potato could do that kind of damage to a car, a plank fence, or a plate-glass window."

Dame Bishop closed her eyes and clasped her hands in front of her face, almost as if she were absorbed in prayer. "I'm not talking about projectile potatoes, and I'm not referring to this life. I'm talking about guilty deeds of the past that have come full circle."

A sickening feeling weighed on Arcona. "I just want to leave. Please tell me how to safely get this amulet back in the box so I can go back to my hotel."

"I can't tell you how to free yourself from the amulet because I don't know the secrets of the Strix."

Maybe those aikido lessons would finally pay off? "I could walk out that door right now with the amulet."

"You could, but you wouldn't get far. Within minutes, you'd walk right back, and you wouldn't even know where you were going until you found yourself back at my shop."

She headed toward the door. "Shall we test that theory?"

"Shall I call the police and report the amulet stolen?"

"Stolen property? Really? That's an interesting concept coming from you."

"We're wasting time. Only a few hours of All Souls' Day remain, and you have yet to explore your acts as a Strix."

Hearing Dame Bishop denounce her as a Strix caused a wave of melancholy and she wasn't sure why. At that moment, Arcona wanted to go home so badly it hurt. Though her tiny bungalow near the beach was practically empty, and there was nothing waiting for her there, not even a pet. "How do I know if any of this is true? I'm not sure I believe in reincarnation, let alone any of the rest of this wild crap."

"It's simple. Everything in the universe recycles itself. You can see it with your own eyes. A human being is a single soul with many facets that returns to life again and again to polish itself. Would you like a chance to look back at one of those facets?"

"Can you do that?" Arcona's mood lifted. Maybe if she placated Dame Bishop and listened to what the *preeminent witch of Salem* had to say, they could cut this nonsense short. Bonus points if she could keep the snarky comments to a minimum. If she played nice, perhaps the old girl would stop giving her the Marquis de Sade treatment and take the damn amulet back. "Will it help? I just want this to be over. At this point, I'll try anything."

Dame Bishop motioned for Arcona to follow her into the front of the shop. "It might help to know what you're dealing with. At least I can offer you that."

She lifted the thong and again it burned like acid, so she dropped it. The amber had shot a spark. Was someone blasting it from some unseen location with an electric charge? Did Tesla invent something like this? Probably not. How was Dame Bishop doing this? What forces were in play?

They returned to the cozy firelit shop. Dame Bishop walked toward the front window and tugged the velvet curtain aside. A blaring red sunset glowed in the west. "It's already nightfall." Bending forward, she retrieved a Romanesque bronze dagger from the front window display. She turned with the polished blade clutched in her hand.

Oh my God, I'm locked in a creepy Wiccan shop with a psycho! Arcona gazed warily at the elegant but dangerous-looking blade pointed at her. "What are you going to do with that?"

"We are going to do some scrying, my dear." Dame Bishop closed the curtains and invited Arcona to sit at a small table.

Holy fuck, more madness. Should I just call 911 for help? She dug into her purse and searched for her phone. "Scrying? I don't know what that is."

"Scrying is the ancient art of divination. Using any reflective surface, one can look forward or back in time and catch a glimpse of the eternal moment. Some scryers sprinkle ashes on water, some read scattered tea leaves in the bottom of a cup, and, of course, there is the most classic scrying tool of all, a crystal ball. I prefer to match my reflective surfaces with my clients."

"Am I your client?" Arcona dreaded debt or further entanglement with this strange woman. "What do I owe you?" Discreetly, she clicked her phone inside her purse. No bars. Dead battery. It should be fully charged. Damn. Was the Silver Moon Scrying Shoppe the Bermuda Triangle of cellular connection? *Now what?*

"You owe me nothing." Dame Bishop held a dismissive palm to the air. "I'll be repaid; don't worry about it."

"I think I should be worried. I'm not enjoying this. Can't we find someone who can remove this nasty thing from around my neck?"

"No. Please sit. We'll have to take a traditional approach."

Terrific. More runaround from a mean-spirited trickster. Arcona pulled a ladder-back chair from the table and sat. She remembered the disruptive knock at the front door and wondered if she could or should trust Dame Bishop. This whole thing had gotten so weird, fast. "Who was here earlier?" Maybe help wasn't too far away?

"An agitated young man who mistook my shop for the bar next door. He was in the wrong place at too early a point in time." Dame Bishop sat opposite Arcona and placed the dagger in the middle of the table. "The problem was corrected. He's now in sync with the proper timeframe."

Wow. Dame Bishop thinks she controls time? She'd said it all with such a straight face, too. What a cuckoo bird. "He knocked on your door thinking it was a bar? Come on, this isn't a prohibition-era speakeasy. Are people accustomed to knocking on bar doors in Salem? It doesn't sound very welcoming or good for business." None of this was adding up. Arcona tugged on the amulet's thong, hoping against hope that she could wriggle free of the wretched thing and run away with the speed of a cockroach fleeing the kitchen light, but the damn thing scorched her again and tangled in her hair the moment she lifted it past her chin. Once again, she was forced to drop it.

"The amulet can't be removed by guilty hands. So stop fussing and give it a rest." Picking a long wooden match from its box, Dame Bishop struck it against the side. A tall flame flared blue before dying down to a pale yellow flicker. She lit a drippy tallow candle jammed into a brass holder. The candle flared to life, accompanied by a delicate swirl of black smoke. "That young man who came by here was in an unusual predicament."

What about *her* unusual predicament? For God's sake, an attention-starved wacko witch and an amulet that heated faster than fuel-soaked charcoal briquette were holding her hostage. "How so? I thought he was just looking for a bar?"

"Next door is an unusual bar named Slayers. It's a private affair and more of a closed gentlemen's club."

Euphemism alert. "A gentlemen's club?" Arcona muttered as she stared at the faint trace of black smoke twisting in the air.

"Yes and no. It's not what you're thinking. Slayers is an unusual sort of gentlemen's club." Dame Bishop picked up the dagger and handed it to Arcona. "If you're curious about what goes on inside Slayers, I'm sure you'd be welcome." A broad smile dimpled her pretty face. "Hold the blade to eye level, please."

Why was she cooperating with this nutcase? Because she had no choice, that's why. *Just bite the bullet and get it over with.* The sooner, the better. A steaming bowl of clam chowder and a glass of wine sounded perfect right now. Arcona raised the dagger in front of her. The hilt was richly tooled with a wolf's head motif, embedded with garnets that resembled tiny droplets of blood. The polished bronze blade reflected her wind-tousled auburn hair and wide, catlike green eyes, but other than those striking features, she looked rather pale and plain.

"What do you see?" Dame Bishop's voice carried a touch of confrontation.

She grinned at her reflection with a rising sense of discomfort. "Nothing special."

"That's not how another might see you." Dame Bishop reached forward, took the dagger from her hands, and tipped the blade over the smoldering candle. The fatty candle wax sputtered and released a steady plume of sinuous black smoke that spiraled around the blade. Watching the twisting stream of smoke flow upward proved hypnotic.

Unable to look away, she gazed at the dagger, Arcona's thoughts turned inward. *What kind of man would wield a blade like that?*

She closed her eyes as a vivid image complete with extreme sensory details filled her mind. The zealous roar of a crazed crowd rang in her ears. The mob screamed condemnations and hurled garbled curses into the air. Her blood curdled from the hateful rage that rang out in thousands of united voices. Where was she? The dank passageway where she stood was filthy and reeked of butchery and death. A man standing beside her wept in silence. Another retched and pissed down his leg, adding to the misery of the place. Her knees trembled. A horn blew a loud, shrill note.

The ominous clatter of a hand-cranked lift thumped behind her. She turned just as an iron cage packed with hissing leopards appeared at the top of the lift. An attendant opened the cage and cracked a whip in the air.

The terrified leopards bolted past the bars, down the passageway, and into the sunlit arena beyond. Hysterical screams of approval greeted the frightened creatures. The startled animals were quick to slink toward the perimeters of the arena in an attempt to hide, but a hail of arrows aimed at the surprised leopards drove the fierce cats away from the walls and brought the cheering crowd to its feet.

The leopards pounced on the fallen and wounded men already lying in the sand, and the screaming started in earnest.

The man standing beside her muttered, "We're going to die."

"Not me." She was surprised to hear the rumble of a deep male voice coming from her lips. "I'm already dead."

"Look at this." Dame Bishop interrupted the vision.

Arcona blinked and looked at the sooty blade of the dagger, feeling a moment of utter disorientation. *What the hell was that about?*

"Do you see it?" Dame Bishop inquired with a sweet tone.

Arcona nodded. The smoke clung to the bronze blade in uneven spiraling patterns. One of the sooty swirls had taken on the exact semblance of a snake, an Ouroboros, biting its own tail. "Do you mean the circular whirl?"

"Yes. Where were your thoughts just now? You had a faraway look."

"I don't really know," she hedged.

"I think the scrying marks are trying to tell you some aspect of yourself has come full circle." Dame Bishop paused. "Are you sure you don't know where your thoughts took you? For a moment, I thought I caught a whiff of blood."

Arcona started. "You saw what I saw?"

Dame Bishop shook her head. "No, not quite. The vision was strictly for you. I was just doing a little etheric eavesdropping."

"What I saw," her admission was soft spoken, "had nothing at all to do with the amulet. I can't possibly see how this is helpful to my current situation. In fact, it seemed like some sort of delusional nightmare, and on top of it all, I saw the world through the eyes of a man."

"Oh, my. That is unusual." Dame Bishop looked delighted with this odd bit of information. "Can you tell me more? Any details would be helpful."

The stench of death immediately came to mind, along with blood-clotted sand and the piteous screams of men. Dear God, had she ever willingly promoted or participated in anything so horrible? "I'm sorry, I don't remember any more." Her evasion sounded unconvincing.

"Are you sure?" Dame Bishop glanced at her sideways. "You look remorseful."

"It's disturbing." She shifted uneasily. "And I'm still not clear about what's going on and how much of this I should believe."

"Can I tell you something?" Dame Bishop set the dagger on the tabletop. "I scry for a living. It's my service to the community. I see and hear sad stories every day. When I sit down with someone, I know one of two things is going to happen. The first, which is far more common, is that a difficult situation is raised where a person has been traumatized, betrayed, or terribly wronged.

"For a number of reasons, it's much easier to accept the role of the victim. The people I perform scryings for readily embrace the pain of the past that was inflicted on them by others. For most people, believing they were victims causes no conflict. They expect to be the victim."

Tension clutched Arcona's gut. "And the second group?"

"The second group has different issues. They tend to resist the truth. As you might suspect, it's not easy to shoulder responsibility for being the perpetrator."

"Oh." The breath whistled out of her. A guilty feeling settled over her. "Are we done?" Desperate to breathe fresh air, she needed to get out of there.

The shop's phone rang.

She flinched.

Dame Bishop bolted upright from the chair. "Excuse me. I'm expecting an important call." She blew out the candle and hurried across the floor toward an old-fashioned telephone with a tangled extension cord. She lifted the receiver off the cradle. "Hello, Silver Moon Scrying Shoppe." Pressing the phone to her ear, a somber expression colored her face. "Yes, it's true we have a long-standing agreement. Rest assured that contract will be honored. I can confirm the names match. All of it is a perfect match, but is it fair…"

Arcona watched the candle smolder until the red ember at the top of the wick flickered out and the blackened wick curled as it cooled. Only the faintest scent of smoke hung in the air. She couldn't resist dipping a finger in a molten puddle of wax. The hot wax scorched her fingertip and instantly hardened, clinging like a tiny cap.

"I won't give my consent on that matter." Dame Bishop sounded concerned. "Use caution. These situations are unpredictable…. How would that be helpful? You do realize I've sworn to harm none." She turned her back on Arcona and whispered inaudible words into the phone.

Arcona took hold of the amulet, intent on freeing herself from the invasive object while Dame Bishop was distracted. She tugged at the thong, but the bronze setting grabbed at her sweater and held tight. Taking direct hold of the setting, she jerked it away from her.

A searing rush of heat, as if someone had poured boiling water across her chest, caused an explosion of pain. "Ooww!" She released the amulet.

"Stop that foolishness!" Dame Bishop swung toward her. "You can't simply lift the amulet over your head and be done with it. If the amulet has chosen you, it's because it has an important lesson to teach. You can't cheat your way out of it."

"This is crazy." Arcona slapped the tabletop as she stood. "I didn't ask for any of this. I'm leaving."

Dame Bishop covered the phone with her palm. "Where do you think you're going?"

"My hotel, the airport, home…."

"Absolutely not. You can't leave with the amulet. It's too valuable. You'll have to stay while we figure things out."

Her spine stiffened. "I don't have to do anything. From my point of view, you pushed the amulet on me and caused the problem. When you figure out how to get it off me without causing pain, the Smithsonian can keep it, but for now, I'm leaving."

"Wait!" Dame Bishop pointed her finger in the air and twirled it in a wide circle like an invisible lasso. "So long as you wear the amulet, I forbid you to leave Salem!"

"What?" Arcona's jaw dropped at the theatrics. "You can't do that."

"I just did." Dame Bishop returned to her phone call and whispered, "I'll be there in a few minutes." She hung up the phone and addressed Arcona with a firm, calm voice. "I must leave the shop. I have a pressing errand I cannot avoid. It will take about an hour, perhaps a little longer. I'll be back as soon as I can with some supper. We'll deal with the amulet then."

Dame Bishop reached for a hooded black cloak hanging from a brass hook behind the front counter and glided into it. Looking like one of Salem's many historical reenactments from the seventeenth century, she tugged on a pair of tight black gloves and grabbed a velvet purse, strode toward the front door, pulled the curtain aside, and drew the latch. "Lock the door behind me," she commanded. "Open it for no one but me."

Arcona hurried to join her. "You're going to walk away, and you expect me to stay?"

"Yep." Dame Bishop gave Arcona a gentle push and closed the front door in her face. From the other side of the glass, she pantomimed locking the door. The wind whipped her flowing cape into the air as she turned and walked away.

Arcona drew the latch on the door and let the curtain fall into place. "Too bad for you, Dame Bishop," she mumbled. "I have no idea how you'll get in the front door since I'll be leaving through the back."

She rushed through the storeroom, stepped past the stuffed goat, and pressed the release bar on the emergency exit. The door swung open, and she stepped outside the shop.

A blast of cold wind swirled around her legs as she peered into an unlit alleyway. Her eyes strained to adjust to the blackness. Damn, when did it get so dark? The temperature had plummeted, too. She let go of the door handle to draw her coat around her.

The brisk wind grabbed the back door of the shop and slammed it shut. The door locked behind her with a distinct *click*, leaving her stranded in a dark alley.

She glanced up and down the alley, seeing only brick walls, wind-scuttled leaves, and shadowy corners, but no clear opening facing a street.

"Terrific," she grumbled. A tense, spooky walk in whichever direction she chose lay ahead, and she still had no idea where she was. She stood frozen on the back step, wondering what to do.

"You look lost," a male voice purred beside her.
She jolted when she realized a tall man with a broad build was standing in the shadows, barely an arm's length away.

Chapter Two

Arcona's heart pounded in alarm. She shuffled backward until her boots slammed into the locked door.

"I didn't mean to startle you." A man with stark Nordic features stepped from the shadows, carrying a crate of clanking beer bottles. The angles of his lean face were severe, yet strikingly handsome. He appeared to be in his early thirties and looked elegant wearing a silky black shirt, dark-washed jeans, and black boots.

She gazed at the man with approval. His dark clothing was in stark contrast to his silvery-blond hair, which flowed past his shoulders. His pale brows and light eyes reflected moonlight. His only ornamentation was a thick silver cuff glittering on his wrist. Overall he presented a complementary palette of masculine black and silver, stunning to look at.

He set the crate on the ground. "I was just taking out the recyclables and saw you standing there."

The man's accent hinted at Northern European origins, but she couldn't quite place where.

"If you're waiting for Dame Bishop"—his pale gaze as icy as a glacier—"I'm sure she's gone for the day. She usually closes her shop at five, but she'll be back tomorrow at nine o'clock."

"I'm done with Dame Bishop. I'm heading back to my hotel." Arcona stepped into the darkness of the alley and hurried a few leaf-crunching strides in the opposite direction of the silvery man.

"I wouldn't go that way if I were you," he called out to her. She turned. "Why?"

"It's a dead end." A sly smile crossed his face. "Unless you're carrying a grappling hook and a climbing rope in your purse, you'll never get over the eight-foot brick wall waiting for you around the corner."

He lifted his hand into the air and motioned for her to approach. "Come here." His tone softened. "A beautiful woman shouldn't be walking alone at night; it's not safe. You can take a shortcut through my bar and walk straight onto a lit street."

She relaxed her tensed shoulders. There was something intriguing about his Nordic beauty that drew her toward him. "You own Slayers?"

"Yes." A proud smile warmed his sharp chiseled features. "You've heard of Slayers? My name's Varn." He thrust his palm forward in greeting.

"Hello, Varn." Too nervous to grasp his hand, she managed a half smile.

"Come inside and stay for a drink if you like."

"I thought Slayers was some sort of private gentlemen's club?"

Varn's brows arched. He laughed as if he enjoyed a private joke. "Slayers is a gentlemen's club by nature, not by choice. We'd welcome the privilege of entertaining an attractive female patron." His eyes glittered in the darkness as if they were casting their own light. "By the way, I'm not sure it's accurate to describe us as gentlemen."

He looked intense but seemed good-tempered, and it was a heady thrill to have such a striking man flirt with her. She loved the whole underworld attraction of ultratough guys, corporate specialist with military backgrounds, but had never found one she could actually trust and relate to; most were just trouble, plain and simple.

A cool breeze funneled through the alleyway and blew Varn's long hair away from his steep cheekbones. This guy sure looked like a big, burly bushel of trouble. His knuckles were raw with scars, like he got in a fistfight every Saturday night and won. Her imagination ran away with her, but what the hell? He was just a bar owner in a touristy town, not a world-class mercenary, for God's sake, though he certainly looked like one. The touch of danger called to her attention-starved libido like a siren song.

"If you don't mind, I think I will dart through." God help her, she was already considering staying for a drink and maybe more. Why rush back to an empty hotel room when a little fun might be had? She tried to be stealthy as she swept her gaze over Varn's thick forearms. His sleeves were rolled up, and he didn't seem the least bit bothered by the chill.

Cataloging each exciting detail in her mind, she loved everything she saw. Solid and steely described Varn to a T. How much would Devon love this guy's Nordic good looks? A lot. She owed it to Devon to at least check this guy out and report on her findings.

"Be careful stepping over the crates." He reached toward her and offered his hand a second time. "There are a couple of broken bottles. I wouldn't want you to get hurt."

She took hold of his hand. His grip was iron, and his hands bore heavy calluses.

Varn grabbed her around the waist and lifted her, almost to the height of his shoulders, with an easy swoop.

A gasp of surprise escaped her as Varn effortlessly elevated her high above the crates and set her down at the threshold of Slayers with care. At no time in her adult life had a man picked her up and lifted her so high with such ease. It left her breathless.

He opened the door for her with a flourish. "After you."

Breathless, she planted her heels on the ground. Men didn't just pick her up and twirl her through the air every day, especially gorgeous ones in black silk shirts. This was a special thrill. What else could this guy do to make her heart race faster? She guessed plenty.

Arcona entered Slayers. The building was chilly and dimly lit by old-fashioned kerosene lanterns in seeming defiance of fire codes. The scent of fresh-cut cedar hung in the air. Her first impression was that Slayers felt like a men's outdoor camping trip.

They walked down a narrow service hallway lined with wooden casks, dark cubicles, and storage closets, passing a small candlelit room strewn with earthy red cushions and a curved lounge before entering the main part of the bar.

Her gaze narrowed as she entered the room. The interior of Slayers was an odd, ultramacho ensemble of themes. Part of the bar was reminiscent of an Old West saloon complete with a naked lady etched into an antique Parisian-style mirror hanging above the bar.

The main room looked like a Viking longhouse with exposed wooden beams and dragons carved into the individual booths. The back resembled a military barracks embellished with Roman shields, medieval swords, weapons, and artillery shells of every description.

"Wow." Every bizarre detail dazzled her. Her restless gaze couldn't settle for long on a single thing. Slayers' decor seemed to chronicle every infamous moment in warfare and mayhem. "Who's your decorator?"

She began to worry she was barking up the wrong tree. When Varn had said gentlemen's club, had he meant gay? This place definitely looked like it was a testosterone-drenched, chest-thumping, dick-swinging, warcraft-loving, all-male celebration.

A few patrons sat in dark booths playing cards and drinking from an eclectic selection of pewter-topped beer steins or wooden tankards. The rough-faced men casually looked up at her before returning their full attention to the card game. There seemed to be a lot of combat boots and leather worn in this place, along with steel rivets and fur. The whole place looked a little too *Road Warrior* for her tastes.

Varn leaned close to her ear and whispered, "Would you like a Humpen?"

His deep voice sent shivers up her spine. "Would I like a what?" she asked in alarm.

Varn pointed toward a row of polished stoneware beer mugs lined up on the bar. He walked toward the bar, picked up a chunky mug, and began to draw a trickle of rich black beer from a keg. "A Humpen is a half-liter beer stein."

His gaze dropped toward the dark liquid filling the mug. "This is Slayers' signature brew. It's an ancient recipe, and the only kind we serve. Call it divine magic at its best. You can't get it anywhere else. I want you to try it and tell me what you think."

He handed Arcona the weighty mug with a tall head sloshing over the rim.

She accepted and fought the impulse to wipe her wet fingers on her pants. "Thank you." Hoisting the drippy mug in a toast, she grinned. "To Slayers." Before taking the first sip, she paused. "Aren't you going to drink?"

"I'm on duty." Varn busied himself tidying up the back counter. "Maybe I'll join you for a drink during my break."

She raised the mug to her lips and sipped past the dense head of foam. To her surprise, the liquid was thick and, despite its darkness, not bitter at all. Distinctly sweet, the beer had strong undertones of honey and tongue-warming herbs. "The flavor's unexpected. What do you call it?"

"I call it the second-best drink in the house."

"What's the first?" Good God, this guy was gorgeous. Too bad her phone was dead and she couldn't take a selfie with him just to prove to Devon that such hunks existed.

His gaze focused on her throat as she swallowed another sip. "You have a sweet tooth, don't you?"

Was his comment an allusion to her round hips? He did keep looking at her with heated interest. Maybe she had a chance, after all. Varn looked like the kind of guy who would prefer a more robust woman. Good for her. She cautiously wiped her lips with her fingertips in hopes of avoiding a foamy mustache. "I suppose I do."

Varn stared at her as if she were standing naked in his bar, and her breath hitched. Nervous, she drank more. Several sips later, the odd beer warmed her blood. Within minutes, the brew lived up to Varn's claims of divine magic. She felt happy and relaxed.

Slayers was filled with hundreds of curious objects, but her gaze kept compulsively returning to Varn and admiring some newly gleaned detail about him. Fascinating to look at, he perfectly matched his bar and resembled some sort of war-dogged hero from another age. His crystalline eyes never seemed to blink yet carried a hypnotic depth to them. Smiling back at him, she felt a strange sense of elation.

"You're a handsome man." Maybe it was the brew, but she couldn't control the nervous laughter that bubbled past her lips. Usually, attractive men left her in stupefied silence but not tonight. For some reason, she couldn't shut up, even though she wanted to. What was up with that? "You should get an agent and go to Hollywood."

Hollywood? Whoops, she did it again. What a cornball thing to say. But damn, she could see Varn in any number of tough-guy ads selling manly things to men like motorcycle boots and razor blades, or better yet, an epic Viking movie with lots of rough, semiconsensual sex scenes. Holy crap, that would be so hot. "I mean it. You should be in front of a camera." She heard her incoherent blabber and couldn't believe she was being so obvious.

Varn looked amused as he stepped from behind the bar and stood beside her. "Why would I want to do that?"

"So everyone can see what I'm looking at." *Where the hell is this bold attitude coming from? Time to shut up, Arcona, before you say something even more ridiculous. Got it?*

He traced his fingertip against the side of her throat. "What do you think you're looking at?"

"A gorgeous Teutonic god." She cringed. Damn, that was an awful line. Out of practice and bad at flirting, she just sounded desperate. "But I'm sure you've heard that before."

Digging his hands into his pockets, he appeared as bashful as a kid in a school play. "Not in those exact words. But thank you."

Oh my God, my Teutonic god to be exact, she sounded like a complete idiot. No sane woman said things like that. Too bad she wasn't carrying a roll of duct tape in her purse. She wanted to place a sticky strip securely across her blathering mouth and stop any more bullshit—like that last comment—from tumbling out. Seriously, what was wrong with her?

Varn smiled back at her. He didn't seem fazed.

She took another long sip of the brew. A warm rush surged through every cell of her body. Everything was lovely, and it became impossible to remain still. "What the hell is in this stuff?"

"Honey, hops, oats, a bunch of different herbs…. To be honest, Slayers' secret ingredient is enchantment."

"Enchantment? You don't read that on ingredient lists very often." Please, no. The visit with Dame Bishop had provided more than enough *magic* for one day. What was with the citizens of Salem? Was everyone a dabbler in the dark arts, even a freaking bartender? Enough already.

Arcona rubbed her temples and sighed. Something didn't feel right. Not bad, just different, as if her world had slipped slightly out of sync and then ascended to heaven. Everything around her was incredibly beautiful and shimmering with light. The highly polished wood on the bar…Varn's broad, sturdy hands… Damn, those were nice hands.

She had skipped lunch. Maybe this was a sugar rush? Making lazy motions, she swayed her hips to shimmering chords of music that played in her head. Closing her eyes, she rhythmically swished back and forth, almost gliding her body against Varn's thigh. "After your shift, do you want to…go somewhere? Alone?"

"And what?"

Why did she say that? She bit her tongue at the unexpected words that darted out of her mouth. This was bad. The beer, or whatever it was, had gone to her head. "I have an early flight. I didn't mean that."

"Too bad." A big, winning smile crossed his face. "My loss." They both laughed. His was hearty, hers nervous.

Toying with her purse strap, she turned to leave. "I've made an ass of myself and said way too much. Thanks for the beer. I should call a cab and go before I say or do something extra stupid." But how could she top what she'd already said and done?

"Wait." He tapped her hand, and the slight gesture brought her to a halt. "You're not stupid, and you're more than welcome to stay. I'm never lucky enough to have a woman visit Slayers. It's a privilege." He made a sweeping motion with his hand. "There are too many damn guys here. When I saw you standing in the alleyway, I couldn't believe it. I thought, wow, she's gorgeous. I wish you wouldn't run away. Relax, finish your beer, and I'll call a cab for you."

The man was so handsome. It might be fun to explore the situation and see if she could keep him smiling. "Okay, but I can't stay long. Go ahead and call the cab, please. I'll finish my beer while we're waiting."

Varn reached for a phone on the bar, picked up the receiver, and punched a long number. He muttered, "Please send a driver to Slayers bar in about an hour to pick up a customer." She started to protest. "An hour? Hey, hold on—"

He held his palm over the phone and asked, "Where do you need to go?"

"The Waterfront Hotel."

He nodded. "It's close. I could take you there."

"A cab would be better."

"Be here in an hour. No sooner." He hung up the receiver and eyed her beer mug. "Want a refill, Miss…?"

"Arcona. Thank you for asking, but I wouldn't dare."

Varn grabbed a bar towel from the countertop and used it to polish some beer steins. "Well, Arcona, I got what I wanted, another hour in your company. Lucky me." He gestured toward a table of men absorbed in a poker game. "As you can see, you're not interrupting anything of importance. What brings you to Salem?"

"I came here for an academic seminar." She made a mental note not to go into too much personal detail, but couldn't stop talking. "And to visit a college friend I haven't seen in ages. We thought it would be fun to get together and tour Salem."

"Was it fun?"

"Of course, it was." She hesitated just a second too long to answer and noticed his gaze flicker ever so slightly. The mini reunion with Devon had been a poignant reminder of all the things that weren't happening in her life. There was nothing to boast about, no new lovers or anything solid on her career horizon.

"Are you sure?" His brow lifted. Hot damn, even the tips of his blond lashes looked like they were dipped in silver. "Which college, Boston U?"

"Yes. Though I did my undergraduate work at Amherst." She reached for the beer, mead, or whatever this delicious drink was and took another sip. A wave of euphoria washed her glum thoughts away.

He looked at her like a big, lazy lion waiting for a gazelle to walk within paw's reach. "So what happens next?"

"What do you mean?"

"Where do you go next?"

"I go back to my hotel and fly home to the West Coast. At an ungodly hour."

"If you have to get up that early, why go to sleep at all?" He grinned. Backlit, he looked at her sideways, his profile stark. Her heart fluttered. Why couldn't she let down her guard and have a little fun for once? "Nice try."

"Do you blame me? You're a dream." He smoothed a strand of hair from her cheek. "Besides, I'm a sucker for red hair."

"My hair's not red." As obvious as his motives were, his compliment and the intense look in his eyes left her glowing. Hearing nice things about herself was really boosting her shattered self-esteem. "It's auburn."

"It's beautiful." He beamed.

Pinned to the spot by his gaze, she was left breathless. "Thanks."

Varn opened his gorgeous mouth and in a subtle and teasing way licked his lips. "Don't second-guess yourself. I say trust your first impulse, especially if it's a strong one. I'm brokenhearted you changed your mind." He laughed, and his whole face lit like a summer day. "Hell, I'd settle for a kiss." What was wrong with her? This sort of thing never happened in her staid world. Stunning men didn't insist on kisses and carefree sex no one else would ever find out about. Could she do this? Being abandoned by Mario for a younger woman had left her wondering if any man would ever find her attractive again. And damn, this guy had a twinkle in his eye if ever she saw one. Should she do this? Maybe just this once to break the ice? After all, she'd been completely celibate since signing her divorce papers. It wasn't like she did this sort of thing all the time…"I wouldn't say no to a kiss."

"If you're willing, come and get one." Varn reached toward Arcona and opened her coat. He skimmed the edges of his knuckles against the amber amulet and lingered near her breasts before slowly traveling toward the collar of her tight sweater.

Her nipples peaked and pressed hard against the lacy cups of her bra. The look on his face stunned her. "You're staring."

His gaze lowered. "I like you."

Really? This was great, and so not her usual behavior. She grazed her fingers across his jaw. The little voice in the back of her head screamed, *What the fuck are you doing?* But God help her, she wanted this.

"How adventurous are you feeling? Do you still want to go somewhere?" Varn stepped closer. He slid his booted foot between hers and pushed her ever so slightly off balance.

The air left her lungs. What did he mean by that? Arcona started to topple backward, but Varn was quick to catch her and wrap his arms around her waist.

74

He leaned her against the bar. His hands tangled in her hair, and pressing his mouth to hers, he delivered a sweet, lingering kiss. Drawing away from her, he looked into her eyes, gauging her reaction.

The kiss was cool, as if he'd just drunk from a chilled glass, but the sensations it provoked were incendiary. Her body blazed like a lit match tossed onto dry straw. She wanted more and wrapped her arms around his neck, locking him against her.

He held her fast against him with a hard bulge pressing between her thighs. "There's a soft, red velvet chaise in the back."

His voice was soothing as a lullaby. This was insane; she knew nothing about this man. The rational part of her mind waved a caution flag but got ignored. "Kiss me again."

"Here, where everyone can watch us?"

"No one cares." What was she saying? Of course, she cared. She'd better be more cautious about what she said. "Of course, I care," she whispered. "I never do this sort of thing." It didn't sound very convincing, and it should have. Her love life had been on life-support for far too long.

Varn dug his fingers into her hair and held her face to his. "Hush. No apologies. No shame. Not here." His next kiss started light, an electrifying brush of his lips to hers, but ended in ravaging claim. Pressing down hard, he took her breath, then nipped her bottom lip until it tingled.

This guy was so sexy he was killing her. "Where did you learn to kiss like that?"

"Valhalla." Pride flooded his husky voice.

She twined her leg around him and clung tightly. "I believe you."

"I know a lot of fun tricks." Varn grabbed her ass and gave it a squeeze. Gliding his lips to the side of her cheek, he leaned close to her ear and whispered, "I'd even be willing to share you if there's another man here you'd like." He paused. "Or I can take you somewhere private, just you and me. Lady's choice."

What an offer. She would never do such a thing, yet her traitorous body was begging her to do it. Excitement soared and she despaired of getting herself under control. It just wasn't going to happen. Her common sense had gone bye-bye. Was she possessed or something? Shocked with herself for even considering it, she turned and looked around. Four men in a near booth were engrossed in a quiet card game and seemed oblivious to her.

Good. No one else seemed interested in Varn's crazy scheme. Hallelujah, she was saved. But it was gratifying to have it offered. Maybe she wasn't a dried up fossil, after all. At least she was interested in living again and had a juicy story to share with Devon on their next marathon phone call.

Then her gaze traveled to a far corner toward an attractive man with tousled sandy-blond hair. The man sat so silent and still she hadn't even noticed him until that moment. He looked Middle European, but his upturned eyes had a touch of the Orient about them. A vicious scar on his cheek marred the pleasing symmetry of his lush mouth and square jaw. The man's build was broad-shouldered and solid. He dominated the booth where he sat alone beneath a Roman long shield mounted on the wall. Undeniably, there was something fascinating about him and she wondered if his voice matched his commanding presence. Damn it. She was almost out of the woods. Why did she have to see him in the first place? Now her gears were spinning.

The second she made eye contact, the man's intense gaze clashed violently with hers. He set down his wooden tankard and glared at her with hazel eyes that radiated hate. His lip curled in disgust.

Stung by his response, she glanced around. It took a moment to fully realize the disdain was aimed at her.

The man's eyes narrowed to slits as he volleyed a look of pure abhorrence her way. He was a lot to be confronted with, and his open disapproval messed with her mind. After all, he was just a stranger in a bar.

She could barely stand to look at him. His wrath-filled gaze repelled her. Unable to bear another moment of his laser-focused scorn, she turned away from the man.

Her chest felt hot. When she glanced downward, for a moment she imagined a tendril of smoke rising from the amber amulet and even smelled the faintest whiff of burning fibers. She clutched the amber; the bronze setting was cool to the touch. The weird sensations immediately vanished.

Varn loomed over her. He brushed a kiss against the crown of her head. "What does the lady want?"

Her gaze returned to Varn. At least she had his admiring attention. One Teutonic god would have to be enough. As a lover, she was badly out of practice and probably couldn't handle two anyway. "I pick you."

Looking pleased, he slid his hand across the hem of her sweater. "I'm good with that."

"Wait a minute." She stared into the half-empty stein. "What's in this stuff? I'll be honest, I have no idea why I blurted those things. That's not how I normally am."

"Too wild? Too much?" Varn leaned away and looked like a big cat lounging against the bar, not the least bit bothered by her flightiness. "You're the one who brought it up. We don't have to do anything. I'd like your company. Finish your beer. No pressure."

Grazing her hand across the open collar of Varn's black shirt, she traced her fingertips against a strip of silky platinum hair disappearing beneath. This guy's muscular build and good looks were just too tempting. "Let's talk." She wanted to do a lot more than talk. "But not here in front of everyone. Take me someplace private."

He smiled. "All right, but I don't want you to feel pushed." An ecstatic buzz overtook her as she seriously flirted with the idea of sex with a charming stranger. She was a proverbial good girl and had never allowed herself to do this sort of thing—ever. This was a super-adventurous first, but there was no way she could enjoy herself anywhere near that hateful man seated in the corner. It was a shame too. With his rugged face he looked so sexy in his distressed leather jacket. Except for his sour attitude, he was exactly the type of soul-wounded, lone-wolf warrior she fantasized about alone at night holding an overheating vibrator between her thighs.

Arcona stole one last look at the man's face. Yep, he was still glaring at her and as pissed off as could be in his own private Idaho. *The dude's probably a nutcase.* She was certain she didn't know this man, yet something about him was familiar, like he'd stepped out of a long-forgotten dream she was just now remembering.

She almost wished she knew him. He had such an intense vibe about him and appeared to be the kind of man who'd seen it all and prevailed. Too bad he was acting like a total bastard.

Varn took the stein from her hands and set it on the countertop. "Follow me." He slid his hand to her waist and steered her toward the back of Slayers.

Her gaze darted over her shoulder as they left. The man in the back booth shot a final dagger-laden glance her way.

What the hell was wrong with him? None of the other men in the scattered booths even looked up as she and Varn left the main bar.

They walked down the same service hallway they had entered through and soon arrived at the open door of the small candlelit room.

Varn pushed the door wide and motioned for her to enter. "What do you think?"

Entering the room, she glanced upward. The actual footprint of the room was small, but the ceiling towered high overhead and ended in a windowed dormer that looked out on a clear, starry sky. Windblown leaves scratched against the glass, and a slice of moonlight glowed above. She shivered. "You sure keep this place chilly."

"I'll warm you up." Varn shut the door. The single candle in the room flickered and nearly guttered out. He reached for her coat, slid it from her shoulders, and tossed it onto a richly upholstered wingback chair.

Trembling from both the chill and high-strung nerves, she paced the room. The thin weave of her sweater clung to the lace of her bra. Her nipples visibly pushed outward. Self-conscious, she locked her arms across her chest and rubbed her hands against her shoulders.

Varn moved closer.

Her gaze drifted toward the wide silver cuff on his wrist embellished with intricate Celtic knots and twisting dragons. The impressive piece of silverwork rose halfway up his forearm and hugged it like a shield. The ornate designs were broken by a large and conspicuously blank oval that appeared to have once contained a stone.

"You seem interested in this." Varn held his thick cuffed wrist in front of Arcona's face. "It's very old. The legend is a witch of the north forged it. She infused her will into the metal and used blood and sex magic to create an army of invincible warriors."

More witches? The tiny hairs on her nape stood. Either the residents of Salem were obsessed or this was the theme *du jour*. "That's quite a tale."

"In the old days they could do that sort of thing." A slight hint of bitterness invaded Varn's voice. "Such acts were allowed. The gods listened and granted boons more freely than they do now." He paused. "It's a shame; I long for the privileges and power of those days to return."

She pointed to the blank oval. "What's missing?"

A frosty gleam lit within Varn's eyes. "It once held a polished cabochon of red amber, just like the one you're wearing."

"This isn't mine," she answered, unsure how much she should say. "It's a loan."

Varn held the cuff closer. "Do the patterns look familiar? Do you know what they mean? Look closely," he demanded. "Take a guess."

Another person wanted her to assess yet another piece of ancient jewelry? Two in one day couldn't be a coincidence. Struggling to focus, she studied the cuff. The tangled, twisting dragons both fascinated and confused her. They seemed to slither over each other in one continuous loop and she could hardly tell where one ended and another began. It was equally difficult to pick out the dragons from the labyrinth of Celtic knots in the background. She tilted her head and allowed her gaze to trace along the sinuous lines of the serpents as she tried to solve the puzzle. The design presented a visual conundrum that left her slightly woozy.

Varn leaned closer. "Ready to take a guess?"

"Not yet." Her gaze almost crossed and became blurry from trying to concentrate on the design. Embedded within the main patterns there seemed to be tiny stylized scenes of an underworld populated with fanged skeletal creatures climbing the roots of a great tree and reaching toward the light. The ancient Norse motif was decidedly creepy.

The black beer she had drunk left her unsteady on her feet. She needed to lie down on the red velvet chaise before she fell to the floor. "I'm dizzy."

"I've got you." Varn pressed her back against the wall and pinned her there with a muscular arm placed on either side of her head. He gazed down at her with an inscrutable expression on his face.

Varn's silvery eyes caught the faint reflection of the flickering candle flame. "I want you to know this is an honor I never dreamed I'd enjoy." His voice remained somber. "We were ready to believe your kind was gone from the Earth."

"What?" She found his statement odd. Varn's tone was polite, but his eyes were menacing. At the moment, his expression was too intense to look at. What had she gotten herself into? He lifted the amulet from her sweater and swirled the pad of his thumb against its polished heart. "I know your secret," he whispered. "I can smell it on your skin. You're of the sacred northern lineage." Taking hold of the hem of the sweater, he lifted it above her bra. He cupped her soft flesh and pressed close. "I'm glad I got you first. I want the lion's share."

A chill rippled up her spine. This was getting too weird. "I don't feel right." The room spun. She slumped against the wall, praying not to fall. "I should go."

"No. You should take this off. It's in the way." Varn glared disapprovingly at her bra. He didn't wait for her response. He reached behind and effortlessly ripped the hooks of the bra apart. It snapped open with a harsh tear, and her breasts bounced free of the cups. She gasped in surprise at his strength.

He lowered his face to her breasts to kiss the smooth curves and nuzzle his mouth against her.

Arcona stepped away but stumbled. Why couldn't she walk? Varn's touch was overwhelming and no longer welcome. He grabbed her and turned her toward him. Her pulse throbbed in her ears as he drew her close and nipped her shoulder so hard she felt the sharp edge of his teeth scrape the skin.

"Stop!" she pleaded, but his grip held her tight.

"You're perfect, and so much more than I hoped for." He moved his ravenous mouth to her throat.

She made a futile attempt to push Varn away, but he was solid as stone and couldn't be moved. Swaying on shaky legs, she felt as if she had fallen prey to a raptor. Her mind fogged. She tried to speak but found the effort too daunting.

Varn pushed her to the wall.

With every shallow breath she took, she grew weaker. That damned black brew seemed to have robbed her of strength and free will. Her eyes drifted shut, and her head tipped back against the wall as all her desire to fight, resist, or reason with Varn fled.

Her only thought was that in a few moments Varn could do whatever he wanted and what he wanted probably wasn't nice. God help her, this was such a stupid mistake. She tried to protest but simply couldn't form the words or even lift a finger to save herself.

"You're mine now," Varn snarled as he effortlessly scooped her up, lifted her high above his head, and flung her across the room toward the velvet chaise.

Arcona sailed through the air and landed limp as a rag doll on the sturdy lounge with a loud *thud*. The breath whistled out of her. It took gargantuan effort to pry her eyes open a crack and shout, "No!"

Varn leaped across the room with blinding speed and almost took flight. He landed hard on the chaise. Crouching above her like a sentinel gargoyle, he glared down at her, malignance burning in his eyes. In a flash, he was on top of her, holding her wrists captive. In a heartbeat, he became the embodiment of death.

She lay half-smothered beneath his weight as he pinned her and parted her legs with his knee, convinced Varn's silvery hair and the glint in his eyes would be the last things she saw in this world.

He settled between her thighs and arched upward like a cobra poised to strike. "I gave you a choice and you came with me willingly." His voice became harsh as acid to her ears. "That gives me the right to keep you to myself and feed from you until I get what I want. You're mine. Beyond this point there will be no sharing. Do you understand?"

Paralyzed with fear, she couldn't answer.

Varn wrapped his hands around her throat and turned her chin to the side.

She squeezed her eyes shut in terror.

"Open your eyes," he demanded. "You must watch."

As she opened her eyes a slit, her body shook uncontrollably.

"This is how it's going to be." Varn held the silver cuff aloft and pressed a tiny button near its center. A single needle-sharp blade popped upward from the top of the cuff. "I make my formal claim on you. You are my blood slave, and you will submit to me freely and with respect." He pointed the blade to her throat and scraped the sharp tip across her skin, but even that light touch stung terribly.

"Don't!" she cried as warm blood trickled down the side of her neck.

Varn used his blunt finger to swirl a few droplets of blood from her skin. Enraptured, he brought the glistening fingertip to his lips and sucked it clean. He inhaled a sharp breath as an ecstatic expression crossed his face. "Strix blood is even better than I expected. It's going to be a fucking challenge to restrain myself." He smiled as his white canines descended to deadly tapering fangs. In the dim light he looked like a slavering wolf.

"Please let me go." Faint words squeaked unnoticed past her lips.

Varn reared back and lashed forward with the recoil of a bullwhip. His mouth and fangs struck her throat with such force her body stiffened and arched off the chaise as she screamed. A searing rush of pain left her writhing beneath him, helpless.

Varn sank his fangs deeper into her throat and sucked, making the lusty, guttural sounds of a hungry animal feeding. The hard bulge in his pants pumped against her leg with an insistent rhythm.

His bite left her stunned and unable to move. She became acutely aware her life was draining away with every gulp he stole. Soon, her heart slowed and it became difficult to keep her eyes open. Her lashes flickered. The space between heartbeats stretched. She struggled to open her eyes one last time.

With her strength fading, she stared upward at the dry leaves blowing outside the dormer window as Varn slurped blood near her ear. She'd been a fool and should have known better than to drink strange brews with dangerous men in Salem. Now it was too late.

Chapter Three
The Island of Nerthus. 78 AD

Arcona woke in dismay to see that the campfire had died to a low smolder. She'd fallen asleep and allowed the worst to happen. If she didn't get it burning soon, she'd have to start again from scratch, and on this damp, foggy morning such a task would be challenging.

She bolted upright too quickly, the violent motion making her head spin. Her arms stung. She glanced downward at the bloodied bits of shredded tunic she'd used as bandages. The cuts were fresh enough to still ache and bleed a little when she flexed her arms.

Why had she allowed herself to fall asleep? Now she was in trouble. The priestess might not come to the island to check on her for another day. She needed to find suitable firewood, not only for warmth but also to send a signal to the shore.

Her duties on the island were finished. A clear choice had been made. Now the real work would begin.

A hellacious vision had been granted. The Romans were coming. Death was on the march. There would be no time wasted on pretense, false talks, or treaties. She'd seen this particular legion for what it was: a band of thieves raping the world in the name of the Empire.

She had to leave the island and warn her people so they could stage an ambush against the legion and wield the first decisive blow. Intending to start a signal fire, she gathered a few smoldering branches and walked with them to the island's shore.

The heavy morning fog made it impossible to see the woods of the mainland or her people's camp, which was only a short distance across the cold, tumbling river. All lay blanketed beneath an eerie gray mist that muffled sound and revealed little.

A faint splash broke the silence. The steady rhythm of an oar dipping into the water moved toward her. The mist thinned, and she saw a small boat approaching the island, rowed by Hedron.

At the sight of Hedron's beaming face, her heart leaped with joy. Just as swiftly, the breath left her body. This was not good; it was a clear sign of betrayal. The gods had not stricken love from her heart in exchange for power. Seeing Hedron caused pain and doubt in her choices. Tension clutched her chest as if a cruel fist were crushing her ribs.

In this pivotal moment, the gods were still testing her resolve. "Arcona!" Hedron hailed her. As he approached, he jumped from the boat and dragged it ashore. He rushed to her with soaked boots. "Be quick! Get in the boat. We must leave." He held out his hand. "Roman soldiers have been sighted in our woods."

"I know." She displayed her bandaged arms. "I saw them in a vision."

Hedron's expression became somber. "What did the gods show you?"

"That I am to be their sacred weapon against Rome." Intense and somber, her voice had taken on a new and unfamiliar tone.

His frown deepened. "What about me? I love you above everything. When news of the Romans came, everyone scattered into the forest, including the priestesses, but I wouldn't abandon you. You belong with me. If you must, become a warrioress and fight at my side, but don't tell me I can never have you."

"Hedron." She stood firm, refusing to take his hand. "The choice has been made. It was decided long ago, but now I'm certain this is the right path. I'm sorry, but you can never have me. I've been called to a higher task. I'm going to take the vows of a priestess and wear the amber. You must accept the will of the divine as I have."

"I don't accept it." Hedron looked dejected. "It's madness! How can a lone woman defeat Rome? Get in the boat. Roman scouts were spotted moving upriver. We're not safe in the open. Come." He offered his hand again. "I'll lift you over the water; you don't have to get wet."

She reached for his hand; it felt solid and tough, just like Hedron's patient spirit. Why did she have to care for him? It made full commitment so much harder. For Hedron's sake, she must send him away without hope. She spoke with deliberate coldness. "I know what must be done, and my destiny doesn't include you. I'm going where you can't follow."

"You're exhausted and not making sense." Determination lit within his eyes. "You belong with me. Let me take you somewhere safe and get you something to eat. Then we'll talk."

"You're not listening." She steeled her resolve. "The gods made the choice for me. I'm merely acting on their desires."

Swoop! A loud swooshing object zipped past her ear and lodged into the center of Hedron's chest with a vibrating *ping*. Hedron staggered backward. Looking stunned, he gazed at the arrow driven deep into his chest. His lips parted, and blood trickled from his mouth. His eyes widened as he swayed to the side and toppled facedown into the river.

She may have screamed, but the shock was so great she wasn't certain. Every fiber of her shook with rage. Deafening shouts rose all around. A volley of arrows flew toward her, sending her scrambling to the ground for cover.

A group of armored Romans rushed forward with bows drawn.

"Stop!" the head legate commanded. He stared at her with dark, gleaming eyes. "It's a woman. Bring her to General Gaius."

* * * *

Slayers Bar, Salem, Massachusetts. Present day

Tyr sat at the back booth of Slayers, allowing Varn to do as he pleased with the auburn-haired witch. Not partaking in the mayhem surprised him. An hour earlier, he'd been raging to take the lead, confront the witch, punish her, and sink his fangs into her flesh while drinking her dry.

Arcona had it coming. She deserved it.

He'd waited nearly two millennia for this chance at revenge against the seductive trickster who had turned him into a blood-craving abomination, and the moment was nothing like what he'd expected. He knew he should feel relieved, even joyful, but he didn't. He felt sick.

Conflicted emotions rose, worse than any he'd experienced in years, and that was saying a lot. His existence as an Upir Likhyi had been nothing but conflicted actions and emotions. He was exhausted from his nineteen-hundred-year journey down a dark road and wanted it to end.

He toyed with the edge of the wooden tankard as a distraction. The enchanted spiced brew was the only beverage a Slayer partook of except for living blood.

Unlike Varn, he hated being a Slayer. He had renounced senseless cruelty and killing centuries ago and fed only on the willing and the doomed, never taking more than needed. He no longer participated in elite military campaigns or violent underground martial games dedicated to Mars. Saying no to those beloved practices left him lonely and suspect within the Slayer community.

He wasn't truly one of them anymore, but even if they disapproved, what could they do about it? He was far stronger than all of them, and infinitely older and wiser. All these long years, he'd managed to keep his precious head on his stubborn shoulders. Like it or not, he was the senior Slayer, the last man standing—or as they joked in the old Balkan countries, the lucky Upir Likhyi.

He didn't feel particularly lucky; he felt cursed, and his prolonged and unnatural existence carried a steep moral price. Along the way, he'd accrued centuries' worth of shame and self-disgust and done things to others he was loath to remember, but had to.

For him, there was no blissful loss of memory and no moving forward with his life. He was forced to live with the detailed memories of every deed he'd ever committed. Even the ones commissioned in the gritty dust of the distant past felt as if they'd occurred yesterday. Every murder, every moment of a victim's terror, the smell of the dying, every desperate cry—all of it remained intact, front and center in his memories.

To be a Slayer was to be trapped in an eternal hell realm of the mind without hope of exit.

With the harshest intentions, Arcona, the cunning Teutoni witch, enslaved and humiliated by Rome, had done this to him. She'd deliberately subverted the most vicious gods of Rome and mated them to her own north forest demons to create new monsters to roam the earth in the name of rage. Arcona had turned him into a weapon of revenge that had far outlived the Empire he was created to disrupt. Of course, the original Arcona had died long ago. Like all souls, she had traveled through the gates of death and rebirth over many lifetimes.

But not him. Such a cleansing had been denied. He was left stranded in a stale existence, a captive of a world that no longer needed him, an archaic public menace and a horror even to himself, and he hated her for it.

Through the flames of a Roman pyre, Arcona's soul had escaped the world, leaving him alone to live a Slayer's eternal nightmare.

But here she was again.

The witch had returned to the human realm. After nearly two thousand years, she had been reborn in a new body, but the soul was definitely the same. So was the name. He found that fact telling. This Arcona so strongly resembled the old one, they could be sisters. And more than a physical match, she also reeked of her history. The tangy-sweet scent of Strix lingered on her skin. He'd sensed the seductive aroma from across the room and resented its manipulative power.

Yes, Arcona deserved what she got at the hands of Varn. Too bad Tyr still loved her.

Her pitiful whimpers drifted from the back room.

Covering his ears with his hands, he snarled to block out her desperate sounds. In anger, he picked up the tankard and dashed it against the wall, splashing black beer all over the booth.

The other Slayers paid him a brief glance to see what the commotion was, but soon lost interest and looked away.

Seething with rage, the past flooded forward. He wanted to forget he'd ever wept tears of blood for her loss. Surely Arcona must know, or suspect, what she was? How could she not? Her long-avoided judgment day had arrived. It seemed fitting that on All Souls' Day, in the city of witches, Arcona would step inside the chalked circle of fate, face her accusers, and pay for her selfishness.

So why couldn't he enjoy the moment? Every one of Arcona's soft pleas floating from the back room made him cringe. He didn't want to hear them. He'd sworn off cruelty long ago, and what he heard Varn doing most definitely sounded cruel. Her frightened sounds stabbed at his conscience.

He shifted restlessly on the booth's wooden bench. Why was he allowing this to happen? This was yet another event sure to hang heavy in his mind and cause an eternity of emotional pain.

Arcona hadn't turned Varn into an Upir Likhyi. Another Nordic witch had made Varn during the long winter of the Dark Ages, but that wasn't of consequence. By Varn's reckoning, all women, especially witches, were useful *things* to draw upon. The Viking had a bad reputation for excessive brutality with his victims. He enjoyed seducing and then turning on them.

She was Tyr's maker, and he was being a coward. Arcona was his responsibility to punish, and his alone. He'd been reckless to allow Varn to do his dirty work. Varn would go too far. Arcona would die before anything useful could be learned. Conflicted emotions built until Tyr couldn't stand them another second.

He bolted from the booth, grabbed a bronze dagger from the wall, and raced down the hallway toward the sound of Arcona's earsplitting screams.

When he reached the locked door, he kicked it to splinters with the heavy sole of his boot. The door burst open, and the candle flickered out, but his keen Slayer eyes possessed perfect vision in the darkness. Arcona lay motionless on the chaise with her thick hair tumbling over the side.

Varn glanced up from his limp prey with enraged eyes and hissed, "Fuck off! I'm not finished."

"Let her go." The threat-laden words chipped off his tongue like brittle bits of frost.

"You're a fool!" Varn laughed. "You had your chance and turned it down." His mouth was sticky with blood. "After the first sweet taste of Strix, there's no way I'd share her."

The determination in Varn's voice signaled he'd fallen into bloodlust and had long since passed beyond reason. To claim Arcona, Tyr had to challenge his strongest rival and take her by force.

Tyr lunged forward and slashed the dagger across Varn's face. The strike made a harsh popping sound as Varn's cheek split. A flash of white molar showed through the fleshy slit. Howling in pain, Varn darted away from Arcona's unconscious body. He leaped high against the wall and clung like a fly, one hand gripping his cheek. "Damn you. I knew you'd change your mind. Weakling. You don't deserve seniority with the Slayers. I do!" Varn sneered. The flesh of his cheek buckled, revealing the shocking damage to his face. "I've made a formal claim on her. The Strix blood I've taken from her will soon make me as strong as you, but I won't be such a fool. I know how to use power." He released from the wall and zoomed toward Tyr, knocking him backward. "She's mine!"

When Varn sprung forward, Tyr ducked. Varn smacked hard into his shoulder, slamming him to the floor. In an instant, all his years of brutal training as a gladiator kicked in. A man down was a man doomed. Rolling from beneath Varn, Tyr shoved him aside with a single swift stroke of his forearm. Lightning-quick, he leaped to his feet, grabbed Varn's ankles, and spun him violently through the air with increasing velocity. Summoning the titanic force centuries of rage had harnessed, he heaved Varn's twirling body higher and released it into flight with a victorious roar.

The hulking Viking sailed into the air and crashed through the dormer window above. Varn continued to soar into the night sky before pausing midair and then sinking back to earth. He landed hard on the rooftop with a crash. Making a noisy clatter, his body rolled across the steep pitch of the roof followed by a heavy *thud* to the alley below.

Pointed bits of broken glass wobbled precariously in the window frame. A gust of wind snapped a chunk of the shattered pane free. Tapering shards of glass tinkled downward like a rain of stilettos. Arcona lay motionless on the chaise directly below the pummeling stream of glass.

Tyr saw what was about to happen and threw his body over Arcona's limp frame to spare her the falling dagger-like shards.

Jagged bits of glass struck his leather jacket, jeans, and boots. A narrow, wedge-shaped piece sliced through his pants leg and pierced his thigh like a knife. He growled in anguish.

In extreme pain but triumphant, he decided it had been worth it. Arcona had to be shielded. If he wanted her alive and repentant, this brief agony must be endured. He could not allow her to die and escape his justice a second time.

The slice in his leg left him groaning, but he knew any damage inflicted on him would heal within days, and he'd soon be all that he ever was. But that also went double for Varn. Though his attack had been brutal, Varn was only stunned and would come looking for vengeance the moment his body healed. More problematic, Varn had drunk from the Strix and taken on some of the witch's transformative powers. Once Varn healed and fed again, he would be an exponentially stronger and even more vicious version of himself. Allowing that to happen had been foolishly shortsighted. Tyr vowed to avoid any more mistakes of such magnitude.

The menacing bits of broken glass stopped falling, and cold air from the outdoors sank onto them.

Tyr lifted his weight off Arcona and turned to examine his leg. A slender spike of glass protruded. He took hold of the shard and yanked it free. Tossing the bloodied piece of glass aside, he rose on a shaky elbow.

He surveyed the damage to the room. The place had been wrecked. He rubbed the blood from his hands onto his pants leg. The jagged gash in the denim would never mend, but he knew from many past experiences that a shallow stab in the thigh was not a permanent problem. The wound was a painful but temporary inconvenience that rest and a couple of blood feedings would easily alleviate.

A faint squeak of a moan escaped Arcona's lips.

For the first time, he took a good look at the young woman lying beneath him. Her eyes were closed, and her arched lips were parted in a peaceful expression. Her smooth skin was pale and cool. Varn had taken a lot of blood from her, but she still had a slow heartbeat and was most definitely alive.

He hadn't thought much of her when she'd first entered Slayers, but gazing at her up close, he had to admit he understood Varn's reluctance to give her up. Something about her created an irresistible attraction. She had the lush curves he'd loved as a man. He remembered how good it'd felt in those days to run his hands across a woman's silky skin, get hard and be able to spend himself inside a soft, willing beauty. *Those days were good.*

The thrill of a blood feed was always exciting, but unlike the other Slayers, what he missed most about his old life was the soul-drenching moment of sexual release. He thought it ironic that it was Arcona who had denied him that human pleasure when she'd changed him into what he was now.

She'd pay a heavy tribute for that loss, he'd see to that.

Icy wind howled overhead. A few stray leaves blew past the smashed window and swirled into the room. Soon, Varn would rise from his stupor. A confrontation was inevitable. They couldn't stay here, but Salem was not his home, and he had nowhere to go.

He examined the bruised puncture marks on Arcona's throat where Varn had done some sloppy drinking. The twin wounds gaped crimson, and the surrounding skin had turned a traumatized shade of purple. He frowned in disapproval. As always, Varn had been too rough. This defenseless woman was less than half Varn's size; using such force was completely unnecessary.

For his own selfish reasons, he had to keep her alive. He leaned down and slowly dragged the flat of his tongue across her still-trickling wounds, knowing his saliva had the power to soothe and heal if he chose to use it that way.

The moment the tip of his tongue swept across Arcona's cool skin, her sweet, floral, and long-denied flavor sent shivers of ecstasy rolling through him. His groin tightened at the first provocative taste of Strix blood, and the light musky scent of her skin slammed into his heightened senses.

A faint growl of pleasure rose from deep within his throat. He tangled his fingers in her hair and pulled her closer for a second taste. Like a hummingbird, the tip of his tongue flickered across her skin. A feeling of warmth, love, and everything missing from his sour existence enveloped him. He paused and then drew away. Tender feelings? Overwhelmed by gentle and unfamiliar emotions, his hands quaked. How strange. Centuries had passed since his heart had experienced a reaction such as this, yet the feelings were not forgotten, striking like lightning bursts inside his hollow soul. Mars never allowed anything like kindness or concern to get in the way of his elite warriors. As a Slayer, the vicious gods of war had held him captive under their thrall for so long, an emotion as delicate as tenderness was not possible for him. Why would he even pretend such an unlikely thing was happening? What was wrong with him?

The unfamiliar sensations left him trembling with want. Arcona's honeyed taste provoked irrational thoughts. For a fleeting moment, he felt like a man again, with a healthy man's desires. His eyes closed in bliss as a bright, coppery intoxication unlike anything he'd ever experienced during a blood feeding hammered him like a heroin rush.

His cock pressed hard against his jeans, demanding release. He longed to give in to the intense pleasure of rubbing between her round thighs as he fed with voracious fervor from her throat. By all the gods, he wanted it so much he lifted his face skyward and howled like a hungry wolf as his fangs lengthened.

"No." He pushed himself away from her with a gasp. A feeding of that intensity would kill her. This situation called for restraint. He wanted her fully awake and conscious of her persecutor when it happened.

Feeling extreme conflict, Tyr's gaze fixated on her throat. The deep gashes on the side of Arcona's neck left behind by Varn's fangs sealed shut and her bruises faded. Another minute passed, and only a few shadowy spots were visible. The healing powers of his saliva had never been this swift. The speed of her recovery was uncanny, and he couldn't take credit for it.

He suspected other forces were at work. Had she used her own sort of enchantment to heal? She wore the amber amulet of the Strix; the hated object had been branded into his memory. Clearly, the new Arcona had fully adopted the ways of the witch in this lifetime, as well.

Reaching out, he dared to touch the translucent amber. A part of him recoiled in disgust. If he weren't careful, he might once again be manipulated and fall victim to her selfish tricks. He drew farther away from Arcona, vowing to remain wary.

She moaned and shifted on the chaise. Perhaps she felt the cold; she struggled to draw the sweater over her, but she seemed incapable of such an effort. The fabric remained rumbled under her arms. A flush of color returned to her cheeks. Everything about her, from her coral lips to her satiny skin, invited his lust-starved senses to give in.

Having her so near was more temptation than he could bear. He ached to leap on top of her, sink his fangs into her soft flesh, and feed to satisfaction. Another rebellious part of him longed to bury his face between her breasts and circle her nipples with the tip of his tongue just to remind himself how it felt.

The struggle of holding himself in strict control left him shaking. In the old days, he'd loved drinking in the sharp flavor of a fallen warrior's blood on the battlefield. Fellow warriors had always been his primary prey, but the man in him still preferred the warm softness of a woman's skin brushing against his chest as he fed. How long had it been since he'd allowed himself to enjoy such an opulent feast— four hundred years, five? He gazed down at Arcona in silence. Varn had destroyed the delicate straps of her bra, ripping the tough fabric like wet paper. Taking hold of the shredded remnants of her lingerie, he slid the tattered garment from her shoulders and tossed it aside. With reluctance he tugged her sweater downward to cover her bare skin, but her other enticing charms still held him enthralled.

He stared at her face, unable to look away from her peaceful pose. Lying beside him, she looked so innocent. If he didn't know better, he might think she was lost in a pleasant dream. The thin sweater without a bra did little to conceal her beautiful curves; if anything, it enhanced them. Almost overwhelmed by the sight of her, he fought the urge to pounce.

A single clear thought lingered. *Arcona, why did it have to be this way?*

He smoothed the amber amulet into place. The original Arcona had worn it close to her heart until the last moments of her life, when a self-righteous Roman master had stripped it from her neck and tied her struggling body to the pyre in the center of the arena.

Not a single spectator in the stands protested the man's actions; most cheered him on with enthusiasm. There had been no public sympathy for Arcona. The crowd was grateful to have one less malevolent witch haunting the slave quarters of Pompeii.

He'd lurked in the back of the frenzied mob and watched the immolation from a safe distance. At the first sight of the rising flames and the sounds of Arcona's piteous screams, even at the peak of his hatred for her, he'd turned away, unable to watch his once-sacred lover and bitter betrayer consumed by fire.

Arcona had snuck into the barracks of the gladiatorial school and forced his lonely heart to love her. She'd deceived him and changed him into something horrible, but watching her burn had brought no real satisfaction or sense of justice. The moment thick black smoke had billowed above the arena, a sense of emptiness he now realized had never faded had settled over him.

Now, he needed answers from her. He wanted to hear from her own lips why she'd done what she'd done, leaving him alone to walk through time as a bloodthirsty monster searching for his next war.

He slipped the heavy leather jacket from his shoulders. His rounded biceps strained the capped sleeves of his snug black T-shirt as he half lifted Arcona and threaded her limp hands through the sleeves of the jacket. The long cuffs hung past her fingertips, and the large garment swallowed her with room to spare. He scooped her off the chaise, hoisted her over his shoulder, turned, and strode toward the door.

The heavy soles of his boots crunched the many chunks of glass scattered across the floor. His thigh stung where the jagged shard had pierced the muscle, and he took lurching steps. The wound was more serious than he had initially thought and would require considerable resources to heal. Too bad his saliva did nothing to help him. To fully regenerate, he'd have to blood feed and do it soon.

With Arcona's arms dangling over his back, he limped forward. Her trench coat and purse lay strewn across a chair. He snatched them as he passed, knowing he would need the jacket to keep her warm. The next step was to get her someplace safe where he could interrogate her at his leisure. This place was definitely not safe for either of them.

Without question, the other Slayers would superficially bow to him as the oldest and strongest Upir Likhyi, but he knew in his heart they would side with Varn. Ever since he had professed his disgust with modern warfare, Varn had risen in a quiet but persistent manner as the unofficial leader of the still-bloodthirsty Slayers who viewed the violence of the modern world as a boon.

It was long past time to leave Slayers bar, a dour place where immortal mercenaries gathered and waited to be called into action by fading gods and chaos-obsessed demons. Most likely, he would never return. If all went as he hoped with Arcona; soon, he would no longer be a Slayer.

Anxious to be away from there, Tyr hobbled faster, Arcona's unconscious body swaying against his back. When Varn woke, they needed to be long gone without leaving an easy trail to follow. There was no way he could effectively fight a fellow Slayer enhanced with Strix blood and deal with Arcona at the same time. A choice had to be made, and he chose the witch.

His car was parked around the corner in the alley. Tyr shoved the exit open with his shoulder. The snap of cold night air bit into his bare arms. He shambled down the steps past stacked crates.

Sprawled at the base of the stairs, Varn's broken and twisted body lay motionless in a heap.

Tyr leaned over the still form lying faceup on the ground. Varn's vacant eyes, the color of moonlight, stared skyward. He wasn't dead; that wasn't possible. As a Slayer, his body had shut down all animate signs in order to concentrate on regeneration. As soon as his injuries healed — weeks, days, or perhaps scant hours from now — Varn would come roaring back, pissed off as hell and with increased strength. Clutching tight to Arcona's round hip, Tyr limped away from the disturbing scene.

Chapter Four

Arcona's head throbbed with pressure as she bounced against something moving and solid. She dug her fingers into the object and felt a brushed-cotton T-shirt.

What the hell?

Struggling to open her eyes, she saw the world upside down. A muscular denim-clad male butt flexed inches from her face. The view from that position was surreal. *Is this a bad dream, or a dream come true?* She couldn't tell. Her head thumped against someone's muscular back, someone who had slung her over his burly shoulder with the same casual ease he might use to carry a sack of grain. She hung limp and too weak to fight as he lugged her across a dark alley toward God knew what.

Weird and confusing images floated in her mind, flashes of silver, fangs, fear, and blood. It made no sense. The mental pictures were so chaotic and disjointed they had to be the residue of a nightmare. Extreme dizziness overtook her. She closed her eyes and willed herself to simply forget all of it.

The next vague moment of awareness came when she was set down on the cushy bucket seat of a sporty car. Someone with broad hands buckled the seat belt around her as if she were a sleeping child. "Thanks, Dad," she mumbled.

"I'm not your fucking daddy," a gruff male voice filled with anger blasted her ears.

Her eyes flickered open just in time to see a handsome but pissed-off-looking man slam the car door in her face.

She yanked her hands onto her lap a split second before the door shut with a loud crash. "Bastard, I could have lost a finger!" Arcona shouted through the closed door, but he'd turned away and didn't hear or else chose not to acknowledge her.

The man hobbled around the front of the car, dragging one leg as he walked.

Glancing around the all-leather interior of the car did not reassure her. A chrome skull capped the racing stick shift, a massive speaker system dominated the car doors, and a fire extinguisher strapped behind the driver seat screamed muscle car and performance driving.

This wasn't her practical, nondescript beige compact with the good driver discount insurance slip tucked in the glove compartment; that was for sure. She looked down at the leather sleeves hanging over her wrists. This wasn't her coat either. Her trench coat and purse lay at her feet. What the hell was going on?

The man flung the driver-side door open and allowed his big body to drop gracelessly onto the seat. He listed his head against the padded headrest with a sigh of exhaustion, closed his eyes, and gritted his teeth. His left leg remained outside the car. He grimaced as he grabbed the leg beneath the knee and hauled it inside, howling as he let go and let it fall with a heavy *plop*.

She gazed at his gashed leg, sticky with blood. It looked bad. "What happened to you? You need a doctor."

He ignored her as he thrust the pad of his thumb against a yellow ignition button. A powerful eight-cylinder engine boomed to life with a sound as deafening as a missile launch. The dashboard lit with an impressive but indecipherable array of dials and lights.

Covering her ears with the leather sleeves, she shouted above the roar, "I want to get out!" Weak, dizzy, and nauseated, she had no business walking anywhere, but she didn't want a ride with this strange man who looked like trouble.

"I can drive myself home." Which was a total lie because her car was at home — on the other side of the country. How had the situation gotten so out of hand? Had they been flirting and drinking inside the bar? It seemed unlikely. Why couldn't she remember anything? "Maybe you got the wrong impression back there. I prefer to be alone right now."

"Shut up!" He looked at her with hate-filled eyes that glowed amber from the yellow ignition light. "Don't talk. Not yet." Her jaw dropped. "Fuck you, mister! What am I doing in your car? I don't want to be here. How dangerously unsocial can you get? You do understand you've already broken quite a few laws. What's your problem?"

"You're my problem." His gaze narrowed to threatening slits. "I can be very dangerous and very unsocial, so don't provoke me."

Throwing her weight against the car door, she tried to jump out; this was a bad scene. Even if she died trying to get away from this man, it would be worth it. She butted her shoulder against the passenger door but it didn't budge, and she felt no buttons or levers on her side that could free her.

"You're wasting your time." He watched her struggles with a self-satisfied smile. "The door locks with a steel bolt and the release lever is on my side." Planting his palm on top of the chrome skull, he threw the car into gear and stomped his boot on the gas. The tires squealed, and the car careened to the side before bursting down the alley like a bullet.

Spinning the wheel, he drifted the car around a sharp corner, pushed the gas pedal to the floor, and shot past a row of stacked pallets that toppled when the bumper smacked them. Splintered bits of wood burst into the air.

He drove like a charging bull. Arcona cowered against the seat. They were going way too fast. Was this the dead-end alley coming up? She covered her eyes and screamed. The car slid sideways and roared onto a paved street.

She jerked her head back to see where they had come from. The entrance to the alley disappeared into the distance. "Eight-foot brick wall my ass—that creep lied!"

"Who lied?" He stared straight ahead as he negotiated his way through the narrow streets with precision.

Why did she say that? Who was she talking about? No names or people came to mind. Awareness that something bad had happened to her that night rose, but she couldn't get a grasp on exactly what. Her memory was muddled. Had she been drinking in a strange bar, or had some of that been a dream? No, she'd been with a weird woman who'd given her something odd to drink. Maybe that was the dream? The pissed-off man to her left looked familiar, but why? She had no clear idea how she had gotten there. The evening's sequence of events remained an opaque fog. The only thoughts to break the surface were of a silky black shirt, a glimpse of pale blond hair, and beyond that, little else.

"I don't want to be here." She studied the driver's face, memorizing the slashed scar on his cheek and his every tiny mannerism, hoping that if she survived the ordeal she might have the privilege of making a positive identification in a police lineup.

"This is kidnapping." Perhaps she could reason with him. "What you're doing is totally wrong and carries a heavy sentence. You'll get zero sympathy from a jury." Pausing for effect, she attempted to sound calm. "I'm not hurt, so why don't you pull over and let me go before anything happens that can't be undone. Okay?"

He didn't answer and continued to stare straight ahead as he drove like a demon. The front bumper clipped a trashcan and sent it hurling onto a lawn.

She jolted in terror and realized she needed to keep talking and trying to reach him if she were to have any chance of survival. "I don't know why you're doing this or why you're so angry, but this is a mistake. I've never done anything to hurt you. You don't even know me."

His beautiful but menacing lips curled with a huff of disgust. "Wrong on both counts, Arcona." He sped faster down a dark lane. A flurry of dead leaves blasted skyward.

She froze. He knew her name. How? Had he snooped in her purse? Followed her from the hotel? Dear God, this was bad. This had been premeditated. She had to do her best to remain a human being in his eyes and not a thing to be used and disposed of. "You know my name, so tell me yours."

He glanced at her, suspicion shining in his eyes. "My name's Tyr." A tense silence hung between them. "Sound familiar?"

The name didn't sound familiar at all. Why would he think it should? It sounded like a place in the ancient world. "Tyr as in tier of a wedding cake, or Tyr as in Tyrian purple dye?"

"I'm more like the dye." An ironic little laugh crossed his lips. "I leave a bloody red stain, and I last a long time." He continued to laugh quietly but not in a pleasant way. "'Dye' — that's very funny." He looked amused by some private joke she was excluded from as he mumbled a few incoherent words in a foreign tongue she could not even begin to identify.

When he nearly struck a parked car, she screamed. This guy drove like a maniac. She clutched the seat as he swung around a sharp corner without lifting his foot off the gas. "Where are we going?"

"I haven't decided yet. I have a safe house in Connecticut and a mansion in Baltimore, but there are other options."

Her heart sank; she was in for hours of torment in this car. "Do you really want to get on an open highway with me and try to cross state lines? That's a huge mistake, my friend."

"I'm not your friend."

"I'm being sarcastic!" She bit down on her lip. This was not the time for sarcasm. Her life might be on the line. *Think.* "If you get on the highway, I'll wave like crazy to every car and truck driver we pass. I'll signal to everyone we see."

"Not if I put you to sleep," he rumbled.

She didn't like the sound of that. Time to pull out all the stops. Dying in a car accident seemed preferable to whatever brutality he had planned. She lunged at him, scratching at his face. "Let me out!"

Her attack left him swatting at her. He lost control of the wheel. The car slid across the road, spun, jumped a low curb, and skidded across a grassy parkway beside an ocean inlet. Fighting to regain his grip on the steering wheel, he pushed her back into the seat with a firm shove. His eyes flashed golden. "Stop it!" He snarled at her and his canines descended to sharp white fangs.

She cringed and drew back. "Holy fuck! What are you?"

"I'm your monster, and I'm battling like hell to keep myself from throwing you in the backseat and sinking my fangs into your throat, so stop it. I'm going to be fair and give you a chance." The car spun its tires as he righted the wheel and steered back onto the dark, tree-lined road. "Even though you don't deserve one."

"What do you think I've done to you?" she asked in utter confusion. "Who do you think I am?"

"You're my maker." An icy grin twisted his beautiful mouth. "Do you not remember?" The fangs retracted as swiftly as they'd come. His broad set of white teeth returned to normal. "It's been a long time, but we'll get reacquainted." He thrust his palm in front of her face.

His rude hand gesture filled her vision and hovered an inch from her nose.

"Sleep," he commanded.

Despite the tension and his abrasive actions, her eyes closed in involuntary yet peaceful sleep. She slid down the seat into the velvety blackness of a strange, trancelike dream.

* * * *

Arcona crouched on the gravel beach. Hedron's body had wedged itself against a rock. As she tried to drag him ashore, she found herself surrounded by the enemy.

Soaked and shivering, she concealed her empty hands in the folds of her tunic and tried to stare the Roman soldiers down, knowing it was only a matter of moments before they realized she wasn't armed and rushed forward. Why had she left her knife by the campfire? It was foolish. At least with a weapon in her hand she could die fighting with dignity.

Making slow, stealthy movements, the Roman soldiers fanned in a half circle around her. Their intense gazes never broke. They stared at her the same way they would an exotic animal trapped in a snare. The icy river and Hedron's dead body were at her back. She refused to glance behind her at them. Her heart couldn't bear it.

Several of the Romans appeared to be her age or younger. She guessed these men were scouts and not seasoned centurions. They had a light dusting of black whiskers on the sides of their jaws and muscular, compact bodies. Their breath came in quick bursts, and despite the cold morning, perspiration glistened on their sun-browned skin. The youngest men possessed a feral, undisciplined look in their dark eyes. Those men scared her the most.

The legate wore a crimson cloak the color of clotted blood, and an ornate sword belt weighing on his hips. Sun-weathered and silver-haired at his temples, he appeared to be the most mature man in the group. "Come here." He coaxed her forward with a wave of his hand. "I want to look at you."

"By Jupiter, their women are dirty," one of the scouts said in disgust. "Look at the filthy rags wrapped around her arms."

"She's been injured." The legate hissed a warning at the man to be silent.

The scout looked sheepish and shut his mouth.

Another soldier darted forward, threw his arms around Arcona, and knocked her to the ground.

Arcona hit the gravel beach with a *thud*. The soldier landed hard on top of her and pinned her. His weight pushed down on her until it became difficult to breathe.

The soldier snarled in her face. "The legate wants to look at you. Don't ignore him!"

The legate strode toward Arcona. "There's no need to shout. She can't understand you." His cool gaze poured over her. A slight smile lit his lips. "She certainly is dirty, but a simple bath will solve that problem." He leaned closer. "Her eyes are a fascinating shade of green, very earthy. They look a bit crazed, but that's probably because she's scared." He knelt and rubbed his fingers against a few strands of her hair. "I can't tell beneath the layers of sooty ash, but I think her hair has a touch of scarlet in it. Lift her tunic," he demanded. "Let's see if the other thatch of hair matches."

The soldier lying on top of her pushed her tunic higher. "I'm hard as stone," he muttered. "Can we take turns with her?"

"No," the legate's reply was cold. "We don't know what we have yet."

Arcona spat in the soldier's face and kicked him.

"She's hurting me!" the soldier complained. He wrestled Arcona into submission. "Get over here and help me!" he barked to his companion.

A mean-looking young scout approached.

"Draw your knife," the legate ordered. "Cut these rags off so we can look at her."

The young man drew a dagger from his hip belt, took hold of the hem of Arcona's tunic, and sawed the blade against the cloth. The threads popped as the fabric ripped higher.

The young man parted the frayed cloth and gasped. "Look at her. She's beautiful." His gaze locked on her. "I'm certain a woman like this has had a man. What sort of fools would let something this tempting walk around and not put their cocks in it?"

The soldier pinning her to the ground looked up at the legate with pleading eyes. "Can I just rub myself between her thighs?"

Fear swept over her. Arcona fought like a she-bear. In a moment of inspiration, she remembered a horrible insult an old man of her tribe who once acted as a Roman scout had dared to teach her. She opened her mouth and screamed, *"Vestri deus Jupiter combibo spurcus gallo of sulum pauper in vicus!"*

The legate reeled in shock. "What did you say?"

"You heard me!" Arcona sneered at the Romans. "Your god Jupiter sucks the filthy cocks of every beggar on the street." She didn't really know what a street was, but the old scout had assured her it was the wrong place for sex.

"Who taught you that?" The legate looked scandalized.

"Ego narro vestri lingua. Volo veneration." She spoke slowly, with as much authority as she could muster. "I speak your tongue. I want respect. Who is your leader?"

The legate looked flummoxed, as if a bird in the treetops had just spoken to him. "Gaius Julius Civilis is our commander."

She drew a bracing breath. "I have a message for Gaius. Unless you want me to scratch your eyes out with my dirty fingernails, take me to him!"

"All right." The legate appeared stunned. "I will."

* * * *

Salem, Massachusetts. Present day

"I can't leave Salem!" Arcona woke clawing the air and shouting. "The amulet's burning me!"

The acrid scent of scorched wool clung to her nostrils. Her eyes were wide open, but she felt as if she were trapped in a waking nightmare. She couldn't tell if she was asleep or awake, if this was real or an illusion, and she couldn't break free and return to a sane reality. None of this should be happening, yet everything around her seemed to be drifting out of sync.

The lights of a highway raced past in a blur. She was held captive in a speeding car with an angry man. Arcona tried to focus on his face. "Who are you?" Leaning closer, she felt a confused moment of familiarity for this stranger. Something about him hovered at the edge of recognition.

"I'm Tyr. I told you that earlier." The man glared at her, his voice drenched in accusation. "I put you to sleep. You shouldn't even be awake."

She smelled char and glanced downward. A faint curl of smoke rose from her chest. "The amulet's smoldering. Stop the car! Exit the highway. Dame Bishop forbade me to leave Salem."

Tyr looked impatient. "You keep waking up and saying that. Why?"

"Uh!" A sensation like red-hot needles prickled her skin. "I'm burning. It's hurting me. Turn around!"

"Fuck!" Tyr stomped on the brake. The tires squealed as the car spun sideways. He righted the wheel and drove the wrong way toward a highway exit. A few startled drivers honked their horns and careened out of the way.

When he turned the car around, the burning sensation ceased in an instant. She sighed with relief.

"No more tricks." His eyes seethed with rage. "You're trying to win my sympathy, and I won't fall for it. I'm not as stupid as I used to be." Gritting his teeth, he smacked the edge of the steering wheel. "I'm putting you under so deep you'll not wake until I command it." Thrusting his palm in her face, he hissed, "Sleep!"

Her eyes closed as she crumpled against the car seat, and the world went black.

Chapter Five

The Book of Arcona

A deep trance, unlike any normal dream, carried Arcona far inward toward her soul's core and down a bright tunnel of racing lights.

In the first disorienting moments, she thought they were merely driving again on a well-lit highway, but she realized she was alone, and this light was too beautiful to be earthly. A river of sparkling luminous fluid flecked with pale rainbows tumbled her downstream. In an inexpressible sense, it was all so familiar. She'd been here before. Many distant places and faces flashed past, old and young, bedraggled and noble. They came and went in a blink.

The amber amulet of the Strix loomed into view. She saw its warm reddish glow and ornately wrought bronze setting floating near. On impulse, she reached out and snatched it. The moment she touched it, the amulet felt like a weighted anchor in her palm. All motion came to an abrupt halt. The river of light stopped flowing. An explosive blinding white flash roared forward and enveloped her like a titanic scream.

* * * *

Pompeii. 79 AD

Arcona woke with a gasp, her face wet with perspiration. She bolted upright on a narrow lounge and straw-stuffed mattress. Furtive glances delivered only faint recognition. Her heart sank once she remembered where she was.

Afternoon shadows stretched across terracotta tiles. A bubbling fountain in the courtyard and bright-hued frescoed walls of the palatial villa were lovely to look at, yet she knew they represented a place of soul-crushing imprisonment.

She reached toward her heart in search of the newly acquired amulet to see if it was safe. It was. She sighed with relief to be assured she still possessed the enchanted charm that would free her from slavery and exact bloody revenge for her extensive losses.

The amulet's dark magic was powerful beyond resistance. In the bleakest moments of the Roman invasion, a precious handful of amber amulets had been forged and worn by the most powerful priestesses in an attempt to turn the wrathful spirits of the forests against the Empire.

By happenstance, or an act of divine will, what should have always been hers had arrived in her possession. Now the enchantment trapped within the amber was hers to command. The amulet would yoke the twin forces of life and death and the belligerent gods of two worlds together and bend them to her will. She had only to perform the proper rituals and activate its power and that task would soon begin.

The best part was her foolish Roman captor had no idea the sort of menace he'd brought under his roof. In a thoughtless moment of smitten behavior, he'd bought the future instrument of his destruction as a gift for her, thinking it a harmless piece of finery.

A crisis loomed and she trembled with a strange excitement. The end of misery was near. She was seized by the sudden desire to see her fellow captives — the ones who would play a triumphant role in her plan.

She walked to the open doorway of her beautiful room and peered into the tiled corridor. For once, there was no one near — no footsteps, no talking, only the splash of a fountain greeted her ears.

This was a rare opportunity to leave her quarters alone, in full daylight, and one not to be wasted. She bolted from the room before anyone noticed her exit and ran toward the back stairs, leaping up the steps as fast as she could.

The slick soles of her delicate sandals skidded precariously across the floor; the fine-tooled leather was so soft, they were more useful as polishing cloths. Her new master had chosen her clothing for its beauty, not practicality.

She climbed the last step and hurried toward the back balcony of the villa. Crossing this threshold had been absolutely forbidden. Her permitted territory was her room and its adjacent garden courtyard. If she were caught anywhere else in the villa, she faced harsh punishment.

Today she didn't care. She possessed the amulet, and soon it would be her oppressors who would the feel the bite of retribution.

She crouched low and crept toward the back balcony that overlooked the ludus, where enslaved gladiators were quartered and trained. It surprised her that there were none of the expected sounds of clashing shields or the *thwack* of wooden practice swords. The drill yard was silent of the usual clang of battlecraft and the sounds of men arguing.

The villa's rear balcony hovered high above the fray, separated from the ludus by thick earthen walls topped with iron spikes and barred gates below, yet it provided an unencumbered bird's-eye view of the daily mayhem that took place in the dirt yard beyond.

The August heat and the scent of men's sweat hung heavy in the air. Arcona peeked over the top of the balcony and into the sunbaked ludus below. Most of the gladiators stood in the shade, leaning against a far wall, their swords and shields cast on the ground.

She couldn't believe the always-strict Cilician trainer, who supervised the school, would allow such slothful behavior. Then she scanned the drill yard and saw the Cilician nowhere in sight.

A dark Gaulish gladiator named Roc stood at the barracks' door, pounding on it with his fists. His loud, angry words were so garbled she couldn't make out what he said.

A small crowd of gladiators gathered around Roc, and they too shouted threats and pounded their fists against the sealed door. She watched the events with interest but couldn't figure out what the enraged commotion was about.

Only one man, a murmillo, the largest and most powerful class of gladiator, remained active on the drill yard. The man had sandy-blond hair and a beautiful sweeping back, breathtaking to look at. She had studied this same man on many occasions and found him fascinating to watch. He was so unlike the others, who tended to clump together in groups and speak as a mob.

The murmillo stood apart. He was quiet and solitary. All the times she had spied on the ludus she had never heard him speak, yet she noticed the other gladiators looked to him constantly as an example, which he provided in his own quiet way. Any martial skills he mastered, the others were quick to imitate.

For such a large man, he moved with power and grace, holding a sword in one hand and a heavy, iron-rimmed shield that stood nearly as tall as he in the other. He advanced with calculated steps across the packed dirt of the yard, thrusting and parrying his blade against an imaginary foe.

He ignored the angry chaos surrounding him and worked through his practice drills with concentrated precision. His skin glistened golden under the noon sun. His focused gaze remained lethal and aloof, making him appear incapable of distraction, as if he occupied an entirely different realm from the others.

Swinging his sword in tight, controlled circles, he stabbed and sliced at his own shadow. He moved beneath the balcony and paused. His sword arm stilled as he held the shield high between him and the others and looked directly at her.

His clear hazel eyes made such forceful contact with her she felt as if she'd been touched. She was left breathless. Despite her caution about remaining unseen, he seemed to possess another sense that alerted him to her presence. Perhaps she was not so stealthy, because he often noticed her crouching behind the balcony while the others remained oblivious to her.

She gazed into his eyes and froze, unable to look away. How was it possible for such a formidable man to have become enslaved?

A slight smile curled the edge of his lips. He gazed at her with scorching intensity, as if he meant to bolt over the wall and grab her.

A flutter of anxious tension and desire rose, and she struggled to extinguish it. Getting involved was not part of her plan.

The barracks' door burst open with a loud bang, and a wailing woman staggered into the yard with tears streaming down her face. Her tunic was rumpled and hung from her shoulders, exposing her back and a breast. She tried to wrap her head shawl around her body to cover herself. She ran straight toward Roc, threw her arms around his neck, and clung to him.

Roc snatched the woman into his arms. He crushed his face against her thick, dark hair and appeared to be sobbing.

The Cilician trainer strode out the open door with a churlish smile on his swarthy face. He gazed at the gladiators resting in the shade. A look of rage hardened on his harsh mouth. "Pick up your weapons, you slothful oxen! Just because I took a pleasure break doesn't mean you get one."

Roc bared his teeth at the Cilician and snarled. "I'll stuff a blade in your gut the first chance I get!"

"I don't think so." The Cilician dismissed Roc with a rude flick of his hand. "By the way, I enjoyed fucking your wife. Tell her to come back next week."

"You're an animal! Her new owner allowed her to come here today to tell me I have a son." Roc thrust his wife aside and lunged toward the Cilician. "I'm going to rip your balls off!" Several other gladiators grabbed Roc in mid-lunge and held him back.

"Don't do it," one man cautioned.

"This isn't the time," warned another.

"Always plotting." The Cilician glared at the gladiators with scorn. "The eternal collusion. I'm not threatened. I've heard it all before. Let's be perfectly clear; there is no hope. Most of you will be dead this time next spring, and I'll still be here fucking your widows."

Roc spit. The stream struck a spot on the ground a hairsbreadth from the Cilician's sandal.

The Cilician gazed down at the spittle and grinned. "I hope the aim of your blade in the arena is as precise. If you fight well, I get paid a bonus, and I'll still go on fucking your wife."

A horn blew a piercing warning and startled Arcona.

A soldier positioned atop a wall shouted, "Dominus Marius has returned!"

Much commotion ensued as armed guards scraped the front gates open, followed by the echoing click of horse hooves striding inside the walled compound.

The gladiators were quick to pick up their weapons and engage each other in various practice drills.

Roc's wife fled the drill yard in haste.

Arcona turned and scrambled away from the balcony on hands and knees. Once she reached the stairs, she leaped up and ran to her room as fast as she could, praying the light patter of her sandals would not betray her.

She entered the quiet, cool fountain room with her heart racing and sat on the bed. Reaching toward the amber amulet dangling around her neck, she gave it gentle strokes as she struggled to compose her agitated mind.

Even though she tried to resist, her thoughts returned to the blond murmillo. Who was he, and how had someone so noble ended up in this wretched place?

"Arcona!" a deep male voice boomed in the corridor.

She flinched at the sound of Dominus Marius's voice and turned toward the doorway.

"You seem surprised to see me." A Roman nobleman with a close-cropped head of steel-gray hair stood in the doorway. He gazed at her with unrestrained lust flickering in his black eyes. "You did remember my wife always visits her sister today? We're alone."

Parting her lips, she started to answer but stopped. They were never truly alone. The villa boasted dozens of specialized domestic servants, not to mention Pompeii's largest ludus stocked with gladiator slaves just beyond the courtyard wall. Any or all of these fellow captives would certainly be able to hear Dominus Marius's pleasure rituals this afternoon as the noise floated into the open courtyard.

She chose to say nothing, knowing it was unwise to contradict Marius, who was equally capable of lavish generosity and pettish cruelty. He had his quirks, some more pronounced than others. After several months living under his roof, she knew them well and planned to exploit them.

Arching back, she tugged her linen tunic over her head with a single graceful motion and tossed it aside, displaying her pale, lush curves. She planted her palms on the mattress as she leaned forward on all fours, allowing her body to sway from side to side as she stretched with the provocative suppleness of a cat.

"Is there something you want to say to me?" Marius unbuckled his sword belt and let it crash to the floor.

With fluid motions she crawled toward the foot of the bed and curled her feet beneath her, chin down, shoulders pulled back, and her full breasts thrust forward in what she hoped was a pleasing submissive pose. She felt a moment of anxiety and reached toward the amulet that dangled between her breasts to touch the smooth, translucent stone and calm herself. "Yes, Dominus, I remembered today is your special day."

Marius's eyes lit with intense excitement as he leaned against the doorframe. "Remember your promise?"

Her stomach clenched with nerves. "I do, and I shall honor it."

His voice was silky with confidence. "As your master, I don't have to ask or bargain with you. I could simply take what I want. You do know that, don't you?"

"Yes. I know." Ever since Roman soldiers had claimed her as a captive over a year ago, many had already taken without asking. One high-ranking Roman named Gaius had treated her well until another man of yet higher rank asked for her services. After that, she was traded between Romans like a jar of wine; she was not a person of worth so much as something of pleasure to be bartered.

Petty revenge had been taken on those men. Whenever she had the opportunity she gathered any or all noxious herbs and roots she could find and steeped them into poisonous concoctions, which she dumped into the Romans' wine supply with joy.

The men's gut-wrenching miseries were her small victories. Her humiliations at the hands of the Romans were many, and that was before she'd arrived in Pompeii's slave market to be sold.

Marius strode toward the bed, shedding the snow-white toga from his body as he approached. Long days spent outdoors and his love of horse riding had left him leaner and more solidly built than most soft Roman noblemen. His ropy thighs were muscular and sunbaked below the knees.

"This is your opportunity to pay me back for that little trinket I bought you." Marius tossed the toga aside and stood naked in front of her with a thick erection pointing toward her face. "Show me your gratitude."

"I'm always grateful, Dominus." She took hold of Marius's flushed shaft and rolled it between her warm palms. In an instant, his cock stood straighter and glistened at the tip. She knew what he wanted from her this afternoon, and she wasn't grateful. She was resentful and actually hated Marius, but she had to do what she must to remain a favorite in this sad villa and maintain some pretense of independence. Today she was a slave, but she was determined she would not die one.

More than that, she vowed every violation her Roman oppressors heaped on her would be repaid a thousandfold. With the help of the amulet, soon her enslaved or fallen kin would have revenge. A new breed of monster would rise, and the Empire would quake with terror. The witch in her would see to that.

She wrapped her fist around Marius's heavy shaft and tugged the foreskin back until the smooth head was fully revealed. She leaned forward and swirled the outstretched tip of her tongue across the crown as if she relished every moment with him.

The only thing she was grateful for was that Marius carried the faint taste of costly spices and was not an unpleasant man to provide sexual service to.

Marius stroked Arcona's hair. "Do you enjoy sucking your master's cock?"

Her gaze turned upward as she swallowed him farther down her throat and gripped the shaft snugly in her lips, hoping to hurry him along.

"My love," Marius muttered. "Except for you, I'm so alone in the world. You're my only happiness. I can't trust anyone in this house, especially not my wife." He closed his eyes and rocked his hips forward. "I hope you care something for me. I care a great deal for you, more than anyone in a very long time."

Tears welled at the corners of her eyes. Over the past months, she'd grown used to Marius's often coarse behavior or thoughtless words, but it was so much more painful and confusing when he was kind to her as he was now.

"It's difficult for me to admit this," Marius whispered. "We're not close to being equals, but sometimes it feels that way."

She cringed. He was right. In many ways they were alike. Despite her hatred of all Romans, she felt tremendous guilt for enjoying sexual games with Marius. He was a harsh soul, but so was she.

"My brother has a villa on Capri." Marius caressed the sides of her face. "Maybe I should leave Pompeii and go there? I'm sure I'd be happier. Would you like to be my traveling companion and see Capri?"

She wished he would shut his mouth and simply allow her to finish him off so he could go away. It tormented her to be spoken to with tenderness by a Roman who treated the occupants of his household as captives to be used and disposed of. Steeling herself, she resisted the temptation to entertain the slightest glimmer of compassion for him.

Marius stroked in and out of her mouth with slow, lazy movements. "I half believe I'm in love with you, but then I remember you're just a barbarian whore. You probably don't understand half of what I'm talking about, do you?"

She fought the urge to bite, knowing such an act would leave Marius enraged, and she needed him to trust her. Remaining his favorite was the only way past the ludus walls. The other domestic slaves were trapped within the villa and never allowed out. Today Marius had the upper hand, but tomorrow matters could change.

"Pleasure me," Marius demanded. "Show me your devotion." Drawing the dewy head of his cock past her lips, she caressed it with her tongue, making as many soft, sweet sounds as she could manage. Until she could perform the proper rituals and sacrifices and rally the dark gods to her cause, this was her only way of being in control.

Marius groaned in bliss as he thrust farther into the heat of her mouth. "Go slow," he demanded. "Just take the edge off. I plan to make full use of you today."

She shuddered. Marius was a healthy man with strong stamina. If he said he would make full use of her, he meant it. Most likely she would be subject to his often-rough touch until sunset unless she could speed him along and find sneaky ways to overexcite him.

Inching closer to the edge of the cot, she grasped her breasts and lifted them as an offering. Marius loved to toy with her breasts and was unfailingly excited by any invitation to indulge in wet, adoring kisses, rhythmic nipple tugging, and even light slapping. Soft, vulnerable flesh got him hard, but there was a catch. The soft one had to be willing and preferably an instigator.

Willingness was a great part of his pleasure. No doubt the condemning glare of Marius's wife had long ago spoiled his favorite acts. His wife did not relish his coarse style of lovemaking, and Marius was a novel type of Roman who needed to believe his partner in abandonment was as lost in ecstasy as he was, so he spoiled his lovers with small gifts, asked permission, and kept them close.

Marius seemed to trust her willing attitude. She was certain that was why he had been so eager to purchase her from the slave block.

The day on the block seemed like yesterday.

Following a long, torturous journey from the north, a vulgar slave broker had acquired her. The broker dragged her onto Pompeii's public dais, stripped her of her tunic, and drew her arms behind her back to prevent her from covering herself with her hands.

The men in the crowded marketplace, especially the ones who could not afford an attractive Teutoni slave, pushed closer to the dais, hoping to get a better look at a foreign woman on display.

A handsome nobleman, made more striking by the strength of his presence, stood in the back of the bustling market, wearing a crimson cape and fine woolen toga embellished with a golden clasp. He stared at her with piercing dark eyes from a distance for what felt like a long while before plowing his way past the other men and demanding he be allowed to touch before buying.

The broker's gaze homed in on the nobleman, and he appeared greatly heartened. "Dominus Marius, it's a pleasure to see you again. Are you going to treat yourself to something lovely today?"

Marius's direct gaze locked on Arcona. "I'm undecided."

She trembled and lowered her head as Marius stepped onto the dais.

He loomed in front of her, casting a long shadow against the bright afternoon sunlight. He skimmed his fingertips across her auburn hair. "She's dirty." A frown of disapproval was leveled at the broker. "A sure sign your slaves have received poor care."

"Not true!" The broker released his grip on Arcona's arms and flailed his hands in the air in a dramatic denial. "She's new to my care, fresh from the northern forestlands of the savage Celts." He pointed an accusing finger at Arcona. "She's the one who's been unkind. I dare not bathe her; look what she did to me. She fights like an animal." He thrust his scratched, reddened forearms into Marius's view. "Believe me when I say she's no weakling. You'll have to be firm-handed with her. This one has plenty of fighting spirit, more than enough to match your own."

"That's encouraging," Marius grumbled. "I enjoy a challenge and hate a wilter." He leaned close and studied her. "The eyes are an unusual color and a bit unsettling. I saw a caged leopard dragged into the arena last week that had a similar look." He ran his blunt fingertips across her lips and gently pried her mouth open to examine her teeth. "Don't bite." The warning was stern.

The all-male crowd cheered Marius's actions and shouted for him to make her kneel and spread her thighs.

With all her heart, Arcona hated each and every ugly face in the mob, so much so her knees shook with rage. If by some miracle she ever possessed the power to slaughter all Romans, she would.

He pretended to be interested in her teeth, which were healthy, but his gaze continued to roam across her flesh, showing special attention to her large nipples. He reached down with his free hand and with a casual action pressed his thumb and forefinger against a rosy tip. "Flat." He sounded disappointed. "Unresponsive. I like stiff little peaks."

Fixing her gaze on Marius's face she noticed that despite his feigned disappointment, likely meant to discourage the slave broker from asking too high a price, his interest in her was intense. His breath was rapid, and his toga strained forward tellingly. She knew this wealthy, self-possessed man was her best chance to escape the dais, and suspected another moment on the slave block or another pair of grabby hands would break her spirit. Self-preservation came first. Honor could wait. Whatever she truly thought of Romans must be ignored, at least for the time being.

Marius finished inspecting her teeth, but his hands lingered near her lips. His eyes narrowed on the broker. "I'm not sure I want her."

She reached out and held on to Marius's wrist before he stepped away, knowing she had to win him over at all costs. She allowed her lips to grasp his probing fingertip with attentive care and sucked the digit deeper into her mouth. With a little moan, she pretended she was swirling her tongue across a juicy bit of honeyed fruit and sucking its rich sweetness down her throat.

Marius's eyes flew wide with surprise.

She slowly parted her lips, drew his wet finger from her mouth. "Take me home with you." She whispered the almost inaudible words in the Roman tongue.

The mob cheered. "She's a lusty one! Mount her! Let us watch!" There seemed to be genuine hope in the crowd that they would be treated to a vicarious show.

Marius removed his crimson cape with a flourish and draped it over her shoulders to conceal her from the disappointed and bitter protests of the crowd. Shouts of frustration and anger rose high into the air. He turned toward the broker and dropped a leather pouch filled with coins into the man's hand. Wrapping his arm around her, he drew her to his side. "I'll buy her."

Her throat went dry. The ploy had worked; she was free of the dais and under the command of this intimidating man. It left her relieved and terrified at once.

Marius stood close, gazing down at her. "Do you speak enough of my tongue that you understand me?"

She nodded mutely but did not speak, feeling reluctant to reveal the raw tone of her voice.

"What is your name?" His voice was soft and caring, as if he were speaking to his favorite child.

Even among friends she had been teased for her deep, husky voice. She was often told she spoke with the authority of a warrior. "I am called Arcona."

Marius reared back. "Great Jupiter, I can barely understand you, but I like the fire in your eyes."

Without even offering her a much-needed drink of water, Marius escorted her off the dais and with swift steps steered Arcona beyond the crowded square and down a shaded arcade.

When they came to the first empty alcove beneath a vaulted stone archway, Marius pushed her into the dark corner that was removed from foot traffic but far from private. Many curious shoppers looked their way.

The alcove was an unpleasant place. Others had recently been there and spilled sour wine onto the pavement. Other disagreeable scents of the busy marketplace hung in the air. Marius pressed Arcona against the alcove's back wall and parted the cape. His gaze traveled over her naked flesh. "You bargained to come home with me." His tone had become gruff. "You didn't have to entice me, but you did." He turned her with a rough twist, eager to inspect her buttocks and thighs. "Very nice," he said with approval. "I'm tempted to fuck your ass right here."

She gasped and pulled away.

"But I'll wait until I get you home where I can give you a proper greasing."

He turned Arcona toward him and thrust her against the stone, pinning her shoulders to the wall.

She writhed in Marius's firm hold but soon discovered the more she struggled, the more excited he got.

A man passing by glanced into the alcove and leered at Arcona's predicament. He stopped to stare.

She tried to push Marius from her. "Please," she whimpered.

"That's right." Marius pressed against her. "Make a little noise, beg…." He skimmed his hands over her thighs. "I'm ready, are you?" In a flash, Marius scooped her up and lifted her hips against the wall. He crowded between her thighs, lifted his toga, and penetrated her with a single determined thrust. Fortunately, she was wet enough from the nervous sexual tension of being displayed on the dais to so many eyes that he slid easily inside, but he was a thick, tight fit.

"This is good." Marius roared with pleasure as he sank deeper, uncaring of the attention he attracted. In fact, he seemed to enjoy that women were fleeing in shock and a few men had now gathered at the edge of the alcove to watch with envy. After only a few thrusts, he came with a loud grunt, then mumbled a few soft but incoherent words near Arcona's ear as he finished.

As quick as the stormy encounter had begun, it ended with Marius slumped against her, both of them in danger of toppling to the filthy pavement. His knees trembled as he eased her toward the ground. Once she was steady on her feet, he smoothed a lock of wavy hair from her face.

"Thank you, love." Marius's intense black eyes now looked soft with gratitude. "I enjoyed you very much. My cock likes you. Did you enjoy me?"

Arcona's heart thumped a wild rhythm from nerves, but she had the presence of mind to nod. Marius continued to gaze at her with a content expression. She realized with a growing sense of shock, shame, and awareness that here was a man who was brutally virile, took risks, but might also be manipulated to advantage, if only she could keep her wits about her.

"Let's go back to the marketplace." Marius smiled. "I want to buy you the finest white stola and a pair of beaded sandals. Now that you're mine, I won't have you looking ragged." He restored the crimson cape to her shoulders with care, making sure her nudity was covered to her ankles. "Walk close behind me and don't dare look at another man. It's not proper," he ordered.

Arcona followed him out of the alcove in disbelief as he led her back into the same city square where she had been displayed like a mare for sale such a short time ago.

The shadows of the arcade gave way to the blinding-bright sunlight of a busy winter afternoon in Pompeii. She found herself staring at the back of Marius's handsome square head in befuddlement. What a contradiction the man was. He seemed to embody all that was distinctly Roman. He was lustful, possessive, and fickle, and seemed both prudish and decadent by turn.

Marius strode straight toward a silk merchant's colorful tent and asked to see his finest fabrics. True to his word, he purchased a fine woolen stola that was so delicate a weave a ghost of her silhouette showed through when she stood with the sun at her back.

A lovely piece of coppery red silk was also purchased that brought out the warm undertones of her hair. Marius seemed to relish shopping for his newest pet and next sought out a cobbler's tent to choose a whisper-thin pair of sandals dyed a watery shade of blue-green and embellished with copper beads.

He turned toward Arcona. "Be loyal to me, pleasure me, and I will buy you many more treasures."

After more shopping for hair combs made of polished shell and copper, and silver bracelets to load her wrists with shimmering elegance, they walked across the city. She was surprised to see the sheer size and complexity of Pompeii with its many fine buildings, ornately decorated public baths, and brothels scattered every few blocks.

The city was far more opulent than the once-astonishing-to-her-forest-bred-eyes Roman outposts of the Danube. By comparison, Pompeii was dazzling, terrifying, and reeked of power, yet there was one place that displayed even greater supremacy.

Beyond the city gates, Dominus Marius's somber villa was an imposing structure built on a hillside at the edge of Pompeii. It stood apart from all other villas, surrounded by towering walls that were unwelcoming, solitary, and fortress-like.

As they approached she immediately realized why.

The loud crash of shields and the shouts of men floated over the walls. She saw half the rambling villa was a ludus, a prisonlike gladiatorial school where the value of physically powerful, condemned men was increased by the acquired martial skills that allowed them to fight to the death in the arena while honoring strict rules. For most of these unfortunate men, the ludus was the next-to-last stop along the road toward a violent, public death.

"This is your new home." Marius beamed with pride as he gestured toward the villa. They climbed the steep steps past several armed soldiers patrolling the exterior. "Welcome, my love, to Villa Lupus Unguis, the house of the wolf fang."

Marius led her into the residential wing of the huge structure. The starkness of the looming walls was buffered in part by the presence of rich mosaics and frescoes wrought by the highest level of craftsmen, yet the villa still felt like an oppressive containment pen with a single, well-guarded exit. She concluded the thick walls and armed guards were there to protect the rest of Pompeii from the many dangers lurking within Villa Lupus Unguis and not the other way around. Her new master walked her toward a back kitchen, which opened onto a walled yard where meat roasted over cooking fires on iron spikes and conical clay ovens baked bread.

"I am waiting!" Marius shouted with impatience for his servants to attend him.

Several startled kitchen staff hurried from the shadows and stood before Marius, ready to act on his next command.

He pointed toward Arcona. "This is my new pleasure slave. I just purchased her. She is to be my amatrix. Prepare a bed for her near the courtyard in the fountain room."

Marius took hold of Arcona's arm, yanked the crimson cloak from her shoulders, and tossed it aside.

Arcona gasped as she stood naked before several unfazed strangers in her new household.

"Feed and bathe her." Marius's orders were delivered to his domestic staff in a gruff manner. "She's fresh from the slave market, so check her for lice." He stripped the toga from his body and tossed it on top of the fallen cloak. "Boil all the clothing and bring her to me clean." He strode away, naked and confident in his own home.

* * * *

"Arcona, your thoughts are drifting," Marius accused. "This is my special afternoon, and you're not paying attention to me."

Marius's firm voice snapped Arcona's attention back to the present. Months had passed swiftly, yet life in the Lupus Unguis household remained a shocking experience. She always kept one eye on the doorway, awaiting one of Marius's thundering entrances, or an ear cocked for domestic gossip or intrigue aimed at her. In this turbulent Roman household, trust did not exist, and one could never truly relax. Here, she lived without friends or companionship beyond Marius's often-brusque presence.

With a sense of unease, she shifted on the bed and stroked the amber amulet. Marius stared at her expectantly, and she dared not tune him out. He demanded her respect, at least for the moment. "Dominus, what would please you today?"

He reached down to grasp the amulet dangling between Arcona's breasts and claimed it from her hand. He toyed with the amulet in his palm. "Even by my standards, this was a costly gift. I hope you're feeling grateful."

Marius paused for effect before allowing his fingertips to stray toward her nipple, giving it a sharp tug. "My appetite today is for a bit of rough play. You've shown me a great deal of resilience and cooperation, and I've often wondered where your limits are. Sometimes late at night I lie awake and wonder if I could go further in our afternoon pleasures without turning you completely against me. What would you say to that? Are you ready to explore a few of my darker secrets?" Taking a slight step away, he withdrew. A tense moment of silence hung in the air. "Before I share more of myself, I need to know you're on my side."

Arcona fought down a terrible sense of guilt that an errant part of her was curious and did want to explore these things with Marius. "Yes, Dominus. I want what you want." It saddened her to hear sincerity in her voice.

A broad grin crinkled the corners of his eyes but his dark stare remained cold and unmoved. "I knew you would." He set a small wooden chest on the mattress and opened it. "We'll start slow with what you're already acquainted with." Reaching into the chest, he pulled out a thick leather collar with a bronze buckle. "Lift your hair."

Scooping her thick waves into her fingers, she drew her hair upward so Marius could secure the leather collar around her throat. A tingle of excitement at what was to come rushed through her.

Part of her wished she could resist him and not cooperate so freely. The heat building between her thighs was a horrific betrayal of her people and training as a priestess. She squeezed her eyes shut in defeat for allowing Marius to bring her so low.

"The graceful arch of a naked woman's throat is a beautiful sight to behold," Marius muttered to himself as he looped the tongue of the collar through the bronze buckle.

Arcona lowered her chin. The collar was not snug but felt immense, and she had to move her head carefully while wearing it.

Marius next lifted a pair of iron manacles from the chest and held them up for her to see. "Place your wrists behind your back."

She brought her wrists behind, drawing her shoulders downward.

"Oh, yes, that's lovely." He gazed with approval at her forward-thrust breasts as he secured a rust-tinged manacle to each wrist and tied them together with a leather thong. He stood back and stared at her kneeling on the mattress in the vulnerable pose with her chin up and her hands secured. "Rise."

As best she could, she rose to her knees on the shifting mattress.

"You are the best amatrix I've ever possessed. None of my other pleasure slaves compare. You willingly endure and I have strong suspicion even take pleasure in what others would shun. I've seen a telling gleam in your eyes. You respect strength in another because you are strong." He hesitated. "You're so like me."

She winced. How was she like him? It was shameful to even be compared. Of all cursed things, he was Roman, and lower than vermin in her mind but he kept catching her off guard and drawing her into his twisted erotic world with a firm hand and a few kind gestures.

Marius spoiled her with plentiful gifts and made her his confidante. He was a dark, corrupt man, yet she provided him with moments of real companionship. On rare occasions, she willingly wrapped her arms around him, snuggled against his chest, and held him while he dozed. He didn't deserve such privileges. It maddened her that she'd allowed him past the unmarked door to her soul that other, more worthy men had been excluded from.

Brushing his lips against her ear, he whispered, "You know I care for you, and I would never harm you or permanently mark your smooth skin?"

She knew no such thing. Marius was often careless and impulsive. The flesh on the backs of her arms pebbled.

"You know I love my horses, don't you? They're beautiful, strong-willed animals, but sometimes they need discipline." Marius lifted a long leather crop from the chest and struck it against his palm. The slender crop was the length of his forearm and had a tiny leather tongue at the tip that made a sharp slap that rang through the air. He dangled the delicate whip between his fingertips. "This is what got me excluded from my wife's bed."

Arcona recoiled, now wishing her hands were free.

He lifted one breast with a tender touch, exposing the rounded underside.

Closing her eyes, she held her breath, waiting for the first stinging strike.

The crop struck her skin with a soft slap. Her eyes flew open in surprise. She had endured far worse at his rough hands.

"See," Marius's tone was reassuring, "No matter how excited I get, I won't hurt my lover."

A heavy sigh crossed her lips. Marius's Roman morals were beyond her ken. She gazed into his eyes with the full realization his definition of "hurt" would never be hers.

He leaned over her. "I want you to know you provide me with a great deal of pleasure. I've been craving this, and I can't put it off any longer. I want you to pay special attention to each stroke of the crop and how it feels. Commit the rhythm and pressure of each stinging slap to memory. By now, I'm sure you're wondering why I would ask this."

The collar made it difficult to nod.

His eyes lit with a fiery gleam. "Not today, but someday soon, I will ask you to put the collar on me and pick up the crop. Would you do that for me without telling another soul? Could we share those harsh pleasures in secret?"

Would he allow himself to be shackled and whipped by her? The revelation shocked her and seemed well worth pursuing.

"Yes, Dominus, your pleasure is mine."

"I do wonder if you mean it." Marius's tone was churlish. "Sometimes I think you're just too good to be true. I've shown you parts of myself I've never shared with another, yet you remain distant. You're thinking things through even as we speak. I can tell you're planning how to get advantage over me. You might be surprised to know I'm not angry." He paused. "I respect it. You've got a fire inside you unlike any slave I've ever possessed." His voice dropped to a husky whisper. "I would never do this to a weakling, but I know your anger and passion are bonded and inseparable. You want this as much as I do, don't you? You want to know with certainty that I am the stronger partner so you can willingly surrender to me without guilt. We share a taste for the same sharp flavors. Am I right?"

"You're always right, Dominus." Arcona shuddered as a blackened emptiness swallowed her for even pretending to agree with Marius. It further sickened her that in many ways he *was* right. He'd made a compliant whore of her. She did enjoy what they shared.

A quiet voice in the back of her mind that had lain dormant for too long spoke. *We should spend our afternoons killing Romans, not cuddling with them. Unleash us. Why wait?*

Her breath caught. Who was *us*, and was she ready to meet them? A flutter of excitement stirred her belly. Yes, she was. In a heartbeat, she knew games with Marius couldn't continue. Another day of surrender to a Roman would drive her mad. Making slow but steady progress, Marius sucked the soul from her body and insulted everything she'd ever believed in, and it must end. Beneath the skin and drenched in every drop of her blood, her ancestors' rage simmered. The path to revenge must be taken without further hesitation. How dare Marius compare himself to her or imply he understood her suffering or losses? The vain bastard knew nothing of what she was capable of, but he would soon.

"Dominus." Arcona lifted her chin and offered herself. "I'm ready." She even managed a sly smile.

Marius's eyes glittered as he drew a bracing breath. He seemed to be struggling to compose his excitement. "Thank you." He took a firm grasp of her breast as he lifted the crop high.

She closed her eyes, held her breath, and tensed, but the first strike of the crop was a mere annoying slap. The edge of the leather tongue provided a slight lick of fire, but the sensation was nothing worse than the swelling of her monthly cycle, which always left her breasts tender and craving to be touched.

The next strike landed lower on her breast and caused a rush of heat to pass over her, but no true pain. The leather tongue slapped again and again as the short, stinging flicks sped and landed all over the undercurve of her breast, making her flesh blush.

"Beautiful." Marius's breath quickened to a pant. "Move if you like, or cry out." The gleam in his eyes made obvious how much he enjoyed what he was doing. The tempo changed as the short slaps of the supple leather tongue rained down on her in swift succession.

A sweet moan crossed her lips when the tongue of the crop came dangerously close to the tip of her nipple. She shuddered, and for a heartbeat, she wished she could feel the lick of leather against the sensitive tip, not to harm but just to savor the many sharper sensations it triggered. Her inner thighs were already drenched. Being the object of Marius's furious passion was undeniably arousing, and part of her hated that fact.

She dipped her chin in shame as an unsettling excitement swept over her at surrendering to these intense sensations she knew she should abhor but didn't. A full-blown feeling of heat and heightened awareness flooded in. Each flick of the crop and every tiny noise in the courtyard beyond loomed large in her senses.

Marius's unbridled excitement spread to her. *Am I like him?* Goddess forbid it. She tried to block the thought. The moment was too private and conflicted to share. She bowed her head and hid her face behind a long sweep of hair.

The stinging tongue of the crop stilled. Marius lifted it high. His hand grasped the back of her hair and yanked her head back. "Open your eyes," he demanded. "I won't be ignored as I'm cropping my mare's teats."

Her eyes flew wide. Indeed he'd made a mare of her. She responded to him in ways she shouldn't. He humiliated her, and she couldn't wait for more.

At that moment, Marius represented everything wrong about Romans. Of all men, she was stunned to respond to him so strongly. It left her soul-sick.

She bit down on her lip. The willing submission must stop. As a Teutoni, she should be slaughtering Romans, not sharing their beds and whispered secrets. The gods had promised to make a weapon of her, and instead, she wasted precious time better spent on revenge. Marius's erotic distractions were stalling the inevitable. She had only to unleash her true self and act. The destruction of Marius's household must start today. Somehow, some way, she'd take everything from him and leave him as confused and bereft as she felt now.

Marius snapped the crop against the side of her thigh. "Tell me you want more," he demanded.

Arcona pressed her lips together tightly, refusing to commit yet another self-betrayal.

"You don't have to say it." *Snap!* Marius slapped the crop against her hip. "I know you do."

Writhing under the crop, she was at the dangerous edge of losing control.

This was it. She had to take action and cause Marius's world to plummet from beneath his feet and leave him reeling, and when he could fall no farther, she'd kill him. Then she would slash at the Empire. It all started today. She vowed to drink in what Marius offered and spit the poison back in his face — later.

Marius raised the crop higher.

She glared at him.

"That look doesn't frighten me." His words were soft. "I like it. It's honest." He struck her again. "I'm trying to teach you that as tough and magnificent as you are, I'm greater."

A lump rose in her throat. *Great Mother Nerthus, don't let that be true.* Hatred was all Marius deserved, if only because he was the epitome of an arrogant Roman. Vicious words tumbled in her mind as she cursed him in silence. *For making me writhe and squirm like a wanton out of control, may the lowest demons of the underworld drag Marius down and suck his blood dry.*

He aimed the crop at her buttocks. "Next?"

Angry words formed on her lips. She nearly told Marius she thought him no better than a rutting dog. She was a scant moment away from snatching the crop from his hand and striking him again and again with impassioned fury so that he might suffer the sting of confusion as he wept in excitement at being humiliated, but her shackled wrists made such actions impossible.

At that moment, she had to stand down and endure. In silence, she promised it would be her last. Her thoughts drifted toward her one hope for revenge. The amulet Marius had been so eager to purchase for her in the marketplace would soon be tested. His generous gift would be the cause of his downfall.

"Are you all right, my love?" Marius set the crop down and brushed his fingertips against her skin. "You feel warm," he whispered. He kissed her forehead as sweetly as he would kiss a beloved child. "Do you need to stop for a moment or get a drink?"

Her skin tingled from the wildly contradictory sensations. She closed her eyes and tried to ignore this difficult moment of Marius's odd strain of kindness.

* * * *

At least once each week, Marius demanded Arcona dress in her finery so he could proudly parade her behind him through the marketplace.

The trips to the market were often her only reprieve from the courtyard room, which had become an elegant cage.

Marius spent lavishly on spices, exotic oils, and any treat that caught her eye. He enjoyed buying her things and often purchased items she did not want. A pattern became clear; he liked being generous because it later gave him permission to be cruel.

Still, she looked forward to the excursions outside the villa with great anticipation and devoted much of her time scanning the many foreign faces in the crowd for fellow Teutoni, but saw none. She wondered if she was the only one taken into slavery to travel so far south. After so many months of isolation, she'd almost lost hope of ever seeing a kinsman again.

And then it happened.

In the crowded marketplace, within a sea of Roman shoppers with dark hair, she saw an old woman who stood apart with gold waves spiked with silver. The woman's serene pale blue eyes were distinctly out of place among Romans. She sat in a merchant's tent filled with exotic oddities such as bumpy crocodile pelts, a bronze platter piled high with orangey-red saffron, and a dish of polished amber.

Arcona was immediately drawn to the amber. She picked up a glossy piece of golden resin and held it to the light. The beautiful stone glowed in her hands like solidified sunshine and felt just as sacred. It made her think of home and her once-focused ambitions to take the vows of priestess and wear the hallowed amber.

Now it was enough just to stay alive and plot petty acts of revenge. Goddess help her, she'd lost her way.

Marius stepped into the tent and stood behind Arcona. He blatantly rubbed his body against the soft curve of her buttocks, making his cock rise beneath his toga. He leaned close and gazed over her shoulder at the amber. "I'll buy it for you."

"This might be more to the lady's liking." The old woman spoke the Roman tongue, but an unmistakable hint of the north colored her words.

The breath caught in Arcona's throat when she realized this was a woman from home.

The old woman reached into a wooden chest and retrieved an object wrapped in a square of crimson silk. With reverence, she brushed the silk aside, revealing a large amulet with a polished chunk of golden-red amber at its center that shone as inviting to the senses as sunset at high summer.

In awe, she allowed her hand to hover above the amulet, feeling too overwhelmed to touch a sanctified ornament of a high priestess. "Where did this come from?"

The woman looked straight into Arcona's eyes with utter concentration, as if she were reading her soul, and spoke with detachment in a calm and measured meter. "The original owner is dead. I'm certain she would be at peace to know another *lady* was wearing it." She placed strong emphasis on the word "lady," which in the Teuton tongue sounded similar to the word for a woman of rank or priestess.

Arcona's lip trembled. Tears welled in her eyes. After all she'd endured and the many weaknesses in her character that had been exposed, was she worthy of such power and responsibility? In that crushing moment, she felt humbled and shook her head. "I wouldn't dare."

"Why not?" Marius snatched the amulet from the old woman's hand. "How much do you want for it?"

"Its value is great, Dominus," the old woman insisted. "The young lady must truly want it before accepting it."

"Don't play games with me." Marius scoffed. "I know how it works here. Just tell me the price. I'm sure she wants it." He pressed a handful of coins into the old woman's palm and kept the amulet.

* * * *

"Arcona." Marius sounded impatient. "Don't ignore me. Open your eyes."

"I'm sorry, Dominus," she whispered. "I was lost in the sensations."

Marius raised his hand. The crop smacked the plump underside of her buttocks.

The strike wasn't hard, but she was so tense she arched back and released a howl.

"Too much?" Marius dropped the crop and was quick to lower his face to her hip. With a tender, apologetic touch he brushed a few kisses to her flesh in an attempt to soothe her. "I'm sorry, love."

She was humiliated that her thighs grew sticky from his light touch.

"Do you want me to stop?" He looked crestfallen.

"No, I want you to finish me." Even as she said it, she couldn't believe such traitorous words had crossed her lips.

"Very well." Leaning forward, he glided his lips against hers. Each swift, shallow breath betrayed his pounding heart. He reached toward the sturdy bronze ring on her collar. His finger hooked inside the ring and pulled her toward him. "Come."

She scooted on her knees to the edge of the mattress, straightened her legs, and planted her feet on the floor. With caution, she stood on unsteady legs.

Marius led her by the collar to a wooden bench polished glossy with beeswax. The bench had been specially made to follow the sweeping contours of a woman's body. It was narrow but heavy and could not easily be budged. It was fitted with a rounded wedge of sloping wood on one side and iron rings and leather straps all around.

He untied her bound arms and allowed her to bring her hands in front of her.

She drew her arms forward and rolled the tension from her shoulders.

"Lie facedown," he commanded.

Arcona lowered herself onto the wedge side of the bench. As she relaxed downward, her chin rested in a smooth little indentation carved into the bench, and her hips were held higher than her head.

Her thighs pressed against two scoops sculpted into the edge of the bench, which seemed to embrace and hold her even without the presence of straps. The shape also forced her thighs apart and prevented her from bringing her legs together. She settled against the smooth bench with her breasts thrust through two polished openings designed to leave her nipples exposed and not crushed against the wood. She did secretly enjoy the knowledge that Marius was intimidated enough by her that he had to strap her to a heavy piece of furniture before he too whimpered like a child, shed tears, and even occasionally whispered loving words in her ear that hinted at worshipful respect.

Marius knelt beside her and slipped a leather strap through the ring of her collar, securing her to the bench.

Instinctively, she tugged against the bonds to test her range of motion. Today there was little. She could barely lift her chin from the bench as her hips flared high behind her.

"Your submission is beautiful, Arcona. I'm so glad I bought you that odd piece of amber." Marius stood at her side, picked up the leather crop, and stroked the tip against the backs of her thighs. "Place your hands in front."

With care, she brought her manacled wrists in front of her face and stretched her arms forward on the bench.

Marius walked in front of her, took hold of her wrists, and using a leather strap, lashed her to an iron ring. He reached under the bench and gave each nipple a gentle tug before standing and taking his place behind her.

Unable to turn her head beyond a slight angle, she saw only a slice of what was happening in her peripheral vision.

Marius walked toward the bed to retrieve the wooden chest, which was filled with the accoutrements of a master. He set the chest beside her then brushed his fingertips against the side of her throat. "Is the collar too tight?"

"No." She wished he wouldn't allow the softer expressions to cross his face.

"I love seeing you strapped to the bench. This angle flatters your curves." He skimmed his hands across the round crests of her buttocks. "I think about you when I'm away. Do you ever think of me?"

She tensed, unable and unwilling to answer.

"It's all right. You don't have to say it aloud, at least not yet. You can tell me later." He leaned over her and planted a soft row of kisses between the tiny dimples in her back, then raised the crop. "*Amore*, I'm going to warm your skin before I take you."

She couldn't bear the lovers' talk, wanting Marius to just use her and get it over with before her traitorous body grew any more excited.

Her muscles tensed and her flesh burned.

He examined the places he'd cropped her. "You're turning pink," Marius commented with pride. "And not a single welt. I'm proud of my self-restraint."

The heat and tension his actions produced were incredible. She was so conflicted she wanted to scream.

"That should do it." Marius tossed the crop aside and reached into the chest.

Arcona couldn't turn her chin quite far enough to see what he was doing, but she heard the faint but distinct scrape of a glass stopper pulled from a jar. The pungent scent of crushed rose petals immediately filled the air. "What are you doing, Dominus?"

"You'll find out." The quiet squish of Marius's finger dipping into the jar and circling the rim made it clear he collected a good deal of something on his fingertip. "Lift up," he demanded.

Lifting her hips as high as the bonds would allow, she waited. A slick dollop of rose-scented something was applied to the tensing ring of her anus and spread by his fingertip in slow, gentle circles.

Closing her eyes, she settled into her thoughts. The swirling pad of his fingertip in this sensitive spot caused intense excitement. The dollop melted into her skin and warmed to thick oil.

Marius leaned toward Arcona and held a delicate, iridescent glass amphora near her face. "I bought this in the market right after you begged for your amber amulet and then wandered away to the next tent to look at fabric."

She bit her tongue to keep from protesting his version of events. He was wrong; she had not *begged* for anything. Marius had insisted on purchasing the instrument of his destruction, plain and simple.

How she had longed to speak to the old woman alone, but immediately after the purchase, Marius had grabbed her by the arm and forced her onward. The old woman had walked away and disappeared within the crowd. Another merchant had taken her place inside her tent, and the opportunity to speak with one of her own had vanished.

Marius held the pale blue-violet amphora to the light. The semi-translucent glass glittered with the beauty of a precious gemstone. "The merchant I bought this from said it came from Antioch. He called it *rosa lacrimae*, the tears of roses, and claimed it was concocted by female magicians, or *Magikas*. It was used in the royal harems as an aphrodisiac and a regenerative that strengthens the body, among other things, but I'm not interested in spellcraft. He boasted it produced intensely lustful feelings in its users, so naturally I wanted to try it."

She heard the soft sounds of his breath as he stroked the rose tears onto his skin. He crowded between her thighs and made light contact as he brushed himself against her with slow, minuscule strokes that made her body hum with anticipation. The rose tears contained a warming ingredient that increased pleasure and seduced the senses when combined with Marius's featherlight motions, triggering an exquisite cascade of teasing sensations. She marveled that a touch so subtle could cause such intense ripples of pleasure to travel across her skin and even make the soles of her feet tingle.

Marius grasped Arcona's hips with oiled hands as he lifted on tiptoe.

She struggled to relax into the penetration and press outward, but even Marius's gentle strokes were searing hot. Rolling her hips, she whimpered.

"Don't move!" Marius scolded.

He was already close to climax and she was glad of it. She moved as much as the shackles would allow, feeling the heat of the stretch escalate along her spine. Experience had taught her the only way past the initial discomfort was to surrender to full penetration. He glided deeper, making her bite her lip to deny him the reward of a lusty groan. A voluptuous feeling of fullness and the desire for more consumed her.

He sank to the hilt and slowly withdrew, moving with caution.

Her eyes flew wide in shame when she realized she was enjoying this. Even Marius's firm downstroke was a stunning pleasure to endure. As she fully comprehended what was happening, she gasped. *Sex as magic?*

This was a terrible new threat. Rose tears were undeniably powerful. An almost agonizing ripple of pleasure racked her. It wounded her to know she'd fallen victim to the handiwork of one of her own. Her begrudging but sincere admiration of the Magika's superior skills grew with each stroke.

Marius thrust deeper with a loud groan.

A sense of euphoria washed over her. No doubt the traitorous rose tears were to blame. The tricky concoction was so different from the practical herbcraft she was accustomed to. Witchcraft and sex were powerful things to harness, yet why had it never occurred to her to do so? Humbled, she now fully comprehended that there were far horizons yet to explore. Then a stunning thought occurred. This was not a defeat; it was a boon. Rose tears were a gift from the gods just as the amulet was. They were both tools of great power handed to her at the perfect moment to be used against Rome. This was not the moment to struggle but instead observe and give in with respect to the Magikas of Antioch and their uncanny potion.

Thrilling heat spread across her skin, and she was helpless to hold back. *Curse everything Roman.* She groaned and pushed into the stroke.

"Don't move!" Marius gritted a stern rebuke for disobeying him. His legs trembled as he dared take a few short, controlled strokes.

The bench was not new to her. She'd been shackled to it many times before. Submission was never easy, but this time, the rose tears added an entirely different dimension of sensation, one that drove her overexcited nerves to the edge of frenzy. Soon, she rubbed wantonly against the polished wood of the bench, shuddering on the edge of climax.

Booming shouts of enraged men and the clash of shields rang through the air. It sounded as if a giant had struck his hammer against the villa, intent on crushing the compound's walls to dust.

The excessive noise startled her. She jolted on the bench. The melee sounded especially loud. This was not a normal day in the ludus.

Marius tensed. His fingers dug into her hips. "What's going on?"

There was a furious slap of sandaled feet running toward them. "Dominus Marius!" a male servant wailed in the hallway. "There's a fight in the drill yard!"

"Curse you!" Marius snarled at the cowering servant hovering in the doorway, gawking at the shocking spectacle of a naked woman strapped to a wooden bench. "How dare you interrupt me when I'm buried in my whore's ass. The men are supposed to be fighting in the drill yard — they're gladiators, you fool!"

"The men have turned on the head trainer." The servant's eyes bulged with terror. "They have the Cilician cornered in the barracks. They're breaking down the door. The men say they don't respect the Cilician, and they're tired of his manipulations. They've promised to slit his throat."

"Well, they can't!" Marius pulled free of Arcona. "Call the guards. Arm everyone with bullwhips. There will be no killing the gladiators. Do you understand? I've invested too much. Drive the men back with the lash of the whip, aim for their faces. Tell the guards to do what they must to get the men under control, but don't kill them. I'll deal with the men later."

Marius rushed to wrap a toga around his waist. Within moments, he too fled the room.

Chapter Six
Pompeii, a temple is a temple, all is sacred

The angry shouts of defiant gladiators and the crash of shields used as battering rams echoed through the courtyard.

Arcona had been abandoned and left shackled to the bench, her body on fire from the aphrodisiac. "Help!" she cried. "Someone help me!"

The sounds of chaos in the courtyard increased. Marius's bellowing voice rang above the din.

A housemaid hurried past, carrying a bundle of laundry. "Stop!" Arcona called out to her. "Untie me."

The woman paused and stared dumb-faced at the sight of Arcona's predicament, but made no move to enter the private quarters.

Arcona rattled her shackled wrists against the bench. "Untie the strap on my wrists; I'll get the rest," she pleaded.

"I'm not allowed to speak to you." Despite Arcona's appeal, the woman's expression remained vacant. "Our master wouldn't like it."

"Are you witless?" Arcona hissed with impatience. "The gladiators are in revolt. The villa could be under attack or burning to the ground any moment. Our master may be fighting for his life. Don't stand there like a stubborn ox. Untie me!"

The woman waddled toward her, dropped the laundry on the floor, and unfastened the leather straps from Arcona's wrists. "If anyone asks, it wasn't me."

"I'll tell no one. Now get out of here." Arcona yanked her wrists free and undid the strap that held her collar to the bench.

The woman picked up the laundry and rushed from the room.

The thick leather collar was the next thing to go. Arcona unfastened it and dropped it into the chest. The bronze buckle struck the delicate amphora from Antioch with a sharp *ping*. On impulse, she grabbed the glittering cobalt vial, hurried toward the bed, drew her tunic over her head, and ran toward the frenzied sounds of shouting and the crack of bullwhips ricocheting against the walls.

Arcona darted up the back staircase barefoot. She crouched low on the balcony and looked outward. Marius's small but efficient troop of armed guards surrounded the gladiators and whipped the worst instigators into a corner. Guards poised with arrows and javelins perched high atop the ludus walls, prepared to strike the gladiators down at Marius's order.

En masse, the gladiators seemed to realize their brief moment of rebellion was over. Many simply dropped their weapons to the ground in surrender, drew their chests forward, and waited for the inevitable piercing tip of an arrow.

The heavy barracks' door was badly battered and hung by a single iron hinge, but it remained bolted shut and functionally intact.

"Be calm." Marius held a snakelike bullwhip poised at his side as he addressed the unwilling residents of the ludus. "I will hear your complaints." He scanned the deadly row of archers on the wall. Once he seemed certain the guards had the drill yard under control, he approached the cornered gladiators. "Is my trainer from Cilicia still alive?" he asked.

"Yes, Dominus!" a frightened male voice floated past the broken door. "I'm alive."

Taking firm command, Marius pivoted and spoke to the gladiators. "What has your trainer done to turn you against him with such fury?"

"Don't listen to them, Dominus!" the Cilician hissed. "They're all terrible liars."

The gladiators remained stoic. They'd already sustained an enthusiastic whipping at the hands of the guards. Their forearms and faces trickled red with fresh blood.

"Answer me!" Marius roared. "What has the Cilician done?"

The biggest gladiator in the group raised his palm, signaling he intended to speak first.

Arcona crept closer to the edge of the balcony and gasped when she realized the man was the blond murmillo. At first she did not recognize him because his handsome face and hair were smeared with blood. An anxious twist of emotion gripped her heart. How bad were his injuries?

The murmillo spoke with a calm voice. "The Cilician steals from us. Any winnings we might earn in the arena, favors or gifts, he keeps for himself. Even the women who willingly come to see us must bed him first." He swiped his palm across his cheek to stanch the flow of blood from the strike of a bullwhip.

A second gladiator scoffed. "The Cilician offered me to a nobleman who admired me in the arena. The nobleman paid a generous fee for one night." He bared his teeth. "And it was a long, rough night. I didn't get to keep a single sesterce. The Cilician claimed it all. The money was promised to my family. They must eat. I would never have submitted to such a thing without payment."

Roc appeared wild-eyed and hysterical with rage. "He raped my wife!"

"Is this true?" Marius glared through the slats of the broken barracks' door. "Have you been whoring out my gladiators behind my back and profiting from it?"

Another gladiator blurted, "The Cilician boasts he can have any of your slaves, even your favorites, anytime he likes. He says he has only to wait until you leave the villa on business."

The Cilician responded with a piteous whimper. "It is more complicated than that, Dominus. Allow me to explain."

"It is simple!" Marius thundered. "Yes or no—have you done what you are accused of?"

"It sounds far worse than it actually is. Please hear my side of the story." The Cilician unbolted the barracks' door and peeked out. "Will I be safe out here?"

"Toss me a dagger!" Marius called out to the guards perched atop the ludus wall.

A guard tossed a gleaming bronze dagger to the sand within Marius's reach.

After picking up the weapon, Marius stood in front of the barracks' door as if he meant to hold the agitated mob of gladiators at bay with a single blade. "Come out and tell me your version of events. You will be treated justly."

"Thank you, Dominus!" The wobbling barracks' door scraped open, and the shaken Cilician stepped out.

The instant the man entered the drill yard, Marius leaped on him, grabbed him by the hair, and slit his throat with a vicious, sweeping slice.

The startled Cilician's openmouthed scream was silent except for the gurgling sound of blood and breath rushing from his windpipe.

His limp body was thrust to the ground. Marius glared at the fallen man before addressing the gladiators. "My actions were just and deserved. He violated the peace and safety of my home and interrupted a damn good fuck."

Marius paused and made eye contact with the apprehensive gladiators. "Be loyal to me and bring glory to the house of Lupus Unguis, and I will see to it your families receive any winnings you might earn when you fight and die for my honor." He thumped his fist against his chest. "That is my pledge to you as a nobleman. Tonight I will have three sheep slaughtered and roasted. We shall feast and put this minor rebellion behind us. Have I made myself clear?"

The gladiators shouted a well-rehearsed arena cry. "Hail, Dominus Marius and the rise of Villa Lupus Unguis!"

Marius raised his blood-soaked hands high into the air in victory. "Let it be so!"

Arcona drew away from the balcony rail before she was noticed, knowing Marius would greatly disapprove of her being there.

Just as she turned away from the railing, she took one last forbidden glance at the men below. The murmillo with the clever upturned eyes and the sticky red gash on his cheek looked straight at her.

Once again, he was the only man in the drill yard who seemed aware of her presence on the balcony. His gaze locked to hers, and a faint smile curled the edges of his arched lips. He saluted her with a clenched fist just as she ducked out of sight.

Before her illicit excursion to the back balcony was discovered, she ran downstairs. The entire household seemed to be in uproar, and no one took note of her doings. Right and left, servants emerged from their hiding places in the many shadowy nooks and corners of the villa. Once it became clear Marius had been successful at avoiding a bloody rebellion and a feast was now underway instead, a jovial sense of relief spread through the household.

The Cilician's name was cursed with fervor. Dominus Marius's decisive actions were praised. It was obvious to all that there was little sympathy for the Cilician among the domestic slaves.

As promised, three bleating sheep were herded into the kitchen courtyard, slaughtered, quartered, and set on iron spikes to roast over a fire pit.

With bribes and deft overtures, Marius regained control of his household. For the rest of the afternoon, he was too preoccupied to seek her out.

Arcona wandered her tiny circuit of liberty between the fountain room and the garden courtyard, feeling restless. The gladiator who had offered the bold salute haunted her. His rugged face, even when it was bloodied, took command of her thoughts. She didn't want to think of him, but couldn't stop.

A full moon rose in the early evening sky. Everyone was so busy at their tasks preparing for the feast, Arcona recognized it as the perfect moment to offer her soul to the gods and appeal to them for vengeance.

While the Lupus Unguis compound was distracted, she hurried to the small private shrine built onto the back of the villa. The miniature temple was decorated with an ornate inlaid marble floor and rich frescoes painted in jewel tones of sapphire, emerald, and ruby.

As was the custom every evening, a servant had lit a row of flickering oil lamps and set them on the stone altar. The slender flames glowed golden in the shadowy shrine, illuminating the many artistic details carved on the alabaster columns and ceiling.

Marius's ancestors and the house of Lupus Unguis were devoted to soldiering and blood sport, so it followed the shrine should be dedicated to Mars, the exalted god of war. A bronze statue of Mars, depicting him as a rough-faced giant wielding a sword in one hand and a club in the other, dominated the front altar.

Arcona frowned at the artificial splendor. The shrine displayed typical Roman arrogance, designed to glorify the wealth and status of a single vain family. Her lips curled in disgust. In her early life in the dense, snowy woodlands of home, she had learned to worship the gods and goddesses of her people while standing beside a river or sitting within a sacred grove of trees. Her gods and goddesses lived, breathed, swayed with the wind, and rooted their eternal souls deep into the soil of home.

To her eyes, Rome was a painted whore mocking the greater truths of this world. She scanned the opulent shrine with disapproval, thinking perhaps this was the wrong place to plead a favor from her forest gods.

She drew a tense breath. Could the goddess Nerthus and the sacred ones of the forest even hear her pleas so far from home? They'd heard her once and answered with a violent vision, but that was on a sacred island far away.

Her worry deepened.

A temple is a temple. All is sacred, a tiny voice whispered within.

Vivid memories of the wise women of her youth flooded forward. She remembered listening to the prophetess of the grove, bedecked in her beautiful amber. The prophetess had divined that the Roman outpost being built far downriver from their land would bring trial and pain. At the time, many in the tribe believed the outposts were distant and posed no real threat to the Teutoni, but that assumption was proven wrong.

The prophetess had made blood sacrifices and pleaded for a vision. She fell into a trance and made the triumphant declaration that the gods of Rome were powerful but not truly their gods. In what had been a shocking revelation to some, the prophetess whispered to an entranced audience, *"There is not a single god of Rome who did not belong to others first."*

The prophetess had insisted the strength of the Romans rode on the spine of the conquered. She'd claimed the Roman gods were borrowed gods and might prove fickle and easily turned if shown another, more appealing source of power.

As a young priestess in training, the subversive statement had meant little but as an enslaved woman, it meant everything. Now it represented the key to freedom. Roman gods were opportunists. She would exploit that fact.

She reminded herself that even though her formal training in prophecy and witchcraft had been cut short by Roman enslavement, she had been born a mighty Teuton and priestess of the river valley, and a deep connection to the deities of home burned brightly within.

For the first time since her capture, a complete plan for revenge bloomed inside. In a breathtaking moment of clarity, all was known to her. She had only to act.

Arcona stared at the formidable statue of Mars. Could he be tricked or seduced into turning on his own Roman sons? He stared down at her with his jaw thrust forward, belligerent and harsh.

A slight smile lit her lips. Of course, he could. At heart, Mars was a blustering, vain god with as many blind spots as his followers.

Pulling the amber amulet from beneath her tunic, she cradled it in her hands. The stone and the bronze setting were warm against her skin. She gazed at the amber's translucent red heart, and the skeletal bronze ravens and owls surrounding it and whispered, "Great Mother Nerthus, you are the goddess who listens and cares. Your children, the Teutoni, have been broken and scattered by Rome. We've been enslaved, slaughtered, and starved. Have you not heard us crying? You are never afraid to intervene in the affairs of man. I plead for your help now. I ask you to guide my hand in becoming a weapon against Rome so powerful that the invaders shall be driven from our land and we might have peace in our forests again."

Clutching the amulet to her heart, she visualized the fiercest, most bloodthirsty god she knew. "Tyr, god of warfare and single combat, I am but one. Take me under your shield and help me to be as mighty as you. Show me how to strike Rome with the force of an iron axe. May I share in your invincible power to inflict maximum damage on our enemies and grant everlasting life to our warriors."

In reverence, she approached the bronze image of Mars and even dared to brush her fingertips across the sinewy calf of his sturdy leg. "Mars." She spoke to him as if she were addressing an esteemed warrior of her tribe. "I know your true heart. Your fierce spirit is far older than Rome and will live long past the time of the Empire's demise. Help me. You are eternal and thrive on passion and bloodshed. I pledge to deliver both to you in great quantity if you will recognize me as one of your own."

The flames of the oil lamps leaped higher and flickered a shower of golden sparks into the air.

Surprised, she stilled. Without doubt, the deities had heard her and were considering her appeal. Her heart pounded with excitement. "What shall I do in your service?" she whispered. "What do you want from me? No sacrifice is too great."

A quick but certain answer floated into her thoughts. *We want blood.*

Even as she trembled with elation, a strange calmness settled her soul. "You are the same gods who spoke to me before?" She shuddered in awe. "Is the time to act now?"

The answer rang in her mind. *We want blood!*

Yes, she knew those voices. These were the same gods or demons that had come to her during the first vision on the island. She had not been forsaken. They were gathering now before her in great numbers. Their tremendous presence filled the tiny shrine with tangible power that shook the very stones beneath her feet.

Her pulse raced. The gods were siding with her, and she had only to follow their guidance. She stroked the slender glass amphora that contained the fragrant rose tears. Staring at the glass vial in her palm, she knew here too lay strong magic, irresistible and sexual in its nature.

She unstopped the glass top of the amphora and dipped her fingertip into the thick, glossy paste, gathering a generous amount. The sweet, almost lemony scent of roses filled the shrine. Reaching high above her head, she stroked the rose tears on Mars's prominent bronze phallus. The metal gleamed brightly in the lamplight. "Enjoy this offering, our lord of violence," she whispered.

An odd inspiration occurred. Instead of resisting, she acted on it. With trepidation, she brought her fingertips to her mouth and rubbed the remainder of the paste onto her lips. "Instead of a sword, I shall wield divine power with my mouth. May my words carry the enchantment of Rome's utter destruction. May my teeth snap the bones of my oppressors. May Roman blood slake my thirst." Even as she spoke, it felt as if a stranger were speaking through her.

The paste smelled lovely but tasted bitter. Her mouth tingled with a burning sensation, and her gums ached as if her teeth wanted to lengthen and become sharp as a wolf's. Clapping her hand tightly over her lips for fear she had inadvertently consumed poison, she moaned. "What have I done?"

The fiercest weapon of the gods is a woman seeking revenge.

Licking her lips to wet them, she chanted, "I'm owed revenge. I need revenge. I seek revenge...."

Disembodied voices murmured in chorus. *We want blood.* Who was this *we*? Mars, Nerthus, and who else? She sensed the presence of spirits so wrathful, the creatures had never seen daylight and possessed no formal names. A hint of hysteria entered her voice. "Dark ones. Faceless ones. Come forward and I will worship you. What do you want me to do? Tell me."

We want blood.

"Then you shall have it!" Arcona smashed the edge of the amphora against the stone altar. Tinkling shards of glass flew everywhere. The freed rose tears melted onto the altar, releasing an intoxicating cloud of floral scent into the air. She snatched a slender wedge of glass from the floor, held the glittering edge to her wrist, and struck hard. The glass cleanly sliced through her skin, tapping a vein. The blood trickled freely down her arm. She held her dripping wrist near the flickering oil lamps and offered her blood to the flames, one steady drop at a time.

"Take my blood. I make my pact with the future." Her sense of euphoria soared. "To feed the gods and quench my thirst for revenge. May I walk in both worlds and make battle with the single-minded strength of Tyr and the passion of Mars. I ask this in the name of every Teutoni man, woman, and child who has suffered and lost at the hands of Rome!"

The blond murmillo came to mind, and it hurt. Anger racked her. How dare Rome treat such men as if they were disposable? Her new pact with the gods would put a stop to that. This had to be done. Good men deserved revenge and power over Rome.

Her wrist trickled blood onto the flames of the oil lamps. She stared in fascination, unable to look away or stanch the flow. The more blood she offered, the more ecstatic she became. A new sense of power rose within. Every drop of blood that sizzled in the flames cemented her pact with the gods a little firmer, until it became strong as iron.

"It is time to act. This was meant to be. I was driven to do this." Soft laughter rolled past her lips. "And the gods condone it. I cast a blood curse on Rome!"

More nervous laughter bubbled out as she held the amulet under her wrist and allowed the amber to become drenched in blood. "May death stand down for us as we offer eternal, glorious battle to Mars."

Hearing herself speak, she sobered for a moment. "What in the name of Mother Nerthus am I even saying? I sound like a madwoman or a demon. I don't even recognize my own words." She suspected another entity had entered her heart and made itself at home. "Are these *my* words?"

If a demon were empowering her, so be it. Giddiness washed over her, unlike anything she'd ever experienced. It was even more intense than her trance state on the island. Part of her longed to stay where she was, simply watching the hypnotizing ruby trickle of blood dribbling into the flames, but another part of her could not be caged for a moment longer in the shrine, which felt too cramped a space to contain the rising storm of emotion churning within. She needed to escape its confines and roam free.

She leaned close to the altar and whispered, "Are we finished here?"

In a frantic dance of flames, the oil lamps flickered, casting dramatic shadows underneath the statue of Mars. The smooth, oiled metal looked as if it were ablaze.

The insistent words, *we want blood*, rang through her mind. She'd already offered enough blood to become dizzy, yet Mars demanded more. The time had come to go looking for blood elsewhere. Yes, that was what she must do.

The paste of rose tears had been reduced to a puddle on the stone altar and shone like a mirror. She plunged her fingertip into the fragrant pool and swirled it in lazy circles.

"One last taste." She brought the rose tears to her lips and sucked the bitter oil from her fingertip. The acrid flavor clung to her tongue.

"Ah." Lustful abandonment washed over her, and her heart pounded as powerful as a war drum. Her afternoon collared and strapped to Marius's bench came to mind. The thought didn't distress her as much as it should. She vowed to capture the passion, pain, and lust she'd felt at the hands of Marius and pass it to another—by force if necessary. Free will would not be considered. Those she chose to become weapons against Rome would have to comply. The rose tears and her firm-spoken enchantment would ensure there would be no resistance.

Dabbing her fingers in the scented oil, she slipped another taste past her lips. Both in fragrance and sensation it was too much, but she couldn't stop. Her body ignited with desire. She wanted to find some man, any man, mount him roughly, and then sink her teeth into his throat. Conflicted images of blood, sex, and bliss tumbled in her mind.

The feeling was so powerful a moment of doubt pricked her. Had she made a mistake by introducing the unfamiliar sex magic of the east to the violent western gods of war? To her knowledge, such things had never been done. The results were unknown. No priestess of the river valley had ever cast an enchantment such as hers. What skewed demonic offspring would result from such a coupling?

A horrible moment of doubt weighed down on her. Chaos had been invited to freely walk Earth. To call on existing wrathful spirits and demons and ask favors was dangerous; offering to birth new ones into the world brought even greater peril. As a priestess she'd just given birth to something wholly new and terrifying in its power. With blood and sex magic, she'd create a race of invincible warriors shaped by dark forces and unlike anything the world had ever seen. She'd become the new mother of mayhem, and Rome would fear her rule.

The risk was great, but her people had never faced an enemy like the Romans. In her heart of hearts, she believed the extreme path must be taken.

Despite the blood loss, she was not weak. Far from it. Something inside was transforming her being, making her as sturdy as tempered steel. Arcona staggered outside the shrine. The first steps were uncertain and shaky but grew more certain with each long stride she took. Soon she ran as if on winged feet, leaping up the back staircase two steps at a time. With every heartbeat, she grew stronger and became more alert. By the time she reached the back balcony, her heart hammered against her ribs. A miracle had happened. She was much more than a mere degraded woman; the gods now dwelled within. Divine wrath was in her blood—guiding her. She stood on the balcony looking outward. The sun had set. Only the faintest hint of crimson colored the clouds on the horizon. The moon had risen.

How long had she been inside the shrine? It had felt brief, but it must have been far longer than she'd thought. Perhaps time had sped unnaturally, or she had been lost in trance?

Every cell of her body felt vibrant as she braced against the balcony railing, gazing at the first faint evening stars that now shone to her sensitized eyes bright as lanterns.

The night became intimate and intense with many tiny sounds she normally would have never noticed. The light scratch of a mouse burrowing near the ludus wall roared in her ears. Her sense of smell was heightened, as well. She caught the musky tang of men in the air, and even a hint of the Cilician's blood spilled in the sand. In a disturbing way, the scent of blood triggered a growl of hunger.

Her awareness had never been this keen. Her pulse trilled in her ears as an odd sense of excitement overtook every nerve. There were men near, and their earthy aroma intoxicated her senses. Her mouth watered. She wanted them and knew she must have them. A shiver of anticipation rippled down her spine at the thought of stalking such high-stakes prey.

Gazing at the now empty drill yard below, she plotted her next step. All the gladiators had drifted toward the second training yard, which was closer to the kitchen fires. The scent of seldom offered fresh-roasted mutton had lured them away. The sound of splashing riveted her attention. Through an open door and buried deep within the shadows of the barracks, she saw a beautifully formed man standing over a basin.

The man dipped his cupped hands into the water and poured it over his head. He repeated the motions again and again until his thick hair was drenched. Then he rinsed the day's salt and dust from his body, and she noticed his hand often returned to the side of his cheek to rinse and rub it.

She looked closer. The man was the murmillo who had saluted her. Her breath hitched from thrilled surprise. He was the exact man she desired, and there he was, standing naked and alone in a dark barracks. Hers for the taking.

With little effort, she sprang over the edge of the balcony, sailed far into the air, and jumped atop a ludus wall. Avoiding the iron spikes, she tiptoed along the thick wall with the grace of a panther until she reached the heart of the drill yard and leaped to the sand below, landing silent as an owl in flight. Though the walls were nearly three times the height of a man, she marveled that entry into the forbidden realm had been so simple.

The muffled sounds of splashing continued as she approached the barracks' door and stole a peek inside. She peered into the dark with newly acute vision that saw details within the shadows with ease.

Sensing someone near, the man glanced up. "Who's there?" Warily, he stepped away from the basin.

His words were a garbled version of the Roman tongue, but she noticed his voice carried a familiar hint of home. She dared hope he spoke a common tongue with her so that they might share a few words. Ducking behind a wall, she rounded the corner, prepared to steal another look.

With stealth, he'd raced across the barracks and was already waiting behind the door to ambush her. He reached out, grabbed her, and wrapped his thick forearm around her neck in a crushing stranglehold. Even with her increased hearing and strength, he'd caught her off guard. Thrashing against his solid body, she gasped in shock.

Quick to realize his mistake, he thrust her away from him. "What are you doing here?" His eyes widened. "Are you mad to trespass here at night? If the others see you, you'll be eaten alive." He spoke an odd assortment of Roman terms mixed with familiar words of home. "Do you understand me?"

She nodded. Gulping shallow breaths, she gazed into the man's glittering eyes, which revealed a resolute soul. He had a strong jawline and high cheekbones that lent an exotic touch to the solid features of his face. Unlike so many other men who got dragged into the demoralizing mire of the ludus, this man appeared to have retained his dignity.

He reached for her bloodied wrist. "You're hurt; let me help you. The medicus keeps clean bandages and ointments in his bunk." This time, he used mostly Roman words. With a gentle hand on her shoulder, he led her toward the back of the barracks, glancing at her from the corner of his eyes all the while.

His cunning gaze seemed to notice everything. "You're Marius's special woman, aren't you?"

"Yes," she said in her mother tongue of the Teutoni.

Pointing to his throat, he grinned. "You sound strange, but I understand you." He brushed his fingers against her bloodied tunic. "Why are you here? Did someone throw you from the balcony?" As he looked her over, concern creased his brow. "Has someone harmed you?"

She couldn't concentrate to answer his questions. To her overwhelmed senses, he was far too attractive. His warm scent and lightly bronzed skin were pleasing. That, coupled with the fact that his thick cock was already semi-hard and rising, made clear thinking difficult.

With a look of wonder on his face, he steered her toward the medicus's bunk. Reaching into a clay jar filled with narrow strips of linen, he retrieved a single long strip and wound it around her wrist several times with firm twists to stanch the flow. "You're still bleeding. Raise your arm." He spoke in the same calm tone he'd used during the confrontation with the Cilician. "Believe it or not, I've done the same to myself." Thrusting his arm forward, he displayed a flat scar on his muscular forearm.

Despite a heavy accent she understood every word he said. "I'm Teutoni," she whispered.

A broad smile warmed his handsome face and his eyes fanned pleasantly at the edges. "We're distant kin; I'm Dacian. You're from the upper river valley, aren't you?"

Unable to break from his intense gaze, she nodded.

He bent lower. His face leveled with hers as he looked deep into her eyes. "I hear there's good hunting there."

"There was until the Romans arrived to trap, spear, and eat anything that twitched its tail. Our forests are not what they were." She didn't bother to mention the obvious truth that the Romans had emptied the river valley of healthy men and women as well as game.

Turning, she glanced sideways at him, and he looked back at her with the same sharply focused gaze he'd displayed in the drill yard. It was almost more intimacy than she could bear. For many moments, they sat in a heavy silence neither dared to interrupt.

He broke the uneasy calm." The bleeding has slowed. You should go."

"May I ask a question?" She didn't wait for his consent. "Why did you salute me?"

His gaze dropped to the floor. "Most days, you're the only beautiful thing I see."

"I've been admiring you, too. I shouldn't even be on the back balcony looking at you. It's a risk but I do it anyway. I needed to come here. I made a choice."

"It's a bad choice." Looking flustered, he settled his callused hand on her shoulder as he urged her to rise and exit the barracks. His voice remained firm. "I'm tempted to keep you in my bed for a few hours. I'd love nothing more, but you should leave."

She placed her hand on top of his and gave it a suggestive caress. "What if I told you I wanted to stay?"

His thick brows dipped. "I'd say that was a dangerous idea. I'm not afraid for myself. I'm going to die soon anyway." He paused. "Do you know what happened to Marius's last woman?"

"No." A chill ran down her spine at what she sensed he was about to say. She had heard vague rumors about something tragic, but Marius had forbidden the household to speak to her about it.

"Marius caught her with one of the guards. They were in love and met in secret. Marius strangled them both with a knotted rope and hung their corpses upside down on the villa's front wall to rot."

She recoiled in disgust. "It's so lonely in Marius's house; no one speaks to me. Now I know why." With a cautious touch, she brushed the tips of her fingers across the varied dips and ridges of his muscular shoulder and then traced lower, down the lean contours of his abdomen.

He froze. "Don't." His warning was stern. "I won't give Marius an excuse to strangle another woman. Especially one from my homeland."

"My name's Arcona." She moved closer, wanting more than anything to press his broad back against one of the many barracks' cots, straddle his lean hips, and sink down on him. The quiet roar of bloodlust rose inside her, and rushed forward like an unstoppable tide. He was perfect for her plan, and so worthy. She needed him, and she wasn't going to take no for an answer. The pact she'd made in the shrine now demanded a sexual act and fresh blood to seal the bargain. The insistent voices within became increasingly shrill.

"Are you unwell?" His expression softened. "You look agitated."

She grasped his hand. "We're wasting time. The others will return soon."

Shifting away from her, he seemed troubled. "If Marius ever sent you to me as an earned boon, I'd welcome you with all my heart and never willingly let you go. They'd have to kill me to break my grip on you. But I don't want to see you punished for this. You broke the rules and came here on your own, didn't you?"

"Yes."

Even in the shadows, his eyes had a warm luster. "Why?"

"I told you, I'm lonely. I've been watching you. You're different from the others."

His lips parted; a moment passed in silence. He seemed to be searching for his next words with care. "What you've done won't be taken lightly. Crossing over the ludus wall could get you raped or killed."

The swell of his chest when he drew breath and the way he moved with natural confidence, enticed her. Who had he been before the Romans had changed the path of his life? Someone of rank, perhaps the next in line to be a tribal chief or king? What a pity. "I'm not afraid of Marius anymore, and you shouldn't be either. Everything you see, all of it, is coming to an end."

With downcast eyes, he shook his head. "You might be afraid of Marius once you see his bad side."

"Please." She skimmed her hand across the side of his solid thigh. His jaw tensed and his cock rose. Naked, he couldn't hide his reaction from her. "I want to be here with you, and I have something to offer."

"Offering me something as harmless as a smile puts your life at risk. It's not worth it."

She slid closer. "You haven't asked what it is that I'm offering."

"Whatever it is, I can't accept it. I won't have you pay the price when Marius finds out."

"But I want to give you a gift." This was more difficult than she'd expected. "Would you say no to certain victory in any battle you engage in, and eternal glory?"

He shook his head. "I would say no to anything that would get a woman strangled."

Her voice rose. "It's my neck. If I don't care who snaps it, why should you?"

With a light tap of his hand to her shoulder, he looked into her eyes. "I lost my freedom but not my mind. Do you know how much it would hurt me to watch Marius punish an innocent woman, knowing I should have sent you away?"

"I'm not innocent." Her voice cracked.

His gaze filled with compassion. "And that's not your fault. I understand. The guilt is on Rome's hands."

"Yes, the guilt belongs solely to Rome, but I have the means to deliver justice. Why aren't you listening to me? I came here for you."

"Arcona," he said with patience, "I'm going to take you to the ludus gate and call the house steward before anyone accuses you of wrongdoing. I'll tell the steward you slipped from the balcony."

"Don't worry about me." Arcona pulled the tunic over her head with languid grace and tossed it onto a near cot. She stood naked before him, wearing only the amulet. "I don't need to leave by the gate."

Visibly rattled by her nakedness, he scoffed. "What are you going to do, sprout wings and fly over the wall?" A tense laugh burst past his lips. "I'd like to learn that trick. I'd do just about anything to get to the other side of the wall."

They both shared a quiet laugh, but hers was flat and joyless. His gaze scanned her bare skin before coming to rest on the amulet. His expression became somber. "You're a high prophetess?"

"I am now, and you're my first sacrament." She gripped his shoulders and shoved him backward. He toppled onto a straw-stuffed mattress with ease. The magnitude of increased strength surprised her as she leaped on his prone body, pinned his shoulders to the coarse bedding, and mounted him.

Shock filled his gaze. "Others are close. We'll be discovered."

"Don't fight me," she whispered. Her gums tingled and her teeth felt longer and sharper than they ever had. Licking her lips, she gazed down at him. "Give me what I need, and I will grant you a boon."

"You look possessed by the dark ones." His eyes widened in horror. "I've seen this look before. What have you done? What bargain did you make?"

"Look at me," she demanded. "I'm doing this for noble men like you. Liberation is within sight." Clasping the amulet, she held it up. "Our people have been wronged and I have the means to make things right."

He averted his face and stared toward the wall. "I don't want the amulet near me. Those amulets were forged in desperation by hopeless souls. Their power is tainted and can't be tamed. Such an amulet corrupted my village; its magic has more to do with strife than honor. The so-called power spared none of us from slavery, did it? I want nothing to do with it. Take it off."

"No." Arcona squeezed his lean hips between her thighs. "I need your strength. You're the perfect weapon. Allow this, and I'll come to you in secret every night and make love to you any way you ask of me. Isn't that what you want?"

He looked anguished. "It's not good for you to wear it. Don't you understand?"

"Do you understand this?" She took hold of his stiff shaft, guided the head of his cock between her thighs, and rubbed it against her. The motions sent a cascade of sharp thrills rippling through her. "Doesn't that feel good?" The moment she brushed him against her, he groaned. Lightning-hot desire shot through her. "Please," she whispered. "I need this. You need this. This is the first step on the glorious road to revenge."

He lay stunned beneath her. "I'm not saying no to you. It's the amulet I want nothing to do with."

"From the heated way you look at me, I thought you desired me."

"I do!" With a gentle touch, he stroked her cheek. "I wake in the middle of the night thinking about you and wondering...."

"Hush." Even with a calming word, there was no calm. "Stop wondering." At that moment her voice was so brutal it didn't sound like her own. "Don't say anything at all." Another force compelled her to speak. "Let me lift you into another realm." She slid him inside her and thrust her hips downward. The first lush stretch stole her breath. Rolling her hips in slow circles, she sought comfort from the burn. Rising on her knees she allowed herself to sink down the full length of the shaft, loving the aggressive act of pinning a man beneath her and taking him. "See? The many blessings of the gods are near. Doesn't this feel good?"

With eyes wide open, he lay beneath her. Rigid tension held him immobile. Arching upward, he locked his hands on her hips with a desperate grip, as if to prevent her from leaving him. He looked helpless to keep her from her goal.

"Move with me." She rode him harder, dropping her hips down on him with a harsh rhythm that built at a steady pace. Driven mad with pleasure, she found just the right angle where his slick shaft rubbed against her sweet spot. Growling like a feral beast, she allowed her hips to pump faster.

We want blood. The voices returned, this time frenzied.

She reached behind her, cupping his heavy sac against her palm, and demanded, "Give me everything!" Leaning over him she brushed the tips of her breasts against his face. The amulet bumped his chin, causing him to wince and turn away. "Look at me."

She waited with the sharp focus of a hawk, watching the breath rise and fall in his chest, the perspiration on his brow, and the dilation of his eyes. When she felt his abdomen tense, she knew the moment to strike was a heartbeat away.

He threw his head back and released an agonized groan, as loud and pained as if she'd scalded him. Tensing, his hips rose off the mattress.

Her mouth tingled in anticipation of what was to come. Her teeth lengthened like wolf fangs with efficient swiftness. They emerged new and needle-sharp against her lips. Squirming on top of him, she was carried away by an escalating excitement that demanded she rear back like a snake and bite his throat with her fangs. With the tension of a plucked bowstring, she recoiled and struck like a whip.

A startled cry broke past his lips.

Her teeth pierced his flesh. Warm blood bubbled to the surface, which she lapped with her tongue to prevent a single droplet from escaping onto the mattress. His blood's coppery tang made her senses scream. She craved more as her bite sank deeper. The sound of his pulse thumped a quick drumbeat in her ears. Digging her fingers into his shoulders, she held him still as she fed with delirious abandon.

Thrashing, he tried to break free of her, but she simply snarled and thrust him back against the mattress with astounding strength.

He pushed back. "Arcona, stop!"

The sound of her name snapped her out of her bloodlust. She released him and drew back, trembling. A cold sweat crossed her forehead, and for a moment she felt nauseated and faint. She gazed down at him, feeling an intense moment of worry and guilt. "Are you all right?" He looked so pale. This poor man. "What have I done? I'm so sorry." For a heart wrenching moment, she saw herself through his eyes, a crazed and ugly demon, cloaked in the guise of a woman. "I swear, I didn't mean to hurt you."

He stared up at her with frightened eyes that for a fleeting moment shone a glowing shade of amber. "You're a Strix," he muttered in horror. "You're cursed, and now, you've cursed us both."

She couldn't bear the look of desolation on his face. "No. Listen to me. Don't be afraid. All is well." She tried to soothe him with her most loving tone. "You don't understand. I did this as an act of devotion to serve the good of our people. This was an offering to the gods — our gods and others, too. Rejoice! I promise it was done with righteous intent. Because of this act, we'll grow stronger and take our revenge against the Romans."

He shook his head. "It won't help."

"You're wrong! The moment of pain was necessary. It will make the unimaginable possible. Someday soon, we'll be free. We'll bring honor back to our people. You'll see." She choked back a sob.

His eyes went liquid with despair. "You don't understand what you've done, do you? I beg you to stop now."

She shuddered. "Please don't look at me that way. I did what I had to. You are better suited than the others to lead a new army."

An eruption of noise echoed through the ludus. It took a moment for her oversensitized ears to realize she heard the joyful shouts of men. The roast mutton was being carried into the ludus on wooden platters, and its presence was being celebrated with raucous cheers.

"I have to go." She bolted off him, grabbed her tunic, and pulled it over her head.

"How will you leave?" He struggled to rise.

"Don't worry about me. I have a new way of moving through the world." She smoothed the rumpled tunic over her hips. "Thank you for your gift."

"Which you stole." He looked at her accusingly while clutching his throat to stanch the trickle of blood.

"Don't complain; there was a hidden boon in the exchange. You will benefit. Get your strength back. After I leave, claim your share of meat." She hurried toward the door but halted, turned, and smiled sweetly at him. "What's your name, my love?"

He seemed to warm to her sunnier tone. "My name is Tyr."

"*Tyr*, the god of single combat?" She released a throaty laugh. "That's so perfect. The gods truly are with us. Thank you, Tyr. We'll meet again soon."

Turning, she dashed from the barracks before the many voices of feasting men drew nearer. She darted across the shadowy drill yard with long, fluid strides that barely touched the earth. A sense of expansion flooded her veins. Feeding from Tyr had not only been exciting; it had left her feeling stronger. As she approached the formidable ludus wall, she bounded into the air like a leopard. With little effort, she alighted atop of the wall with graceful agility.

The balcony was an easy ascent, as well. A powerful leap sent her sailing upward. She grabbed the railing and jumped over the barrier, making a silent landing on the back balcony on the side of the villa where she belonged.

She peeked over the rail one last time and gazed down into the drill yard. It was now filled with jovial men chewing on hunks of mutton. None of them seemed to have noticed her swift escape.

Tyr stood in the barracks doorway with his mouth gaping in shock.

She blew him a kiss. He'd certainly felt good. Tyr was all man. Soon, she'd have to visit him again to enjoy his strong body and feed on his blood just for the pleasure of it.

Turning her back to the ludus, she hurried toward her room. The blood in her veins felt heated by a multitude of ecstatic sparks. A warm tingling sensation shot through her that bordered on euphoria. The powerful feeling brought her joy. The sad captive girl from the snowy forests of the north had vanished, and in her place, a formidable priestess of the highest order had risen.

Without effort, she could pin a strong man down and do as she desired. Leaping a once daunting obstacle like the towering ludus wall had been accomplished with breathtaking ease. Her magic-enchanted body adapted and acted on a whim. She stared down at the slashes on her arms and saw the improvised bandages had fallen away, and the slash marks were nearly healed.

This was the true power she craved. She suspected sex was the key to the magic — dark, desperate, and lusty. Sex magic was the sacred life force twisted and pierced like an arrow into the heart.

Already wanting more, she'd soon have to repeat the pleasure of mounting a beautiful man and drinking his blood so she could grow even stronger. Were there limits to this new power? She considered that perhaps there were none. Now she possessed the strength of a mountain storm and the heart of a lioness. In no time, Rome would crumple beneath a foe like her.

The Romans would look back in bitter regret on what they had done to her and her people. She marveled that in less than a day, her fortunes, and indeed the fate of the Empire, had been drastically altered. With the enchantment of the amulet and the new blood pact with the gods, everything was possible.

At last she'd found her true calling, and it was well worth the wait. As a Strix, she'd harness the visceral might of the old gods and give rise to the new. Seducing, bleeding, and transforming the oppressed were the new orders of the day. It was time to give birth to a world without Rome. She wanted to throw her head back and roar in victory, but the restless demons within whispered to act with caution.

Mulling over what she should do next, she vowed that tomorrow Marius and the entire city of Pompeii would feel her wrath.

Chapter Seven

Salem, Massachusetts. Present day

Tyr stood at the foot of an elegant eighteenth-century wrought iron bed, gazing down at Arcona's sleeping form sprawled across the mattress. Finding an empty bed-and-breakfast inn under construction had been a lucky break. Now he needed to get his head right.

Nothing about this confrontation with his nemesis had gone as expected. His long-plotted plans had been ripped off their rails. He had to be careful. Where Arcona was concerned, anything could happen. The strategist in him knew he'd better come up with a plan B or even a plan C, and fast.

The shifting emotional terrain had thrown him off-balance. Who would have guessed he was still capable of feeling anything, let alone suffering the embers of tenderness and, goddamn her, even love as they struggled to ignite within his long-hollow heart? The unwelcome revelation left him feeling like shit.

What to do next?

Arcona would continue to doze under his sleep thrall for a while longer, but he didn't dare leave her alone in the small, overly warm room for fear she'd wake.

At least he had that angle covered. Even if she woke earlier than expected, the thick leather wrist cuffs and straps he'd used to shackle her to the headboard made it impossible for her to get up and go anywhere without him.

Like some sort of dark, twisted guardian angel, he stood near, watching over her. Arcona's chest rose and fell as she slept. The gentle rhythm of her breath held him to the spot as securely as if he'd been nailed there. He stared in fascination, wanting to turn away but finding himself unable to. She was the last woman he'd loved as a man, at least he thought he'd loved her, and she still held sway over a deeply buried part of his heart.

He couldn't look at her or be close and not be reminded of his past. In his vividly preserved memories, the heartbreak and betrayal were as fresh as if they'd happened yesterday. Bitter emotions and a touch of childish hurt hovered just below the surface, threatening to burst forward.

Gazing at the glossy waves of auburn hair on the pillow, he asked himself if he could remain persistent in his questioning in order to learn her secrets. Of greater importance, could he torture her if he had to?

Earlier, he'd been all for it. He'd even been willing to share her pain with Varn, but now, he wasn't sure. Listening to her cries in the back room of Slayers had not brought the expected sense of satisfaction; instead, it cleaved his heart. God help him, he still cared about her. That was a fucking unwelcome surprise.

Matters had been handled foolishly, and his regrets were immense. Now the situation was in free fall, and the necessary path of action had become unclear. Arcona was the one cuffed to the bed, yet she was more in control than he was. The biggest threat to the goal came from one of his own kind. Inviting his oldest frenemy, Varn, into the picture could prove to be his worst mistake.

Rubbing his hand on his chin, he studied her. Those few tense minutes with her in the car had revealed she was not the woman he remembered. Arcona—this Arcona—now seemed vulnerable and genuinely clueless about his realm.

A true Strix with lifetimes of guilt on her hands could be spotted with ease. Europe in the Dark Ages had been rife with them. Back then, he'd been able to sense their inner demon fire across dense forests and stalk them like rabbits in the snow.

Something was awry. This Arcona felt fresh and unmarked by guilt. She'd proven difficult to track in this lifetime, and impossible, at least for him, to trap. He wasn't sure what to make of it, so he'd been forced to seek the help of an outside agent.

Over the centuries, he'd learned a few valuable tricks. The easiest way to catch a Strix was to have another witch set a trap for her. It never failed. Why waste lifetimes of energy hunting elusive prey when you could get another vengeful woman to do most of the work for you? A few threats, maybe a favor, and voilà, he'd always been able to recruit a witch willing to cast a circle of enchantment and draw one of her wayward sisters to her doom. The technique had worked well, until Strix became rare and eventually faded from Earth. Lately, he'd sensed Arcona was near, but didn't know where. He was certain she was walking the Earth again, but he couldn't find her. It had been time to employ the old ways, at least until he could narrow down the field and start the hunt in earnest on his own terms.

He'd approached Dame Bishop and asked her to cast a circle of fate and notify him once the prey had stepped over the line. Dame Bishop was cagey as hell and difficult to get a clear reading on. What sort of witch was she? Good or evil, he was never certain of whose side she was on, but others in the occult community had told him that she got results. To gain her assistance, he'd dangled a carrot in front of her face.

Not surprisingly, Dame Bishop had agreed to his scheme. At great cost, he'd arranged for her to be given access to a silver chalice from King Arthur's court. That part was easy. Over the centuries, he'd accrued a fortune, and knew where to find such treasures.

When the amber amulet was unearthed from its tomb of ash in Pompeii, it was immediately brought to his attention. Being a patron of the dig had its perks, and the bureaucrats in Naples were no challenge to corrupt. That was the final piece of the puzzle. It had all come together. After almost two millennia, he had the ways and the means to end his agony. The final requirement demanded of him was mustering patience to allow events to unfold.

Dame Bishop had cast the circle to draw Arcona in, and the amulet had been the bait. Now, he had Arcona where he wanted her, helpless and strapped to the bedposts. She wouldn't get away from him in this lifetime.

This should have been his perfect moment of personal triumph, but it wasn't. Walking the earth for as long as he had, bewilderment was a rare event, yet he was bewildered by his reaction to her. Without doubt, this was Arcona's soul in a new body but she had changed greatly in nineteen centuries. He sensed her core essence; the slight tang of Strix was present, but this incarnation of Arcona seemed so innocent and far removed from damage and wrongdoing. That discovery left him confused.

He'd expected to confront a monster that had grown worse with time and imagined the stain on her soul to be blood red with shame, but no such thing was in evidence.

A disturbing thought occurred. Had this Arcona been cleansed by the many crashing waves of life, death, and rebirth over and over again? Had her soul been forgiven and refined over the centuries into the stranger now shackled to the bed?

Perhaps. And where did that leave him?

His gut clenched. What a fucking tragedy he was. Envy, like he had never known rushed in just as his last flicker of hope bled out. Maybe his plan was doomed. He had to find out. Arcona was not who she had once been, but his tattered excuse of a soul was everything it once was, amplified. Unlike her, he'd been trapped in a single life experience and hard-bonded to the past. Yet another reason to hate her.

Running a palm through his hair, he stroked the crown of his head in agitation. When she woke, what should he do with her? Bleed her? Frighten her? Threaten her? Let her go? He had no idea. Things were far more complicated than he'd ever dreamed.

Arcona moaned in her sleep and turned her face against the pillow.

Tyr focused his unwavering gaze on her throat. Varn's puncture wounds were closed, and the bruising had lightened. The curative properties of his saliva alone couldn't be credited with such a miraculous healing. Hell, he wished it worked so well; he'd lick his own wounds. The gash in his thigh was killing him. He was healing, but far slower than she. Even for a Strix, her recovery was exceptional, and he questioned why. Was this Arcona a new and improved sort of witch, or had she been offered extra protection against just such an attack before Varn attempted to drain her? Either way, her prompt healing raised more questions than answers. The other puzzling thing was the amulet. During the car ride, he'd tried to lift the amulet from her neck and examine it, but despite being in a state of deep hypnotic sleep, Arcona woke screaming and clutched it tight every time he touched it.

The cycle had been repeated a few times. He'd put her in a thrall state, each time at a much deeper level, but the moment he lifted the amulet to her chin, she woke in panic.

No one broke past his sleep thralls—ever. It was unheard of, but as they reached the city limit, Arcona woke from the state, shouting hysterically. The amulet itself smoldered against her sweater. The scent of burning wool had shocked him. Arcona thrashed against the car seat as if she were in terrible pain and even managed to briefly surface long enough to groan the words, "I'm not allowed to leave Salem."

She'd become anxious enough that he'd let go of the amulet and stopped trying to take it from her. Her reaction was so violent that he'd had no choice but to turn the car around in the middle of the highway. The moment he did, the amulet stopped smoldering, and Arcona relaxed and dropped back into an uninterrupted sleep state.

He'd never seen magic quite like that, and he'd seen a lot of fucking strange magic in his time. Some unknown dynamic was at work, and he had to respect it. Apparently, the magic handicapped Arcona, as well. In many ways, she seemed to be its captive as much as he.

Was all this a side effect of Dame Bishop's enchantment, or was something more pervasive at work?

In a fleeting waking moment, Arcona had said another man's name, *Hedron*, and he'd felt jealous, which surprised him. All he should feel toward her was hate; he had no right or desire to feel jealousy, but he did. During all these centuries of existence as a Slayer, he'd never coveted another. Jealousy was a painful emotion to revive but it roared back to life with shocking strength.

Exiting the highway, he'd driven toward Salem Harbor and along the coast. In a remote area beyond a willow grove, he saw a picturesque Federal-era townhouse converted into a bed-and-breakfast. Every window was dark.

A cheerful painted sign in the front yard read OPEN FOR BUSINESS THANKSGIVING WEEKEND. A chain-link security fence stretching all the way around the property attracted his attention to this inn as a usable but currently uninhabited building.

Slowing the car, he'd scanned the surrounding area. The tree-lined lane appeared quiet and unpopulated. He pulled over and parked behind a large dumpster filled with scraps of lumber, where the car was hidden from view. Reaching under the driver seat, he retrieved the leather wrist cuffs he'd placed there in anticipation of confronting Arcona.

Any one of his safe houses would have been ideal. They were soundproof, secure, and well stocked with everything he might need. This site was a greater risk, but the inn would have to do. He hadn't anticipated staying in Salem, but it didn't really matter where this confrontation took place, so long as he got what he needed from the witch.

Limping to the passenger side, he'd released the bolt and lifted a still-sleeping Arcona to his chest. Favoring his injured leg, he kicked down a section of the chain-link fence and carried her inside.

The entryway of the downstairs was a mess. Raw stumps of electrical wiring poked from jagged holes in the drywall. There was still plenty for the contractors to do, and he harbored doubts that this place would be open for business by Thanksgiving.

Climbing the narrow flight of stairs with his leg on fire and an unconscious woman dangling over his shoulder, he soon discovered the second and third floors of the townhouse had been restored with exacting care. Each room was furnished in what appeared to be genuine eighteenth-century pieces. He'd noticed a tall brick chimney from the outside, and carried Arcona toward a small room at the far end of the hall, knowing it would likely have a fireplace.

He opened the last door and not only saw a fireplace stacked with quartered logs and chopped kindling but also a sturdy, iron-framed bed piled high with quilts. Luck was with him. It all seemed made to order.

Using the leather wrist cuffs, he'd secured Arcona's arms to the iron posts of the bed frame and then started a fire in the brick hearth. The room warmed, and she halfheartedly kicked most of the covers off in her sleep.

Standing over her, he noticed her forehead perspiring. Varn had taken so much blood from her, he knew he had to get her something to drink or else she would wake ill and dehydrated.

He walked into a small bathroom, which was already set with stacked towels and a beribboned basket filled with tiny cakes of soap and apple-scented bottles of shampoo. Just the sort of silly crap he imagined ladies would enjoy.

Turning the sink faucet, he waited for a brief blast of rusty water to clear. Filling a glass, he returned to Arcona, lifted her head, and brought the glass to her lips. "Wake." His command was stern.

Arcona opened her eyes, looked up at him, and gasped. "What's going on?" Her wrists rattled against the headboard and her legs kicked. Panic crossed her face. "What are you doing with me? Have I been drugged?"

"I'm trying to give you a drink of water." The fear in her voice made him squeamish. Being the cause of her anxiety felt awful. "Why do you think you've been drugged?"

"Because things have been so fucking outrageous, that's why! I can't tell what's real and what's not. I'm having the most horrible hallucinatory dreams."

Sitting on the edge of the bed, he tried not to crowd her. "Calm down and drink. You'll feel ill if you don't."

"Why do you care, Mr. Glaring Fucking Kidnapper? I remember you. Don't pretend to be nice to me, you psycho bastard!"

"Please drink," he insisted.

"Why? Do you get off on trying to coax me into cooperating with you? Is that part of the thrill? You're a manipulator. So what if I drink water? What possible benefit could there be for you?"

An exasperated exhalation sputtered passed his lips. "As soon as you're recovered, and judging by your hotheaded attitude, you're almost there...." He hesitated. "I must drink your blood. That's my benefit."

"Go to hell!" She thrashed against the wrist cuffs so hard she almost flopped off the mattress. "You're crazy. You're all crazy!"

He smiled, knowing Varn's thrall spell was wearing away, a good sign. "Who's crazy?"

"The Viking dude, the good-looking one who owns Slayers. I remember everything now. He took me in the back room and...." Her face blanched. "Holy crap, please don't tell me that was real?"

Tyr nodded. "It was real. All of it."

"No fucking way! You and your friends are into some ugly shit. You've drugged, brutalized, and kidnapped me. Stop now, or you'll be facing lethal injection when you get caught, and you know you will. I'd forget about the blood drinking if I were you. Do you know how fucked-up that will sound to a jury? You're already in enough trouble. Take these cuffs off and let me go."

"I'm sorry, Arcona. I can't." He was surprised that he genuinely did sound sorry.

"Let me go," she pleaded. "It's easy. You don't have to act on anything but your conscience."

"My conscience?" He scoffed. "You're in no position to take the high ground."

"Why would you drink my blood? That's just sick! What are you expecting to get from it?"

"Answers." His tone became somber. "Your history and the veiled memories of everyone you've ever been courses through your bloodstream. You're a Strix. You carry your history in your blood."

"This is total bullshit. My blood doesn't have any special message hidden in it."

"It does. You're different. Once a Strix, always a Strix."

"What is with the goddamned Strix business? I'd never even heard that word before today. Are you connected in some way to Dame Bishop? You must be. She got freaky on me, accused me of all kinds of weird shit, and tricked me into wearing this damn amulet that won't let me take it off. The sucker burns if I try to lift it over my head."

Couldn't or shouldn't take it off? What was going on? "You mean like this?" Tyr leaned forward, took hold of the amulet's leather thong, and attempted to slide it over Arcona's head. He didn't get far. The moment the thong tangled in her hair she gasped in pain and acted as if he had dashed hot coals on her chest.

"Stop!" she cried. "I can't take it off, and I can't leave Salem."

An interesting development. He'd gotten his chalice's worth from Dame Bishop. "Did the witch at the scrying shop tell you this?" He allowed the amulet to drop back into place. "Was the curse on the amulet her doing?"

"Yes. No. I'm not sure. She tried to blame me as the guilty party." Arcona struggled against the cuffs. "Ridiculous madness. She read my fortune with a Roman dagger held over a flame, put me in a trance, looped this damn amulet around my neck, called me an instigator and a Strix, and forbid me to leave Salem."

The twitch of a half smile curled his lips and couldn't be repressed. "Did she?"

Her green eyes flashed in anger. He remembered that look well. "Don't play dumb. What's the use? It's too strange of a coincidence. Just admit you're working hand in hand with Dame Bishop."

He might make use of a witch, but he'd never trust one as a partner. "Dame Bishop means nothing to me," he heartily denied. "This is between you and me. By the way, Dame Bishop's right. You are an instigator and a Strix." The hurt in his voice startled him.

"All the despicable suggestions she foisted on me set me up for this wave of Roman hallucinations that are unbearably vivid. I'm just not understanding why you're doing this to me!"

Poor thing tried to be brave, but he sensed she was so scared. So was he. Part of him wanted to lie beside her and share a good cry. Damn her, she was drawing him in again and making it hard to think. Softer feelings he no longer knew how to handle messed with him.

Maintain focus. Don't let down your guard.

"It's not a hallucination." He maintained a hard-won veneer of calm. "Everything you're seeing was part of your past, and it's all true. You're carrying the story in your blood."

"You're wacko! I do historical research for a living. Believe me, my head's already full of this crap. Examining and cataloging antiquities is what I think about all day, so a drugging, trauma, and a fucking kidnapping can only make the hallucinations all the more real. That's what I think!"

He offered her the water.

"Fuck no!" She turned her face away.

"They're not hallucinations." He stilled, so overcome with temptation to jump on her throat and feed that he was barely able to look her in the eye. "They're real memories coming to the surface. I know because I already tasted your blood and saw them."

"What? You're a sick bastard. Get away from me."

"I was trying to help you after Varn's attack."

She rattled the cuffs. "You knew what Varn was going to do and you just sat in the fucking booth glaring at me and let him do it. That makes you an accomplice."

"Listen to me. I regret allowing Varn to do that. I came to help you."

"That doesn't make you a hero." Thrashing against the cuffs, she tried to sit but couldn't. "Your idea of help was abduction and scaring the shit out of me with an insane story about tasting my past memories in my blood! Who believes this sort of crap? If you regret this, prove it. Let me go!"

"I can't!" he snapped. "Don't ask. I've waited too long for this." Now he was pleading with her and he hated the desperation in his voice. Looking at Arcona and being near her was so difficult. For a horrible moment, he fought the impulse to wrap his arms around her and cry for joy that their two battered souls had been reunited.

Fresh resolve flashed in her eyes. "If you truly regret what you've done, and judging by your expression you do, you have to let me go. It's the right thing to do."

Grazing his palm over his face, he shook his head. He begrudgingly admired her ability to reason her way through a challenge. But then again, she'd always been clever. "Absolutely not."

"I don't remember all that Varn did to me, let alone anything you may have done. But I'm sure I need to go to the ER."

His gut wrenched with guilt. Why should it be this way? She was the Strix—*his* abuser, not the other way around. "Arcona, it's okay. I got there in time. You've lost blood but that's—"

"Yes, I've *lost* blood! Can you hear yourself? Have some compassion. This is not normal, healthy, or acceptable in any way. I can see by the look in your eyes that this is bothering you. Be a decent man. Stop talking about drinking my blood and let me go."

"The blood drinking will happen." He hissed with frustration. "It's something I must do."

Her face collapsed in despair as she swallowed a choking sob. "Christ."

Arcona's agony was a knife in the heart. Bullying a woman. Not good. He felt lower than shit. If he weren't careful, he'd end up curled in a ball crying too. "I don't have to harm you." The words were out before he could stop them. So much for being dominant and maintaining control of the situation. "I'll be careful. There are ways to buffer a feeding."

She kicked the mattress with her heels and shouted, "I don't want the experience at all!"

"It doesn't have to hurt."

"Varn was a fucking nightmare. I'm lucky I'm still alive!"

Waving his hands like the caution flags at the racetrack, he sputtered, "I'm so sorry about that." There he went again. She melted his resolve to stay tough and get what he needed. "It doesn't have to be awful."

Tears rolled down her cheeks. "Drinking my blood? Of course, it's awful! Why do it at all?"

"I already told you. Your past memories are bonded in blood and hidden. They might be buried, but they're there. I also need your blood for added strength."

"Eat a steak! Stay away from me. You keep saying there are memories in my blood but you can't be sure. It sounds like pure bullshit. What if you're wrong?"

"I'm not wrong."

"Based on what?"

"I've already done it," he muttered.

She shook her head, her hair billowing around her face like a cloud. "You bastard!"

Shifting his weight off his injured leg, he thrust his hands into his pockets. "I licked your wounds to stop the bleeding and caught a glimpse of your memories. We knew each other in Pompeii. Deep down, you remember me, I'm certain of it, so please don't lie and say you don't."

"This is mega insanity. You claim you can see my hallucinations, too?" Arcona appeared shaken by his comment. "Okay, you got one detail right. Pompeii. But it might have been suggested to me under hypnosis or drugging, or whatever a blood-swilling wacko bird wants to call it."

"Don't call me a wacko bird." Damn it, she had him on the ropes. This Arcona had the same sharp tongue as the last one. *Some things never change.* "I was a warrior, then a gladiator, and finally a Slayer, thanks to you. I'm Tyr. I know you remember me."

"You actually believe you're Tyr, the Dacian gladiator?" She sneered. "If he was ever a real person, Tyr lived a long time ago. Explain this to me. How could any of this be real?"

"I'm not completely sure. All I know is that in our time, the lesser gods were closer to us, as were the demons and the Djinn. Any desperate human offering a soul was snatched up and taken advantage of. You still carry an echo of a pact made with dark forces. I can taste it in your blood and smell it on your skin. The curse I'm under can't be broken until I know exactly how you made me. I'm tired of my existence as a Slayer."

He looked into her eyes. Would she ever truly understand what she'd done to him? And what would happen if she didn't? "I'm spent." His throat tensed from an unusually high level of emotion and left his voice ragged. It had been so long since hope had even entered his thoughts; he didn't recognize the voice as his own. "I want what you have—a fresh start with a clean slate. I need war, death, and bloodshed out of my heart and gone from my mind. After nineteen centuries, I'm ready to move on."

"And you think I can do that for you?" Her voice cracked. He pushed away from the wall and paced at the foot of the bed. "I hope so. You're my maker. No one else can."

By firelight, her eyes were wide and wild. "How exactly am I expected to perform this miracle?"

"By sharing blood and memories with me. It won't be pleasant. In exchange for your memories, you'll have to see what's inside me; it's all part of the same thread of creation. What you see might sicken you, but what the hell—you made me. You should know what I am and take some responsibility for what I've been through."

"That's one crazy story."

His leg ached like a sonofabitch. "It's a fact."

"Why would I believe you? *Sharing* my memories is a mighty bold claim. I need more proof than you simply saying it's a fact. Where do I know you from? Say it."

Leaning over the mattress, he wished the scent of her skin weren't so enticing. "In Pompeii, we were both captives in Dominus Marius's ludus, Lupus Unguis, the house of the wolf fang. One August night, you came to me in the barracks. Your wrists were bleeding. I felt pity and bandaged you. I wanted nothing to do with the amulet or the acts of a Strix. You started this. Is that specific enough for you?"

A tense silence hung in the air that neither dared interrupt. Shaken by his admission, he couldn't look her in the eyes. For what felt like an excruciating pause, she stared into space, lost in thought. "Except for the modern clothes…" Not to mention the meticulously shaved jaw with the perfect amount of stubble, and tousled day-at-the-beach, GQ-worthy haircut. "…you look exactly the same as you did in Pompeii."

When the breath whistled out of him, he realized he'd been holding it. Spare her or pounce? What to do? Nearly two millennia of waiting, hoping, and fearing it might never happen had come to a head. His conflicted emotions soared. Knotting his fingers together, he felt like his chest could explode. "I am the same. That's the problem."

"This is too creepy. I don't know why, but I almost believe you." Arcona looked at him, not with fear but with a moment of recognition, her eyes glistening with compassion. "And what will happen after you drink my blood and break the curse or whatever you want to call it?"

The enthralling aroma of Strix drew him closer, like a siren song luring him toward the rocks. "I'll get what I've longed for. I'll become a man again, and I'll die."

Her gaze lingered on his for an uncomfortable stretch. "You look very much alive to me. Are you sure you want to die? Maybe you're not seeing other possibilities."

The genuine concern in her voice ripped at his soul. This Arcona was a completely different woman indeed. His heart softened to her, and it worried him. Getting attached was wrong. His original plan had been to bleed her and drag her with him into death, but after talking to Arcona and seeing her transformation, that simply wasn't an option.

As he looked at her, something unsettling happened. The subtle tenderness he'd felt earlier became raw and profound, pushing his Slayer instincts aside. She was cuffed to the headboard, helpless, and he was worried for her. Worry for another was a very un-Slayer-like thing; it wasn't strategic, practical, or logical. He hadn't experienced true worry for another in ages and the sensations left him nauseous.

Arcona had messed with him. Was this the result of a new sort of witchcraft? Every moment that passed made it harder to stay focused on the goal. A few faint pings of warm emotion passed through him, like depth charges cast into the abyss. Misgivings about his methods rose and confused the hell out of him. Not at all pleasant.

He couldn't afford to blow it. This was his only chance; he and Arcona might never cross paths again. It had taken two thousand years for this cycle to arrive. He had to move through his transformation with extreme caution; gentle emotions could muddle the process. Blood and lust had cast the enchantment in the first place, and no doubt blood and lust led straight toward the exit he craved. Anything else was a tremendous risk he didn't dare explore.

"I'm certain I want to die." He picked up the glass of water and held it to her lips. "Drink, so I can drink from you."

She shot him a condemning glance. "Why don't you just steal it from me and get it over with?"

"Because Varn has already fed from you, and I will need to take at least two feedings. That's how many you took from me. I must faithfully reenact the pattern."

She appeared sickened. "How much are you going to take?"

"I don't know." He hated the look of fearful revulsion that flitted across her face. "I'll try to go easy on you. It won't be anything as harsh as what you went through with Varn. I promise."

What the hell? He couldn't believe those reassuring words had just come out of his mouth. His entire attitude toward her had turned around so quickly that now he was backing off on his deepest desires and thinking of her comfort and safety. He was used to living with the reactions of a Slayer, which were always direct and self-serving. A Slayer did not take time to explain himself to a victim, so what the fuck was this about? He felt as if both feet had just stepped into quicksand and sucked him down fast.

Arcona parted her lips with a sigh. "I don't even know why I'm saying this, but if you truly are the man I saw in my past-life flashback, hallucination—whatever you want to call it— Tyr the Dacian was a decent man who had integrity."

"*Was* is the operative word." A touch of irony crept into his voice. "I once *was* a decent man, but I lived on for nearly two millennia doing many indecent things and that changed me. Do you understand?"

She stared at him in silence. The quiet calmness of her face became troubling to look at, and he wondered what she was thinking. After many long moments, she lifted her head from the pillow. "From what I saw, you haven't changed that much. I'm going to make an appeal to the part of you that has integrity. I want to live. I'll cooperate and do whatever I have to do to survive this situation." She gazed into his eyes in direct confrontation. "Give me the water. I'll drink it."

He carefully held the glass to her lips and helped her drink. "I just want your memories of how the pact with the gods was made."

She finished the contents of the glass in several gulps. "I'm so thirsty. I need more."

He hurried to refill the glass and returned with it, suspicious of her newfound cooperative spirit. He offered the water.

"Can you remove the wrist cuffs?" She strained her arms against the bonds. "You don't need them."

"I can't risk you running away."

"Even with an injured leg, I couldn't possibly outrun you. Please, my arms ache." She winced. "And I need to use the bathroom."

Was it a mistake to give in to her? "All right." He loosened one strap and then unbuckled the cuff. "Don't make me regret this."

The moment her wrist was free, she yanked her arm inward and wiggled her fingers. "Ouch. My hands are numb."

He unbuckled the second cuff.

She sat on the bed and rolled her wrists. "Thank you." She smiled in relief. "See? We don't have to treat each other badly."

Her smile stabbed him straight in the heart and left him stunned. She rose on shaky legs and walked into the bathroom.

"Leave the door open," he demanded.

She slammed the bathroom door shut and locked it.

"Terrific." He frowned. She was already manipulating him, and he was helpless to stop it. *Welcome to fucking Pompeii all over again.*

He waited patiently until he heard her turn on the bathroom faucet.

"My God!" Her scream rang through the bathroom door. "What happened to me? I look awful. My throat was torn open. Did Varn do this?"

"I'm sorry you saw that." He cursed himself for forgetting about the bathroom mirror. He seldom noticed or used them, knowing he never really changed. "Your healing has been incredibly quick. It's already much better than when I took you from Varn an hour ago."

"An hour ago? Are you trying to mess with me? It won't work. I can see what kind of damage was done. How can skin heal like that in only one hour?" She groaned in disgust. "Is this how your kind feeds? Is it always this violent?" Arcona fell silent.

He waited for her to come out, and when she didn't, he continued to be patient. A faint scraping noise and a *thud* seemed out of place. "Are you all right in there?"

"Yes," she squeaked. "I just need a minute to get myself pulled together."

The sounds of soft thumping and the *click* of a latch raised alarm. He bounded from the bed, kicked the bathroom door in, and saw Arcona standing on top of the commode with one leg thrust out an open window, ready to throw herself to the ground.

"Don't!" Tyr lunged forward, grabbed her, and pulled her back into the bathroom. He locked his arms around her to prevent her from thrashing, which she did anyway. "It's freezing cold, and that's a three-story drop onto a pile of jagged lumber scraps."

"I don't care!" She hammered her fist against the raw gash in his leg.

When her pummeling fist connected with his wounded thigh, he felt as if a lightning bolt of white-hot pain had struck him. His mouth opened wide and a pitiful bellow roared out. He almost crumpled to the floor in agony but somehow managed to keep his arms locked around her and remain standing.

"You shouldn't have done that." He snatched her close to his chest, dragged her back to the bedroom and threw her on the mattress. With swift motions, he leaped on top of her, buckling one wrist back into the leather cuff and then the other. "It's clear we can't trust each other." Glowering at her, he bared his teeth. "Thank you for reminding me of how badly I need to feed so I can heal."

"I'm sorry," Arcona pleaded. She looked sorry, too. "Please don't hurt me!"

"I'm disappointed. I wanted to trust you, and for a moment, I thought I could." He glared at her as he grabbed the back of his snug T-shirt and tugged it over his head.

She gasped. "What are you doing?"

"What does it look like?" He took hold of her sweater and pushed it above the rounded crests of her breasts. "It's been a long time since I've given in."

Her wrists strained above her head as she kicked against the mattress. "Don't do it!"

He lifted his head. Her pulse visibly pounded on the side of her throat, sending his bloodlust soaring. "I haven't done *this* in almost five hundred years." He stretched on top of her, brushing his bare chest against hers. Her nipples grazed his. The warm scent of her skin promised exceptional pleasures that made his breath race. "I usually avoid situations like this," he whispered. "I enjoy contact with warm flesh too much, and I'm always tempted to go too far."

She whimpered and tried to wiggle from beneath him but couldn't.

"Hush." He stroked her hair with his fingertips before moving to the side of her throat, pushing the collar of her sweater and the amulet aside. He pressed his knee between hers and parted her legs, feeling the heat rolling off her skin. He allowed himself to sink between her thighs.

A furious erection rose and thrust hard against the zipper of his jeans. The usual intense desire and discomfort washed over him, yet he couldn't remember it ever being this bad. He reached down to adjust himself before he burst the seams. Sexual frustration was a huge part of his anger. He could want her and clearly remembered how good it felt to thrust inside a woman, but he also knew there would be no release, no satisfied moment of bliss, no end to the erotic torment he was in now. It ebbed but never truly ended.

Life as an Upir Likhyi offered only bloodlust and the semi-satisfied fleeting high that came from an act of violence or a prolonged feeding, both of which he'd tried mightily to avoid.

But he did need to feed. Hovering above her exposed throat, his fangs descended to their full wolfish length.

"Oh God." Arcona squeezed her eyes shut and turned away. Tangling his fingers in her hair, he held her still to prevent her from flinching away from him and ripping her skin. He chose the side of her throat untouched by Varn. Gazing down at her bruises filled him with shame. He hissed in self-loathing that he'd been foolish enough to allow Varn to taste her. That misstep was certain to become a problem later. Arcona should have been kept in his exclusive care from the beginning.

He pinned her beneath him, and with focused caution, bit into her throat. To his sensitive ears, her skin made a barely audible *pop* the moment it was punctured. The sound alone drove his cock harder against his jeans. A warm trickle of blood welled to the surface. Swirling his tongue across her skin, he lapped each ruby droplet. The flavor was salty sweet and laden with mysterious undertones, intoxicating in their complexity.

She moaned a string of soft, indecipherable sounds and writhed in his arms.

His grip on her tightened, but only enough to secure her. He ground his hips against her, working his body closer to the source of all pleasures. Drawing a slight sip of blood over his lips, he shuddered from the intense reaction she provoked in him. The moment pushed dangerously close to abandonment. For a moment, he almost believed he could experience the long-lost pleasure of gliding inside a woman just for the pleasure of it. By all the gods, he wanted to be a man again so badly he wept.

Drinking from a Strix and tasting the long repressed but never forgotten flavor of his maker was a contradictory experience. In an odd way, it was comforting to be reunited with the one who had been the direct cause of his pain.

Her back arched off the bed as she continued to struggle.

Withdrawing his fangs, he cupped his hands around her throat and whispered, "Relax. I won't hurt you." His muted words were so faint, he wondered if she even heard him or cared. He continued in a semi-dream state of pleasure. Feeding from his Strix provided a rush unlike anything he'd ever known. No victim had ever tasted this delicious or incited such mixed feelings of tenderness and carnality. One bead of crimson blood after another crossed his tongue, and for once, he was content to move slowly.

Feeding on a battlefield or back alley meant he was free to take what he needed in avid gulps and leave without any sort of emotional involvement taking place. Were he to give in and feed with abandon now, he doubted he could control himself and feared what would happen if he did surrender to bloodlust.

The tang of blood rose in his mouth, and he became lightheaded. Arcona's blood was too potent and affected him like a drug that he could easily grow addicted to. He tried to resist the impulse to gulp, but he wanted more. Drinking from the Strix who had made him was a conflicted sort of homecoming.

Arcona stopped struggling and lay still, and he wondered if she'd fainted. Careful not to be greedy, he sipped. With every lap of warm blood that washed across his tongue, the pain in his wound lessened. He had taken very little from her, but changes had already begun. His senses were keener, thoughts clearer. Even the gash in his thigh mended with tremendous speed, and it no longer hurt to rub his injured leg against hers. Reveling in the heated sensations she provoked was almost as exciting as being a man again and being able to simply enjoy the pleasures of sex without some cruel god of war getting involved and demanding his share of the bounty. His gaze riveted on a scarlet trickle of blood on her skin. Pressing his mouth to her throat, he tasted her again, allowing his tongue to linger.

While gathering a sticky-sweet sip of blood on his tongue, Arcona's long-enduring and many-faceted soul mingled with his. The breakthrough came with the same blunt force as a glaring searchlight trained inside the darkest cave. Instantly, his pleasure turned bittersweet. The clarity of what he saw surprised him and was unlike anything he had ever experienced. In the next breath, he and Arcona melded into a single consciousness, blurring all boundaries between them. He saw the original Arcona, defiant and desperate, barely floundering above her tragedies. He'd been a slave of Rome too. His understanding of how she felt was absolute. How perfect that they could be one.

An elated sense of anticipation flickered in his mind, and he hoped it meant his days as a Slayer were drawing to an end. He licked another few droplets from her skin that seemed especially pleasing. The coppery warmth elevated his senses. Arcona's soul memories spun through his mind like a stormy whirlwind. Flashes of dense forests. The deaths of her parents. Her time training to be a priestess. A man floating facedown in a river. Vivid and chaotic, the images and emotions from her distant life proved almost too much to bear. He couldn't make sense of anything and pulled away in despair.

With eyes closed, she shifted slightly beneath him.

An uncontrollable tremble shook his limbs. Details came into sharp focus. Arcona's memories sorted themselves out with the same ease as if he'd always possessed them. He'd never experienced this sort of clarity drinking the blood of another; vague emotions were usually the most he caught, but this was like watching a movie or, better yet, living it. Long-ago glimpses of her childhood on the Rhijin River clicked past like a slide show complete with scents and sounds. But soon, the images slowed.

He worried the initial effects were fading and thought that might be the extent of the shared experience, but a heartbeat later, Arcona's memories overwhelmed him with all the intensity of a baking sun in a dry summer sky. In a flash, he knew that she saw his world, as well. Their two lives had blended. In a blistering instant, they were one shared heart and mind without distinction, and he couldn't tell if he was experiencing a moment from Arcona's life or recalling a memory from his own.

Chapter Eight

Book of Tyr

Arcona lay beneath Tyr, stunned. Nothing was as it appeared. She'd expected fear, pain, and something morbid and unbearable, and instead the act of sharing blood with him had been ecstatic. Tyr's warm mouth pressed against her throat held her in a rising state of excitement, like an orgasm that kept building but refused to crest.

Through magic or some unknown force, her thoughts slipped inside his and could not be untangled. Every bit of his inner conflict, excitement, and even his intentions to be careful with her were clearly read. That intimate knowledge transformed the shared encounter from terror to bliss.

Her consciousness floated inside his head, privy to his every thought as his solid body shifted restlessly between her thighs. She sensed how difficult it was for him to feed without losing control. He needed the blood and meant no greater harm to her. In his own way, he followed strict ethics. She was certain of that now and relaxed into the strange coupling that she shouldn't desire but did.

Her soul drifted backward in time; years and then centuries sped past at an ever-faster rate. Awash in a river of blazing white light, she was thrown into a dark barracks, dank with the scent of many men. In this place she was no longer herself. She was Tyr.

* * * *

Pompeii. 79 AD

Tyr lay in his bunk, hands folded beneath his head. Unable to sleep, he stared at the low ceiling of the barracks, imagining mocking faces were hidden in the whorled plaster and the cracked beams. The Romans, by their own deliberate and devious design, had built the roof of the gladiator quarters many inches too low to fully accommodate the tall men of the north. As if their position as condemned slaves was not humbling enough, they were also forced to stoop indoors or risk scraping their scalps against the lintels.

He shifted on his bunk. The thin straw mattress provided little comfort to his large frame. A long day of sparring drills in the yard left his shoulder aching and his hip bruised by a clumsy parry from his own drill partner, who should have been guarding his flank.

Many days had passed since the death of the Cilician. The head trainer's demise had brought upheaval to the ludus. Aside from their often absent master, Dominus Marius, no one was officially in charge of Villa Lupus Unguis, and the wolf pack ran wild.

Overnight, once-minor rivalries had exploded into a house divided. The Germani did not take orders from the Gauls, the Gauls did not respect the Egyptians, and so on. Fights broke out in the training yard that only the threat of a hearty whipping by the house guards could quell.

With the Cilician gone, Tyr had done his best to unite the ludus and remind the men to save their ire for the arena. With firm words and by setting a stoic example, he calmed a potential storm and convinced the men to train hard for the upcoming games and earn their chance for freedom and fortune. He wanted both but harbored no hope of being able to do it alone. Victory in the arena was ultimately a group effort.

The day had ended peacefully enough, but he knew the same problems would return with the sun.

His biggest concern was Arcona. After their brief but intense tryst, the scent of roses in her hair, and the glint of mischief in her eyes haunted him. For many days in a row, she'd not appeared at the back balcony, and he'd been deprived of his daily glimpse of beauty.

Worry for her safety mounted. Even with her Strix-enhanced strength, she was still a captive and outnumbered in a compound of armed men. If Marius grew suspicious of her, all was lost.

Closing his eyes, he dreamed of winning in the arena and being awarded the palm branch and purse of coins, or the most coveted gift of all, the rudis, a wooden training sword signifying to all that he was a free man at last. Somehow, someway, he'd secure Arcona's freedom, too. Days of forced combat and slaughter would end, and in their place, shared liberation would rise. Once they fled beyond the reach of their enemies, there would be nothing but hope and peace between them.

Mulling over the sweetness of such a prospect, he dozed.

In a near bunk, Roc snored. One of the Egyptians, a young man named Renni, barely old enough to be called a man, had smuggled a couple of wine sacks into the barracks and passed them around.

Tyr hadn't bothered pursuing a share, knowing tensions were already high and the goatskin bags would likely be dry by the time it reached him.

After the last oil lamp had been extinguished, the barracks became quiet but for the varied sounds of sleeping men. Soon, exhaustion claimed him.

A soft hand on his shoulder woke him.

Startled, he sat with a jolt. Was this a dream, or had desire for a woman he could never have finally driven him mad?

"Tyr," Arcona whispered while pressing a delicate finger to his mouth. Leaning closer, her lips brushed his ear. "Meet me in the training pit." The heavenly scent of rose water and amber resin rolled off her skin.

Goddess help him, he was already hard just from the sultry tones of her voice. She was really here; her warm flesh and cascade of glossy hair stood apart from everyone else like a lone flower on a trash-strewn lane. This wasn't good. The other men were sure to wake and shout rude comments. Her visit to the wrong side of the ludus would be discovered and she would be punished.

Bracing for the worst, he grasped her hand. "You shouldn't have come here."

Her eyes glittered against the semi-darkness and so did the amulet around her neck. She turned and motioned for him to follow. Her movements were so subtle and quick she strode through the barracks like a phantom.

Rising from the bunk, he followed. None of his fellow captives stirred; it was as if they were swaddled in a cloud of enchanted sleep. On a typical warm summer night, the men were surly and woke with ease, so how was that even possible? He suspected Arcona's skills as a Strix might be to blame.

Crossing the training yard, her steps were so light and swift, she appeared to be floating. The hem of her fine stola fluttered around her like the wings of a butterfly. In silence, she darted down the stairs of the training pit, disappearing from view.

Crunching pumiced sand beneath his bare feet, he marched after her with the same desperate fervor as a bleating calf chasing its mother. What was she doing? If Marius or a nosy servant were to notice, they would both face execution. Fear for her rose and choked his heart.

The moon was high and painted the walls of the ludus in icy-blue light and indigo shadows. He raced down the steps and saw her already leaning against the equipment shed with a sly smile on her face.

"That was even easier than I thought." She bit down on the lush cushion of her bottom lip. "Come over here."

He approached, half alert for a cry of alarm from the house guards, who should have been patrolling atop the walls on lookout for just such a breach of security.

The pit was exactly what its name implied. Downhill of the training yard, a basin had been dug into the earth and reinforced with stone blocks and concrete. The floor was covered in sand and provided a shallow arena where trainers, observers, or potential buyers might watch men fight at close quarters and critique or praise them from the relative safety of a raised seat.

Most days, the pit served as a segregated portion of the training yard where small groups of gladiators were taken aside and taught specialized skills. With Arcona's graceful frame leaning against the wall, the normally stark space took on the illusion of a temple graced by the presence of a goddess. His breath caught. "You took a terrible risk. We shouldn't be here."

Her gaze locked on his. "It's worth the risk. I had to see you. Besides, I have a good reason for doing this."

Standing so close to her, his heart hammered against his ribs. He couldn't wait to tell her his plan. "I have a good reason for seeing you, too, but I don't want to put you in danger."

For a moment, she looked sad. Her hand brushed his cheek. "Don't worry about me, my love, this meeting couldn't wait. I'm running out of time, and there's so much yet to do."

Panic gripped him. "Running out of time? What's wrong? Has Marius threatened you?"

"No. I'm fully committing to the work of the Strix. The process has already started. I'm changing. Nothing frightens me anymore. My human heart is fading, but not completely gone. Once it's extinguished, I'll be truly free to act."

"Act on what?" The moment he spoke, he feared it was too loud.

Her eyes lit with a terrible gleam. "Revenge on Rome. I have a plan—"

"So do I. Please listen to—"

She shook her head, making her auburn waves ripple. "Whatever it is that you're about to say, I can guarantee my plan is far grander."

"We don't need grand!" Desperate to reach past her defensive exterior, he cupped the sides of her face. "We need each other. I can help you. I want a woman of my own."

A brittle, unhappy laugh rushed past her lips. "You don't even know me. If you did, you'd be disgusted."

"I want to know you, and I would never be disgusted." He took hold of her shoulders and forced her to look at him. "Do you think I don't understand? I've done horrible things, too. We all have. A captive has no choice. I'll admit that I want freedom so badly I'm willing to do worse than I've already done. But there is hope. The gods of the world yet to come, know of our plight. Whatever it is that you've done, they'll forgive you and set a place at their table. If I win in the arena, I can choose my reward. Say you'll come with me."

Sounding distraught, she wrung her hands. "Don't offer me false hope. Marius would never let me go."

"He might have to. Before he died, the Cilician trainer got drunk one day and muttered something about Dominus Marius's debts and his need to sell or surrender the ludus to his brother-in-law. If he's truly in debt, he might be willing to sell you."

"To whom?"

"To me!"

"Ha! That is a fantasy that will never happen." She looked stricken, as if his words were as unwelcome as a knife in the throat. "Romans slaughtered my family and scattered my people. Even if the gates of Villa Lupus Unguis opened wide and Marius said 'go,' I would still not be free. It would never be enough."

"What do you want?"

"I want blood, fire, and destruction brought on my enemies! If innocents die in the process, so be it. My hate alone could lift mountains and send them crashing down on Marius's house."

Stepping closer, his leg brushed against the fine linen of her stola. "Those are the words of a demon."

"They are my words and my deepest desires." Her voice trembled.

"I don't believe you. You hate because you're hurt. I'm hurting, too. Everyone I've ever loved is gone. Listen to me. If you give in to bitterness and stop caring about others, the Romans win."

She shook her head. "They won't win in Pompeii."

"What are you going to do?"

A sickly smile crossed her lips. "It's a surprise."

Reaching toward the amulet, he dared to touch it. A tiny static spark shot from the polished surface, and he recoiled from the sting. "The amulet feels angry. You should take it off before its power consumes you."

"I'll do no such thing. I'm an adept prophetess and entitled to wear it."

"Arcona, I've seen this stubborn attitude before. Amber is a sacred thing. It preserves life and stops time. But when the wearer is desperate or soaked in rage, it can only deliver more of the same. I warned you of this before; my village splintered over such an amulet. The priesthood and our warriors clashed over how to handle the Roman threat. We battled and killed our own kin. By the time the Romans arrived, we were divided and weak."

Her eyes flashed. "Warrior or priesthood? Whose side did you take?"

"Does it matter? In our case, they were both wrong, and the result was my people being slaughtered or pressed into slavery when we should have stood together."

She lifted her chin in defiance and looked away.

"Arcona, I fight men all day. I don't want to fight with you. Please." He brushed his hand along her arm. "You've given me something to strive for and more hope than I've had in a long time."

Wanting to tell her more, he stopped himself, too afraid to sound foolish. Perhaps he was a fool. Few men survived the arena and bought their freedom. No gladiator he knew of had dared purchase his master's concubine and lived to boast. Were his dreams of freedom as outlandish as her thirst for revenge?

Tense moments passed, and nothing more was said. Wishing for a truce, he sat at her side on the stone bench. The surface still radiated the heat of the day against the backs of his thighs. Under the intimate veil of moonlight it would have been a good time to kiss, but her petulant expression put a damper on his prospects.

Being near a woman so lovely brought impatience. He'd hoped they would not waste the chance to lie together and feel the only joy this wretched place offered. He'd left the barracks dressed only in a loincloth and was now forced to cross his hands over his lap to hide the obvious. "Talk to me a little more before you have to go."

She smirked. "There's no rush. Marius is asleep, as is the rest of his household. They won't be waking anytime soon."

Something about the way she said it alarmed him. "Have you killed them?"

"Not yet." Arcona stared at the starry sky as if committing it to memory. "You'll know when it happens. Death won't sneak quietly over the walls in such a peaceful manner. When it arrives, the Dark Slayer will make itself known to all."

"Who is the Dark Slayer? I do not know this deity. Is he a father god of the Teutoni?" No wonder she was so warlike. With a dainty gesture, Arcona folded her hands in her lap. "What makes you think the Dark Slayer is a *he*? The Slayer is a new god of my making."

Tyr balked. "Do not say you've created a god. It is arrogance. Our gods will be cross with you."

An impudent sideways glance proved she did not appear the least bit apologetic. "I made the Dark Slayer and I am not afraid to say it out loud. At this moment, the Slayer is gathering strength and waiting to be fully born into our realm."

The tone of her voice had shifted. Something cruel and strident spoke through her. Real alarm left him tense. "How was this task accomplished?"

Madness shimmered in her catlike eyes. "With magic from the East and West wedded as one."

"You used the amulet of the Strix, even after I warned you of its capriciousness?"

"Yes. In a trance, I went to the edge of the abyss and shouted down to any and all malevolent spirits who wished to join me in the righteous punishment of Rome. They responded with a howling battle cry. A thousand faceless demons rushed forward hungry for slaughter, clutching at the opportunity with bony claws. I yoked these starving, misshapen creatures to the more powerful gods who walk in the light. Something new was formed. My child, my only child, the Dark Slayer will be invincible. Rome and the rest of the world have never seen anything like it." Her refined laughter was as menacing as the slash of a battleax striking too near his face.

He'd heard similar talk before, and with an aching heart, resolved to reason with her. Madness and despair haunted any ludus. Waiting for their inevitable turn on the tip of a blade broke the strongest of men. Causing the death of a friend they'd been forced to train with and bunk beside broke the rest. Cooperating with such conditions caused guilt as destructive as swallowing ground glass. Fervor and wild claims that salvation was near were just part of coping with something too brutal and unwieldy to grasp. "Slaughter will only rend your heart further. I know. I'm forced to do it every festival day. Killing strangers will not return your lost loved ones."

Her gaze fixated on the stone steps. "What is it you think I want?"

"You need hope, Arcona, if only for the next world."

"Is that the cure?" Looking down at her hands, she appeared agitated. Tears welled and slid to the tips of her lashes where they clung, stubbornly refusing to fall. "I'm beyond anything as delicate as hope."

"No, you're not. You're alive. I care for you and understand."

"Care and understanding will not free us." With restless motions, she crossed and uncrossed her slender ankles. Her pale hands smoothed the hem of her stola into place as she planted her feet firm on the ground, prepared to rise. "A well timed act of vengeance might."

Half afraid she'd leave before he made his point, the words rolled past his lips in a desperate flurry. "Have you ever loved another?"

Turning, she looked at him as if he'd dashed cold water in her startled face.

"I have." He persisted. "Just the sight of her got me through the day." A tense grin strained his lips. "But she didn't love me back." His voice was so raw the last words faded in a raspy whisper.

"Her loss." For a breathtaking moment, a warm and genuine smile lit her face that made the corners of her eyes crinkle in the most charming way. For a fleeting second he was provided with a dazzling glimpse of what she might have been had tragedy not burdened her so. "Who was she?"

"You. I've been looking at you since Marius brought you here last winter and paraded you on his back balcony."

"Don't be foolish." Her smile faded. "Any woman wearing silk is eye-catching."

"I wasn't impressed with the silk."

"You're lonely. Even a leper with half her limbs and some of her wits would appeal."

"You're cruel to say so." His gaze skimmed the ramparts that should have been patrolled by armed guards at regular intervals but were not. "This is a dangerous place to be. We'd be easily seen from above. What are we doing here? Waiting to become moving targets for the night guards?"

She grasped his hand and moved closer. The fine weave of her stola brushed his bare thigh, making the tiny hairs on his legs prickle. "Don't worry about the guards. They are sleeping with the poppies, and I wish them all nightmares."

The amulet glittered against the moonlight, riveting his attention. "Did you cast a spell?"

"I drugged their wine. It's one of my most dependable tricks. Rain or shine, the Romans never forego their beloved *vinum*. Tonight, I added a little surprise. Marius keeps a large and costly amphora of sticky black paste from the East in his sleeping quarters. Many nights I've watched him rub it under his tongue and fall into a dazed stupor he cannot be roused from."

"Is that where Marius is now, in his quarters in a dazed stupor?"

"Unless he drank too much. Then he'll be crossing the River Styx."

"Styx? Where is this river? Is it near here?"

Her lips curled into a mean little smile. She appeared to be reveling in a private moment of amusement. "The Styx is always near, especially in a ludus."

"I don't understand."

"Marius told me the Styx is a treacherous river beneath the earth where the newly dead gather on the bank and pay coins to unspeakable monsters to ferry them to the other side."

"Oh." He nodded. "Their souls do not take a boat west into the setting sun and go to the great feast?"

"No." A look of disgust twisted her pretty mouth. "They burrow into the earth like vermin and go searching for their gods below. Yet another example of how warped the Romans are."

"I would rather go to the feast and eat my fill of roasted meat and drink." A deep laugh rumbled free that he hoped no one beyond Arcona heard.

Leaning closer, she twined her arm through his and rested her head against his shoulder.

Starved for tenderness or anything close to normal interaction between a woman and a man, he tensed, on high alert for her next move.

Arcona faced him, and with breathtaking gentleness, traced her fingertips across his jaw and then along the bridge of his nose. She looked into his eyes with such strange intensity that he found her examination almost unbearable.

"Tyr." Her voice was low and sweet, and her lips ripe as summer berries. "You will never go west on the boat of souls and your feast will be one of blood."

He recoiled. "Don't say that. Not even in a jest."

"I didn't say it to be amusing."

He had no idea what to make of her odd comment. "Every man must die. For me, it could be soon. I would not want to be denied a proper homecoming."

Mischief flickered in her eyes. "That's because you don't know of other options."

"There are no other options for me. I want to live, and hope I do, but if I perish in the arena, I pray I die well. I'm not afraid of it. Everyone I ever loved, except you," he dared to add, "is already at the feast."

"You don't love me." The silver filigree of her earrings shimmered when she shook her head. "Please don't say it."

"I think of you constantly, and I'm certain we could love each other if you gave me a chance."

She drew away from him. "A ludus is no place to plan a happy future."

"I know." He grew quiet. "But why give in completely? Must I surrender my dreams to the Romans, as well? Isn't that the ultimate conquest, to hand over hope before it's even been taken? If I do win in the arena, and I could, the victory may come with a prize. I've heard of gladiators who walk free and have enough Roman coins to buy a herd of horses or a farm. It's rare but possible. I would use my winnings to buy you."

With an angry gesture, she swiped her hand through the air, making her wristful of bracelets rattle. "Forget that."

The amount of noise her jewelry was making made him nervous. "Why?" he whispered. "The prizes can be large. As I said, rumors have spread that Marius is in trouble."

"It doesn't matter. Marius could give you his blessing to take me away, and I still wouldn't go with you."

Soul wounded, he gritted his teeth. "You'd choose life as a captive over life as my woman? If you don't want me, why do you seek me out in the dark of night? I don't understand."

"I'm needed here. The gods have put me in place and empowered me to carry out their will. I have a mission to fulfill, and when it's done, I'll have my revenge. That's all I expect. I don't care about little things the way I used to. My life as a woman was meaningless, but as a Strix, I'll have power."

"No." He rubbed his hand across the gritty stubble on his jaw. "You care. I've seen it in your eyes when you watch me from the balcony. You don't watch the others the same way. If I take a blow, you flinch. Even now, you're asking yourself if I'd be good to you. Put your heart at ease. I would."

Her gaze met his. Her expression softened and her eyes became glossy with tears. "I admit, I allowed myself to consider that possibility, but only for brief moments. I have only to endure a short while longer. Soon, all doubts will fade. The emotions I feel today will not be there tomorrow. It's best to let them go willingly rather than suffer the pain of having them yanked from my heart at once."

"You're not making sense."

"Tyr, events have been put in motion that cannot be halted. The call has gone out. Power is building. Once a stone is hurled at the sky, it must fly in its arc and fall."

Burying his face in his hands, despair overwhelmed him. This was not lovers' talk; it was painful. Arcona would not even allow him to clutch the filaments of a dream. She had to stomp the embers out of his heart like a soon-to-be abandoned campfire. "Why did you rouse me from my sleep? Did you need to prove to me that I mean nothing to you? Perhaps this is the amulet talking. The wretched thing has turned you mad."

"You're wrong." She clutched his wrist with such strength that his hand tingled. "You mean everything. I'm putting all my expectations on you. I came tonight to tell you something important. Earlier, I overheard Marius making plans for tomorrow's games."

"Tomorrow?" He winced. This was all too much at once. "He's not replaced the Cilician. We have no trainer."

"Nor will you. You were right. Marius is greatly in debt. He's scrambling to hang on to what he has. Even his wife is plotting a lethal blow against him. An ornate spectacle is to take place with several high-stakes fights. With big wagers, Marius is gambling on Villa Lupus Unguis to relieve him of debt. If it doesn't work, he must surrender the ludus to his wife's brother, something he is loath to do. He would rather empty the barracks of valuable gladiators and watch them bleed into the sand than see them given to his hated brother-in-law."

"And you've come to warn me?"

"Yes, my love. You need to be prepared."

"How will this *spectacle* take place on such short notice? Are we to be woken at dawn and marched to the arena?"

"No. You will be marched there at noon."

"Are you sure? This isn't funny."

"You can see by my face I'm not laughing." She patted the amulet. "The mark of the Strix, which you claim to hate, may be the very thing that spares your life."

He drew away from her. "I put no stock in it."

"That's because you are a warrior. You must do what you do best and allow me to do what I do best." She stood and offered him her hand. "Come."

Grasping her hand, he followed her into the shadows. When they reached a private spot behind a wooden shed filled with sparring equipment, she turned to face him with her hands braced against the planks. "I begged the gods to strike love from my heart and give me power instead. The first time I asked, I failed. Now I understand why. The sacrifice wasn't great enough. Poor Hedron." Her gaze softened. "Then I saw you, so straight and strong, the perfect weapon. You are my final test, my greatest sacrifice."

Alarmed by her tone, he brushed a strand of hair from her cheek. "Who is Hedron?"

"A good man who died trying to save me. I vow I will not allow that to happen to you." She slid her stola from her shoulder, exposing a pale breast. A flock of freckles graced her collarbones. The small but endearing details were a pleasing surprise. She was human, after all. For so long, he'd thought of her as perfect and as removed from life as the alabaster statues set above the gates of the arena. A series of reddened marks on the side of her breast caught his attention. With a light touch, he traced the pad of his thumb across the raised edges. "Does Marius hurt you?"

She looked away with lips parted and conflict on her brow.

"We take turns hurting each other, but I'll have the pleasure of taking the final strike."

Confusion and disgust with Marius grabbed hold of his thoughts and clung like tar. "What do you mean?"

A chilly expression loomed in her eyes as if she were watching future events from a distance. "It's nothing that needs to be discussed."

"Yet another good reason to leave this wretched place and come with me."

Her voice was a husky whisper. "You don't even know where you're going yet."

He made a weak attempt to bring some levity to this uncomfortable conversation. "True, but I'd love some company wherever it is."

With a featherlight touch, she fussed with a lock of his hair and then tucked it behind his ear. "You're naturally kind, aren't you? That's a shame. How have you survived?"

This was not the moment to spill his own self-loathing and regrets at her feet and confess to every unkind act he'd ever committed. Terrible things had been done just to guarantee he ate that day or did not die.

Tangling her fingers with his, she gave his hand a squeeze. "Why aren't you as damaged as me?" Lifting her face to his, she licked her lips. The sight of her darting pink tongue added to his rising nerves. For a heartbeat, their gazes locked. Had he ever seen eyes that caught and reflected the light with such mirror-like intensity? He doubted it.

She pushed the stola lower, allowing it to slide past her hips and glide down her legs to the sand. Holding an effortlessly graceful pose, she stood naked. He beheld the stunning sight in awe. Every curve was lush and inviting, a celebration of all things feminine.

The wild look of madness had fled, and a soft, almost somber expression took its place. A haze of tears glimmered in her eyes. "This is my final act as just a woman. After tonight, there's no going back. Show me everything good that I'm giving up." Her breath hitched. "Break my heart."

He didn't truly understand what she meant, but the sadness in her voice struck at his core like a cleaver to the butcher's block. "You don't have to give up anything for me."

Arcona wrapped her arms around his neck and pressed her soft body against his. The bronze setting of the amulet scraped his chest like the tip of a dagger and sent a chill racing down his spine. Once her thigh brushed against his, the rest of his body rioted to get closer. Hard to the point of discomfort, he wanted her so badly he would have snapped the neck of any man who dared to interrupt. "I'd fight and kill for you, but most of all, I'll wait for you to come to your senses. I won't demand. Anything you offer is welcome."

"Anything?" A burst of nervous laughter bubbled free of her. He worried someone might hear and quickly brought his hand to her mouth. "Arcona, practice caution."

"You forget, Villa Lupus Unguis is under enchantment."

"And by your doing, also drugged."

"Yes, that too, but my Strix enchantment is stronger than poppies. I could scream at the top of my voice, and the sleepers on the other side of the wall would merely hear the screech of an owl on the hunt or the squeak of bats. I'm becoming a shadow creature, unseen and silent to men. After tonight, there will be no need to practice caution. I'll soon be free to roam Pompeii. Then I'll head to Rome and inflict my judgment there."

With unease, he watched her expression grow colder. If it helped her survive the unendurable, why should he care if she needed an illusion of power? Didn't everyone in a ludus believe they might be the lucky one, the fish that slipped through the net and lived? "So, you are committed to the path of the Strix and all the strife it will bring you?"

Cupping his face, she held him captive with only the barely there pressure of her fingertips. "My commitment is absolute." A moment passed as she allowed that fact to sink in. She took hold of the edge of his loincloth, made quick work of unraveling the fabric, and flung it onto the sand. Caressing his hipbones with warm hands, she whispered, "Your legs are shaking. Why is that?"

Standing stripped and hard, her blunt actions left him vulnerable in a way no one else could. Desire battled with reason. Why couldn't he just let her rant her fill about magic and Dark Slayers while he enjoyed her beautiful body? Instead he spoke his truth. "Arcona, I'm worried for you. The Romans hate *barbarian* witchcraft, especially when it's practiced under their roof. Do what you must, if it gives you peace, but don't parade it in front of Marius. Mad talk and calling on the amulet is sure to provoke him. I don't want to see you hurt."

She twined her leg around his and pulled him close. "You're the one who sounds provoked, and that's not what I intended. I came here tonight to share pleasure with you, not an argument. You have my word that I'll put talk of the Strix aside, at least for now. As I said earlier, this is my good-bye, and I want it to be a sweet one."

He wrapped his hands around her hips. Her skin was soft and scented with fragrant oils. "We don't have to say good-bye, not yet."

With her face tilted upward, her eyes glistened. "Tomorrow the world will be an altered place." Taking hold of his hands, she gently kissed each of his fingertips one by one and then guided them to her breasts. "The evening's grown cool. Keep me warm." Her hand slipped to his nape and held him close. He kissed her mouth, tasting a hint of exotic spices and a floral fragrance that he could not name. With soft lips and the sweep of her tongue, she returned his kiss. "Tyr," she whispered, smoothing a few wild strands of hair away from his face. "You are the strongest and the best." She traced her fingertips across his jaw and then lovingly stroked the outer edges of his ears, like she was fawning over a cherished pet. "I had to choose you." The shared kiss melted into playful nips. Her motions were tender and yielding, filled with the affection he craved and had feared he'd never experience again.

Pressing closer, he pinned her against the sun-warmed wall, her breasts heavy in his hands. He wished he could have wrapped her in furs and lain with her in the safety of a shepherd's cabin high in the mountains of home, far from Roman danger. Despite her claims that the house slept, he knew the pit was not the place for lingering tenderness. Someone was bound to wake and once they did, his time with Arcona would evaporate in an instant of panicked flight. He seized this sweet moment of life in the same way he would likely die, with his bare feet planted firmly in the sand. Parting her thighs with his knee, he slid his hands lower and caressed the dip of her waist and the lush flare of her hips. Stroking the sides of her rounded thighs, he lifted her to his level. He pressed between her legs, and his cock grew wet when it grazed against her. For a breathless second, he nearly lost control.

Locking her arms around his neck, she twined her legs around his hips. "Go slow," she murmured. "So I can enjoy you." She looked bashful, and the slight scrape of her teeth against her full bottom lip drove him mad. Of course, he wanted to please her and longed to hear her say his name during a breathy rush of pleasure.

Grasping his shaft, she guided him closer. Her soft sighs hijacked his senses, and her hips pressed down in the most provocative way. With a slow, careful thrust, he glided inside. The heat of her silky grip enveloped him. The first second of wet friction was so luscious and filled with joy, he came to a tense halt for fear it would end on the initial searing stroke. She leaned her head against the wall with eyes closed and lips parted. "I've dreamed of this every night. If I could, I would have left Marius's bed to find you." Her eyes opened. Moonlight bathed her face. "Tyr, you're the only man I've willingly lain with."

The way she said it cleaved his soul. There was no anger or the thundering bravado of the Strix in her tone, only the heartrending honesty of a young woman who'd suffered so many misfortunes. The statement brought honor to him to have been sought out but added tragedy to know that she'd been forced to share herself with others not of her choosing. Goddess willing, he would fight well and end their days in slavery.

"Move with me." Her hands gripped his shoulders and her nails scratched his flesh. "You don't have to be gentle. No one else is."

They both deserved gentleness. He kissed her throat, allowing his mouth to linger on the pulse point below her ear. "I want to be." His voice was ragged from the exertion of holding back and he was surprised he'd been able to say anything at all. Arching her back with grace, she rocked her hips against him. The look on her face was pure abandonment. With his heart hammering, he dared to risk a few steady strokes, prolonged and cautious with breath held. In the center of great pleasure, his mind churned. Could he keep her? How long did they have?

Arcona buried her face against his chest and made tiny sounds that were impossible to decipher. She might have been sobbing or reaching climax; he couldn't tell. Brushing her hair aside, he whispered, "It's all right," even though he knew it wasn't.

She drew away just enough that she could look at him. A languid haze of pleasure glowed on her face. He stared into the bright sparkle of her eyes, and for a heartbeat, got lost enough to forget who he was and who she was; they were simply one.

"Arcona." He whispered her name through gritted teeth. Thrusting deep, he came so hard stars flickered in the corners of his vision. Every fiber of his body released into the white-hot moment of bliss, the pleasure almost too much to bear. He hoped he'd been quiet and not cried out, but he wasn't sure. Panting, he braced a hand against the wall, trying to catch his breath.

Lifting her chin, she smiled and it was as if the sun had appeared at midnight to light his world.

Pressing close, he planned to remain inside her for as long as he could, but every breath he gulped and each small motion put him in greater danger of sliding out of her. She wriggled in his grasp, and he did slip free.

He thought of their last coupling. There had been no smiles and sweet moments of peace after they finished. She'd been aggressive with him, rough. He rubbed the tip of his nose against hers. "I didn't hurt you, did I?"

"No, love. All is right."

Hearing her use her softest voice melted his heart. "You didn't bite me."

The smile returned but had a sly edge. "I'm saving the bite for next time."

He couldn't tell if she was teasing. Women were always a challenge to understand, but Arcona was even more so than most. "Will there be a next time?"

"Oh, yes." She smiled.

Easing her feet to the sand, he asked, "Are you cold? Do you want your stola?" He wondered if it was possible that they could make love again before they had to part, and was reluctant to grab the discarded garment. As he reached down, a low rumble passed through the ground. The sand shimmered and chattered off the floor of the pit like grain winnowed from the chaff. The walls swayed and he was quick to pull Arcona away from the unsteady stack of earthen bricks. He drew her against his chest to protect her.

"Look!" She glanced at him with an odd gleam in her eyes. "Even the ground beneath our feet wants to throw the Romans off its back."

Within the villa, the sounds of pottery smashing to the floor roused a few startled servants. Shouts and calls of alarm rang through the air as the world rattled.

Giving him a gentle push, she urged him to pick up his loincloth and flee. "Not everyone drank wine. Go, before anyone sees you."

Wrapping the stola around her, she dashed up the steps and disappeared around a corner. Her exit was as stealthy as steam rising. Everything happened so fast, he stood speechless as the last ripple of movement traveled across the yard.

Half in shock, he returned to the barracks with plodding steps. As violent as the shaking had been, he was surprised to hear no one awake. The varied sounds of men snoring provided evidence that all had slept through the disturbing event. Stepping over empty wine sacks left strewn on the floor, he approached his bunk and lay down. Stretching across the mattress, he stared at the ceiling and saw the same mocking faces etched into the plaster and cracked wooden beams that had snarled at him earlier.

Arcona had made love to him, opened up and revealed a kinder, more accessible facet of her heart. He desired her more than ever, yet their situation remained impossible. Everything had changed, and yet nothing had changed.

Chapter Nine
Hours later, Pompeii. 79 AD

Sleep finally came for Tyr at the same time the house guards staggered into the barracks at dawn.

The senior guard, a pockmarked Roman named Felix, banged a bronze dagger against a shield. "Wake up, unlucky bastards!" The obnoxious clatter of the blade pounding the steel disk rang through the barracks with earsplitting intensity. "On your feet! Your day of glory in the arena has come. Double rations in the kitchen yard. No nervous puking. Every man eats."

Still exhausted from the night before, Tyr rose on one elbow, rubbing his sleep-deprived eyes with the heel of his palm. Arcona had been right. Marius had been planning to take his gladiators to the games, and they were not prepared. Everywhere he looked, men lay sprawled across their bunks, refusing or unable to stir. Only a handful managed to open their eyes or muster the energy to complain. The poppy-infused wine still held sway, and he worried Arcona may have done more harm than intended.

Felix signaled to his fellow guards to line up four abreast. A battery of burly men stomped through the barracks like angry oxen, overturning cots and dumping the dozing occupants on the floor.

"Everyone up!" Felix bellowed. In the low light, his unblinking eyes glistened as cunning as a rat's. "Dacian, on your feet. Set a good example for these shiftless snails."

Tyr stood as straight as he could under the low ceiling and rewound his loincloth. All the guards looked as bleary-eyed and tired as he felt. All signs indicated the ludus was headed toward misfortune. With heavy steps, he walked across the drill yard and made a beeline for the kitchen.

The newly risen sun tinted the sky a fresh shade of blue. The grinding heat of an August day had yet to come. As he approached the kitchen, which was situated outdoors in summer, the grainy scent of millet porridge greeted him. Each morning, the bubbling caldron of vegetable-enriched porridge was a monotonous and unavoidable constant. But today, a heaping platter of chopped cold mutton accompanied it, along with golden loaves of bread steaming from the oven.

He grabbed a wooden bowl from the stack and filled it to overflowing, intending to eat his fill now. Once inside the arena and subjected to the many stomach-churning sights and smells within, there would be no appetite. Exhausted or not, he had to fight his fellow captives, but he did not have to fight them while hungry.

Choosing a stone block as his seat, he faced the sun, allowing the soft rays to bathe his face. He tore a warm loaf of bread in half, dunking a portion of it into the hot bowl of porridge and using the crust as a scoop. Every few moments, he scanned the back balcony, hoping for a glimpse of Arcona, but the villa on the far side of the wall displayed no signs of activity and remained silent.

Had she slept after they parted? Was she thinking of him as often as he thought of her? Were her strong words signs of madness brought on by the hopelessness of their situation? Surely the cure for such delusion was freedom and a stable life far from Roman conflicts. With luck, he could offer her a new beginning with open hands. He dreamed of saying, *I am the victor. It is done. Come with me now.*

Looking around, he began to worry about his fellow gladiators. The few men who were on their feet shuffled around the training yard in a daze and seemed incapable of focusing their thoughts long enough to eat breakfast. He had no intention of losing in the arena today, wolfing his portion of cold mutton and then going back for more.

After finishing his meal, he returned to the barracks to wash at the trough set in front. He rinsed the salt and dust from his skin and sought the clay pitcher that contained bitter green oil to rub into his skin, but it was not in its usual place or any logical place a man might have set it down. Always in short supply, perhaps it had been stolen? His salt-stiffened leather armor had to be oiled as well or else it would hamper his range of motion. Obviously in the Cilician's absence, the small but important details were going unaddressed. Vital practice drills were not being performed. Blades went unsharpened. No one was offering prayers. Without doubt, they were marching into disaster.

And where was Arcona? Was she all right? Had a jealous Marius caught her sneaking back onto the right side of the wall? Not knowing her fate was torturous. Looking at the lethargic state of the men around him, he realized it was time to take matters into his own hands and make sure the day had a decent outcome.

Tyr approached the cook. "I need a dish of oil."

A look of disgust flooded the cook's face. The usually uncommunicative man who prepared their bread and porridge was a slave himself, yet he appeared offended to be forced to deal with one of the lowest of the low: a damanti, a man condemned to the arena. "I can't just give you things because you bark for them!"

"Someone has stolen the oil pitcher."

"That's not my problem." He turned his back. "You're all thieves. That's why you're here."

That wasn't why Tyr was there. "We face the arena today."

"And I've done my part. You've gorged on mutton. At least you got a last meal. Go away."

"Don't be a fool," he snarled. "I need to oil my armor and blade if they are going to be well used. Shall the house of Lupus Unguis fall today because a petty cook refused to share a measure of oil? Do you know what I think? I think you steal and resell the oil. If you care to take the argument further, I will talk to the guards and make sure Dominus Marius knows his gladiators were unprepared because of a cook's stinginess."

"Wait!" The visibly rattled man hurried inside the dank cave of a room that functioned as a winter kitchen and returned with a clay amphora sealed with wax. "Take it."

He accepted the amphora with a curt nod and headed back to the barracks to prepare. It irked him to think that his life might depend on something as trivial as a splash of oil, but that extra bit of oil might mean the difference between a glancing strike and a lethal blow, or his sword sliding free at a crucial moment. Just another unfair detail going unaddressed in this very unfair place.

Tyr finished his tasks with precise efficiency, then performed a few basic drills. The day grew hot. Hours passed and Marius did not appear in the drill yard to announce which teams of gladiators would be paired together for each fight. Soon everyone became weary from being on high alert and having nothing happen. There were so few signs of real preparation that hope grew among the men that the games might not take place that day. The gladiators who had unwittingly drunk the drugged wine halfheartedly dragged themselves through the tasks at hand, as did the guards.

Finally, at long past noon, the men were lined up, shackled together, and loaded into carts pulled by oxen. A separate cart carried their sharpened weapons and battle gear, safely contained in sealed trunks, all lorded over by heavily armed house guards.

The great iron-trimmed gates of the ludus creaked open, and the carts fitted with human cages clattered over stone pavement headed toward the city. The day was bright and clear but for a haze of smoke from a multitude of hearth fires that hung over Pompeii.

Tyr squinted against the sight. For a man whose tribe preferred to disperse and live in small groups of hundreds at most, the sheer density of Roman cities awed and terrified him.

With increasing frequency, he looked over his shoulder, expecting to see a dour-faced Dominus Marius riding to the front of the procession, but the man and his towering Egyptian steed were nowhere in sight. Was he not accompanying his gladiators to the arena? This seemed ill-advised. Perhaps he'd ridden ahead? Tyr both worried and hoped Arcona would be present today to watch him fight from the safety of Marius's viewing box as she had in the past.

The procession rumbled through the city's Vesuvius Gate. The ramshackle cottages and lean-tos of the poor on the outskirts of Pompeii gave way to grander structures owned by the affluent merchants.

They passed a fine plaster home. A young woman with flowing dark hair and a bundle in her arms darted from the doorway and ran alongside the carts.

"Roc!" she called out in a bleating voice. When she lifted her face, Tyr recognized her as Roc's wife, Janna, a young slave from Gaul who'd been separated from her family and sold to another master.

A house custodian exited the door and hurried in pursuit, his face purple with exertion. "Stop!" he demanded.

Janna ignored the command and ran toward them, faster. Eager to greet his wife, Roc rushed to the far side of the cart, dragging a row of shackled men with him. He gazed through the square grid of iron bars with his body quaking. "Janna, what are you doing on the street? Don't get yourself into trouble, my love."

Tears streamed down Janna's cheeks. Taking staggering steps, she clumsily unfurled the bundle to reveal a baby with wispy dark curls. "Look at your son. He's so like you." Her pace slowed as she held up a bright-eyed baby for him to see. Her voice broken, she called out, "I love you—we love you! You'll not be forgotten."

Roc opened his mouth to speak but sobbed instead. He stared at Janna with his jaw so tense his teeth could be heard grinding above the noise of the wooden wheels crunching bits of debris as they rolled along. "I'm so sorry." He gritted the mumbled words.

"I'll have a stone carved for you." The child in Janna's arms cried out in hiccuping gasps. "It will say 'Roc of the mighty Ambarri, always valiant, beloved of—'"

Roc struck his forehead against the bars. "Don't waste coins on a stone."

Despair washed over Janna's face. Her lips trembled. "I must do something."

The custodian caught up to Janna, grabbed her by the arm, and dragged her back toward the house. "You don't have the master's permission for this. These men are criminals. Stop making a scene and bringing shame to a respectable household."

Janna turned and shouted over her shoulder. "Roc!" She lifted her fist in salute. "I've named our son *Roc*."

Roc wilted against the bars, refusing to move or even blink as Janna was led away.

For a moment, no one dared to speak. Such a scene was all too familiar. Everyone inside the cage had recently buried a loved one or had one snatched away.

For a moment, Janna and the custodian argued in the street. The custodian grabbed hold of her hair and gave it a yank. "Stop stalling. Return to the house."

The cart clambered forward as Roc watched helplessly, his fingers clutching the bars so tightly it appeared several digits were in danger of being severed.

Within moments, the custodian shoved Janna through a doorway, and she disappeared from view.

Bowing his head, Roc wailed a heart-piercing note so raw and jagged it barely sounded human. In a pulse pounding instant, a wave of bone-jarring emotion spread to every man in the cart. All reacted. Some eyes went vacant, and some fists clenched until fingernails pierced the palms. The moment became shockingly real. This was it. Caged like animals, they were rolling toward their deaths, and nothing short of a miracle could change that.

The top-heavy cart swayed as it rolled along the paved city lanes that led to Pompeii's amphitheater. Frightened children too wary to make eye contact with the men behind the bars and disinterested old people who'd seen it too often and no longer cared stared from their doorways as they passed. Everyone else looked upon the condemned with mild distaste. As they approached the great amphitheater, the crowds thickened and the carts were forced to slow for the bustling foot traffic. In this part of the city, taverns and brothels were rampant. Bawdy frescos painted on the exteriors made it clear what one could expect inside.

He'd fought at the amphitheater before, but the first sight of the arena always took his breath. A large statue of some proud Roman with outstretched hands was set atop the front gate. The massive structure was grand beyond anything his people were capable of building and yet it remained tawdry in so many ways. Heaps of garbage had accumulated everywhere. Murals of battling and bleeding gladiators ornamented the walls. The graceful arches were painted blaring shades of red and yellow and filled with many coarse and unseemly things. Vendors hocked roasted meat and wine and even strange souvenirs like vials of gladiator sweat or bits of a shattered shield from a particularly engaging match. Prostitutes, young and old, male and female, occupied every foot of ground near any entrance or exit and serviced their customers in the scant shadows.

The carts were pulled alongside the amphitheater, and the door was unlatched. In groups of six, the shackled men were unloaded and escorted under guard through a dark archway that led into the arena. They marched in an orderly row with leg irons clanging. Once they had crossed to the other side, sunlight bouncing off the pale stone momentarily blinded him. The smell of a crowd of thousands on a summer day and of blood clotted in the sand assaulted his senses.

One by one, Felix released the men from their shackles and handed them dull wooden swords to practice with. "Entertain them. Get the crowd cheering!" he shouted above the din. "Perform some exhibition drills."

Tyr glanced around warily. The arena was filled to capacity, more than he'd ever seen it. "Large crowd."

"This is a special day." Felix beamed. "The people have been promised something spectacular."

A shudder of apprehension gripped him. "I need my armor."

"You'll get your armor along with everyone else. We haven't unloaded the carts. Meanwhile, your job is to stomp around on the sand like a stallion, swing your sword, and show yourself to good advantage. Make our master proud. They're still taking bets out front, and the bookies are encouraging everyone to plunk down their coins."

His gaze scanned the arena boxes, seeing no one inside them. "Is Dominus Marius here?"

"Our master has been here for hours." Felix frowned. "It's not any of your concern, but Marius had important business to discuss with several senators. He's with them now."

"When will he be back? Who will organize us?"

"Don't give it a thought." Felix gave him a shove. "All you need to do is get out there and break some hearts and spill some guts." He winked.

Tyr padded into the center of the arena. The grit of hot sand rasped between his bare toes. The smell of sweat and the sound of clashing shields hung heavy in the air. Once the crowd noticed him, they screamed heated insults and impassioned adorations from the stands.

Needing water and wishing he could spot Arcona in the stands, he parried and stabbed at an invisible foe, allowing his strikes to become fluid. The drill went on without break for what felt like an eternity. No one asked him to stop. If he weren't careful, he'd wear himself out. Why wasn't someone taking charge? The men around him eventually ceased their practice drills and leaned against a far wall in a spot of shade while the crowd jeered at them.

A lone figure appeared in Marius's viewing box. The other gladiators made quick work of slashing the air with their swords and making themselves look busy.

"Stop!" Marius swept his hand through the air as he looked down at his gladiators from the safety of his privileged perch, which clung to the curved wall of the amphitheater. Protected from the sweltering sun beneath several layers of colorful silk awning, he remained untouched by direct light or common men.

Tyr and all the other gladiators of the house of Lupus Unguis halted their practice and turned to face Dominus Marius.

The crowd, now eager for lethal entertainment, roared their approval at this auspicious sign the main games were about to begin.

"Come here." Marius leaned over the side of the observation box and called his team of gladiators nearer. Lording above his men, he addressed everyone in a firm but subdued voice that prevented others across the way from eavesdropping.

"Today's events are crucial. We have much at stake. The citizens of Pompeii are here today to enjoy quality blood sport, and we will not disappoint them.

"This city is filled with low-minded gossips. Everyone already knows what became of the Cilician trainer."

Agitation creased Marius's brow. "In past days, much has been said against the house of Lupus Unguis. The average dull shopkeeper is babbling that without a skilled trainer the wolf has lost its fangs. I'm deeply offended by such idle speculation, and you should be, too. They say my gladiators are an undisciplined rabble. The crowd has bet heavily against the house of Lupus Unguis and the odds are shocking. They expect all of you to crumple on a rival's blade and bleed into the sand."

Pointing toward the impatient Pompeiians milling in the stands, Marius snarled, "Are you going to allow that to be said of you?"

"No!" Tyr shouted.

"Good!" Marius bellowed back. "I like your spirit, and I have something special planned for you, Dacian."

"The odds against the house of Lupus Unguis have never been so grim." Marius's voice strained with tension. "Every fight is a fortune at stake. I cannot impress this enough. Fight well today, for you are not only fighting for your lives but also my honor. At the end of the day, I will pay a purse of eighty thousand sesterces and grant freedom to every man left standing!"

A hearty cheer rose from the gladiators.

Though only midafternoon, Marius already showed signs he'd been drinking heavily. His face was flushed, his words slurred. He hung over the side of the viewing box and gestured so enthusiastically he was in danger of toppling to the sand below. "Those of you who are so inclined may carry on as freemen and paid combatants for the house of Lupus Unguis!"

Wild shouts of approval rose among the gladiators, but Tyr remained silent. The promise was an empty one. With bad odds, the house of Lupus Unguis would have to retaliate with extreme novelty fights, nearly impossible to survive.

He looked at the men around him. All were strong, brave men and true warriors, but the Celts were unaccustomed to Roman ways. Their fury and strength were often used against them in the arena, which demanded skilled strategy and luck.

The Celts, especially the Germani warriors, placed their sole focus on personal valor and killing the highest-ranked man in a fight. Each Celt fought a solitary battle. They did not function well as members of combat teams against well-trained and highly cooperative Numidians and others who fought with tight precision in organized packs.

Offering the men their freedom was a farce. Many of the gladiators surrounding him, and possibly he himself, would not see the sunset. Just when he believed his thoughts could sink no lower, an ominous rumble passed through the walls of the amphitheater.

A buckling chatter rippled across the shivering sand beneath his feet. The viewing box where Marius stood trembled. Dust and small bits of debris sifted down. People in the stands shouted curses and prayers.

Tyr glanced over his shoulder toward the source of the foreboding sounds. East of Pompeii, a faint plume of black smoke hovered above the great cone-shaped mountain of Vesuvius.

A communal gasp rose from the crowd. Frightened spectators got up to flee, but when the movement stopped and did not resume, everyone seemed content to settle down. Once the ground stopped trembling, those who'd fled soon returned. Only the wine vendors seemed pressed by any urgency to distribute their product to the flustered throng with efficient swiftness.

Arcona appeared in Marius's private viewing box and hurried to his side. She stood at the railing looking disconcerted but lovely in a white stola. The amber amulet was looped around her neck, her auburn hair worn down and brushed smooth in the style of a concubine.

At last, there she was, the woman who beguiled his heart. For all the gods, he had to help her. Staring at her in Marius's presence might prove deadly, but he didn't care. His gaze locked on her and no amount of reasoning could force him to break it.

"Vesuvius is restless, and so am I." Marius grabbed Arcona and drew her close. "I forgot to mention," he blustered to the gladiators below. "Tonight there will be a woman waiting for every man who returns to the house of Lupus Unguis a victor!"

Another robust cheer rose from the gladiators, but again Tyr remained silent with his full attention trained on Arcona. He willed her to look his way, but she didn't. She stood at Marius's side with a stoic expression on her brow, refusing to acknowledge him. A terrible sense of jealousy and utter frustration built.

Marius pushed Arcona to the front of his private box. "This is what the victors will get." He bent Arcona over the railing, parted her thighs, and lifted her stola to her hips. "Of course, you can't have this one." He laughed. "I never share."

Tugging his toga to his waist, he thrust himself inside Arcona. A faint whimper crossed Arcona's lips as Marius closed his eyes in bliss, taking Arcona like a dog on the street in full view of anyone who happened to look. He satisfied himself with crass self-indulgence as the gladiators below him watched. Arcona dipped her chin downward and glanced away from the men.

Marius grabbed her by the hair and forced her chin upward. "Go ahead," he hectored her. "You can look at them."

Pointing at Tyr, he shouted, "See that handsome blond Dacian with the scar on his cheek? Most likely he'll be dead by the end of the day. I have a three-against-one fight scheduled for him. If he survives, I'll win a fortune!"

Looking into Arcona's eyes, Tyr saw how humiliated and angry she was. He wondered why she did not do to Marius as she had done to him the first night and simply overpower him with her uncanny strength.

For a moment, he wished he could see her as merely the beautiful woman he'd admired every day on the back balcony, not the victim or madwoman. He wanted to forget he'd ever seen the crazed fire of the Strix in her eyes, but he understood more clearly than ever the forces that had placed it there.

Risking Marius's wrath, he managed to catch Arcona's attention and silently mouthed, "I'll fight for you." But at that exact moment, she closed her eyes, and he wasn't certain she'd noticed his gesture.

Now he was even more determined to save Arcona and leave this cursed place. Today was a day to kill with flourish and win freedom for them both.

Marius smacked his palm against Arcona's ass. "Pull yourself together and fetch us some wine," he ordered. "Let the games begin!" he shouted jovially.

Arcona rose from the railing and tugged her stola into place. Pointing at a towering rough-faced Celt, Marius barked, "You with the ugly face, what's your name?"

"Gundomar," the man grumbled.

"Gundomar?" Marius frowned. "How dull. I'm going to change your name and bill you in the first fight as 'Bear Claw the Berserker,' and by Jupiter, you'd better show the crowd a good fight, or else you'll be dragged from the arena on the tip of a meat hook." He paused. "You look rather dim-witted. Are you sure you understand me?"

"I understand." Gundomar nodded with a scowl on his face.

Everyone understood. If a man fought bravely, the crowd might spare him, and even if he were victorious but mortally wounded, he might enjoy the fleeting honor of being carried from the arena on a litter and allowed to die in peace in a shaded corner of the amphitheater. Matters were far worse if a man displeased the crowd or fought poorly. A man like that could expect to be slaughtered on the sand and have a hook sunk deep under his arm; his carcass dragged from the arena like trash. Such an ignoble death was something no gladiator desired.

Marius scratched Gundomar's new name onto a slate along with a few brief notations and handed it to a slave boy, who quickly ran toward the viewing box of the editor of the games to deliver it. He turned his attention toward Tyr. "You." He pointed at Tyr. "You'll fight the second match as a lone murmillo."

A faint but audible gasp rose among the men. A murmillo fighting alone was simply never done. Everyone knew in that moment that Marius was struggling at his task. The Cilician trainer, despised as he was in the barracks, at least understood the skills and strategy of the arena and did his best to keep the gladiators alive.

Obviously, Marius didn't know what he was doing, or was being deliberately reckless.

"Will I not be paired with a thraex?" Tyr knew his mouth was gaping in astonishment but couldn't stop. Murmillo armor was the heaviest in the arena. He depended on his thraex, who was always a smaller, lighter man, armed with a small round wrist shield and a curved blade, to dart between him and the annoying retiarii, or "net men," who cast their lead-weighted fishing nets at the murmillones' ankles in hopes of toppling and overwhelming the larger men.

"It's not that kind of fight." Marius beamed. "This will be something truly special, and certain to have everyone in the marketplace talking for weeks to come about the glory and honor of the house of Lupus Unguis!"

Marius made an impatient shooing motion at Tyr. "When the gladiator parade starts, while you're still handsome and in one piece, I want you to walk in front of the stands and let the ladies and a few of those eyelash-batting senators get a good look at you. I want maximum sympathy and interest in the fate of a beautiful Dacian man. It might spare you a sharp nip of iron, if you know what I mean."

Tyr nodded. He knew exactly what Marius meant. Despite bravery or skill, the editor of the games often made the final decision of who should live or die. An arbitrarily condemned man would be asked to kneel, calmly expose his throat, and await the lethal blow.

The melancholy sound of a tibia being blown in the editor's box signaled it was time for the gladiators to line up and the parade to begin.

"Already?" Marius glowered. "I haven't finished planning my lineup." He frowned at Tyr. "You don't yet have an arena name. How about 'Golden Boy'?" Marius smeared his palm through the air as if to erase a misspent thought. "No, a murmillo should never be called a boy, even if he is one." His gaze narrowed on Tyr. "How old are you?"

Tyr answered, "Twenty-eight winters."

Marius hesitated, his expression blank. "I know. I'm going to bill you as 'the Dacian Dagger.' It's perfect." He scribbled the name on a slate. "Runner!" he called for another slave boy to deliver the slate to the editor.

A young boy dashed forward and took the slate from Marius's hands.

Marius addressed the boy. "Tell the scribe to chalk this name on the front gate of the amphitheater where everyone can see it in large letters." He scribbled a bit more. "Be sure to include the house of Lupus Unguis in the title. Now go." Shooing the boy away with a slap on the back, he commanded, "Hurry!" His gaze focused on the gladiators standing below. "Don't just stand there with your mouths hanging open. Get yourselves lined up behind the palm branch at the Gate of Life and start the parade!"

Cheers and laughter rang through the packed amphitheater as several black bulls were herded in the arena, with graceful young men clinging to their sweeping horns and vaulting over the bulls' shoulders. The bulls and riders circled the arena, performing astounding acrobatics.

"Look!" Marius gestured in disbelief. "The bull leapers are already doing tricks and clowning around. Gather up the wooden practice swords and bring out the sharp iron. Quick, cut somebody with the iron blades so the crowd knows the swords have sharpened edges and they are seeing the real thing."

Glaring at Marius in disapproval, Tyr gritted his teeth. Without the Cilician to show the way, Marius appeared confused about how to lead his gladiators into battle.

"Come with me." Tyr gestured to the other gladiators and took charge. "There's no time to waste. Let's get the parade over with so we can at least have the opportunity to properly buckle into our armor and say our good-byes to the world." He turned and marched the men toward the far side of the arena where oiled, naked slaves were waving palm fronds as signs of peace and victory. Musicians with flutes and lyres played a high, strained tune he did not recognize or care for. The triumphant beat of the drummers was more to his liking. Tyr and the other gladiators of Lupus Unguis arrived at the Gate of Life wearing only simple loincloths and the salt on their skin.

236

Other teams of gladiators were already lined up, looking splendid and battle-ready in gleaming armor ornamented with feathers and leopard-skin trim.

Several panther-like Numidian swordsmen glared at Tyr with large dark eyes ringed with kohl.

Gundomar leaned near Tyr's ear. "It's no wonder the odds are against us. The Cilician was an ass, but without a trainer calling the strikes, we have no chance. Marius was a fool to exhaust us with endless practice drills and coining pet names. Bear Claw the Berserker." He sneered. "I could belch a better name."

"The crowd wants blood." Tyr sounded far calmer than he felt. "Make an open appeal to everyone seated near the editor; he's sure to hear their cries loudest. I don't know what Marius has planned for us, but I want those eighty thousand sesterces and my freedom." He paused and made sure the other gladiators standing in line were listening. "And I won't let peacocks in fancy costumes steal my victory."

The Numidians glowered at Tyr and thumped their shields. The bulls and bull-leaping acrobats were led from the arena to make way for lethal sport. The tibia blew again, and the gladiator parade commenced.

Roman husbands grabbed their wives and led them higher into the stands where they could not easily shout to or flirt with condemned gladiators or be mistakenly molested by drunken or overexcited blood sport fans.

Bewigged and rouge-cheeked prostitutes immediately took the wives' seats, knowing the sights and sounds of human mortality drove the male crowd into a mindless state of lust. The only women who did not have to shift seats in the arena were the vestal virgins, distinguished by their bright saffron-gold stolas, whom the law declared inviolable and no Roman dared touch. They sat serenely near the high-stakes carnage in relative safety.

Tyr looked into the stands. The seats were filled with an odd mix of wild-eyed fanatics already on their feet screaming for blood and other Romans who looked bored. He thought it strange these Romans had decided to spend a summer day baking beneath a blistering sun, swilling wine, and fighting back the rising stench of death in their nostrils for pleasure. Parading barefoot across the hot sand with his fist raised triumphantly in the air, he shouted and waved to anyone who glanced his way. He fervently wished he were anywhere but there and promised himself that if he survived the day, he would never wantonly fight or kill again.

Freedom would mean a return to the mountains of home and a horse herder's life and, if he were fortunate, a wife and children, too. In Marius's current desperate state, it was possible eighty thousand sesterces could purchase Arcona's freedom with plenty left over. If Marius refused to sell her, other means could be explored. He would find some way to save her, and even considered bribing the guards of Lupus Unguis and taking her by force before Marius's brother-in-law took command of the ludus.

The gladiators circled the arena with the chaotic music growing louder and shriller. He returned to Marius's viewing box and looked upward to salute.

Marius didn't even glance down at his own gladiators' parade. He hovered at the back of his box, too busy fawning over a Roman nobleman's wife who sat beside him. His hands were all over her. Tyr knew the woman was a wife and not a concubine by her ornate hairstyle of coiled braids. The nobleman sat tipsy and bleary-eyed in the front of Marius's viewing box. The foolish man had been imprudent enough to not only bring his attractive wife to the arena but to also get drunk and turn his back on Marius.

His gaze searched the viewing box for Arcona. Where was she? He needed to see her one last time. She was the closest thing he had to a sweetheart, and he wanted her blessing before he faced the unknown.

But she was nowhere to be seen. How could he confront death without first dedicating his battle to her? A thousand tortured thoughts streaked through his mind. He needed to salute her or just look into her eyes, and he wondered if she would be sad to see him die. He almost shouted her name but thought better of it, not wanting to call the wrong sort of attention upon her.

The parade marched on, and he was forced to move forward with the others. Soon, they were standing before the editor's box. Today's editor was merely a wealthy Roman magistrate sponsoring the games in hopes of gaining popularity and being reelected to office.

The editor stood and hoisted a cup of sloshing wine high into the air. "Fight bravely," he slurred. "And tell everyone to vote for Lucius Caspar Sulla for magistrate!" He plopped down into his chair and refilled his cup.

Tyr glanced over his shoulder toward Marius's viewing box, still hoping to see Arcona, but he did not. She was gone. Her absence left a crushing void. He wanted her to at least smile at him one last time. The moment felt empty and incomplete. "Arcona, where are you?" he mumbled.

Without the slightest inhibition, Marius rubbed himself against the nobleman's wife. He wasn't even watching his own gladiators' dedication march intended to honor him.

The gladiators strode through the Gate of Life, which was a passage in the amphitheater wall that led to a curving subterranean chamber filled with staging equipment, plus cages of wild animals, horses, and condemned prisoners waiting to be executed in any number of novel ways to further entertain the jaded crowd.

As Tyr descended the sloping torchlit corridor, the stale air below was heavy with the scent of men and animals. A row of horses was tethered to the wall.

He approached a chestnut stallion and stroked its muzzle. The horse whinnied and enthusiastically nuzzled his palm, hoping for a treat, but he had none to offer. He loved horses, and in the past, had owned a respectable herd of one hundred. The horse reminded him of everything that had once been good about home.

"Get away from that horse!" A harsh-faced man with a thick silver braid dangling over one shoulder pushed him away. "Are you the Dacian Dagger?"

Tyr nodded. He did not recognize the man.

"Come here. I'm a trainer from the house of Mars. Call me Jude. Marius has hired me for the day." He reached for a pile of leather straps and body armor. "Let's get you prepared. You fight after the Gaul."

"Gundomar is not a Gaul. He's Germani," Tyr quietly corrected.

"Today Gundomar is a Gaul. It's what the crowd wants. We're dressing him in scaled Gaulish armor with a fish insignia on his helmet. He'll look like a Gaul, and I certainly hope he knows how to fight like a Gaul." An uneasy laugh broke free of Jude. "Gundomar will be cast in today's fight as a secutor, though he seems far too slow and clumsy to succeed as a chaser. He's sure to make the crowd laugh. He'll look like a big, loutish fish flailing around in the arena, and he'll probably get speared by the retiarii right away."

He did not like the man's attitude. A true trainer helped preserve lives, not add to a man's risk. Tyr stood still as Jude buckled a fluted leather shoulder shield under his sword arm and wrapped a heavy leather belt equipped with a dagger around his hips. His wrists were encased in layers of sheepskin laced with slender leather straps that could be tightened and used as tourniquets should he sustain a blow.

"Where's my helmet and shield?"

"You don't get either." Jude was already looking around for the next man to prepare for the arena.

"What do you mean I don't get a helmet or shield?" Panic crept into Tyr's voice. "I'm a murmillo. I do most of my fighting with an iron-rimmed shield."

"Not today you don't." Jude looked befuddled. "I think Dominus Marius is taking this bad-odds tactic too far. He's dreamed up a few unlikely spectacles guaranteed to make people talk. Too bad for you."

Jude turned to the side, and Tyr noticed two tiny bruised puncture marks on the side of his throat. He immediately touched his own throat and felt the small twin wounds Arcona had left on him their first night. His gaze simmered on the trainer's wounds as a poisonous wave of jealousy washed over him. "How did you get those marks on your throat?" His voice quaked.

Leering, Jude nodded. "Marius's beautiful whore has been roaming around down here all morning, lifting her stola and sharing the bounty with any man she can grab. She's a rough slut, likes to bite, but I'd happily take another turn with her."

Rage spread through him like wildfire. Tyr snarled at Jude and shoved him to the ground. "Liar!"

Jude's brow arched in bewilderment; he spat at Tyr. "What's wrong with you?"

In a flash, a team of other trainers was on top of Tyr, pulling him away.

"Get him off me!" Jude flailed on the ground before scrambling away from his attacker. He stood and straightened his sword belt with an indignant tug. "He's gone mad."

Tyr broke from the trainers' grips and staggered backward, feeling sick. It couldn't be true. Arcona wouldn't do that. His world spun in dizzying swoops as he retreated as far as possible into the dimly lit bowels of the staging chamber. More than anything he needed to be out of everyone's sight and collect his thoughts. He headed down the narrow curving corridor, which seemed to lead nowhere.

In the shadows ahead he heard the breathy, lustful noises of what sounded like a man being pleasured. The man's seemingly agonized cries echoed against stone.

The corridor came to a dead end. Arcona stood in a dark corner beside a flickering oil lamp. Her white stola drooped off her shoulders as she pressed a young gladiator against the wall.

"Arcona?" Tyr's voice cracked. "What are you doing here?"

She drew away from the gladiator's throat and turned. Ruby droplets of blood clung to her lips. Her stola was tugged to the side, exposing a pale breast. Gazing at Tyr in calm silence, she licked her lips.

The young man slumped in a stupor against the wall. He had a clean-shaven head and dramatic eye paint. Tyr knew him from the ludus; he was an Egyptian slave named Renni, whose slender build betrayed the fact that he was more of a boy than a man. His loincloth was partially unwound and tugged down his lean hips. With eyes closed, he swooned and crumpled forward.

Arcona stepped back and simply allowed Renni's limp body to slide down the wall and land on the floor with a soft thud.

"Tyr, I've been waiting for you."

"It doesn't look that way." His voice filled with pain.

"The others mean nothing." She beckoned to him with a graceful wave of her hand. "I did this for you. I've been gathering their strength. Come closer. I have a gift to share."

"How many others?" Glancing deeper into the shadows, he saw several men lying splay-legged and motionless on the ground.

"Does it matter?" With the feral expression of a wolf, her eyes glittered against the sputtering flame of the lamp. "I have found a way to secure victory over Rome, and these men are part of it."

Tyr looked at the many bodies strewn in the shadows. "Did you kill them?"

"No." Arcona's laugh had a razor edge. "Did I kill you? They will rise again, and when they do, they will be much more than they were." She stroked her fingertips against the amber amulet dangling around her throat. "I drained these men of their passion and life force, and I'm going to give it all to you."

"What?"

A hint of hysteria crept into her voice. "The blood of the gods shall be yours. You shall fight fearlessly with the skill of an immortal." She paused. "After today, you will be invincible."

"This is madness. No man is immortal." Anger welled within him. "Arcona, I know you have no say over what Marius does to you. It grinds at my heart to see him use you. If I win today and earn my freedom, will you come with me? I'll buy your freedom—"

"No," she snapped. "I'm going to stay and continue what I'm doing until I've made an army of immortal warriors to turn against Rome."

One of the men lying on the floor moaned and shifted position.

A sickening feeling of despair came over him. "Did you bed them all?"

"Yes." Her lips curled with insolence. "Sex is essential to the magic. Blood and lust bind the spell. At night, I leap over the villa walls and hunt down slaves and even foreign merchants asleep in the town square. Any able-bodied non-Roman will do. I straddle their hips and ride them hard, and at the moment before they spend their hot seed inside me, I bite their throats and drink their blood. Their strength becomes mine, and at my discretion I can share it." She hesitated. "That reminds me; I've not yet had my turn with the condemned men, but I'll get to them next."

Tyr shook his head. "I don't like you this way."

"I did enjoy you. Our time together was worth the risk. With you, I felt things I thought were lost to me. You were my favorite." A tortured smile crossed her lips. "This wasn't easy. Last night, you almost convinced me that there was hope for us when we both know none will be offered. I begged the gods to strike love from my heart so that I might act with precision and focus, and you nearly spoiled that bargain."

Was she blaming him? Daring to approach her, he held out his hand. "What do you mean? Arcona, you sound crazed. I believe the amulet has driven you mad. It's a wicked thing. Take it off and leave. This is no place for you."

"You're a man of my homeland and by far the best of Lupus Unguis. You are deserving. Let me gift you immortality." She held out her delicate hand. "Hurry. We have little time."

Shaking his head, a sob of frustration escaped. "I don't need an illusion of immortality. All I need to win today is a fucking shield! Arcona, I want more from you. I want a life of freedom together. Forget about the blood and witchcraft. It's dangerous. Eighty thousand sesterces can get us both home with enough money to buy horses to breed."

He stepped closer and grazed his fingertips across her cheek. "Do you remember that life? Herding the flocks from summer to winter pastures, living simply with our gods and our ways? It was a good life."

For a moment, Arcona looked stricken. Her eyes welled with tears. "I remember nothing before the Roman invasion." Her voice trembled. "You do realize there's nothing to go home to, don't you? The Romans have taken our land and burned our villages. Look at me! After what I've been through, I can never go home. I'm contaminated and would poison anything decent I touched. Just as water cannot run uphill, the forced journey south pointed me in one direction only. My focus and my fate shall be in destroying Rome. If I die trying, I accept that. I can't run away and be a herder's wife, so please don't ask."

One of the trainers in the front bellowed, "Where is the Dacian Dagger? He fights next!"

The breath hissed out of Tyr as if he'd been kicked in the chest. "I have to go." His gaze riveted on Arcona. He knew how she felt. He was angry too, but he wanted her to know he would have given her his heart.

"Arcona, please give me your blessing." Every warrior entered the world through a woman, and every warrior with the opportunity asked a woman he loved for the goddess Nerthus's blessing before he entered battle. "Please? Your blessing, my love — that's all I want from you."

"I can do better than that." Arcona lunged forward and grabbed Tyr's wrist. She yanked him against the wall and pressed herself hard against him.

His nostrils flared at the heady scent of sex and other men on her skin, and he felt a twinge of shame that he was so aroused by the wantonness of it. "Arcona, we have no choice about what others do to us, but we can choose—"

"The Romans are in the wrong," she blurted. "I feel justified in doing whatever I must to bring the harshest curse possible upon them. I'll start with Pompeii, and I'll finish in Rome. I want the Romans to look with dread upon the day they invaded our lands and brought us captive within their walls." She stroked the amulet, becoming wild-eyed. "The vision I have glimpsed of Pompeii's future is far worse than anything the tortures of the underworld could offer. They'll suffocate beneath a burning rain of ash. The gods have promised me this! I feel no pity for them. They deserve what's coming."

A shiver of dread rippled up his spine. "What's coming?"

"A caldron of fire shall cook them alive!" Arcona laughed. "And the Dark Slayer will walk their paved roads." She gripped the sides of Tyr's face with the strength of a man and pressed her mouth firmly to his, lavishing wet, languid kisses on his lips.

He gasped and tried to break free of her grip but couldn't. Her overpowering anger and lust brimmed at the surface. She sounded and looked crazed, but against his will his rebellious body reacted to her. He wanted to give in and fuck her with full fervor. She was seductive and repellant at once as her tongue swept across his. Below the faint flavors of rose water and wine on her lips, he tasted the coppery tang of another man's blood and drew away.

"No." Arcona grasped the back of Tyr's neck and held him against her with surprising strength. "Don't pull away, my love. You're my favorite and first made."

First made what? He had no idea what she was talking about. Tension for the impending fight built. His heart pounded in distress.

She pushed the edge of his loincloth aside.

"I can't." Tyr weakly held her at bay. "I have to fight in the arena."

"All the more reason." Arcona reached inside his loincloth, her fingertips skimming his warm skin. "Take it off." She deftly unraveled the linen; most of it unfurled toward the floor, leaving only one edge tucked into his sword belt. His lean hips, jutting cock, and solid thighs were exposed.

"That's better." Arcona fondled his heavy sac, squeezing it against her palm until it rose higher.

"Don't." A sense of despair hung over him as his free will drained away. "You've already been with so many men." He sounded bitter. "I had it in my heart I was in love with you."

Her beautiful mouth curved into a snarl. "We don't need love. We need revenge!" Arcona released him and lifted the hem of her stola to her hips, displaying an auburn tangle of curls.

"This is the blessing you want. It's what you need. Claim it."

He looked at her round thighs and drew a tense breath, willing every thought in his worried mind to stop so he could enjoy one last pleasure. His heart hammered against his ribs as he picked Arcona up and shoved her hard against the wall. He crowded between her thighs and eagerly pressed against her.

"Lie to me," Tyr pleaded. "Tell me I mean something to you."

"No," Arcona whispered. Her soft tones were more disturbing than angry shouts. "I won't lie to you. We are engaged in a battle with Rome, and you are my weapon of choice, nothing more." She guided the head of his cock inside her with a sweet moan and began to rock her hips with aggression. "Be quick, my love," she panted. "Give me everything."

He thrust fiercely inside her, ashamed for doing it but couldn't stop. Anger and desire whipped him forward. By all the gods, she did feel good. A pleased groan floated past his lips as his hips pumped faster. He made one final appeal. "Let me save you."

"Hush," she hissed.

"Where is the Dacian?" Jude's voice echoed against the walls as he wandered the stone corridor. "Is he hiding? It wouldn't do him any good; there's only one exit."

Tyr's breath quickened. He knew he was about to be interrupted and wrenched away from Arcona. On the brink of climax, he stroked faster. "I love you."

"Be silent." Arcona grabbed Tyr's throat and held him captive. Baring her teeth, she lunged at his flesh. The sharp tips of her canines pierced and tore his skin. Hissing like a snake, she fought to hold on to his thrashing body with her teeth. She bit harder, puncturing his throat, and left him arching backward in shock as she sucked blood in greedy gulps.

The pain was intense. Tyr's thoughts hovered at the searing edge of consciousness. Sweat beaded on his brow as panic overwhelmed him. For a moment he thought he might faint. His skin prickled as if it were aflame, and then he stopped feeling anything at all.

The world around him went black. Within a heartbeat, he simply did not exist as a living, breathing man. A whispering numbness too subtle to describe chilled his blood, and he wondered if this was how death introduced itself in polite stages. His rational mind knew he was beneath the amphitheater, but he felt as if his body had dissolved and was now as light as vapor drifting in a starry sky. The moment was timeless and spacious and completely independent of the squalor of the arena.

For what felt like an eternity, his heart did not beat, and his breath stilled. Adding to his disorientation, Arcona had hoisted him higher and he could not feel the floor beneath him; his feet fluttered midair like a moth caught in a spider web. Dazzling patterns danced before his eyes. Only the wet, juicy sounds of Arcona's lapping tongue filled his ears. Like a lioness brooding over a fresh kill, she violently slurped warm blood from his throat.

Unable to move with his back pressed against the cool stones of the wall, he remained trapped in a terrible life-and-death moment. His lungs were ready to burst for want of fresh breath. Unbearably rigid, he was long past ready to climax but couldn't.

Arcona drew her teeth from his throat and released him. Lowering him gently, she returned his dangling feet to the gritty floor. She chuckled, a high-strung unhappy laugh as her hand fished into his leather hip belt and retrieved the dagger. "The final step must be taken, and I'm doing this only with you."

He stood frozen against the wall, helpless to act of his own volition.

"Watch." She held the dagger to her throat and traced the well-honed blade across her skin, making a shallow cut. A crimson slash of blood oozed forth. She thrust the dagger back into his belt. With trembling hands, she took hold of his face and forcefully guided his mouth toward the gash. "Drink," she commanded. "This is the gift."

The moment he pulled away, she yanked him back. This madness had to end. He was willing to do anything she asked to end the torment and then flee. Bowing his head toward her throat, he dipped his tongue into the warm trickle and tasted her.

As her blood washed across his tongue, a shocking jolt of sensations rocked him. In an instant, his heart grew cold, devoid of love or anything tender. His soul shrank or fled, he couldn't tell which, and another malevolent presence swooped in to fill the void. A massive specter appeared before his startled eyes, seeming to dominate the corridor and rise to the heavens beyond. The vivid image of an enraged god with fiery eyes and breath foul as a battlefield snarled in his face with the ferocity of a violent mountain storm. With eyes wide, he gasped.

"You belong to the god of war now," Arcona whispered. "Drink. You shall be his companion in combat, his lover, and blade in hand until the end of time."

With all his heart, he wanted blood; it was the only thing that mattered. He stared at the scarlet trickle on Arcona's throat and then dived at it, lapping and biting at her bleeding wound, not caring if he harmed her.

"That's right!" Bitter laughter rolled past her lips. "Be vicious. Drink and be reborn as something eternally lethal. Rome's worst enemy was born today!"

He hardly listened to Arcona's ranting as he furiously drank her blood. The initial moments of pleasure had gone stale. This act was empty. It tormented him that he was still hard as iron yet unable to climax and end the agony. Squeezing her soft breasts, he thrust deeper and faster, willing himself to climax, but nothing happened. A worrisome sense that something irreversible had occurred crept over him.

What was wrong? He pulled away from Arcona and looked at her with utter dispassion, as if she were a stranger, and realized with disturbing clarity that she was. He didn't know her, not in any real sense. She was just like any other damaged soul with a pathetic agenda. Disillusioned, his heart now felt nothing for her. He was hard-pressed to believe he had ever asked her to run away with him and share his future. Why would he even want a wife and children in the first place? That long-cherished desire now seemed ridiculous.

She gloated. "There is nothing but anger in your eyes. The gods have accepted you as their weapon. Our accomplishment is complete. The future has been rewritten."

Closing his eyes, he sensed he had no future except for the intense craving to see and taste more blood. Something horrible had happened to him, and she had called it a *gift*.

"What have you done to me?" His voice shook.

"I did what had to be done." Arcona cupped her hand against the side of her throat to stanch the flow of blood. "I know in my heart that on this day there are other Strix like me making other Slayers like you. Together, we shall grow in number and know victory over the Empire."

Hanging his head, he sighed. The Strix was back in all her blaring glory, as shrill and bombastic as a battered trumpet. Arcona was wild-eyed once more, but this time he didn't pity her or care. He stared at her, unable to pinpoint or name the terrible transformation that spread through him like a spring frost, claiming and killing all tender signs of life. He was changed to his core, but how? Had she stolen his soul? Was he dead and standing unaware on the other side of life's shore? What had happened to him?

"Dacian!" Jude yelled as he rounded the corner. "Get out there!"

The sight of blood dripping from Arcona's fingertips nearly drove Tyr mad with want. He longed to lick the dainty fingers clean or bite them off, and he couldn't tell which he most preferred. A new disturbing savagery colored his thoughts.

"There you are." Jude lumbered toward Tyr and Arcona. He gazed at Tyr's unfurled loincloth. "I see you've been poking Marius's whore." He glanced at Arcona's bleeding throat. "It looks like fun time got too rough." His gaze dropped toward Tyr's naked lower body and prominent erection. "There's no time to finish. Get your loincloth on. The crowd is waiting." Wasting no time, Jude reached for his own loincloth and began to unwind it from his hips. "I'll finish for you." He shooed Tyr aside. "I'm more than ready to fuck her again."

"Go." Arcona firmly pushed Tyr away. "Take your gift into the arena."

Tyr stood dumbly beside her, too shocked to react in a sane manner.

Arcona's slender hand was on Jude's shoulder in a flash, pulling him near. "You know what I want," she whispered in the trainer's ear.

Jude moved his braid aside and bared his bruised throat to Arcona as he slid between her thighs.

Tyr watched, feeling a horrid blend of detachment and the harshest rage as Arcona bit Jude's throat and drank his blood, allowing the man to pump freely inside her and climax after only half a dozen fast thrusts and a piteous groan.

"I'm finished with you." Arcona brusquely shoved Jude toward the wall and tugged the stola over one shoulder, barely covering herself. "I want more. Bring me a condemned man."

Hatred and disgust on a colossal scale consumed him. Tyr's knees trembled. He loathed Arcona and everything she was doing, yet his body raged to be inside her again and drink more blood.

Jude turned and glared at Tyr. "Why are you still standing there like a fool? Do you want to be prodded into the arena with red-hot irons? Get going!"

Hurt and anger paralyzed him.

"Pull yourself together. This is your day to seek glory." Jude pressed Tyr's fallen loincloth into his hands. "Cover that fleshy blade, pick up a real dagger, and get yourself into the arena."

His gut ached from a rising sense of nausea. Death in the arena sounded easier than standing immobile and watching Arcona fuck another stranger. Distracted and reluctant, he wound the strip of linen around his hips and between his thighs. Being so hard made the task more difficult, but nothing seemed to calm his passions, not even brooding, vengeful thoughts.

"Go!" Jude grabbed Tyr by the arm and roughly ushered him through the shadowy corridor toward the sun-drenched entrance to the arena.

As he passed, the chestnut horse whinnied and stomped its hoof in greeting.

He glanced into the horse's large dark eyes as Jude marched him forward to the edge of the gate.

Just as he reached out to pet the lovely creature, the horse reared away from him with a startled snort, as if it sensed a threat.

"I'm not going to harm you," he whispered. But the spooked horse stomped its hooves and clambered backward to escape his touch. Even the beast sensed something uncanny and rejected him.

Walking onward, he hung his head. The horse's reaction was disturbing. Tyr stood at the threshold of the Gate of Life, squinting outward at the heat mirage shimmering on the sand beyond. He stepped forward.

"Wait," Jude commanded. "Don't enter yet. Gundomar's still on his feet. I don't know how it's possible, but he won the first battle, and he's moving on to round two."

He gazed into the heart of the arena. Miraculously, the towering Germani was still alive. Gundomar was dressed in silvered armor that glittered brilliantly under the harsh sunlight. His helmet bore the skillfully hammered head of a fish. The gleaming scales of the armor mimicked the skin of a salmon and rippled as he moved. He indeed resembled a giant fish looming over a fallen man lying bloodied and facedown in the sand.

Gundomar raised his gore-smeared sword high into the air. "I have won!" he thundered.

"Bear Claw! Bear Claw!" The crowd cheered Gundomar's win with wild, whooping shouts. Flowers and coins were tossed into the arena.

Two attendants, one dressed as the god Mercury, approached the fallen retiarius. The attendant dressed in winged sandals and helmet held a red-hot iron pike to the fallen gladiator's feet. When the prone man did not respond in any way, a hook was struck beneath the man's arm and the attendants dragged the corpse toward the Gate of Death to be disposed of.

Gundomar turned in a slow, victorious circle, relishing the crowd's praise.

The crowd in the amphitheater rose to its feet and enthusiastically screamed their approval as a large wooden ship was rolled from behind a piece of scenery and into the center of the arena.

Glancing over his shoulder, Gundomar watched the ship roll closer with a look of shock on his whiskered face.

The prow of the ship opened and four nimble retiarius gladiators dressed as fishermen leaped out, swinging lead-weighted fishing nets above their heads and brandishing tridents.

"Come closer, big fish!" the retiarii taunted. "Jump into our nets." The men circled Gundomar and attacked from all sides, flinging their heavy nets into the air and allowing them to land all at once, tangled atop a thrashing Gundomar like lethal spider webs.

Poking his sword through the nets, Gundomar took haphazard slices at anyone foolish enough to step near.

The retiarii yanked the tangled nets away, knocking the larger, heavily armored man off balance.

Falling flat on his back, Gundomar landed hard.

Rushing forward, the retiarii took vicious stabs at Gundomar with their tridents anywhere a lack of armor had left exposed.

Writhing on the ground in agony, Gundomar managed to hold onto his blade and fight back with focused intensity. A trident was knocked from the hand of a startled retiarii.

The blood-crazed crowd flailed their arms in the air and screamed for a decisive conclusion as they worked themselves into a state of unbridled fury.

The tibia was blown. The editor of the games called for the retiarii to halt their attack.

The retiarii planted their tridents in the sand, where the sharp prongs could do no harm, and stepped back to await the editor's verdict.

"What shall it be?" The editor appealed to the spectators with dramatic flourish. "Life or death for Bear Claw the Berserker?"

The crowd answered with loud shouts in favor of both verdicts, but a few more showed the thumbs-down signal, expressing their preference for Bear Claw's life.

"Life it shall be!" the editor shouted. "The weapons shall stay down." A tibia was blown in celebration.

The retiarii abandoned their tridents in the sand and turned toward the crowd to salute.

Gundomar was sweat-soaked and blood-drenched as he struggled to stand.

The crowd cheered in support as he rose.

In a flash he turned and butted his full weight into a distracted retiarius, knocking and pinning the smaller man to the ground. He lifted his sword high and thrust the blade into the startled man's throat.

The retiarius kicked with futility on the ground but died with expected swiftness.

254

Gundomar rose and staggered toward the crowd with his arms raised valiantly. Blood and sweat trickled down his face. "This big fish has a stinger!" he hollered.

The crowd loved it. They screamed their approval that a fish caught a fisherman. More coins showered onto the sand.

The editor beamed from the safety of his viewing box. He stood and shouted to the stands, "If you enjoyed this novel battle, then don't forget to thank the man who sponsored today's sport, by whom I mean my humble self." He piously crossed his hands over his heart. "Show your gratitude for today's fine entertainment by voting Lucius Caspar Sulla for magistrate!"

"You fight next." Jude shoved Tyr's shoulder.

The wooden ship was wheeled away and the dead retiarius carried off.

Gundomar gathered a few coins from the sand and arduously limped his way toward the Gate of Life. The trainers greeted him with shouts of joy and by thrusting a wine sack into his hands.

"Give him to me." A disheveled Arcona stepped from the shadows. "I'll revive him." Her grasping hands were reaching toward Gundomar before he even entered the gate.

Tyr turned to glare at her.

"Don't look at me like that." She frowned at Tyr. "You'll soon be thanking me for what I've done."

"I doubt that." His balls ached and he was taking a plank-hard cock into the arena.

The tibia blew.

"Get out there." Jude pushed Tyr into the empty arena and barred the way back with his broad chest. "Walk into the center of the sand."

What kind of fight is this? Tyr drew himself upright and strode into the blindingly bright light of an empty arena, disoriented by the howling cheers of the crowd and the occasional boo. What was he doing out here without a thraex fighting at his side or a shield to hold his foes at bay? He drew his gladius from his belt and gripped the hilt with mounting ferocity.

He strode toward the desolate heart of the arena, feeling soul-naked and doomed. Thousands were watching and shouting, yet he was as isolated as if he were cast adrift on an endless sea of sand. He lifted the blade toward the sky and hailed the crowd as they screamed for blood.

A sound like thunder rolled behind him. He turned. Three black chariots pulled by double teams of handsome black horses ornamented with sooty black ostrich plumes entered the arena. The fluffy feathers quivered in the air, producing the visual suggestion of dark smoke rising from a team of supernatural steeds.

The charioteers whipped the horses to a furious sprint and charged straight toward him, each driven by a Numidian swordsman brandishing a gleaming hooked blade.

Two of the chariots rode close together. Their drivers linked blades to create a single speeding weapon intent on cleanly decapitating Tyr and trampling his body into the sand.

Tucking himself into a tight ball, he rolled between the closely spaced chariots. The hooked blades remained tangled together as they whizzed by a handbreadth over his head.

He drew his limbs inward to avoid being struck by the chariots as he somersaulted upright. He almost didn't make it. A wrist was nearly crushed by a whirring wheel, but he snatched it back a split second before his arm was caught and ripped from his shoulder.

Tyr rolled to his feet, blade thrust outward. The two linked chariots slowed and made a wide sweeping turn. *Where is the third?* He glanced over his shoulder.

The third charioteer was pointed straight at him with a team of agitated horses poised to charge.

He made eye contact with the charioteer. The man had black eyes ringed in kohl. In bright sunlight, the Numidian's eye sockets looked hollow, lending his lean face a cadaverous appearance.

The Numidian hoisted an iron-tipped javelin in one hand and whipped the chariot reins against the horses' backs with the other. The horses bolted forward and pounded full gallop toward Tyr.

"Give him the iron!" The crowd was hysterical with excitement. "Give him the iron!" they screamed.

As the chariot sped toward Tyr, all he could think about was that the iron tip of the javelin was pointed straight at his heart. If he hesitated too long, it would pierce his chest. If he moved too soon, it would sink into his back. The other two chariots had completed their turn and were now heading in an unswerving path toward him, ready to trample his body to pulp the moment the javelin pinned him to the sand.

"Give him the iron!" the crowd roared.

The Numidian raised the javelin higher and steadied his aim as the chariot bore down on Tyr.

Tyr forced his feet to remain planted until he saw the charioteer's shoulder muscles flex during the first moments of the throw. Time slowed as he watched the ripple of muscle travel down the Numidian's sleek arm as he released the weighted javelin into flight.

Swallowing a tense breath, he leaped backward; his body spun sideways with a sharp twist, but it wasn't enough. The javelin pierced his side and sank deep. He gulped air. Pain of unimaginable magnitude burst through him. Falling hard onto the sand with a rib-crushing grunt, he stared upward at the blinding bright disk of the sun. He was struck; it was over. A gurgling gasp rose in his throat as the chariot clattered past.

"He has it!" The crowd shouted their approval. "He's taken the iron!"

A thousand crazed voices echoed in his ears. The horses' hooves thundered across the ground. They were heading toward him. He was about to be trampled by fine horses, and he thought it ironic that something he had so loved during his life was about to end it.

"Get up!" Arcona's harsh cry somehow rose above thousands of others, clear and strong. "Don't lie there. Get up!" She ran from the Gate of Life onto the arena sand, waving a blazing torch above her head and using it to startle the horses.

The two chariots set in a deadly trajectory were forced to split and veer away from the swinging torch in opposite directions. Tyr was momentarily spared.

The crowd became enraged that a woman was running loose in the arena, ruining the games.

The trainers rushed forward to grab Arcona by the arms. The torch was wrenched from her hands and tossed to the sand.

"Stand up and fight!" Arcona shouted over her shoulder to Tyr as the trainers lifted her under her arms and dragged her bodily across the sand. "You are one with the gods and share their blood. Believe what I say. No man can stop you!"

Tyr squinted against the sun. Why had she said that? Was it just more of her madness? How could he possibly stand? He'd been dealt a mortal blow and should already be dead. He melted against the sand, waiting for the inevitable.

"Stand!" Arcona screamed. "I made you mightier than the rest. Fight!"

He drew a deep breath and realized with astonishment that his heart was still beating steady, and he wanted to live. Perhaps he could stand and fight.

Grasping the javelin, he laboriously tugged it free of his flesh. It made a horrible wet sucking sound as he withdrew the iron tip. The pain was so great he roared in agony, but once it was out, he discovered he could easily stand. His legs were solid beneath him, perhaps more powerful than they had ever been. *Is this a dream or a delusion during the final moments of death?*

It wasn't either. A moment later, not only could he stand but he could run. This was real. He was still alive and had never been so strong or fast. He pointed the bloodied javelin at the horrified Numidian who'd delivered it to him and threw it with such force and speed across the length of the arena that the iron tip pierced the Numidian's body and ripped through the other side.

The Numidian wheezed, fell from the chariot, and crumpled to the sand. The team of horses ran off with a driverless chariot bouncing wildly behind them.

The crowd gasped, shocked and thrilled by the unpredictable turn of events. Cries of "Freedom!" coupled with the thumbs-down signal for mercy rang through the stands.

The tibia blew, calling a halt to the games while the editor delivered his verdict.

The other two charioteers drove to the far side of the arena, beyond the range of a javelin, and waited.

The editor stood in his box, visibly tipsy from too much wine, his body swaying precariously from side to side. "It is my right as your magistrate and sponsor of today's games to grant life and freedom to the Dacian Dagger!" With a lazy flick of his wrist, he tossed a laurel branch, a leather pouch of coins, and a rudis onto the sand below, the wooden sword signifying to all who could see it that Tyr was now free and would never again be asked to publicly fight for his life.

Tyr ignored his prizes and stared at the blood trickling from the speared Numidian's body. There was no sense of relief or joy that he'd been spared death and had his greatest wishes delivered.

He was free but it no longer mattered. Instead, a new sort of slavery had arrived. A hunger rose inside, one that craved unwholesome things. His empty heart rumbled within like the pleading muttering of a starving beggar.

He raced toward the bleeding body of the Numidian and pounced on it like a hungry wolf. His teeth felt long and lethal as he tore at the man's throat with unflinching viciousness. He was eager to rip into the warm flesh and drink blood. The taste fed a raging void within. Wanting more, he ravaged the Numidian like a wild beast as a mindless bloodlust swept over him. In the first horrible moments he felt as if he could never drink his fill.

A startled gasp rose from the crowd, followed by silence as they stared at the uncanny spectacle.

"The Numidian is dead, and you have won." Jude strode toward Tyr with a look of concern. "Don't do this. Rise and thank the crowd for your freedom before they turn on you. Come away from the corpse. Salute the editor and thank the crowd. That is what you must do."

Wanting only to be left in peace as he drank every drop of warm blood from the freshly dead Numidian, he hunched over his prize, glaring.

Jude placed a gentle hand on Tyr's shoulder. "You're the victor, not an animal. Stop this feral behavior."

He furtively glanced upward at Jude and snarled in the man's face like a crazed jackal shooing a fellow predator from its kill. Jude blanched and backed away, a look of abject horror on his face. "What's wrong with your teeth? You have fangs! What are you?" He turned and ran in terror. "The Dacian is under an enchantment!" he shouted. "He's become beastlike and gone mad!"

The spectators in the front rows leaped out of their seats and fled to higher ground in a state of chaos. Frightened cries of "Plague! Demons! Witchcraft!" echoed through the air.

The Numidian's blood felt cloying in Tyr's mouth, yet he wanted more. He felt sickened and thoroughly disgusted with himself for drinking it but couldn't stop. A still logical part of him knew he should rightfully be dead from the javelin thrust, but instead he was a living monster, consumed with rage, looking for the next throat to slash, and he knew exactly who to blame for this horror — Arcona.

He rose on powerful legs and turned toward the Gate of Life. Arcona hovered at the threshold of the gate, gloating. She shouted across the sand, "It is done, and it cannot be undone!"

Tyr pointed his bloodied finger at her. "Witch!" He strode toward her with confusion, hate, and horrid desire rattling his gut. "What have you done to me?"

She laughed a sour laugh, and inclined her head toward the bowels of the amphitheater. "I made you the strongest Upir Likhyi. I cast a blood enchantment on the others, too. They've already received the gift, but they do not possess your superior strength. You're the master Slayer. I'm proud of what I've done. All the newly made Upir Likhyi will be on their feet stalking Romans by nightfall, and tomorrow I'll make more."

The ground rumbled and shook violently. A blast of black smoke rose high above Vesuvius. A heavy bronze statue of Emperor Titus set atop a marble column wobbled and crashed to the ground in a cloud of dust.

Startled people scattered in all directions. The sand in the arena shivered like the surface of a windswept sea.

The crowd screamed in terror and fled toward the amphitheater's exits.

Tyr ignored the turmoil surrounding him and strode toward Arcona. "I don't want your gift. I want nothing to do with you. You're an unfeeling, malevolent Strix!"

The shaking earth rocked the wooden stands of the amphitheater.

He struggled to hold his balance as the world rolled beneath his feet. "You have no heart. You'll fuck, bite, and bleed any man you can grab and turn him into a monster!"

Arcona gasped for breath as if she'd been slapped across the face. "You will not thank me?" Disbelief shone in her eyes. "You're an ingrate!" Her gaze hardened to steel. The trembling ground left her staggering to hold her balance. "I did it for the freedom and love of our people. I did it for you! If not for my gift, your trampled body would be cooling behind the Gate of Death. You're alive because I made it so!" The last fragment of his unblemished soul rose up in rebellion and screamed, "This isn't the life I wanted!"

"But it's the life you'll endure." Her eyes sparked with anger. "There is no other choice!"

The earthquake subsided. The wooden structures surrounding the amphitheater stopped creaking. A disturbing silence filled the dusty air that no living creature dared interrupt for many moments. No one spoke or cried out; not even the usual chattering sounds of opportunistic birds circling the arena could be heard. All was eerily quiet.

Marius stepped from the shadows of the Gate of Life, looking ashen and dazed. He glared at Arcona with suspicion as he approached her. "Why is the Dacian saying these terrible things?" He loomed beside Arcona, his fingertips grazing her bloodstained stola. "Is he telling the truth? Are you a blood-drinking Strix?" His voice strained to breaking. "What have you been doing down here with all these men?"

Arcona glowered defiantly and said nothing.

A troubled look crossed Marius's brow. He raised his palm into the air, prepared to strike Arcona's cheek, but froze. His face purpled with rage, and his hand trembled. "Fate protect you, Arcona. You were a great favorite of mine, but if I find out you've humiliated me behind my back, bedding low-caste men and drinking their blood... I swear, I'll tie you to a pyre and burn you alive."

Chapter Ten
Salem, Massachusetts. Present day

Arcona opened her eyes with a start. The steeply angled ceiling of the cozy Federal-era room was unfamiliar. This wasn't her little bungalow in California, and this wasn't Pompeii. Where the hell was she?

The setting was deceptively serene; a fire in the hearth had died to red embers, leaving the room warm with a soft glow. A pile of quilts clung to the foot of the bed, poised to slide to the floor. The sight should have been comforting but weird memories surfaced, none of which made any rational sense. Most unsettling, there was a man lying at her side.

Her arms ached from being trapped in one position for too long. Hijacked by disorientation, she glanced around in alarm. It took a moment to fully absorb the odd chain of events. A crazed man in Salem had kidnapped her and brought her here. Pieces of the picture fell into place and formed an insane mosaic. It all flooded back. Holy crap, could any of it be real? What the hell was coming next?

Tyr lay peacefully facedown beside her on the big iron-framed bed with his heavy arm cast across her shoulders, as if he meant to hold her captive even in his sleep.

She shifted beneath his weight and discovered her wrists were still shackled to the headboard. Tugging at the leather cuffs, she winced in frustration.

He stirred on the mattress, lifted his head, and gazed down at her. His eyes bore a sleepy, satiated expression. Tyr looked at her with less of his former anger or menace. His expression radiated calm.

"You're awake?" He sounded surprised and still seemed drowsy as he pulled himself onto his elbows. "I seldom sleep so deeply. It almost never happens," he mumbled. "It felt wonderful."

"You don't sleep?" Her voice was hoarse.

Rubbing his eyes, he sat. "Not like you do, but I did tonight."

"What was I seeing?" Each shaky syllable filtered through a heavy layer of caution. Did she really want to know? "It wasn't a dream. The experience was too vivid. Was that truly your life in Pompeii?" She gulped a labored breath. Damn, her world had gotten weird. "Do you even know what I'm talking about?"

"Those were my blood memories." His answer was quiet. "Everything you saw happened."

Her logic wanted to reject his statement as ridiculous, but every cell of her body screamed he was telling the truth. Was this her secret guilty act, the one that floated in the back of her mind muttering, *You're not worth anyone's time. You're a bad person all the better to be rid of.* "Did I really do those things to you? Did I make you into what you are?"

"A Slayer? Yes, you did." Tyr nodded. "You didn't even ask me, and it wasn't what I wanted." Rolling onto his side, he tugged the waistband of his jeans lower and pointed to a flat, faded scar above his hip. "The javelin should have killed me that day. This was my last mortal wound — my exit wound, inflicted while a shred of me was still a man. I'll always bear a trace of it."

A strong sense that what he said was fact and she was responsible for another's displacement and discomfort for two millennia was overwhelming. "I'm so sorry." She genuinely meant it. "If I'd known the results of my actions, I would never have gone down that path."

A wary look crossed his face. "Are you sure of that? You were very determined back then."

Dame Bishop had been right; she was an instigator and wrongdoer. Shame welled to the surface and she recognized *the facts* as something vague but real that had always been part of her, haunting her thoughts. "I was damaged and wanted revenge."

His gaze simmered. "You certainly were, and you damaged me."

Despair rose within her, as powerful as a storm gathering on the horizon; its full effects were as yet unfelt, but repercussions were coming. Her actions as a Strix were something that could never be changed or forgiven. For a horrible moment she wished he'd just kill her and get it over with. "How could I have known?"

A smug grin tugged at his mouth. "A trained prophetess who doesn't know that bargaining with blood-swilling entities and mixing violent rival gods might be a bad idea? Bitch, please, you're not very convincing."

Desperate words poured out of her. "The person I am today would not do what I did to you in Pompeii. Never!"

Tyr stilled. "I know." His steely gaze indicated he was mulling over options. "And it's become a problem."

"What are you going to do with me?"

He remained silent as tension built between them, more forceful than torrential waters pushing against a fragile dam. The fire crackled and the ashes of a smoldering log collapsed with a loud *slump* and made her flinch.

Tyr reached for his T-shirt and tugged it over his head. Thrusting his heavy arms through the sleeves, he shifted on the bed and faced her. The slightest hint of vulnerability simmered beneath his petulant expression. "In Pompeii, you were so desperate for revenge you didn't give your actions a second thought. I paid the price with my soul. What about my revenge? Am I not entitled?"

Her limbs went to jelly. "I'm sorry! You're right. There's nothing I can say or do that would be apology enough for what I did to you. But I've—"

"But what?"

"I saw what I did and—"

"You haven't seen anything yet!" He sounded despondent as his mouth twisted in a sneer. "So far, you've only glimpsed the *how*. By the way, Pompeii wasn't the worst of it." He stared at her for many long moments. "Lucky for you, I see things differently, too." His eyes glittered in the dim light of the fire. "During the blood feeding, I saw you were an angrier, more broken soul than I ever imagined. For ages, and I mean that literally, I believed you'd tricked me and made me your victim. I remembered you as being formidable and in control, but you weren't. You really didn't know what you were doing, did you?"

"If the blood memories are accurate...." She struggled to construct a solid argument, sensing this was not the time to ramble or sound hysterical, though she wanted to freak out and sob. "I thought I was doing the right thing for our people who had suffered at the hands of Rome."

The situation was impossible. She'd been a selfish monster in one lifetime, and was the captive of a pissed-off blood-drinking immortal in this one. Not good. "Someone needed to take action." The weight of the past and fear for her life in the present pressed down like a steel-toed boot stomping on her chest. If she started crying now she'd never stop. "Past Arcona thought only of revenge and didn't care how she got it, but I'm not that person. I swear it."

Rubbing his hand against his jaw, he stood and paced the room. "Where does that leave me? I'm in limbo." Taking long strides toward the fireplace and back, he reminded her of an agitated tiger trapped in too small a cage.

Tyr stopped and glanced down at his leg. "Damn!" He stroked his hand against his thigh. "The wound from the broken glass has healed." Looking perplexed, he poked his finger through the ragged gash in the denim. "It was deep, but there's not even a scar. I've never regenerated an injury so quickly. Your blood must be very potent." Worry creased his brow. "But that means Varn will quickly regenerate, too."

She glanced at his healed thigh peeking through the slash in his pant leg, then looked a little higher and saw a prominent bulge pressing hard against his jeans.

Tyr noticed where her gaze was focused. "That never completely goes away," he said sheepishly. "I'm always left hard and aching, especially after the pleasure of a good blood feed." His gaze traveled over her body.

Her face flushed. "Never?"

"Yet another nasty side effect of being a Slayer. The last time I came like a man was that night in the sparring pit with you. I've had no satisfaction since."

More torment caused by her? She collected her thoughts. The bad news didn't stop. "When you say no satisfaction, you mean what exactly?"

Anger flashed on his face. "Isn't it obvious? I can't finish anything. I'm neither dead nor alive but stranded on the edge, always hungry for more sex that can't satisfy me, more blood that will sicken me, more violence that will rot the last fibers of my soul I might still possess. For me, nothing comes to an end and it's a nightmare."

"Never finishing? That was part of becoming a Slayer?"

"Yep." His response was pure sarcasm.

"Holy crap, I'm so sorry."

A sad smile flitted across his face. "You should be." He hesitated. "You made me immortal, and I hate it. I miss being a man and enjoying a hard fuck just because it feels good and not having blood or violence involved. I'm tired. I want this existence to end. I've had more than enough of the little it has to offer."

The pain in his eyes was a crushing confrontation. The muscles of his jaw tensed and then released in a subtle nervous twitch. He looked into her eyes with an odd mix of hope and anxiety. "How do I end it, Arcona? Tell me, how do I die?"

Her breath caught. "I'm sorry, but I have no answers."

"You must." He bit his lip, frustration flashing in his eyes. "You were the prophetess and the Strix. You cast the enchantment. It's on your soul imprint carried in your blood. You must have some sort of memory or intuition."

She slowly shook her head, but could she help him? He deserved answers and she had none. A sense of despair swept in like icy water pooling at her feet. "The original Arcona was lifetimes ago. She's a complete stranger to me. I don't think or feel the same way she did. I couldn't even guess what was in her heart or mind. That's the truth."

Tyr hissed in disgust. "I'm jealous. I wish I could say the same. Nothing changes for me. I'm exactly as I was, preserved like an insect in amber."

The glow of the fire lit his hazel eyes ochre. At that moment he didn't look menacing; he looked as sincere as a lost child appealing for help and sulking that none was offered. She stared into his face and simply studied him as the handsome man he was. He'd once been human, until her actions changed the course of fate. Something had to be done for him.

"Unshackle me," she whispered. "Please."

Her comment was dismissed with a look of disappointment. "You already used that trick. You tried to leap out a third-story window and proved you're not trustworthy. Do you really think I'd fall for it twice?"

Straining against the cuffs, she lifted her head from the pillow. "I thought my life was threatened."

"And you've changed your mind?"

"Yes. You need me alive, don't you?"

A smirk curled his lips. "Don't get ahead of yourself."

"I'm right. You need me alive. If the answers you're looking for were offered as easily as drinking my blood memories, you'd already know them, wouldn't you?"

He sat beside her on the edge of the bed and brooded in silence for a few tense moments. "I admit that matters are more complicated than I expected."

She gazed up at him. "Tyr, look in my eyes. This night has been the strangest and scariest thing that has ever happened to me. I'm in shock. I can't explain what forces might be at work, but I accept that it's real and I have to deal with it as rationally as I would any other serious problem. I want to help you but I also want to live. I'll cooperate, but you need to reassure me that there isn't going to be any more brutal crap or forced blood drinking. I'm at my limits and I can't take any more. Okay?"

The line of his mouth drew tense as he nodded. Remorse and, dare she say it, even compassion showed on his face. For the first time she grasped real hope that she might survive this weird experience. "Maybe we can help each other?"

"Let's hope so. I won't lie. When the night started, I wanted you to suffer like I've suffered." He appeared uncomfortable as he bowed his head. "Forget it. I can't even bring myself to say it."

"Say it! Go ahead. I want to know."

His chest stiffened as if he were holding his breath. "I planned to drink your blood and throw my ugly life as a Slayer in your face and make you choke on it."

"You did that, and I deserved it." Desperate to reason with him and secure her life, she also had to question why she felt so badly about her own acts. They were selfish and horrid. "But you still have a problem, don't you?"

Running his hand across his wavy hair, he rose and paced the room again. "I still have a fucking big problem. I waited almost two thousand years, praying every day we'd cross paths again. Now here you are, and I'm no closer to knowing how to end this shell of an existence. Nothing will come of it. We're just going in circles."

"I disagree. This meeting was a slap in the face. I had no idea I was a Strix and that anything like a Slayer existed. Would you believe me if I told you I want to help?" It hurt to face the fact she'd ever been so selfish. "I think I owe you."

Tyr shrugged. "You don't really believe that."

"I do. I can see I did wrong by you. In the ludus, in Pompeii, I chose you because you were the best, the strongest and most decent of all the men. In a perverse way, turning you into a Slayer was an act of admiration. As much as I was capable of, I did care for you."

"I cared greatly for you. Too much." His voice was raspy. "What you did to me was a sickening betrayal."

"I can't even imagine how bad it was through your eyes, but that was long ago. We should be thinking of the present and what I can do for you now. The old Arcona is gon-gone…" she stammered…"but I'm here. Tyr, what can I do for you?"

He leaned against the wall with the heel of his thick-soled boot scraping the wallpaper. "You have no idea how confusing it is to hear you say those words. You're Arcona, my Arcona, and my maker. You look like her and sound like her but your attitude is so different. In that way the two of you are night and day. I don't know what to feel."

She shifted against the pillows. "We may not be able to solve the big stuff yet, so let's start with the small things. How do you feel right now?"

"Confused."

"Me, too." She said, voice wavering.

In an anxious gesture, he tapped his clenched fist against the wall. "I'm not angry with you anymore. I don't know what I feel."

"That's good!" Her voice brightened. "Anger and violence won't solve anything. See, we're getting somewhere. I'll treat you with respect and you treat me with respect."

A few moments passed and nothing more was said. The dim light of the smoldering fire cast a crimson glow over Tyr's rugged face.

Finally, he pushed away from the wall. "Respect is a good word. I like it." He returned to the side of the bed and sat, making the mattress squeak. Hunching forward, he clasped his hands under his chin and rested his head on them. "You have my word I'm not going to harm you. I can see it's the wrong thing to do."

Tears of relief rolled down her cheeks. She broke into a sob. "Wow, I didn't realize how scared I was until… I stopped being scared."

Making eye contact with her, he appeared contrite. "I'm sorry."

"It's okay. I need a good cry." Now she was choking on tears and wished she weren't trapped on her back. "It's not every day that your past shows up to confront you with the horrible things you didn't know you'd done."

"We've both done horrible things." Tyr's eyes filled with liquid. "I'm so tired of it all." Tears slid down his lashes and clung like crystalline beads. He daubed at his eyes and studied the moisture on his fingertips. "Look at this, real tears." Touching his fingertip to his lips, he tasted it. "Salty." He seemed surprised. "I haven't cried in two millennia."

"You don't cry?" She sniffled.

"I can't. Yet another item on a long list of can'ts. I can't eat either. A little blood now and then is all I need, but I still dream about roasted meat or fresh bread. It's torture. Nothing stays down, and blood is the only flavor I crave, so food remains another can't."

"But you're crying now. Your cheeks are wet. Something has changed."

"I couldn't tell you what."

"Tyr, I am full of regret for what you've been through. It's hideous to know I'm the one who did it to you."

His face glistened. "Arcona, how do I stop being a Slayer? What do I need to do to die?"

She shook her head. "I have no idea."

He reached for a box of tissues beside the bed, took one, and used it to gently blow her nose, which made a juicy sound. "That's gross." She wished more than ever her hands were free to blow her own nose.

A hint of a smile warmed his face. "I've seen worse leaking out of people. Trust me on that."

A nervous laugh bubbled out of her. "If you took the cuffs off, I could do that myself."

He hesitated, appearing wary. "I'm not sure I can trust you." Sadly, he had a point. She wasn't at all sure how she felt. "You can."

Setting the tissue on the nightstand, he rose from the bed, walked into the bathroom, and turned on the sink.

Glancing sideways, she peered through the open door. "What are you doing?"

"Getting you a glass of water."

"Thank you." She wriggled her wrists against the cuffs, hoping against hope there might be a way to slide free of them. There wasn't. "I'm thirsty. That's very kind of you."

"No need to thank me. I'm just being practical."

"Practical?"

"Varn took a lot of blood from you. I took some too but not as much." He turned off the faucet and walked back to the side of the bed and sat.

Her suspicions grew. "And you want to take more from me?"

His gaze skimmed her throat and lingered. "Not now and not by force."

She felt as safe as a rabbit in a lion's den. "Why? I'm shackled. I couldn't stop you."

"Because drinking from you was the greatest pleasure I've known since I was a man. Sharing our memories of a common past, even if they were difficult, felt good."

A lump of tension rose in her throat, almost smothering her words. "That's how humans are. Sharing things, even if they're painful, brings us closer."

He winked. "But I'm not human. Did that fact slip your mind? I'm a Slayer. I'm cursed to remember every moment of my miserable existence down to the last gory detail and relive it again and again for all eternity. Having some company in my personal hell realm was a real treat."

She shrank away from him, unable to tell if he was merely being sarcastic or allowing his earlier belligerence to hold sway.

He slid his hand behind her nape, lifted her head, and pressed the rim of the glass to her lips. "Drink."

Parting her parched lips, she drank. The water was like life pouring back into her body. Until that moment, she had not realized how thirsty she was.

Tipping the glass, he made sure she got the last drops. "More?"

"Yes, please." Her request was breathy.

Tyr returned to the bathroom to refill the glass. When he came back, he was grinning, and she had no idea what that sunny smile might mean. Holding her head gently, he offered her the water. After she finished the contents, he set the glass on the nightstand.

He brushed the side of her face with his fingertips. "I know we got off to a bad start. I was rough with you, and I had a few wrong ideas." A slight smile twitched across his lips. He appeared uncharacteristically nervous. "I don't want you to fear me or run away. I like being near you. It's been so long since I've enjoyed a conversation with a woman or shared a thought...."

She saw a way to buy time. "We can talk. What do you want to talk about?"

"Anything. I like hearing your voice. I spend most of my time alone, or reading."

Damn, why did he have to look so pleasant and approachable when he said it? "You like to read?"

"Yes. God knows I've got plenty of extra time for it."

"Do you have a favorite author?"

Tyr leaned onto his elbows. "I have a lot. Lee Child and John le Carré get reread often."

What did she think an ex-gladiator would read? Taken aback by his taste in classic airplane-fare books, it was easy to imagine a typical male's cluttered collection of paperbacks stacked on an end table and poised to topple. "You like action adventure, spies…. Why am I not surprised?"

Brushing the pad of his thumb against the full swell of his bottom lip, he paused. "I read the Brontë sisters, too."

Her mind reeled. This was getting surreal. "You do not!"

"I do! On top of it all, I read the books when they were new. It's not light reading. *Wuthering Heights* is loaded with angst. Heathcliff dug up Catherine's dead body from the churchyard and lay beside her, for fuck's sake. That's not exactly a Nicholas Sparks novel. It's so obsessive and beautifully twisted."

"You're right." Okay, she'd misjudged the reading tastes of a Dacian gladiator. She'd thought a lot of the same things he did, but loved the book an insane amount. "Wait a moment, you read Nicholas Sparks?"

"I found a copy of *The Notebook* at a bus stop. Most nights I can't sleep, so I'll read anything."

"This is messing with me bad. You read romance? I'm not sure why but that's as hard to believe as the fact you're two thousand years old. You look like such a…"

"Such a what?"

He looked like a steel SEAL. "For an undead Slayer from the Iron Age, you seem very up-to-date."

Tyr's deep voice became gentler, as if he were speaking to a frightened animal— which at that moment she was. "I'm here, walking the same streets as everybody else. I make an effort to blend in. I've had all the time in the world to learn a new language or skill. I drift along outlasting everyone and everything, just trying to fill my days."

For a breathless moment, she simply looked at him, saying nothing.

He looked at her with a faint, wistful smile, and she wasn't sure what it meant.

In a heartbeat, the invisible barrier between them dissolved. Maybe this was Stockholm syndrome in spades, but she began to believe she and Tyr had made an essential connection. Was it possible she had a chance of surviving this crazy-ass night, after all? "So, you reread favorite books?"

"Love to. Books are the one thing I can forget and enjoy again. Interactions with people, never. That shit's branded on my brain."

"I reread, too. I have trouble remembering stuff from two years ago, let alone two millennia. Have you read Bram Stoker's *Dracula*?"

"Of course." He appeared wary. "But it frustrated me. I was hoping there might be some mention of the ancient myth or secrets of the Upir Likhyi that could free me. There wasn't. All I got was good entertainment."

An odd desire to open up to him overwhelmed her. "In my teens, *Dracula* was my favorite book, but now I'm questioning what that was about. Was my past dictating my choices or not so gently reminding me of what I'd done, creating Slayers?" As soon as she said it, she regretted it.

Tyr became quiet.

The ease that previously passed between them evaporated.

"So." He stared at his hands as he spoke. "Deep down...you always knew you were a Strix?"

"Not in a clear-cut w-way," she stuttered. "No. It was more of a fascination with the ancient world and dark stuff."

A spark of hope lit in his eyes. "Do you think that somewhere in the back of your mind, there might be more?"

She needed to be careful about how she answered. One wrong word and matters could turn sour again in an instant. "You mean the answer to undoing your situation?"

"Situation?" A huff of disgust passed his lips. "Why so polite? Call it what it is: a goddamn curse."

"Tyr, I don't know. Probably not."

His shifting weight on the edge of the mattress made the bedsprings creak. "But you're not sure? There could be something lurking in your blood memories?"

The breath whistled out of her. "I don't like the sound of that."

His gaze took on a curious quality. "In my long life, I've met a lot of witches, even a few Strix. I used to hunt them. In the early days, there were many to be found."

Swallowing hard, her throat ached from anxiety. "You hunted witches?"

"Yes. Back then, it was as easy as a bloodhound following a well-marked trail. You see, blood magic leaves a heavy residue, or shadow, if you want to call it that. Those connected to blood magic, or made of it as I am, naturally attract. If I were within walking distance, I could locate one of my own kind as certainly as a compass needle points north."

Not really wanting to hear the answer, she asked anyway. "What happened when you found a Strix?"

"Typically, a number of things happened, none of them nice. During the first centuries, I traveled the Roman Empire, watching it slowly fall apart and searching for witches who might know the secret. I found them too, lonely, sad women, soul damaged in their own ways. Most created Upir Likhyi to atone for some injustice that could never be made right."

"What did you do to them?"

"I interrogated them. Sometimes heavy-handedly. Did they know how to reverse the condition? What sacred words were spoken to bind the spell? If they wore an amber amulet I pursued my line of questioning with brutal fervor. They always seemed so surprised that a bit of their own handiwork had reared onto its hind legs and turned on them."

"What did you learn?"

He slapped his palm against the mattress. "Almost nothing. Beheading is the only way most Slayers can be killed. But a master Slayer, a sort of firstborn like I am, is immortal unless his maker chooses to end his existence."

"And how would she do that?"

"For fuck's sake, I never found out!" The dying fire lit his eyes crimson. "All that trouble for nothing, can you imagine? The witches knew how to create a monster from anger and vengeance but they didn't know how to unravel the beast. By the Dark Ages, the myths and tales had become so garbled any information a Strix might possess was nearly useless. Soon even the broken folktales faded and no one spoke of them."

"I'm so sorry."

"You should be." Tyr smirked but it wasn't malicious; it had a defeated, beautiful-loser quality about it. "Every day that passed condemned me to an ever longer eternity."

"So you have no idea how this works?"

For the first time in many minutes, he made direct eye contact with her. Something indefinable shimmered in his gaze. "Only that you and I are tied by blood and fate. I've been chasing you a long time."

Chasing? "What do you mean? How the hell do you chase a departed soul?"

Planting his boots firmly on the floor, he curled forward, resting his elbows on his knees. "You departed and came back. Sometimes I'd get a sense you were walking the Earth at the same time as me, but I didn't know where. I never quite caught up to you and it was maddening.

"Once, I did come close. In 1792, I sensed your presence and hurried to catch you, only to find a fresh grave on the edge of a Scottish village. Believe it or not, you were a man in that life, a country doctor trying to help people. You fell ill while treating the sick. Dozens of mourners showed up at your graveside to weep. That was the first inkling I had that your soul was improving and moving on without me."

Outrageous as Tyr's claim was, it merited serious consideration. The idea that she'd ever been a man or lived in Scotland was a familiar one. As a child, she'd often dreamed of living near rolling heath and watching over a herd of shaggy white sheep with black faces. Another frequent dream was of sitting on damp earth with a heavy journal balanced across her lap, committed to copious study while sheep grazed in the distance. The dreams were so innocuous yet vivid and hardly worth mentioning to others but she did. Her mother enjoyed reminding her that when she was a toddler she often shocked guests at family get-togethers by telling them she used to be a boy named Allaster. "How did you find me today?"

"A witch alerted me that you had stepped inside a sacred circle. I knew then my luck had changed."

"A witch? Are we talking about Dame Bishop?"

Looking guilty, he glanced away. "No comment."

"You said it yourself, you've used a 'heavy-handed' approach in the past with witches. Why would she or any other witch help you?"

"Dame Bishop is not your average witch. For your information, I stopped making war on witches long ago. I had something she wanted and we arranged a trade. Without her help, we wouldn't be talking."

"A trade? That's all this was?" For some reason, that news was disappointing. There had been moments when she was convinced Dame Bishop might actually care about her, in a pushy tough-love sort of way. How sad was that? "I knew she was up to something but I couldn't figure out what. I can't say I'm favorably impressed with her. She set me up with a cursed amulet and caused a lot of trouble."

His smug grin reappeared. "To be fair, you've caused a lot of trouble for me."

He was right and so far, Dame Bishop was too. She strained her arms against the cuffs in exasperation. "I want to get past this. What do you need to hear?"

"I'd like to hear that you're sorry about what you did to me, and I want to know how to die. That's all. I'm not even interested in revenge anymore. When we're done, you're free to go, which is more than fair. It's foolish of me."

"Go where?" she gasped. "I'll spend the rest of my life, which might be damn short, looking over my shoulder, waiting for your lady-killer friend, Varn, to pounce. I'm pretty sure that guy would be willing to bleed me white just to see if he could find any blood memories you may have missed."

Alarm registered on Tyr's face. "It wouldn't do him any good. Blood memories are only passed between a Slayer and the witch who made him." His mouth drew taut. "I know because I've bled a few witches white trying to learn something from them."

That was a disturbing image to hold in her mind. Just when things were looking up, they looked down.

Bracing his elbows on his knees, he glanced at the floor. "It took a while, but I finally realized those women didn't know much of anything of the old ways. A few magic words and wrong ideas were all that survived. The legends of the Strix, the amber pendants, even the collective memory of the Roman invasion faded. Everyone had new enemies to worry about."

Genuine regret about what she'd done to Tyr soaked in. She'd driven him to despair and stranded him in a position where he was bound to commit soul-corrosive acts. This was something no apology could make right. "What happens next?"

"I don't know." He shook his head. "I was hoping this would be easier to figure out."

"Easier for whom? I've been kidnapped, brutalized, and bled. I've done nothing harmful to you in my current life. If I can help you, you have my word I will. I just want to be treated with basic decency. Take these cuffs off and we'll talk."

He appeared leery. "We're talking now."

"The way I see it, you have a problem and I have a problem. You need my help, isn't that true? As long as I'm captive, I won't be able to relax and think clearly. The other witches couldn't unravel the Slayer curse, but maybe I can."

"Don't fuck with me, Arcona. How many times tonight have you pleaded innocent and claimed to know nothing? I lost count."

"But tonight, for the first time, you saw more of my story through my eyes. You watched me work the magic and felt what was in my heart at the time. All that was new to you, wasn't it?"

Leaning away from her, he looked troubled. "Yes, it was."

"I'm wondering if intentions are as important as words when casting or dissolving a spell."

He glanced at her sideways. The glow of the fire lit the tips of his lashes golden. "What do you mean?"

"In Pompeii, you worried about me. You wanted to save me, spare me. You tried to put me first and that was noble of you. What would happen if I showed you the same level of care and respect that you showed me before the betrayal?"

His breath caught and his lips parted but no words came out. She shifted carefully on the bed. Poor man, she'd messed him up good and set him adrift in the river of time to float downstream alone. "I think I know what to do. Unbuckle the wrist cuffs. I want my hands free."

A skittish little smile crossed his lips. "Is this a trick?"

"No, I promise. I had a thought. Blood and lust cast the spell, so maybe blood and lust handled differently will undo the magic." She gazed at him. "Please take off the cuffs so I can touch you."

He resolutely shook his head. "It's no good. It never works. I'm caught where I am, always hard and denied climax."

"Not sex. I meant an affectionate gesture. I could touch your face or stroke your hair. You know, the everyday stuff people who care about each other do naturally."

"Do you think I haven't tried?" Anger flooded into his voice. "I've tried a thousand times. It will end badly. I can't have casual contact with others. It doesn't work for me anymore. I'm frozen out of my feelings. The desire to drink blood will overwhelm me." His voice cracked. "And I'll hurt you.'

"You sound pretty emotional right now and you've been fairly restrained with me."

"This is different!" Tyr's eyes flashed. "I've waited centuries for this. There's so much at stake, and it looks like I'm not going to get what I want after all. I'm stuck in my own bloody hell realm."

"Then you have nothing to lose, do you? You haven't tried with me." Tyr's clashing blend of vulnerability and danger appealed to her. "You asked what my intuition told me, and this is it." She melted against the mattress. "I'll willingly let you drink from me again — just a little, not much. No struggle, no fear. You're sure to get some pleasure from it. What's the harm in trying?"

Like a dog that had been mistreated too often, suspicion glimmered in his eyes. "Why would you agree to that?"

For some reason, she was reluctant to admit she'd gotten a lot of pleasure from his first blood feeding. If she knew the whole tale, she might spot a way to break the Slayer curse. "Sharing blood memories and knowing more of the story might be helpful."

"You would do that for me?" Almost holding his breath, his body tensed. "You would allow me to lie with you and drink from your throat, voluntarily?"

"Yes." She tugged against the cuffs. "But free me first. I want to wrap my arms around you."

"I'll admit it's a very tempting idea, but it could go terribly wrong." He tilted his head and a wisp of regret shone in his eyes. "It has in the past."

Something crucial about their story was almost within reach. To not look deeper would be like leaving a theater before the most compelling movie she'd ever seen ended. "I want to try."

"You're certain?" He sounded intrigued but his doubts raised concern.

"Yes." The confidence in her voice surprised her.

"Can I take my pants off?"

"Uh?" What had she gotten herself into? "Is that necessary?" Flustered, her confidence flew out the window. She should probably be more worried about his sharp fangs than his nakedness, but what the hell.

His eyes shimmered. "I want to lie skin to skin with you like I did in Pompeii."

She tensed. "Tyr, am I going to be safe with you naked and feeding from me?"

"You're the one who offered."

His voice was silky rich and she wondered if karma had decided it was her turn to be seduced by a monster. "I know I did, but now I'm scared."

Tyr brushed his fingertips against her cheek. "Be scared of what you might see in the blood memories, but don't be afraid of me. I'll only take a little."

Perhaps this was a mistake. He'd admitted to hunting and killing witches before. A hint of hysteria crept into her voice. "And if you're lying, there's nothing I can do about it anyway."

"If you're fearful about me turning you into a Slayer, don't be. I can't. It doesn't work that way."

She hadn't even thought of that but now it was a worry. What poetic revenge that would be.

"I knew it was too good to be true." Disappointment tugged his brows downward. "You've already broken your word. You're no longer willing and you look terrified."

"Do you blame me?"

"I don't. I thought you were mad to offer in the first place. Forget it." He turned away. "I didn't expect you to go through with it."

"I haven't changed my mind," she said, too loudly. "Showing you the respect and affection you deserved hasn't changed. I just got scared by—"

"Me, taking off my pants."

"Yes." The word hissed between her teeth.

He smoothed his hair with the stroke of his palm. "We've been lovers before."

"That was another Arcona, not me, and it was a long time ago."

"In my mind, it was yesterday. You look almost identical." The sudden dip of his chin to his chest made him look crestfallen. "But you don't act or think the same, do you? I'm having a very hard time with this."

"I'm confused, too. I shouldn't have soft feelings for you. We're strangers and you're some sort of freaking vampire. I can't believe I'm saying that in a conversation. I shouldn't care about you or feel responsible, but I do."

"See! Arcona, I always knew you had a warm heart. You hid it so well. I wanted to love you so badly, and you wouldn't let me."

The look on his face was heart-wrenching. She had to be more careful of what she said. Clearly, he wanted to stay in the past. "Tyr, let the old Arcona go. Mistakes were made, but none of them have to be repeated. Not between you and me."

"How do I let her go?" Tyr glanced at her, distracted and agitated. "You were my last love. I wanted to believe that you cared about me and that we could have escaped together."

"That wasn't me," she gently corrected him. "The woman you knew has been dead for twenty centuries, and we both know why she did what she did."

"But...."

"But what? Regardless of the witchcraft, which I admit was a horrible thing to do, you took a javelin strike in the side. In 79 AD, that meant certain death. You and I were never going to escape anything. You would have died on the sand and I might have gone on being tormented by Marius a little longer, at least until Mount Vesuvius blew to bits. That life was never going to have a happy ending. You need to own that."

Burying his face in his hands, he groaned. "I know. I've played that scenario in my head a million times. It never changed how I felt about regret, betrayal, and loss." With a pained expression, he smacked his hand against the mattress. "Why do you look the same and have the same name? Was this fate's way of torturing me a little more?"

"Perhaps there was a reason for it. All of this can't be a coincidence. I'm here on All Souls' Day, talking to you. That has to mean something." A fleeting thought surfaced. "What time is it?"

"What does that have to do with anything? I don't wear a watch, never got used to it." He glanced out the window. "We've been here a few hours. It's probably close to midnight. Why do you ask?"

"At midnight, All Souls' Day becomes All Saints' Day."

A bitter laugh burst free of him. "There are no saints here."

"No, just old souls. Tyr, maybe I'm here today to help you."

He tensed. "Didn't we already decide that there was nothing to be done?"

Finally feeling like she could relax, she kicked her legs straight on the mattress. "Maybe we are supposed to discover the secret together."

"How?"

"Retrace our steps." She hoped she sounded braver than she felt. "Tyr, drink from me. I'll trust you to be careful. Show me where our story goes. I want to understand what I did and see the repercussions."

"Why? What good would that do? I've known the details for ages. Nothing changed for me."

"I'm your maker, and I didn't know. I need to see it."

He ran his hand along his jaw, back and forth with a nervous motion. "Arcona, you've already been bled twice tonight."

"I don't feel weak."

Worry hardened the sweeping lines of his mouth. "You should."

"But I don't. I think you were right. There might be a clue hidden in the blood memories."

Clenching and unclenching his hands, he looked anxious. "I'm not sure I want to see them anymore. Everything's changed between us. What if I see that the only way for me to die is take you with me?"

Dear God, she hadn't thought of that.

"A few hours ago, I would have been all for it. I would have cheered us both to hell."

"What changed?"

Conflicting emotions raced across his face. "I care." His voice went husky. "Even before we ever spoke to each other in Pompeii, I'd see you on the balcony and think, 'That poor woman. She's in danger.' I'd fill my nights dreaming of stealing you away from Marius and saving you for myself. The way things ended between us was tragic, with me screaming in rage at your betrayal. Of every memory I'm forced to relive, that one is the most painful."

"Tyr, you've been forced to carry and relive a large chunk of history. What would happen if you shared it?"

Biting down on his lip, he shook his head. "I have no idea."

"I think those memories may fade."

"Or grow stronger." A huff of disgust burst free of him. "I'm not sure I could bear that."

"I know it's a risk. The memories are strong because you want to remember. You need to stay angry. I suspect it's part of the spell that has bound you to the gods of war and kept you immortal, but I think we can get past it."

"You think?" He glanced away. "I wouldn't count on it."

She mulled over all she'd seen that night. "The old Arcona only saw part of the picture, but I have the advantage of seeing it all in the rearview mirror. The vision on the island of Nerthus was important."

"No shit. It was the root of madness. Until tonight, I knew almost nothing of your past. Only what you told me in the barracks, and that wasn't much. This is just another tragedy to carry on our shoulders."

"My experience on Nerthus's island is the first piece of the puzzle. We had to see it to solve our problem."

"How could it help?"

"The vision was a prophecy, but also some sort of contract. The dark forces or whatever they were cried out, *we want blood,* again and again. I slashed at my arms and gave them small amounts of my blood. In rage and desperation, screaming for blood equals death, but I've been ignoring an obvious point: blood is life. It's pure life!"

Tyr squinted in irritation like someone had kicked sand in his face. "Where are you going with this?"

"Blood bound you to never-ending servitude to the gods of war and strife. Perhaps blood will dissolve the contract."

"Blood is blood. Why spill more?"

"Tyr, I was so angry when I made you." The words flew out of her mouth. "I thought only of revenge. The price you'd bear and any future damage to your soul didn't even enter into the equation. What I did to you was selfish and wrong. I take full responsibility for everything you've suffered as a Slayer."

"By the gods," he muttered. "Hearing you say it is like waking from a nightmare." He drew a rushed breath. Tears welled at the corners of his eyes and threatened to flow.

"If I take full responsibility for the horrible things you were compelled to do and if you can forgive me, there won't be much holding the spell together."

"And the spell would be broken with blood?"

"Yes, but not in anger or any of the darker emotions. Let's be done with that."

His brows met and for a moment his face reflected the same innocence as a hopeful boy. "Could it work?"

"Why else are we here? I think we met again so we could release each other from the past."

In silence, he gazed at the wall as he considered her statement. A troubled expression twisted his mouth. "Are you asking me to surrender to my maker to be unmade?"

"Yes. Tyr, I know what to do. This time you can absolutely trust me." To her astonishment, she sincerely believed every one of her swift-spoken words. "Take the cuffs off me and drink."

Chapter Eleven

"Do it." Arcona's voice was firm. She'd committed, yet a telling touch of anxiety chipped away at the strength of her resolve. Her desire to help Tyr was absolute, but could she deliver on her promises? Freeing him from an ancient curse was a mighty big claim and far outside her wheelhouse. Worst-case scenario, this could become Pompeii part two and she'd just set him up for yet another crushing disappointment. Tyr gazed at her, raw emotion displayed on the surface. By firelight, his lashes cast long shadows on his cheeks. "Did you remember something important, more of the spell?"

The space between them, and perhaps it was merely emotional distance, shrank. "It's more of a feeling than anything else, but I know what the next step is." Where was the confident tone coming from? She had no special knowledge of witchcraft that might be helpful.

"So, what happens now?"

"I know it sounds easier than it really is" — Arcona settled against the bedcovers — "but try to relax and get comfortable."

"This whole night has me pretty keyed up." He held out a trembling hand. "Relaxing might be tough."

"How do you chill out when you're alone?"

"I take my boots off." He grinned and glanced away, looking bashful. "And my pants."

Her face warmed. Tyr was a gorgeous guy, but having him naked might be too big a distraction. "Feel free to take your boots off."

"What about the pants?"

"Best not to."

"Damn. How about my shirt?"

She hesitated. "What the hell. Go ahead."

Perched on the edge of the bed, he kicked his boots off. He took hold of his black T-shirt, bunched it in his hands, and tugged it over his head. With a careless flick of his wrist, he tossed it aside. "Are you going to take anything off?"

Her eyes widened at the solid perfection of his muscular torso crisscrossed with faint scars. "The cuffs?" The sight of him left her breathless. "Take them off."

"In a moment." He removed her boots and chucked them on the floor. "I want to look at you." His warm hazel eyes betrayed the slightest hint of pleading. This was not the look of a blood-crazed psychotic.

A sense of vulnerability prickled Arcona's conscience. He was being so trusting. What if she'd given him false hope? "How long has it been since you climbed under the covers with someone and shared a warm bed?"

His throat tensed. "I stopped trying ages ago because it just left me depressed and frustrated. Not to mention Slayers usually only get intimate with the dying. A battlefield triage is not very romantic."

"I have a feeling this will be different." She crooked one leg and slid her foot across the bedding. "Come here."

When he stretched out beside her, his big body dented the mattress and made the bed squeak. He carefully unbuckled the wrist cuffs one at a time. "I'm not going to harm you. You don't have to jump out any windows. Please, promise me you won't."

"Tyr, I saw what you wanted from me in Pompeii." He deserved a sincere apology. She paused, searching for the right words. "I'm sorry the person I was back then mistreated you. Betrayal is a terrible thing. I'll try to be as honest with you as I can."

Tossing the discarded cuffs against the headboard, he smiled. "I like you so much better than the old Arcona." He glanced at her with clear, bright eyes. "It's the strangest feeling in the world, but I'm not angry anymore. That's saying a lot because Slayers are always angry. Could the rage have finally bled out of me?"

Once her wrists were free, she drew them in front of her and rolled the joints in lazy circles to bring circulation to her tingling fingertips.

Tyr waited patiently for her to shake the blood back into her hands. "I would love to feel your arms around my neck." He grazed his fingertips against the amber amulet dangling between her breasts. "I hate the sight of it. I wish you could take it off."

"Don't. It will burn me. Just ignore it."

"It's hard to ignore the cause of the problem."

"Maybe it wasn't the cause. What if an angry person willing to trade souls for revenge was the real source of the curse? I know I've changed, so maybe the curse can change too."

She gingerly grasped the bronzework as she attempted to lift the amulet over her head. Stinging sensations like the bites of swarming red ants scorched her skin. Immediately, she dropped the amulet back onto her chest. "Can't do it!"

He covered the amulet with his palm, a flicker of regret shining in his eyes. "Leave it." He reached for the hem of her sweater. "Take this off. Please."

Was it wise to undress in front of a Slayer? Every moment that passed drew her further down a path without an easy return. She sat and allowed him to pull the sweater over her head. The amulet was left in place. Her hair fell to her shoulders. He smoothed a few of her stray locks into place. "Slide under the covers before you get cold."

A surge of unexpected emotion gripped her. He was behaving like a man with real feelings and caring thoughts. They were worlds away from where they'd been a short time ago. His tender gestures left her optimistic that something good might come of this.

She pulled the coverlet back and climbed underneath, a little awed by the sheer intensity of the moment. There was nothing casual about Tyr. His presence commanded respect and provoked strong emotions. She thought it sad that the last time they were lovers there had been little love, at least on her part.

In that instant, she knew what was missing. Love had not factored into the original Arcona's decisions, not really. Her ranting and pleading with the gods to strike love from her heart had been transferred to her warped creations, the Slayers. Poor Tyr had borne the brunt of that dark appeal. The full weight of her omission sank in. That was probably her worst offense as a Strix. Her actions had maimed him.

Today was an opportunity to make it right. There had to be deeper meaning and purpose to Tyr's long life. The academic in her was thrilled by the prospect of having a real gladiator in her company. Inspiration filtered into her thoughts. "You're living history, aren't you? You've seen everything."

"Unfortunately, yes." Slipping beneath the covers, he settled on the mattress beside her. The bulge in his jeans brushed the side of her thigh. "History? Is that all you're interested in?"

"Historical research is what I do." She placed her hands on his shoulders and drew him close. "You could teach me so much—set the record straight on so many things."

"Like what?" His voice was soft as smoke. "Nonsense like the Virgin Queen was technically no virgin? Everyone already knows that."

"Not everyone." The academic potential made her head swim. Tyr was a literal godsend to researchers.

Leaning closer, he pressed a featherlight kiss to her mouth. "Don't bring your work to bed."

She parted her lips, loving the lush cushion of his full bottom lip brushing against hers. With a light touch her tongue swept his.

He drew back. "Normally I only taste blood, but I just tasted an unusual spice on your tongue. It's slightly floral. There was a hint of it in your blood, as well. What did you eat tonight?"

Once he mentioned it, she realized how hungry she was. "I didn't get dinner." Looking back, the evening was one shocking blur of events. "Except for the dark brew at Slayers, I've had nothing.

"Wait." There had been something else. "I drank some sort of exotic spiced cider at Dame Bishop's shop. It's funny. I think she mentioned *rosa lacrimae,* as well."

"Rose tears? That's an ancient term I haven't heard in a long while." His brow knit. "That's interesting."

She grew concerned. "Is the taste unpleasant to you?"

"No, just the opposite. That taste was on your lips the first night you came to me in the barracks." He kissed her again, but that time he slid on top of her and pinned her beneath him. "I like what it's doing to me."

Tyr parted her thighs with his knee and settled his weight on his elbows. "I'll be honest with you. Right now, I'm more interested in fucking you than drinking your blood."

Arcona shifted beneath him. "Is that a bad thing?"

He brushed his lips against her throat and allowed them to linger. "No. It's just unusual."

Draping her arms around him, she allowed her fingertips to tangle in his hair. "I know you need blood." Arching her throat, she offered herself. "So go ahead. Take it."

Every muscle in his broad back tensed. "I can't."

A shiver passed over her. The tension left her breathless. With eyes closed, his lips parted for a muffled sigh. "You feel so good to be near. It's been so long."

"It's all right." She sensed he was scared to unleash his appetites and allow himself the freedom to fully enjoy her. Sliding a foot up his leg, she whispered what she hoped was an irresistible offer. "Kiss me, then feed gently."

He cupped his hands against the sides of her face. A tiny muscle on Tyr's jaw tensed. "I don't want to lose control and hurt you."

"If that were true, it would have already happened."

Worry shone in his eyes. "Slayers aren't lovers."

"Are you sure?" She kissed the soft swell of his bottom lip and gave it a teasing nip. "You feel like a lover."

Remaining hesitant, he made no further moves.

She released her hold on him. "Switch places with me. Lie on your back. I'll be on top."

He appeared dubious of her suggestion but pulled free of her and rolled onto his back.

Kicking the covers aside, she climbed on top of him and straddled his hips. His broad shoulders pressed to the pillows provided a stunning sight. "Put your arms above your head," she commanded. "So I can keep an eye on you."

A brilliant smile warmed his face as he raised his arms over his head. His knuckles rapped against the headboard. "Will this make you feel safer?"

"No, it will make you feel safer." She smiled back. "Should I cuff you to the bed?"

"I don't see why. I could easily shred the leather cuffs and bend the iron bed frame."

"In that case, I won't bother." The sweeping contours of his expansive chest were the same as they had been back in the days when he hefted an iron-rimmed shield and swung a sword. She spread her fingers across his broad torso and firmly pinned him beneath her. "You're the most physically fit man I've ever been with. That's for sure."

He looked at her with an enraptured expression. "Too bad I'm undead. I'd give anything to be the man I was again."

God help her, she wished the same thing. Stroking her hands along his solid torso she leaned over him, allowing a few silky strands of her long hair to brush across his chest. "If I could spare you all you've been through, I would. I swear it."

"Do you mean it?" He reached for the sides of her face to draw her close, a spark of excitement glittering in his eyes. "Really?"

"I do." She kissed his mouth with a soft whisper of a touch. His lips parted and she kissed him with long, voluptuous sweeps of her tongue as she rubbed herself against his chest like a purring cat.

He shuddered and arched off the mattress. "Hold on."

She broke the kiss and drew back.

A look of surprise was branded on Tyr's face. An intense luster shone in his eyes. He tried to speak but couldn't. Then a few broken but joyful-sounding foreign words tumbled out. "Tyr, what's wrong?"

"Nothing's wrong." The soft-spoken denial did nothing to veil his look of confusion. "It's just…while you were kissing me, I was thinking how silky your skin was and that I could feel the hair on my chest teasing your breasts and…." He smiled like a fool.

"And?"

"For a second, I was convinced I was about to climax. The way I used to. Like a man is supposed to." Laughter roared out of him.

She laughed, too. "Why are you laughing?"

He grabbed hold of her shoulders and rolled her beneath him in a graceful swoop. "It felt good! No blood, violence, or rage, just pleasure."

Arcona stretched onto her back, feeling flushed and extremely happy for Tyr. "Would you like me to kiss you again?"

He settled his weight on his elbows with his body pressed against her, a wolfish grin on his lips. "I demand it."

Slow and tender, she kissed him again, taking extra pleasure in brushing her breasts against him and teasing her nipples. Her hands slid across the broad swoop of his back and cupped his solid ass. Luxuriating in the feeling of his big body on top of her, she wrapped her legs around him, locking him in her embrace. "How does that feel?"

With eyes closed, he appeared breathless and tense, as if hovering on the brink. "Amazing."

The joy in his voice allowed her to dare to hope the Slayer curse could be broken. "What changed, and what do you think will happen next?"

"I don't know." An ecstatic expression lit his face. "I cried real tears. I can taste different flavors. My body reacts to a beautiful woman like it should." Nuzzling her throat, he gave her a gentle kiss. "By the way, I still want to fuck you." He paused as if lost in thought. "Maybe I'm finally dying. The gods know I'd welcome death."

"Death?" A chill passed through her. "Are you sure that's what you want?" It wasn't what she wanted. Not now.

He gazed down at her. "It's what I deserve. I've ended so many lives. My death is long overdue."

They had just come to a hard-won understanding. It would be so tragic to watch him die. Could she bear it? "What if life offered you something unexpected?"

"Like what? Is someone reopening gladiatorial schools? I think I've already overstayed my welcome."

"No, I meant another type of challenge." Was it her place to talk him out of what he'd longed for? "Never mind."

"It seems straightforward to me. We break the curse. I die. I move on to the next life. I think that's the best I can hope for." A touch of defensiveness crept into his voice. "I know I can be better than what I am. I did learn something during my overextended lifetime. It hurts to remember the things I've done to others. I'm so burdened. I just want this existence to be over, so I can have what everyone else gets—a fresh start. I want to wake in the next life cleansed of the past. I don't want to remember anything."

"You don't want to remember any of it?" Alarm rushed through her. "You're such a rarity. You've seen so much. Some of it must have been good."

"Some of it was, and that made the rest tolerable." His voice lowered. "You know what's strange?" He tapped a hand to his heart. "I didn't realize how much the softer emotions were missing until I felt them again. This stuff hurts. Knowing you're invulnerable is numbing. As a Slayer, I knew I couldn't die, so I never worried about my welfare or anyone else's."

Had they come this far only to usher Tyr through death's door? Even if he wanted it, the option seemed tragic. But was it her place to meddle with his fate a second time? "I saw how much the old Tyr cared. Maybe you could be that person again."

"That was so long ago." Doubt clouded his expression. "My existence as a Slayer was pleasureless. I had no friends, only fellow Slayers. I couldn't enjoy something as simple as a meal, or take a lover, and I certainly couldn't fall in love. New people and situations took on a monotonous tone because I couldn't really take part. I was forever on the outside, pretending to be human and waiting to take advantage of death."

"The enchantment was my doing, and not your fault."

The mood grew maudlin, as he remained silent for many tense moments. "Not all of it was your fault. For centuries, I willingly served the gods of war. There was a time when I needed little persuasion to kill. I followed misery all over the globe, traveling from one conflict to the next as an ambassador of strife."

She tried to look into his eyes, but at this angle his face was lost in shadow. "The day you walked into the arena in Pompeii, you wanted my blessing, but I didn't give it." Shifting on the bed to better see his expression, she placed her hand on his face. "I'm sorry you had to wait so long, but would you accept the goddess Nerthus's blessing now?"

"I would." He appeared puzzled. "But what difference would it make now?"

"You said I carried the secrets of the Strix in my blood, secrets you wanted to know. I feel this is the right thing to do. I'll give you my version of the blessing now. Would you agree to that? You might finally get what you've always wanted."

Moments slowly unspooled as Tyr gazed at her in contemplative silence. "All right." He nodded. "Do it."

"You'll have to shift positions with me." Pressing against his shoulder, she guided him onto his back. "If you pass out" — she avoided saying *if you die*, but she thought it — "I don't want to be crushed beneath you."

"It's just a blessing." His brows creased. "Why would I pass out?"

Lifting the amulet, she carefully searched with the pad of her fingertip for the bony beak of the largest bronze bird. The thinnest edge of the bronze work protruded like a tapering needle and was easily located. She brushed her fingertips against the side of his throat. "Lie down and close your eyes. I need you to trust me."

Tyr looked wary. "Be careful, Arcona. I don't want you to join me in my realm. This is no place for a loving soul like you."

"See." Her heart ached for him. "That proves you're a better person than I was. In Pompeii, I used you as an extension of my pain, yet your first impulse is to spare me the same suffering." She glided her hand against the side of his throat and pressed down with the lightest pressure. "I don't need to be spared. I'm strong enough in this life to take responsibility for the acts I set in motion."

"How?"

She cast one leg across his hips and straddled him. "There must be a reason I was born once again as Arcona, the historical researcher. I'm going to do what my blood tells me."

His eyes widened. "What is your blood telling you to do?"

A nervous burst of butterflies stirred in her belly. "To drink your blood and take back the original act."

Horror filled his gaze. "No! It may damage you. Don't do it."

She leaned down and whispered close to his ear. "It will be all right. The blood flows one way. That's clear to me. I was the Strix and I made the pact with the gods. My blood can taint yours, but you can't harm or transform me. No Slayer has ever created a Strix or another Slayer, am I right?"

He nodded. "But what if you're wrong?" His voice cracked.

"I'm not," she said more confidently than she felt. "The enchantment of the Strix was not completely angry and vengeful; rose tears and the mother goddess Nerthus were present, too. I'm going to call on the loving and erotic properties of both to break the enchantment."

It must have sounded plausible because something akin to hope flickered in his eyes. "You know how?"

"Based on what I've seen of my past, I know I did love my people. I longed to restore their homeland and dignity the only way I knew how. I did wish for love, but I wouldn't admit it." She brushed her hand against the side of Tyr's brow. "I could have loved you so much, but I wouldn't allow it. So you see, love was smothered beneath everything I did wrong as a Strix. Admitting it will set us free. Now all I need to do is put things right in this lifetime."

She held the sharp tip of the amulet to his throat and gave it a firm push.

He flinched and shook his head. "No!"

"Shush." Her soothing whisper trailed off. "Don't move." The bronze tip pierced Tyr's skin and made a tiny slice below his ear that dripped blood.

"You shouldn't do this." He physically recoiled. "You'll drink in a lot of me that isn't wholesome."

"Don't fight it. The old Arcona wasn't very wholesome, either." She pinned him to the mattress and leaned down to lap his warm blood onto her tongue. It tasted thick and salty and not to her liking, but she persisted, hoping it would do him some good.

"Arcona, stop," he weakly protested.

She didn't and instead bore down on him with all her strength. The taste of blood in her mouth left her repelled but determined. As she drank, Tyr surrendered beneath her with his long limbs sprawled limp across the bed.

A hum rose in her ears that blotted out all other sounds. Marshaling all her will, she silently chanted her intentions. *Let's go back. Let's make this right. Please let me free this man.* Tension crackled between them like a fallen powerline in a storm; his beautiful body was almost too dangerous to touch. As his blood washed across her tongue, a sort of sensuality overwhelmed her that was more than sexual; it was the essence of magic.

She closed her eyes and braced her trembling palms against Tyr's shoulders as a tunnel of brilliant white light opened in her mind's eye. The irresistible phenomenon drew her forward like a leaf rushing over the lip of a waterfall. Once again she was in the river of light, but this time she saw events from Tyr's life. Vivid images flashed past, people, landscapes, and even flavors and scents, but soon all sensations slowed and the images came to a jarring halt.

The first impression that caught in her mind's eye felt like a bittersweet welcome-home kiss. The memory was a conflicted one she sensed Tyr had always possessed, but had been unable, or unwilling, to access for nearly two millennia. Like a hawk circling overhead, she looked down and saw Tyr as a boy of five or six, dressed in leather leggings and a wolfskin vest. His hair was a child's shade of buttery blond.

In the next heartbeat, she was Tyr and saw the world through his eyes. He stood among a milling herd of whinnying horses on a steep mountain meadow, holding a swaddled newborn child in his arms. He held the warm, squirming baby so his mother could have her hands free to toss a leather rope around a mare's neck.

Tyr's mother, Valynda, was tall and beautiful with flowing auburn hair. She darted between the horses, chasing down the mare she wanted to ride. With raucous whistles and stomps she deftly lured a chestnut-brown mare close, lassoed the horse, and reined it in. In what looked like a single graceful motion, she grabbed the mare's mane, threw her long leg over its back, mounted, and rode. Her silky hair floated on the wind, shimmering like copper in the sunlight. Within moments the mare trotted in a slow circle following her commands.

Valynda rode close. "Hand Malyka to me." She held out her hands and waited for Tyr to hand her the baby.

Tyr offered his newborn baby sister upward as high as his little arms could reach.

His mother gathered the baby into her arms and tucked Malyka into a woven sling strapped across her chest. She looked at Tyr with worry brewing in her uptilted hazel eyes. "Tyr, now that Father's dead, you're the man of the family. Be brave and stay put. I have to leave you here to guard the horses. Blow the horn only if you need help. I have to do a task. Roman soldiers are camped below our grazing land. I need to know what they want from us."

He nodded.

As his mother rode away a chill passed through him. It was his earliest and last memory of his mother and sister. He never saw them again. Beyond that point, all feelings of love and trust seemed to drain from his life.

The image faded, and another took its place. An older Tyr of about sixteen appeared in the memory stream. He was handsome, tall, and lean with little hint of the lethal qualities his body would later display. His hair had deepened to a dark blond. Though he was still young, he was no child. His cheekbones and jaw displayed the first strong signs of maturity. His mouth was almost pretty in its arching fullness, but there was a fierce toughness shining brightly in his eyes.

Alone on a hillside, he sparred against an imaginary opponent, striking the trunk of a great tree again and again with a herding staff with such ferocity that his palms blistered and bled. He ignored the pain, knowing the practice drill was toughening his grip and preparing him for what had to be done. He knew he must hone his battle skills, take up arms, and help bring about the destruction of Rome.

There was sound reasoning behind such a monumental goal. By no choice of his own, he lived in a village of angry old men. The Romans had come that spring as they always did, bringing their desperate requests and broken promises with them, but this season was different.

Usually, the Romans came each year to buy horses and recruit local scouts to spy on the neighboring tribe, the Medes.

His people had no love for the Medes, who provided nothing but generations of combative competition over the same fertile slopes. Spying on the neighbors and allowing the troublesome Medes to take the wrath of Rome had become a reliable source of income for his people. The old men of his tribe accepted bribes, often ignoring what the Romans were most notorious for—stealing women.

Tyr knew firsthand about Roman treachery. A Roman legate had kidnapped and claimed his mother as a prize. To keep the peace, the tribe was later compensated with a few amphorae of wine and assorted Roman luxuries. At the time, no one flinched because Valynda was alone in the world with no man to protect her from her fate, but this spring, a different set of circumstances had played out.

A new group of Romans came, even more aggressive and arrogant than the last. They pretended to be interested in a stable alliance with the Dacians and invited everyone to a feast in their camp.

He had not been allowed to attend because it was once again his turn to guard the great herd of horses and drive them toward summer pastures.

The Dacian warriors who did attend the feast were systematically surrounded and slaughtered en masse. Every young Dacian wife, daughter, or sister was rounded up and taken as the property of the Empire to be shared or sold to fellow Romans. Those few left behind buried the dead and plotted revenge.

There was a lot of revenge to be had. Taking part in his first war party, Tyr distinguished himself by strangling a Roman guard. Then he snuck into a legate's tent and sliced the man's throat before turning on the rest of the sleepers.

Many Romans died in the raid but not enough to stop their malignant presence in the river valley. Even at his young age, he knew more Romans always appeared with the next snowmelt.

He struck the tree with thundering force, making his knuckles ache. He vowed when the Romans returned, he would be stronger and ready to fight.

A fresh memory came.

Tyr was a powerfully built man, riding horseback through a windy mountain pass. His solid thighs gripped the brushy coat of his horse. The rocky trail was narrow with many sharp bends. He rounded a turn and came face-to-face with a scouting party of Medes accompanied by a few Roman soldiers.

The men looked upward and spotted Tyr.

The Romans bellowed the order to attack.

The Mede warriors reached for their bows and poison-tipped arrows and aimed at Tyr.

In a sharp moment of clarity, Tyr realized the Romans completely distracted the people of the river valley by paying them to spy on each other while the Romans did as they pleased.

For the first time in his life, he felt inspired to speak civil words to the long-abhorred Medes.

"Brothers!" Tyr shouted in a clear voice that echoed against the mountains. "The enemy is beside you, not before you. We both know the truth. Think before you shoot."

The Medes froze and did not shoot. Several tense moments passed.

Tyr knew a Mede arrow was deadly at that range. Even if the iron tip missed a vital organ, the poison would pass into his bloodstream and leave him crippled or stunned while the Medes raced forward to finish the task with a club or dagger. He was trapped on the pass. The trail was too narrow for him to turn his horse and flee. He held his breath, waiting for the first volley of piercing arrows to take him down.

To his surprise, the Medes turned on the Romans, killing each man with an arrow and then slitting his throat for good measure.

The leader of the Medes shouted, "Dacian, help us hide the bodies from the ravens and ride with us against Rome!"

The scene faded, and another horrible memory rose of Tyr being captured by Roman soldiers and brutally beaten. Tyr had retaliated, injuring a high-ranking Roman officer and leaving the man lame.

For this transgression, he was taken into slavery and condemned to the arena. Everyone he'd ever befriended was taken from him. Land, dignity, and future were gone. There was nothing left to him but the gladiator's vow to willingly accept the iron.

With a resolute sense of calm Tyr accepted the vow, knowing short of taking his own life, which he was loath to do, the arena was the quickest route to the next world. He had no fear of death and was ready to embrace it.

Over many torturous weeks, he was marched or dragged like an animal to the marketplace of Pompeii to be sold as a gladiator; an event so degrading Tyr had blocked it from his mind.

Soon, the tone of the memories changed. The river of light seemed to slow and thicken, as viscous as honey. Arcona sensed these were the memories Tyr cherished most. She guessed he'd returned to them often, carving them ever deeper into the streambed of eternity.

Within the next memory, he saw an auburn-haired woman standing on a back balcony overlooking the ludus where she should not have been.

She experienced everything Tyr felt for her.

Tyr watched her unseen from just inside the barracks' door. He looked for her every evening on the balcony, hoping she'd appear and add a measure of joy to his day. He thought Marius's new woman was lovely, with wavy hair that rippled freely on the wind. He couldn't stop staring or thinking about her.

The evening was warm, and he thought her fortunate to feel the breeze above the steep confines of the ludus walls. There was a glint in her eyes that reminded him strongly of someone, but he couldn't place exactly who. All he knew was the moment he saw her, a long-denied part of his heart opened, and he wished there were no walls between them. After that first glimpse of her beauty, his monotonous days in the ludus were endurable, as long as she, whoever she was, walked the back balcony in the evenings and looked down on the drill yard where he could briefly look up at her.

Sometimes he could actually sense her watching him from some hidden part of the balcony. He'd look up and there she would be, as surely if she'd called to him. Sadly, there were many other men looking also, and she never seemed to notice him. Until one day....

Arcona, you scorched my heart black. I don't want to think of you.
The memories leaped forward in time. Tyr was now wealthy and freshly freed from the arena of Pompeii, but all was not well.

Fleeting images of a great pyre being hastily stacked in the center of the arena filled his mind. He watched Marius drag Arcona by the hair across the sand and chain her to a plank. The crowd went wild when Marius shouted to the masses that at sundown a witch would burn.

From a safe distance, he stared at the tears streaming down Arcona's face. A hideous death awaited her. He had helped denounce her and been the first to shout *witch*. Why didn't he feel anything? This wasn't right. Knowing he should care but didn't haunted him.

Events could have been stopped. Despite the javelin strike, he had miraculously recovered. The wound had sealed and he felt strong enough to pick up both Arcona and the hulking wooden plank and walk off with them if he chose to, but he did nothing. It puzzled him. He lurked at the back of the crowd and watched as an enraged Marius lobbed the first flaming torch, and wondered why his heart was so numb. When the screaming quieted, which gratefully did not take long, he left the arena. The heavy pouch of coins rattled against his thigh. He was rich. A part of him wished a bold thief would rush forward and snatch his guilt-drenched winnings away, but no one dared confront him.

A merchant offered him a sack of wine. He tossed the old man a coin and gulped the dark liquid down in a single draft. The world spun, and he felt sickened. His gut refused to accept the liquid, though he was thirsty and had drunk little all day. In a startling rush, his stomach muscles clenched violently and the wine came back up. Tossing the empty sack to the ground, he went looking for water.

Cupping his hands under a fountain, he took a trial sip. The water made his belly ache and it too came up with a choking sob.

He strolled through the marketplace. It was now long past dark, but the balmy night had lured many onto the streets in search of a breeze. Roasted lamb rubbed with fresh herbs was being sold near a tavern. The succulent juices dripped off the spit. How often had he dreamed of eating his fill of fresh meat and not having to fight other men for his share? He could afford as much as he wanted now, and it astonished him to realize he wanted none of it.

Instead, he found a stall that sold sturdy sandals and warm cloaks to affluent Romans. At least his body did not reject the new clothes.

Lusty women stood in tavern doors. Making bawdy remarks they invited him to drink with them, but even the most voluptuous among them provided the least bit of temptation. What was wrong?

All he craved was the chance to take part in yet more violence and witness yet more death. He was not himself; these were the thoughts of a monster. Blood became something he actually hungered to see and smell. He knew it was wrong. The desire for blood left an ugly residue on his mind that sickened him beyond belief. What had happened to him and how long would this horrible situation last?

He had escaped the arena but was now captive to something new and dreadful. In this state, blood and violence were an irresistible temptation. Arcona had just died, the smell of her pyre still clinging to his nostrils, and all he could feel was anger. He knew he should feel more, but he didn't.

The first night of freedom was spent stalking back and forth in escalating conflict along the dark arcade that ran the length of Pompeii's amphitheater. He knew he should not be there. It would have been wiser to immediately leave the city, but he'd been unable to tear himself away.

The underworld was there, and that was where he now belonged. The air of the arcade reeked of soured wine and sex. Beggars, thieves, and prostitutes of every description took shelter in the many shadowy niches and corners of the looming structure.

His fine pair of newly purchased sandals crunched against the grit of the pavement as he roamed the arched galleries, looking at the world through the eyes of a raptor. He no longer pitied the many desperate people he saw. Truthfully, he didn't feel his heart at all. He was not himself; he was changed, and there seemed to be nothing he could do about it. Horrific desires and dark thoughts dwelled within. He was cursed. His body and soul had passed through the gates of certain death and arrived in a limbo realm.

Walking in the most disreputable part of the city, he felt safe and invincible in the darkness. His keen eyes were sharper than they had ever been, and the shadows held no terror — only opportunity.

A plump and pretty young man with a carmine-stained rosebud mouth and the tucked-up skirts of a girl accosted him from the shadows.

"Greetings, soldier." The young man clearly mistook Tyr for a Roman legionnaire in his tall sandals embellished with bronze buckles and finery. "I know what you want." Sweet, flirty words were whispered. "I understand." Lifting the hem of his skirt higher, he skimmed his fingertips across his rounded thighs and flashed a glimpse of bare buttocks. "I'm fun, and I'll let you play rough. So let's be friends, handsome." He beckoned Tyr closer. "Tell me where you've been and what you've seen. I love a bit of military gossip."

Tyr shook his head. A chatty young man wasn't what he wanted.

"Oh come on! Don't walk away. Tell me your name, handsome." He followed Tyr. "My favorites call me Bellus because I'm so pretty. I'll bet I could even charm a tough guy like you." Stepping closer, his brows arched in astonishment. "Praise, Jupiter! You're the Dacian Dagger," he murmured with reverence. "I cheered for you in the arena and tossed you a rose." His mouth gaped in awe. "I watched you pull a javelin from your side. You're a god!" He stood frozen to the spot, staring dumbstruck.

A loud snarl and a blur of motion struck Bellus violently from behind. Blood spurted from his ripped throat as Renni, the Egyptian gladiator, pounced on the young man with fangs bared like a jackal.

Renni was vicious and used none of Arcona's seductive finesse. He stalked his prey, attacked, and drank blood with the ruthlessness of a ravenous beast.

Tyr watched in fascination and disgust as Renni ravaged Bellus's limp body with a gorging mouth that shredded flesh and lapped blood. The gory spectacle triggered overwhelming blood hunger and perverse desire. All of it was in conflict with what he knew to be right.

After he finished feeding, Renni flung the lifeless body to the ground and confronted Tyr. "Was he yours?"

"It doesn't matter now, does it? Poor man."

A sneer lifted the edges of Renni's bloodstained mouth. "That's what I thought. You were stalling. If you had wanted him, you'd have taken him. Would you like to hear a bit of advice? Don't prolong the kill. There's no need for conversation; it's cruel. Strike and be quick."

"You thought I was being cruel?" Tyr glared at Renni. "Is this what we are now, stalking predators?"

"Don't look at me like that. I saw what you did to the dead Numidian in the arena." Renni wiped the blood from his mouth. "You must know by now what has to happen." He paused. "No matter how hungry you get, food won't stay down. I tried. It doesn't work. Stop fighting it. We're newly born creatures. You have to blood feed. If I were you, I would just get it over with. You'll feel better. It gets easier too." He pointed at the body lying sprawled on the pavement. "He was my third tonight."

A shudder passed through Tyr. "Why so many?"

"Because I enjoy it!" Renni's eyes gleamed. "Gundomar and Jude were in a brothel wasting time just like you. I brought them two lovely women, and they wouldn't kill them and drink. They don't want to face the truth either. Maybe you should join them. The three of you can cower together and whimper."

Tyr lashed out and struck Renni across the cheek so hard the man spun backward.

Renni quickly regained his balance and lunged at Tyr with shocking strength. "I claim Pompeii as my hunting ground!" he snarled. "The city is mine. Go elsewhere if you don't have the stomach for what you are."

"Let go of me." Tyr remained calm. "I'll leave Pompeii. You can have it." Revulsion and horror washed over him. He wanted blood and knew what Renni said was true. Part of him wanted to rush to the brothel and claim the victims Gundomar and Jude had spared.

He shoved Renni away from him and strode into the darkness toward the marketplace, wishing to be rid of the taint of the amphitheater.

Walking in circles, he found himself once again in the marketplace. It had not been a conscious choice to return, but something inside instinctively steered him toward concentrations of people. At night the marketplace was quiet but not abandoned. Merchants slept in their stalls. The varied aromas of exotic spices mingled with the scent of rotting vegetables discarded in the gutters and picked on by squeaking vermin had been dulled by his blood-focused senses.

Tyr strolled the paved lanes, becoming acutely aware of the scent of salt on sleeping men's skin. He noticed with discomfort that he was beginning to sniff at people like they were food. The truth was disturbing. He was hungry for blood but reluctant to act on his desires. What he'd done to the Numidian was still vivid in his mind and filled him with loathing.

Near the city square, he heard the gentle sound of two women laughing. He felt drawn toward the soft voices and found himself standing at the doorway of one of Pompeii's many brothels.

The brothel was nearly empty of customers; only two of the curtains were drawn across the tiny brick cubicles the prostitutes used as semiprivate rooms. Heavy breathing and the occasional gruff male voice distracted him until the muffled sounds of two women giggling drew his attention to a dimly lit back room.

He cautiously approached and stood, barely concealed, behind a curtain merely a stride's distance from the women, yet they remained oblivious to his presence.

One was slender and fair and looked far too delicate to survive long in her trade. The other was robust and dark with a round, friendly face and prominent bosom.

Standing so near, he wondered why the women didn't notice him until he smelled the acrid scent of wine on their breath. The fair woman extended a trembling hand. "Molina, hand me the jar."

The dark woman picked up a clay amphora and gave it to her friend. "Haven't you had enough, Flora?"

Flora tipped the wine to her lips. "Today was horrible. I had a line three deep outside my stable all afternoon. The day was one endless fuck."

"It's true." Molina's gaze drifted toward a row of abandoned cubicles. "I never saw daylight."

Flora wrapped her arms around Molina and gave her a clumsy hug. "I've been with men all day, and not one of them was the least bit satisfying." She caressed the side of Molina's face and brushed a brief kiss across her lips. "Are you too tired?"

"No." Molina tangled her fingers in Flora's rumpled hair and drew her deeper into a kiss. The two kissed, teasing each other with just the tips of their tongues, making sweet little sounds.

Watching the two women left Tyr overwhelmed. The suggestive scents on the women's skin drove him mad. He fought the impulse to leap from behind the curtain and pounce on them. His foot involuntarily shifted forward.

"What was that?" Flora whispered.

Tyr froze.

"I didn't hear anything." Molina drew Flora closer.

Flora's lips parted to Molina's kiss. She grasped Molina's tunic and slid it from her shoulders, exposing smooth brown skin and heavy breasts glossy with aromatic oil. She traced her fingertips across Molina's lush curves.

Molina closed her eyes and leaned against the wall as she stroked Flora's hair and held her close.

"What's going on here?" a belligerent male voice boomed through the back door.

Molina and Flora leaped apart and tensed.

A coarse-faced man with a lumpy nose strode into the back room of the brothel. "If you're done for the day, I want my money."

"I already paid you." Flora sneered.

The man's heavy jowls sagged beneath a frown. "I say it's time to pay again."

"Lupi, half is too much," Molina protested. "On top of the fact we service you, as well."

"Which I'd be happy to take advantage of now." Lupi lifted his tunic to his hips. "But first, I want my money."

"You charge too much." Flora glowered.

"It's my wine shop." He loomed closer. "When you can afford to buy your own wine shop, you can set the rent."

Molina yanked her tunic upward to cover herself.

He slapped Molina's hand. "Don't bother. You'll be taking it off again in a moment."

Flora squared her shoulders. "What if we refuse?"

Lupi's face melted into a nasty scowl. "You earn good money because this establishment is respectable to the merchants near the marketplace. If you think you could do better in some shabby little niche along the arcade of the amphitheater, try it. You'll soon find out what a low caste of whore ends up there."

Flora tossed the man a small leather pouch filled with coins. "Take it and leave."

He cracked an ugly grin. "You're being surprisingly reasonable." Focusing on Molina, he grumbled, "What about you? Where's your share?"

Flora's gaze narrowed with rage. "I paid you everything I had. It's more than enough. She owes you nothing. Now leave us alone."

"It doesn't work that way." Lupi shook his head. "I'm owed some coin and a good fuck from both of you." He lifted the hem of his tunic higher. "Come here. I want both of you to take off your clothes and kneel in front of me like the obedient whores you are."

Flora and Molina exchanged reluctant glances.

"Stop making sour faces," he demanded, "and kneel."

Tyr couldn't stand the man's arrogance a moment longer. He burst from behind the curtain, grabbed him, and cleanly snapped his neck with a loud *crack*.

Lupi's eyes bulged and remained open in a look of utter shock.

Tyr pinned the brothel keeper tight against his chest, but there was no struggle. The man's hands dangled limp at his sides. The heady scent of salt and wine on his skin was both disturbing and enticing, and left him dizzy with want. Tyr's mouth tingled with an odd burning sensation as sharp fangs shot downward.

The women gasped in horror and dashed into a corner as Tyr sank his fangs into Lupi's throat, tore the flesh, and sucked the warm, iron-rich blood as it welled to the surface. He greedily gulped the first swallows. Doing something so heinous and having it deliver such profound gratification brought him to the verge of tears.

He fed voraciously, a terrible pleasure fraught with disgrace. He was relieved to be feeding his dark craving at last. Blood and lust were now entangled in his being. Intense shame gripped him, yet he was driven to continue. His tongue lapped blood with relish. Now he knew he was no better than a demon, and perhaps that was what he was. The hunger inside demanded this behavior. He no longer had a choice. Arcona had done this to him. She was entirely to blame, and he hated her for it.

Tyr drank his fill, then allowed the spent body to fall to the floor with a heavy thud. During the act he'd been so consumed in the feeding he'd not given thought to the outside world. With furtive glances, he wondered who had witnessed his trespass.

The two women cowered in the corner, trapped.

He drew closer. The light musky scent on their skin called to him in a deeply provocative way. With all his heart, he wanted to grab one of them — he didn't care which — and drink her blood. The strength of his desire left him shaking.

By sheer force of will, he wrenched his attention away from the women and knelt beside the ravaged body on the floor. He studied the dead man's face, committing each detail to memory. Whose life had he ended? Clearly this person was not a good man, but was the life his to take?

With trembling hands, he plucked the leather pouch Flora had been forced to surrender from the floor and tossed it to her. "Get out of here!" he snarled at the women. "Run!"

Flora snatched the jingling coin pouch from the air. The terrified faces of the women were pale as linen as they turned and fled onto an empty street.

Unbearable tension left him shaking. Killing the brothel keeper had been too easy. Sparing the women did little to alleviate the rising sense of self-loathing. The incident proved he was not the worst of Pompeii's monsters, but he'd become a monster nonetheless.

A horrible certainty welled within: sooner or later, he would do it again. An obnoxious whoremaster had blundered along at the perfect moment and provided a better option than the women. That close call was a moral convenience he could not afford. What if it had been a child? He wanted to retch at the thought and worried the day might come when he wouldn't care.

He had to face the truth, find the boundaries of his needs, and learn to honor them. He vowed to resist becoming as callous and vicious as Renni, which required being choosy about whom he killed.

Pompeii was a wealthy and cultured city but small. He needed a vaster hunting ground and knew Rome, with its many criminals and constant warfare, would better suit his needs until he could free himself of this abominable condition. *Tomorrow*, he promised himself. *I will travel to Rome.*

Chapter Twelve
Salem, Massachusetts. Present day

The present moment returned with the same shocking abruptness as a balloon bursting in her face. One moment she was Tyr, drenched in self-loathing in a brothel in Pompeii; the next, she lay cushioned in quilts on an old-fashioned bed. This business of snapping back and forth between parallel worlds left her disoriented. Arcona knelt on the mattress, hovering over Tyr's throat. The sharp tang of blood coated her tongue, leaving her sickened. She gazed at Tyr; his eyes remained closed as he stirred restlessly beneath her. His lashes fluttered and he looked ready to wake.

Bracing her palms against the big iron-framed bed, she fought to stay in the past a moment longer and see more of Tyr's story. There were so many questions deserving of solid answers and memories she wanted to unburden from Tyr's mind, but his world faded beyond reach. The little she'd seen of his existence as a Slayer was tragic enough.

She gazed down at him. "What brought us back to the present?" she murmured. "I wanted to see more."

Tyr opened his eyes. They were clear and especially bright. "I woke us. You saw enough. I thought I should spare you."

Brushing her hand against his cheek, she wondered if her actions as a Strix could ever be undone. "Valiant but misguided, considering I'm the direct cause of your shame."

"You saw plenty." He wrapped his arms around her shoulders in a loving gesture. "Stay close."

She drew the bedcovers overhead, creating a protective cocoon, and snuggled against him. She rested her face against his chest; he radiated body heat where earlier he had felt almost cool to the touch. "You feel warmer."

"I've been next to you."

Lying against him, she rode each deep swell and fall of his chest. "I felt the hunger for blood and the whole struggle. Did you ever learn," she hesitated, "to tame it?"

"There is no taming it." His voice remained flat.

"I meant control it."

"You mean deny it? Yes, but that came centuries later."
Leaning on one elbow, she traced her other hand across the
patch of silky hair on his chest, swirling a few long strands
around her fingertips. "You spared those two women in the
brothel."

"I always spared women and children. Only the Strix were
treated to my wrath, and that's bad enough. The poor fools
never knew anything anyway."

They lay together in silence.

Her emotions did somersaults in her heart. The old Arcona
had done terrible things to Tyr, but he'd learned to minimize
the damage from something as consuming as the Slayer curse.
How many other men could find the strength to pull out of
such a vicious nosedive? In Pompeii, she'd been a willful and
destructive person, but did she still possess the power to
transform others? Was such a thing even an option?

A tiny voice in the back of her mind whispered, *Maybe.*

The clear but unexpected answer jolted her. Like the old days,
were there really voices talking in her head? Was this a good
or bad thing?

It's a good thing. The voice spoke with reassurance. *You've
changed. Power is eternal, and you still have it. Use it.*

Now there were voices in her head with strong opinions?

"Terrific," she muttered.

Tyr stretched his arms overhead. "What's terrific?"

"I'm going to try something."

He looked concerned. "What?"

She stroked the amulet. "I'm going to call on an old friend for
help."

A sleepy smile crossed his lips. "Go ahead."

Using a firm tone, she spoke directly to the great mother goddess from the distant past. "Goddess Nerthus, I take full responsibility for setting events in motion. May I be allowed to see and take on as many of this man's burdens as I safely can so he might be free of them."

Even as she spoke, she questioned where those sentiments had come from. Though she had great respect for the ancient past, she was no pagan goddess worshiper, yet the plea to Nerthus felt completely sincere, as if spoken by a true believer. More than that, her voice was uncharacteristically deep and raspy, as if the original Arcona were speaking her truth. A stab of emotion struck deep in her heart. Could this be *her* redemption too?

With eyes wide, Tyr studied her face. "I know that voice."

"We both do." Tears welled and slid down her cheeks. "She's so sorry for what she did. I can sense it." Leaning close to his throat, she gently kissed the tiny wound she had made with the sharp edge of the amulet. She licked a droplet of blood from his skin.

"I owe you." The words were mumbled so softly she doubted he heard them. A drop of blood floated across her tongue. She swallowed. This dark sacrament carried the echo of the ancient ritual of the sin-eater. A beggar would be invited to partake of a feast set upon a dead man's chest and expected to consume the sacramental meal, to cleanse the deceased of any residual sin they might accidently carry into heaven. This felt no different.

Sin-eater? If only it were so easy. The little voice sounded amused. *Drink it all in. Take the final draft.*

"Tyr, don't try to spare me and wake us too soon. I'm strong enough to do this and I want to. Allow me to see what I need to see, and we'll let it go together." With the tip of her tongue, she swirled another droplet of blood from Tyr's skin. Its slightly metallic flavor went straight to her head. A high-pitched vibration rang through her bones and a rising sense of dizziness left her clutching the bedcovers to keep from falling off the edge of the mattress. It became impossible to remain upright. She wilted on top of Tyr, gripping his shoulders as his life as a Slayer flashed before her eyes.

The intensity of the visions pouring uninterrupted into her mind at ever-increasing speed left her reeling. It felt as if her mind had been stretched and forced to swallow the entire two-thousand-year epic in a single profane mouthful.

As the images slowed they began to make sense, and she saw the world through Tyr's eyes.

He stood on a paved road surrounded on either side by vineyards. The Roman sandals on his feet were the same ones purchased in Pompeii. A white milestone came into view marking the site as the *Via Appia*, the Appian Way. If he continued walking at a steady pace, Rome was several days' journey north.

A drover strolled past, leading a pair of yoked oxen. The young man had curly dark hair that hung in ringlets to his shoulders. The torn collar of his tunic partially exposed his robust, sun-browned chest.

The scent of salt on the man's skin caused Tyr to stop and sniff the air. Blood hunger rose within like an unwelcome but persistent suitor. His hands shook. The brothel keeper had been his last blood feed and every hour his need for more grew stronger.

With stealth, he turned and fell in line with the drover. The clattering bells looped around the oxen's neck covered any sound the crunch of his sandals on stone might have made. Like a wolf stalking its prey, he focused solely on choosing the perfect moment to pounce. He drew nearer.

A loud rumble distracted him. Sharp tremors like the footfalls of an angry giant stomped across the landscape. With deafening force, a plume of smoke thick as tar shot skyward and blotted out daylight. A blast of fire rocked the world and made the pavestones beneath his feet shiver like clamshells shaken on a plate. The ground continued to tremble as a lacy veil of soot darkened the horizon a murky shade of umber. Filtered through a tempest of heavy smoke, a weak sun glowed ruby red and transformed the far landscape into an eerie ghost world.

The drover brought his oxen to a halt, muttering unintelligible words of shock. When he noticed Tyr standing so close behind him, he seemed doubly surprised and gasped. "By all the gods!" He looked thunderstruck. "What has happened?"

What has happened indeed. He fought to compose his shattered nerves. "This is what revenge looks like from a distance." Desolation took hold. Arcona had not been mad after all. The gods truly had spoken through her. A chill passed through his already cold heart. Her prophecy had come to fruition. "Behold the face of the Dark Slayer."

Appearing confused, despair shone in the drover's eyes. "What are talking about?"

"The new gods are angrier than the old ones." Tyr focused on the man. An artery pulsed on the side of the drover's throat, the heartbeat visible, nearly driving him into a frenzy. Should he strike like a viper and take the man down or let him live? He decided to let him live. Sounding far calmer than he felt, he said, "You're headed south. Do you have family there?"

Worry creased the young man's face. "Yes, a wife and two children in Oplontis."

His gums tingled and threatened to descend into fangs. Waving his hand in a dismissive gesture, he shooed the man away. "Go to them."

Urging his spooked oxen forward, the drover hurried onward.

Tyr scraped his palm down his face, trembling from the need for blood. The drover had been spared death by fangs but he was not a lucky man. One tragedy had been averted but another was certain to greet him further south beneath a mantle of ash.

The cloud of black smoke rose heavenward, casting a shadow across the land. Had the people of Pompeii been cooked alive in a cauldron of fire and the city destroyed as Arcona had boasted? Staring skyward, he stood fixed to the spot, a witness to abject horror yet unable to feel anything.

The scene faded. Others quickly followed.

Tyr traveled the Empire looking for Strix to free him from his curse. Sometimes he was a foot soldier marching the wooded hills of Gaul. Other times, he was simply a cloaked stranger in Rome's underworld. His existence was entangled in slaughter and death, yet he remained exempt from it.

For a century or more, he sometimes took up the iron shield and became a gladiator again, always moving from city to city and changing his name with the seasons. As a voluntary, paid combatant who could not perish in the arena, his fortune grew.

One battle bled into the next. Deep down, he hoped the arena would surprise him and provide release. With sword in hand, he'd flirt with death in the most outrageous ways, often turning his back to an armed opponent and pivoting at the last possible moment to strike him down and send the hysterical crowd screaming to their feet. Over time he'd become as addicted to the cheers of his former oppressors as he was to blood, and that too added to his shame.

Eventually, Rome fell. The many roads he used like arteries to reach the next large group of people showed wear and crumbled. He traveled constantly with no home or attachments. Centuries drifted by, everything about the world changing except him. Nearly a millennium passed before he discovered he wasn't alone.

One day, as he trudged through a silent wood, knee-deep in snow, an odd feeling overwhelmed him. A certain scent and electricity hung in the air. He returned to his lonely fortress on the Rhijin. The Romans had abandoned the outpost long ago and parts of the timbered fort had fallen to ruin.

Few dared to confront him due to his reputation as a berserker, a lone warrior too vicious and mad to be reasoned with. Craving privacy as strongly as blood, he did nothing to dissuade people from that opinion.

He opened the heavy oak door to the sole room of the fortress that still possessed a solid roof and four walls. The fire he'd left burning that morning roared, remarkable in itself. Beside the hearth stood an uninvited visitor. A towering man with silvery blond hair plopped himself gracelessly into Tyr's favorite chair.

Enraged at the man's gall, his fangs dropped as he prepared to attack. "That's my chair! Who are you?"

"Your brother." The man had perfect teeth at odds with his mean grin. "I've been waiting all day for you to come home." Clutching a horn-handled knife, he moved his fur cape aside, exposing bare skin, and plunged the blade into his lean torso with a loud grunt. He made a pouting face. "Ow, that stings like a wasp."

Tyr watched in confused revulsion as the burly Norseman with a wicked expression stabbed himself in the gut with a dagger and pulled out the blade with gleeful flourish. He stood frozen in disbelief as the man impaled himself again and again, withdrawing the bloodied dagger with apparently no consequences.

"You're staring, brother." The man's face lit with a sickly smile. "Have you solved the puzzle yet?"

"Upir Likhyi?" Tyr approached with caution. "How?"

"You know how." The man held his hand high and tugged his sleeve down his wrist to reveal a thick silver cuff with a large piece of red amber embedded in it.

Tyr parted his lips in horrified awe. "Where is the Strix who made you? Is she near?"

A brittle laugh broke free of him. "Don't bother looking. I've already killed her."

"Why?" He'd been searching so long. Crushing disappointment consumed him. "She might have known how to reverse the curse."

"Exactly." The man toyed with the knife, twisting it between his fingers. "This is all I've ever wanted to be and so much more. I was born to be a Slayer, and I won't have some fickle woman take that privilege away from me."

Had they misunderstood each other? Did this man with cold, almost colorless eyes actually embrace the curse? "Being a Slayer is a harsh life, brother."

"It's not really a life, is it?" He adjusted his wolfskin cape and stood. His wound had already sealed shut. Only a vicious red scar and a smear of blood betrayed any trauma had taken place. "It's more of a divine calling."

Tyr recoiled. "How did you know I was here?"

"Don't you know when a brother is near?" He grinned. "I always know. I felt your presence in the woods and walked straight to your fort." Tapping the tip of his elegant nose with his finger, he looked smug. "I have a sense for fellow Slayers. You're a firstborn or master Slayer, aren't you?"

He nodded. "Yes." He was in awe that there were others like him walking the earth. Perhaps other Slayers had escaped the wrath of Mount Vesuvius or the zealous demon hunts to purge them after the fall of Rome.

Tyr reached for the hilt of his sword and drew it from the scabbard. "Are we to do battle?"

"No. I've come to follow you and learn."

The breath rushed from his lungs. "Why would you follow me?"

The man's eyes lit with keen interest. "How old are you?"

"I'm not certain," he answered uneasily. Was it wise to have this conversation with a stranger? "I'm far older than this Roman fort."

The man rolled his eyes and bowed in mock reverence. "You're immortal. I'm not. At least, not yet. I was made a Slayer only this autumn as an afterthought. In disgust, I watched my maker, my Strix, destroy her firstborn. Her callous actions convinced me I had to kill her before she turned on me."

Hope rose. "How did she kill him?" He sounded breathless.

"No, no, no." He wagged a finger in the air. "I'm not telling. You'll have to earn that morsel of knowledge. I don't want to die—ever. I need a brother to fight at my back. We could help each other." The man wiped the bloodied knife on his leather leggings and sheathed it. "I've come to invite you to the games. My name is Varn. I served in the Varangian Guard in Byzantium. There are still a few of us in the north."

He'd been alone for so long he knew nothing of this. "Upir Likhyi?"

"Slayers," Varn corrected. "Our numbers are not great, but that could change. Another foolish Strix might come along who's stupid enough to believe she's going to make pets of raging, blood-drinking warriors."

Tyr's blade remained pointed at Varn's throat. "What sort of games are you talking about?"

"Odin's games. A wild hunt of wanted men for fun and profit." Varn's gaze swept over Tyr. "You can play on Mars's team if it makes you feel more comfortable, old man."

The discipline of the ludus remained deeply engrained in him. "What are the rules?"

"This is high-stakes blood sport for the entertainment of kings and gods. We're blades for hire. There are no rules." He shrugged. "Why not? What else would you do with these long winter days, spend them knitting?"

Lonely for company of any caliber, Tyr agreed. "When do we start?"

"Now."

* * * *

Arcona woke from the trance state. She sat astride Tyr, shivering as if hypothermia had set in, unable to breathe or think clearly; both were too painful. Too much had been taken in too quickly.

Tyr opened his eyes. "What's wrong?" In a panic, he grabbed hold of her and rolled her onto her back. "Arcona, are you all right?" Worry furrowed his brow. "Say something!"

Her lips parted, but she couldn't speak. Her thoughts were a scattered blur of Slayer images and bloodied battlefields. The carnage was more than she could stomach. Centuries of bloodshed pressed down so oppressively she could barely draw breath.

Tyr scooped her into his arms and lifted her off the bed. "Arcona, what have you done? My memories are not yours to bear. I'd never ask you to do it."

He darted into the small bathroom and turned on the shower while still holding her close. Water streamed from the faucet. "Please have warm water," he mumbled.

She gulped shallow gasps, her first breaths in what felt like an eternity. Her lungs burned. It hurt but she fought to take a deeper breath. Racing glimpses of violence and warfare throughout time left her head spinning. Slowing her thoughts proved impossible as a terrifying collage of exotic places and appalling acts on a titanic scale overwhelmed her.

Tyr had participated in and witnessed a lot. The historian in her wanted to capture and possess each and every memory, but it was just too devastating to absorb. A whimper of surrender crossed her lips.

"Thank God you're breathing." Tyr tested the stream of water with his fingertips. "It's getting warmer."

"What are you doing?" She was finally able to speak.

"I'm going to try to wash some of it away before it does any permanent damage to you."

She scoffed. "I don't think soap and water will rinse the guilt away."

"Don't laugh; these enchantments are clingy and strange. Sometimes, the smallest things can disturb them." He frowned as he stripped his pants off and then began to undress her.

Batting at his hands, she pulled away. "What are you doing?"

"Don't talk." His words were gruff. "Take off your clothes."

"I'll pretend you said that a lot nicer than you did."

A wild mix of emotions displayed on his face, but mostly he looked pissed off. "You had no business taking on so many of my memories. I accepted your blessing, but not this. If I'd realized what you were doing, I would never have allowed it." He unbuttoned her jeans and slid them down her legs. Locking his arms around her, he dragged her under the warm shower spray. "It could have killed you."

"But it didn't." Defiance made her sound braver than she felt. "I don't regret it. I think I was meant to do it. I was the Strix. I started this, and I have to make it right."

"How?" Tyr looked confused. "It's already happened, and it will never be right."

* * * *

Water streamed down on them, drenching their hair. The shower stall became steamy. Tyr held Arcona close under the torrent of warm water, feeling genuine worry, irritation, and very loving toward her all in the same moment. It had been so long since he'd cared in this way about another, he almost didn't recognize what was happening.

He was used to the single-minded goals of a Slayer—make battle, kill, and feed. The rites of Mars were demanding and merciless. The many complexities of love were never present. This was so different.

The emotions he had for Arcona were varied and hard to identify or tease apart. Confusing as hell, but it still felt good. A quiet laugh slipped past his lips. It had been a long time since he had laughed with any sense of joy.

"What's so funny?" Arcona turned toward him.

"Are you feeling better?" Tyr moved back and allowed her to stand beneath the lion's share of warm water. The amulet glistened against her skin.

"My head's not spinning like a carnival ride anymore. The images are still awful, but they've died down to a manageable roar. I can almost deal with them." Arcona reached toward him and traced slow, looping lines across his chest with her fingertip. "Your crazy idea worked. Standing in the shower did make me feel better." She paused. "But the memories aren't exactly washing away. I sense a subtle shift. They're not driving me mad like they were. It's as if I can choose to stand back and observe them without getting pulled into them."

"Really?" Tyr leaned his head under the spray and kissed her wet hair. The warm water felt heavenly on his skin. Having a beautiful naked woman within arm's reach wasn't bad either. "I'm not sure what you did, but I feel lighter. Whatever you did, whatever passed between us.... I don't know how to say it, but I think it did me some good. I feel amazing."

"You look amazing." She cupped her hands beside his temples. "There's a different light in your eyes." Leaning close, she brushed the tip of her nose against his. "Tonight was a strange experience to share. I crossed a huge gulf of time. Now I know almost everything about you and you know more about me." She hesitated. "Did you experience any of that or am I just imagining it?"

He felt all that and so much more. "There's always more to know, isn't there?" There were no words for the transformation he'd undergone. For certain, she'd changed him. The difference between his existence as a Slayer and how he felt now was night and day, and beyond comparison.

Lifting her into his arms, he pressed her against the warm tile wall. "Do you know what I want to do to you right now, and keep on doing?"

She wrapped her legs around his hips and clung to him. "Tell me."

"Let's do what I've wanted to do for two thousand years." He guided his cock between her thighs. Looking hopeful, he paused. "Do you want me?"

"Yes. But can you? Won't it just frustrate you?"

"I don't care it if does." The soft tone of Arcona's voice and the loving look on her face melted his heart. She'd willingly drunk in his worst moments and unburdened him from their poisonous residue. He needed to show her with body and soul what he had no words for. "It has to be you, Arcona. I don't want anyone else."

Gazing into his eyes, she pressed against him. "You're going to express gratitude for my courage and ingenuity in our bizarre situation by fucking me senseless?"

Anticipation of how good she would feel wrapped around him brought him right to the edge. "Something like that."

"Thank you." She smiled. Tilting her hips forward, she gently guided him closer.

Breathless, he slid inside her and moved his hips slowly, giving her a chance to stretch and accommodate him. The initial sensations of gripping heat were so sweet he closed his eyes and drank in every scintillating moment of contact. His overstimulated senses reeled. Rocking his hips, he was eager to know if he could climax inside her the way he used to and prayed he could. Every instinct raging through his body told him it was possible. He ached to start thrusting, but he didn't. This was for her enjoyment, too. In a stunning moment of passion, he realized he was thinking of her first and liked how it felt.

Loving contact and the hope of sexual release were things he'd never thought he'd enjoy again, but here it was, full-blown bliss, better than anything he could remember, and he was getting it between Arcona's thighs of all places. It seemed so unlikely, but it was true; his nemesis was now his redeemer. Explain that?

She brushed a light kiss against his lips. "You feel wonderful." He opened his eyes; her gaze was already locked on his. "This is so good." His voice became rough as he moved faster. As he pressed her against the slippery tile, he thought he'd lose his mind from bliss and could hardly believe he was free to take this much pleasure without causing harm or drawing blood. "Hold on to me."

Arcona locked her arms around his shoulders. Ecstasy radiated on her face. She closed her eyes and allowed her head to tip back. Her unintentional yet provocative display bared her slender throat and the faded bruises left by Varn. In the past, the sight of an exposed throat at close quarters would have triggered a moral-shattering guilt-inducing attack on his victim, but not this time.

Something within him had changed; he wanted her now simply because. His heart opened and flooded with once familiar feelings. This Arcona was a lighter soul with a kind heart willing to share everything with him. An undeniable connection had been made. They had found each other again and forgiven the wrongs each had done. The lost world of just being a man and loving another reopened and the parched landscape of his soul flooded with an overwhelming sense of gratitude.

Taking long, slow strokes, he moved with her, enjoying every second. This was real. While floating in breathtaking moments of pleasure, a blinding climax snuck up on him. First scorching hot shock and then joy rushed through every cell as he clutched tight to her hips and finished. Throwing his head back, he released a victorious growl that echoed against the tiles.

Through every last shudder of pleasure, she caressed his back and covered his face with kisses, making the moment perfect. Beneath the shower spray, they pressed close each panting. Her gaze met his. "I don't need to ask, do I?"

His throat tightened with emotion. The act had been better than anything he ever remembered, made all the more wonderful by sharing it with her. He tried to speak but couldn't.

She held him tight with a beautiful smile on her face.

"Thank you," he muttered. Words were so inadequate.

"What happens now?" A bit of fear crept into her voice.

"I don't know." This was so unexpected. Had he been selfish? Could there be repercussions? He was out of his depth. "I know modern women have ways to… you know…."

Her face paled. "I don't know? Just say it."

"Have ways to avoid pregnancy. I hope you don't think I'll behave dishonorably."

"Holy crap! We didn't use a condom. You're two-freaking-thousand years old; I didn't think we needed to. What was I thinking?"

He kissed her forehead. "It's all right. I have wealth. I can support many children."

"Tyr, I'm not breeding stock."

Was she angry or worried? He couldn't tell. "I'm just trying to be responsible." Wanting to stay inside her for as long as possible, he pressed her body against the shower wall and hoisted her higher but stopped when his arms trembled from strain. "You feel heavy," he whispered in surprise.

Her eyes opened wide. "What?"

"Not in a bad way." He carefully lowered her to the floor and stared at his shaking forearms. "I just meant I could feel your true weight."

Looking irritated, she turned off the faucet. "Do I want to hear this? Perfect moment — ruined."

"That's not what I meant to do. Varn is six-foot-three and solid muscle. I threw him twelve feet into the air."

She crossed her arms in front of her. "Okay, I see your point."

"Now my arms ache after holding you for a few minutes. What does that mean? Along with all the good changes that are happening, I don't seem to be as strong as I was. Maybe this is the beginning of my real death?" He pressed his palm against his belly and his stomach rumbled. "I feel lightheaded and empty, too."

A crooked half smile appeared. "I think you need to eat."

"I don't eat." His stomach growled in contradiction.

"Maybe you do now. You can try it. I'm hungry, too. Why don't we get dressed and find someplace that's open and get a hamburger, breakfast, anything."

"Hamburgers? I've heard constant talk of them."

"Because they're great. Actually, I should have said cheeseburger. They're even better."

Arcona grabbed a plush towel off the top of the stack and dabbed her skin dry. "I'm chilly, and I want to get dressed. Where are we anyway? I know everyone's trying to save money these days, but this is ridiculous. They certainly keep this hotel on the cool side. A little heat would be nice."

A stab of guilt made him break eye contact. "It's not really a hotel." He stalled, trying to think of the best way to explain matters. "When I discovered I couldn't drive you past Salem city limits without the amulet burning you, I turned around and went to the first place I saw."

"So where are we?" Her tone was innocent.

"I broke into a construction site. We're in an unfinished bed-and-breakfast."

Her face blanched. "What do you mean, you broke in? Are we trespassing?"

"Yes."

"Oh my God!" She looked panicked. "We used the shower, messed up the bed, and we...all over the place." She opened the bathroom door and darted into the bedroom that still glowed by the light of a smoldering fire. "We're vagrants. Let's get out of here before we get arrested."

He laughed. "I do this all the time. I never get caught."

"I don't do this kind of thing at all because it's wrong." She rummaged beside the bed, looking for as many discarded bits of her clothing as she could find. "I'll have to give this bed-and-breakfast a really great rating when they open." She struggled into her discarded jeans and sweater. "Where's my coat?"

He pointed to a delicate turn-legged chair. "Over there, beneath my leather jacket, which you're welcome to wear."

Arcona grabbed her trench coat and slipped her arms into the sleeves. "Hurry." She turned to confront him. "Put your clothes on so we can leave."

She grabbed hold of a hair dryer attached to the bathroom wall, turned it on, and gave her damp hair a burst of warm air while she stepped into her boots.

Padding naked into the bedroom, he dressed halfheartedly, already wishing he could tumble her back onto the warm bed and take his time with her. "I rushed in the shower." He glanced at her sideways, wondering what she was thinking. "I owe you one, sweet and slow."

Shouting above the drone of the dryer, she flipped her hair. "I can't believe I fucked a gladiator. I've got a coworker or two who would be so jealous if they knew."

The playful joy in her voice left him beaming. "I wouldn't tell them if I were you."

A bright smile burst across her face as she leaned down to zip her boot. "I'd be happy to take a rain check someplace where we aren't breaking and entering." She turned off the dryer and set it back on its holder.

Tyr dressed quickly, pulled on his boots, and grabbed his coat. He walked toward her and offered his hand. "Let's go."

For a moment, she hesitated and merely gazed at his outthrust hand. "Isn't it odd that a few hours ago we were complete strangers and yet we were never really strangers? We had a hidden history all along. It's weird and overwhelming if you think about it."

Surprised by how alarmed he felt when she didn't immediately take his hand, he stilled. He had already begun to consider her *his*. "Do I still feel like a stranger?"

"No." She grasped his hand.

"I should ask." He dreaded the next question. "Do you have a man in your life? Is there someone at home you care for?"

Appearing uncomfortable, she glanced at the wall, the floor, anywhere but his face. "There's no one."

They were both alone in the world and needed each other. He was relieved and too terrified to say anything more that might frighten her away. The old-world Dacian in him felt possessive and wanted to demand a promise or some sort of oath from her, agreeing she was his and only his, but he caught himself with the silent reminder women of this era would not appreciate such an attitude.

He pulled her close. "I'll walk ahead. The inn is dark, and I don't want to turn on any lights that would be visible from the street." Striding into the hallway, he slammed the toe of his boot against a table. "Ouch." He winced. "I didn't see that."

She huddled close. "It's so dark in this corner. How can you see anything at all?"

He'd seen everything on the way in and always saw well in the dark, but not now. Squinting into the blackness, he was going to have to do what everyone else did — go slow and feel his way along. Taking hold of the banister, he descended the first flight of stairs with Arcona clinging to his free hand. There was a patch of moonlight on the next flight that made the descent easier.

"The moon's still up?" Arcona mumbled. "What time is it? I thought it was nearly dawn."

In his early days as a Slayer, he'd liked the anonymity darkness provided and preferred to hunt and ambush men at night. Night was his ally, and he'd always had a strong sense of the approaching dawn. "It's about two o'clock, but no later than three. Sunrise is hours away."

"Is that all? It feels like an eternity has passed."

"It has." He laughed.

They descended the last flight of stairs and headed toward the rear of the inn.

"Do you know where you're going?"

"Yes," Tyr lied, his voice calm as he turned a doorknob and pushed the door open, hoping he wasn't opening a closet and leading her inside. When he found himself in the kitchen facing the back door he muttered a quiet, "Thank God."

He opened the door and looked around. The night was still and the damp chill of ocean fog rolled toward them threatening to blot out the brightest stars. An odd tingle prickled the hair on his arms, so he paused at the inn's narrow back porch, searching the darkness for movement.

"Is something wrong?" Arcona crowded closer.

"No," he lied again, not wanting to alarm her. Over the centuries, he'd perfected the art of sensing when danger was near, and he sensed it now, but where? He couldn't get a fix on it. His gaze swept the stacked pallets of lumber and the shadowy tangle of willow groves beyond, but he didn't see anything suspicious.

"Look." She pointed. "There's a lit diner down the road. I thought we were in the middle of nowhere. There're a couple of eighteen-wheelers parked in front, and if the food's good enough for truck drivers, it's good enough for me. I'm not nearly as picky." She stepped off the porch and headed toward the restaurant.

His first instinct was to yank Arcona back and fling his body between her and the diner as if he were a shield. "Be careful."

A startled expression crossed her face. "Is there something you're not telling me?"

He scanned the surroundings, unable to pinpoint any possible source of threat. "No."

"We were doing great. We were talking, and we'd established some trust." She looked disappointed. "Is this going to get weird again? I hope not. I just want something to eat first."

He set his anxiety aside and smiled. "Then let's go." He put his arm around her shoulder.

"Should we take the car?"

"No." At the moment, his Mustang, painted the same glaring shade of yellow as an angry hornet, was well hidden from view behind a dumpster. For all he knew, other Slayers sympathetic to Varn could be combing the streets of Salem, looking for him, or more accurately, looking for Arcona, the last fabled Strix. Why had he been so foolish as to include Varn in his plans? "Let's leave the car where it is for now." With his arm locked around her, he held her tight until they walked away from the wooded area that had triggered his suspicion.

Chapter Thirteen

On the brisk quarter-mile walk to the diner, nothing was said. The only sound to disrupt the silence was the quiet crunch of gravel beneath their boots. Soon the rumble of an idling truck engine and lights in the diner window filled the night with cheerful signs of life long before they actually reached it.

"I have to ask." Arcona squeezed Tyr's hand. "Back in Pompeii, what happened the day I died?"

It hurt to think about that day now and he did not want to dwell there but he owed her some closure. "When the games were over and the crowds were still crazed, Marius had you bound, brushed with oil, and dragged into the middle of the arena. In front of everyone, he ripped the amulet from your neck. I'll never forget the conflicted torment on his face. In his own horrible way, he believed he loved you, too. With tears trickling down his cheeks, he begged you to deny your acts or ask for forgiveness but you wouldn't. You remained defiant and shouted curses about the Dark Slayer's imminent arrival.

"The evidence of what you'd done was everywhere. The trainers were quick to point an accusing finger at you, especially after Marius flogged everyone to extract confessions. He was so humiliated he lit the pyre himself.

"Marius would have sent me to the pyre with you, except Lucius Caspar Sulla, the magistrate, forbade it. The gladiators of Lupus Unguis were the heroes of the games. Sulla feared if we were punished, the city would turn on him. I was given my freedom and allowed to watch from a safe distance."

Arcona looked straight ahead as she spoke. "I've had a lifelong phobia of being burned alive. Coming to Salem and constantly being reminded of witch persecutions really set me off. Since I was a kid, the image of a burning woman has terrified me." A sad smile crossed her lips. "There's something liberating about knowing it's over. It's already happened and all I have to do is acknowledge it and let it go." She shrugged. "Of course, I can't tell anyone about it. They'd think I was bat-shit crazy, but somehow it's a relief to know I don't have to worry about it anymore."

They approached the tiny diner, which appeared no larger than a railroad car. Despite the late hour, there were a fair number of customers inside, most of them perched atop steel column stools lining a single countertop. No one did more than glance up from their heaped plates of food as Tyr and Arcona entered.

The low ceiling was steeply curved and paneled in wood. The walls were covered in utilitarian white porcelain sheeting. The diner resembled a ship's cabin, and in a harbor town such as Salem the decor seemed appropriate. The retro-style interior was clean and beautifully preserved but appeared as if it had remained untouched and unimproved since WWII.

Once inside, the curved ceiling made the diner feel smaller than it actually was, and Tyr had to crouch as he walked toward one of the half-dozen small booths lining the window side of the aisle. "Feels like a ludus barracks in here."

"Hush." She patted his back.

"Coffee?" A blonde waitress with her hair neatly scraped back in a pink rubber band approached and motioned for them to sit at the middle booth.

"Yes, please." Arcona sat.

Tyr slid onto the seat on the low side of the curved ceiling, feeling cramped by his height. He realized that was why all the other men had chosen to sit at the counter where the ceiling was tallest. Turning toward Arcona, he asked, "Would you like to sit at the counter?" He hoped she would.

"No." Arcona settled into the seat. "I like sitting in a booth. It's cozy."

His elbow struck the wall. The booth was a little too cozy. She was happy, though; so he bit his lip and said nothing.

The waitress set two coffee mugs on the table and poured. "We serve breakfast all night." She had a hoarse voice that wavered and cracked on the *K* in breakfast.

"I suppose that means no cheeseburgers." Arcona sounded disappointed.

"Sorry." The waitress shook her head. Her baggy brown velour jogging suit left her looking like a cuddly carnival-prize teddy bear. "But the grilled cheese is really tasty."

Arcona glanced at Tyr. "I think we need to look at a menu." The waitress grabbed two menus off the countertop and set them on the table. "I'll be right back." She walked away to check on an order.

Arcona picked up a small ceramic pitcher and poured cream into both cups of coffee. "Try it. It's good with sugar." She dumped several spoonfuls of sugar into hers. "I gave blood. I'm not counting calories today."

Tyr grasped the menu and looked it over, overwhelmed by the columns of tiny type. He wondered how such a small place could possibly offer so many choices. He squinted at the blurred type and held it at arm's length.

"Do you need some help reading it?" Arcona whispered.

He shook his head. "I read eight languages. I have libraries full of books." He moved the laminated card farther from his face. "I just can't read this." He tipped his head and squinted at the menu once more. "Damn, my eyes won't focus."

"Maybe you need glasses?"

His identity as a keen-eyed hunter was being challenged and he did not like it. "Eyeglasses? Never."

She lightly brushed her fingertips across his hand. "You'd look very scholarly in the right frames. In fact, you'd rock a nicely tailored suit, too. It's something to consider."

The minuscule type danced in front of his eyes and provoked a headache. "I give up." He handed the menu to Arcona. "You choose."

She scanned the selections. "It all sounds good. I don't think we can go wrong here."

The waitress returned. "What would you like?"

Arcona quickly sipped her coffee before answering. "Two 'everything' omelets with, of course, everything, home fries, and two large orange juices."

The waitress scribbled it down. "Coming right up." She turned and walked away.

Tyr waited until the waitress was beyond earshot. "I certainly hope the food won't be 'coming right up.' My last meal was roast mutton and barley gruel, but that was two millennia ago. I'm not sure what my stomach can handle, and I have no idea what to expect. What exactly is an 'everything' omelet?"

"It's a surprise wrapped in eggs." Her tone was droll.

"Ah." He was profoundly disappointed with her choice of breakfast, but he didn't want her to know it.

She picked up the thick ceramic mug and sipped with a content expression on her face. "What do you think of the coffee?"

He tasted it. The liquid was so shockingly bitter he recoiled. "You drink this every day?"

"I love it." She gazed out the window onto the dark street. "I must have a cup first thing in the morning or else I'm a grouch." She turned and seemed to study his face.

He found it flattering that she seemed so interested in introducing him to her world. Lifting the mug to his lips, he dared a second sip and winced. "This is an acquired taste, isn't it?"

Reaching across the table, she picked up the tiny pitcher and poured half its contents into his coffee mug. "Cream buffers the bitter." She smiled and a tiny dimple appeared on the side of her cheek. "You mentioned you have a library. Really? I was picturing a wobbling stack of books on a nightstand sort of setup."

"I take my books seriously." He laughed. "My brownstone in Boston has a beautiful mahogany-lined library. That's where I keep most of my first edition books."

"Mahogany? That's a rare wood these days."

"It wasn't in 1893, when I had the library installed."

Her hands cradled the mug, absorbing the heat as it radiated off the thick porcelain. For some unfathomable reason he found the gesture so endearing. "Besides the Brontë sisters, what else do you read?"

"I read a bit of everything. Jules Verne and Robert Lewis Stevenson are favorites. I like science and mechanical journals, too. I'll read anything with an engine schematic."

She tucked a strand of hair behind her ear and toyed with it. "You can figure all that out?"

"I have the time."

Arcona sipped her coffee with such elegance. "Do you read history?"

"Not much." He chuckled. "What's the point? So much of it is unpleasant or inaccurate. It's never how they say it was. I've read a lot that just made me angry."

"I thought so." She wagged a finger in the air. "I work in UCLA's antiquities research department. We date, identify, and authenticate artifacts from all over the world, but sometimes all we can do is take a guess at exactly how some of these objects were used or what they really mean. I was just thinking how invaluable you'd be as a research partner. I'll bet you'd have a whole other take on things. Having your opinion would be fantastic."

Straightening in the booth, he nearly bumped his head on the curved ceiling. "You want to put me to work?"

"Maybe." Her eyes gleamed. "If you want to."

"I can tell what you're thinking, and the answer's no. I've already been enslaved to the Roman Empire and the gods of war. I'm not going to be enslaved in a research department, sitting in a tiny cubicle with a pair of glasses perched on my nose, studying musty old things."

She giggled. "You are a musty old thing."

He froze.

"I'm joking. Your experience and what you've seen of the world would be such a unique gift."

"And how would I explain this 'unique gift' to the historical research world? I can't afford to be too honest, can I?" He flashed her a side eye. "Arcona, you've offered me a 'gift' before, and that didn't work out so well. Remember?"

Setting the mug aside, she reached for his hand. "This time it will be completely your choice. Do only what you want."

Leaning forward onto his elbows, he looked into her eyes that were the same calm shade of green as desert sage. "Who knows how long I'm here for? I've already begun to change so quickly. My corneas are already shot. I shouldn't make plans. I could be dead by sunrise."

Her brows knit. "Dear God, let's hope not."

"Excuse me." The waitress set two glasses of fresh orange juice on the table and smiled anxiously before walking away.

"I wonder how much she overheard." Arcona glanced over her shoulder to make sure no one else was listening or near. She leaned across the table. "What if you don't die, at least not right away? How will you live your life? Are you going to take part in the modern world or just ignore it?"

"If it's my time to die, I won't fight it." Instinctively, he picked up a table knife and tested its sharpness with a tap of his thumb. The round tip of the blade was so dull as to be useless as a weapon. "I've already been everywhere and seen most everything. I just want to enjoy a normal life, if it's offered. *Normal* is the one thing I haven't tried."

She sipped the orange juice and squinted. "God, that's sour." Setting the glass down, she gently pushed it away. "Does anything special interest you?"

He tasted the juice and frowned. "It's too sweet. I don't care for it." Immediately, he reached for the coffee mug and took another sip. "I think I could get used to this. It's bitter, but I like how it makes me feel — really alert." He gulped more. "I'll admit some of the modern world is interesting. I love the muscle cars. I did all the work on my Mustang by myself. Back in my arena days, I could have made good use of a tricked-out V-8. The crowd would have loved it."

She laughed and her entire face lit. Despite a rough night, she still looked pretty and bright-eyed.

He swept his palm through the air. "You wouldn't believe how quickly all of this, everything you see, will crumble or vanish. Even the things that seem so important will be antiques or curiosities before you know it. Most of it will be forgotten. That's the nature of the world. Things pop into existence and then slowly fade away, and no one notices."

She clutched the coffee mug. "Like Strix and Slayers?"

"Exactly. I think Strix and Slayers should fade away. The world doesn't need them anymore. It's an unfortunate fact that Slayers don't stop being Slayers unless someone takes their heads."

"What happens to Strix? Should I be worried? Don't you think it's interesting only the women were given the power to grant immortality, yet they were denied it themselves? Did you ever find a living Strix?"

"No. I only met desperate women who thought they were Strix." He looked away. "Real Strix led brief, violent lives, and most died at the hands of someone they'd turned."

"That's very sad."

"In the past, you wouldn't have thought so. You would have blustered about sacrifice and glory." His gaze returned to her. "You've changed."

"It was a difficult situation then." Arcona set the coffee mug down and crossed her arms in front of her in a defensive manner. "I believed I was doing the right thing, and I did it wholeheartedly."

"Actually, you did it heartlessly, and that was the biggest part of the problem." He still sounded wounded and that surprised him.

"I'm glad you brought it up. Let's get it out in the open. I know you're still angry with *her*." Arcona's gaze locked on him. "But are you angry with me?"

He gripped the edge of the table as if he feared falling into the abyss. "I don't want to be angry with either of you."

"Good, because the old Arcona's not running the show anymore; I am, and I won't tolerate violent gloating crap anchored in the past."

A tense laugh burst out of him. "That's a lucky coincidence, because I think I'm finished with violent gloating crap, too."

"What's happening here? You seem so changed." Her shaky smile betrayed her nervous tension. "Which is every woman's dream, by the way, to see a man change for the better. Do you know of any scenario where a Strix or a Slayer stopped being what they were and moved forward without anyone facing a hideous death?"

His mouth drew taut. He didn't.

The waitress approached with two plates heaped high with food delicately balanced on her forearm. "Here you are — two 'everything' omelets with home fries. Enjoy." She set the steaming plates on the table.

Arcona glanced at the waitress. "Thank you."

The waitress scooted away from the table with a troubled expression.

"Oh, dear." Arcona frowned. "We've got to talk softer. I think we're creeping out that poor woman." Looking at the steaming plate of food with admiration, she slid it closer. "I hope you'll like it." She reached for a tiny bottle of pepper sauce, unscrewed the green cap, and dribbled scarlet liquid over the top of her omelet.

"What is that?" Tyr pointed suspiciously at the red droplets that looked exactly like blood.

"It's a spicy condiment from Louisiana." She stabbed a fork into the bulging omelet. "It makes the food taste *hot*."

He gingerly touched a fingertip to the steaming omelet. "I don't understand; the food is already quite hot. Why make it hotter?"

"Hot flavor, not temperature. It makes your tongue burn. I'd skip the pepper sauce on your first meal if I were you. Some people can't handle it. Try it another time." She bit into her omelet and looked consumed by bliss. "Wow, this is so good. Smoky. Tangy. There's cheddar cheese, bacon, ham, mushrooms, spinach, tomatoes — everything's in here."

Having never tried any of those things he had only a general idea what she was talking about. Feeling vaguely offended by her comment, he snatched the bottle of pepper sauce off the table and sprinkled it over his omelet with a heavy hand until the top was glossy red. "Why would you think I can't handle it? I'm Dacian; we're made of leather and iron."

He thrust his fork into the omelet several times, trying to get used to wielding such a delicate utensil, and finally speared a decent-sized portion of food.

"Be careful," Arcona mumbled through a mouthful of omelet. "Have some orange juice ready."

He pushed the sauce-soaked forkful into his mouth. In an instant, his tongue sizzled in torment and his face flushed. Perspiration beaded on his brow. His sinuses burned as if he had inhaled fire, the searing sensations in his mouth building until they were excruciating. "Holy Mother Nerthus!" he roared.

The startled occupants of the diner halted what they were doing and turned toward Tyr.

"Are you okay?" The waitress peeked from behind a coffeemaker with wide eyes.

"I'm fine." Tyr grinned. "It's delicious." And it was. The moment the pain died down from the initial burn, he wanted more. Pain and good food was an odd craving to experience. "I like this pepper sauce." He sprinkled more on the omelet. "They need to put it in bigger bottles."

"They do." Arcona laughed. "Try the home fries; they're wonderful."

He tasted the fries with relish. They were crispy golden on the outside and moist on the inside, with a seasoned salty crust flecked with fragrant herbs. Glancing up from the plate, he saw Arcona was enthralled, watching his reactions to the food. It was strangely reassuring to see she was so fascinated by everything he did. He was curious to know more about her. "Why doesn't a smart, kind woman like you have a mate?"

"I was married," she answered with quiet unease. "But we divorced a year and a half ago."

He speared a chunk of ham and brought it to his lips. "Was he a poor provider?"

"No, that wasn't the problem."

The ham melted in his mouth. How had he lived for so long in the same world as ham and not known of these things? Tragic. "Did you care for him?"

"Yes, of course. I married him for love's sake. Nobody forced me."

"Why would you let go of a mate? I know it happens, but I don't understand it."

"My husband was a professor at another university. He'd been married before and already had two grown children. He wanted me to join his life, but he wasn't too crazy about a few things I wanted."

"Like what?"

"I was much younger than he was and ready to settle down. I wanted a house with a fenced-in backyard, pets, and children. He wanted to live abroad and travel to archeological digs six months of the year, and he definitely didn't want the responsibility of caring for a newborn on the remote Mongolian steppes. He made it very clear only after we were married that he didn't want any more children. I thought he might change his mind, but he didn't."

She shrugged. "I learned my lesson. People don't change their minds about the big stuff. We had a breathtaking courtship and a really miserable two-year marriage. I think we were both relieved when it ended."

Arcona stared out the window. Her own reflection looked back. "A weird thought just occurred to me. You know what's funny? My ex's name was Mario. It sounds suspiciously close to Marius, doesn't it? It makes me wonder how tangled the big mystery is. If Mario was the same soul as Marius, he wasn't perfect in this life, but he certainly was a big improvement over Marius. I wonder…."

Tyr dunked a fry into a crimson puddle of pepper sauce and swirled it around, mopping every last bit of liquid on the plate. "I think he was a fool."

"Thank you. I think so, too." Arcona glanced over her shoulder and tilted her mug toward the waitress. "May I have some more coffee, please?"

The waitress walked toward them holding a freshly brewed pot. She carefully refilled both coffee mugs.

Arcona reached for the pitcher of cream. Her grip slipped, and she accidently sloshed cream onto her lap. "Damn!" She grabbed a napkin and blotted it. "Why did I do that?" She glanced at the waitress. "Where's your ladies' room?"

"We have just one bathroom." The waitress pointed toward the front door. "It's a bit of a hike. Walk out the front door, go around the back, and climb down the stairs. The bathroom is at the bottom of the stairwell, but the light switch is inside."

Arcona rose. "I'll be right back."

He slid to the edge of the seat, prepared to follow.

The waitress looked panicky as she took a step toward the door.

Arcona gave him a gentle push back into the seat. "You'd better stay. Our waitress thinks we're going to dine and dash."

"Dine and dash?"

"Eat but not pay," she whispered. "After our little bed-and-breakfast adventure, let's not draw any unnecessary attention to us that would cause someone to call the cops. Okay? I'll just be a minute."

"Be quick, or I'll come and get you." He remained in the booth.

Two men seated at the counter looked at Arcona with interest as she passed.

Tyr felt a distinct stab of jealousy. One man who wore a Red Sox cap and jacket especially provoked him. He appraised Arcona's curves with wolflike eyes.

Part of him desired an immediate end to the insult and longed to bolt from his seat and strangle the man for committing such an offense, but by some miracle in this night of miracles, he managed to control his Dacian temper and stay put.

Instead, he took another sip of coffee, barely able to believe that if he chose to, he had control over his impulses. He didn't have to strike at or slaughter anybody if he didn't want to. He could ignore harmless behavior and sip coffee or eat home fries and the gods of war didn't scream for revenge. He liked this new horizon.

* * * *

Arcona stepped into the cold night, cursing herself for not bringing a coat with her. The moon had sunk below the tree line and provided little light to the gravel parking lot and dark woods beyond. Crunching dry leaves while unable to clearly see where she was headed added to the creepy atmosphere.

She turned the corner and groaned. The stairwell behind the diner was narrow, steep, and lit with a single glaring bulb that illuminated upward instead of downward where light was needed, leaving the stairwell cast in shadow.

"Do they want a lawsuit?" She hesitated to take the first step into darkness.

A branch snapped in the woods.

Startled, she looked behind her but there was nothing there. With a burst of nervous energy, she darted down the steps, deciding to just get it over with, but it was a mistake. The farther she descended, the more claustrophobic the stairwell became. The bathroom wasn't even at the bottom; she had to enter a dark little foyer and feel her way along the wall for the doorknob and the light switch. By the time she'd entered the bathroom and turned on the light, her pulse pounded in her ears with the fervor of a marching band.

The overhead light in the bathroom shone a ghastly yellow. She opted not to look in the mirror to avoid getting upset. Unzipping her jeans, she tugged them down and hovered above the edge of the toilet seat to pee.

Something made a weird scraping sound against the bathroom door.

"Who's there? Tyr, is that you?" She prayed it was.

No one answered.

In record time, she finished and pulled her pants up. She rushed toward the sink to wash her hands and rinse the spilled cream from her pants leg, but there wasn't much cream to worry about. She even considered just leaving it alone and bolting up the stairs and back into the diner, where it was well lit, safe, and within arm's reach of Tyr.

There was another harsh scratch at the base of the door.

Tension rippled down her spine. "Stop it!" she shouted as she turned off the faucet. "If you're out there, say so!"

Silence followed.

How was she going to get past whoever or whatever was out there? Her anxiety rose. Walking away by herself had been a bad idea. She was trapped alone down here and should have brought Tyr to stand guard at the door. Now what?

She stared at the crack beneath the door for what felt like ages, but nothing happened. There were no more suspicious noises, but her heart beat like a rabbit's.

A sound akin to the brittle scrape of fingernails grazed the door. She froze.

Tonight, the world had revealed itself to be an inexplicably strange and disturbing place. Nothing would ever be the same. In her new reality, the only place that felt safe was next to Tyr, and she longed to get back to him.

"I can't stand it." She flung the door open, expecting a confrontation with God knew what, but was greeted by a light whirlwind stirring dry leaves in a merry circle at the bottom of the stairwell.

Groaning with relief, she stomped her boot on the largest claw-shaped leaf, crushing it to crumbs in the sprint toward the staircase. Flying up the steps as fast as possible, she ran back inside the diner with her heart thumping in her throat.

"Is everything all right?" The waitress looked at her with concern.

She offered the waitress a curt nod. Heading straight for Tyr, she crowded next to him in the tiny booth.

Tyr was quick to wrap his arms around Arcona and draw her close. "You're shaking. Are you all right?"

"I'm fine. It was a cold, dark, creepy walk to the bathroom, and I scared myself."

He kissed the top of her head. "I should have gone with you."

"Yes, you should have." Was this a glimpse of her new reality, always on high alert watching and waiting for the next monster to leap from the shadows? She slid her hand beneath his jacket and allowed her fingers to caress his torso. He felt wonderfully solid and she burrowed closer to his chest, taking comfort in the calm sound of his breath.

The waitress walked toward the table and set the check facedown. "Can I get you two lovebirds anything else?" Arcona glanced sideways at Tyr. He had literally cleaned his plate. Some of her food remained, but she couldn't eat another bite. "I think we're fine. The omelets were great."

"Everybody loves our food, but nobody likes our bathroom." The waitress chuckled in a good-natured way as she pointed to the amulet. "You like big jewelry, don't you?" She smiled with approval. "Me, too. If that's real amber, I know a few ladies in Salem who would kill for that necklace."

Arcona shrugged in agreement. "The necklace seems to encourage killing. That's probably its biggest fault."

The waitress recoiled. "I'll top off your coffee. Stay as long as you like; there's no rush." She hurried away with confusion on her pallid face.

Arcona turned toward Tyr and smiled. "I was just being honest, but I think I said the wrong thing."

Tyr took hold of her hand and brushed an adoring kiss across her fingertips. "Is this wrong?" He guided her hand beneath the table and between his thighs.

She felt a hard bulge in his jeans and cupped it in her palm. "It feels right to me."

He leaned close to her ear and whispered, "I wish you were lying beneath me in a warm bed right now. I can think of at least a dozen things I would love to be doing to you. Maybe we should go back?"

"To the bed-and-breakfast? No, I don't want to go to jail."

"The car is back there."

The waitress's gaze was directed toward them, so Arcona lowered her voice. "We should definitely move the car before the police notice it."

"I meant my car has a soft leather-upholstered backseat. You can climb in the back, wrap your legs around my face, and let me have you for dessert."

It sounded great. She couldn't wait to enjoy Tyr again. "Are we paying with cash or credit?"

He reached into his jacket and pulled out a thick fistful of bills. "I don't know the money rituals with food."

Her eyes bulged at the stack of large-denomination bills. She capped the money with her hand and pushed it below table level. "I'm afraid to ask how and why you're carrying so much cash. Please don't tell me you stole this wad off a dead guy in New Jersey named Guido."

Tyr looked offended. "I have legitimate means and reasons to carry cash."

"I'd like to hear about them — another time. Meanwhile, don't flash so much moola. It's not a good idea."

His chin rose. A defensive expression hardened on his brow. "I own property that I pay taxes on. I put gas in my car. I'm not a complete hermit."

"Obviously, you're not afraid of being mugged." She plucked several bills from his hand. "Let's leave a generous tip. Waiting tables is hard work. I did it all through college. My feet hurt just thinking about it."

Tyr urged Arcona out of the booth. "Stand in front of me as we walk."

"Why?"

Clearing his throat with a gruff grumble, he whispered, "Because my little gladiator has gone thumbs-up."

"Oh." She grabbed Tyr's hand and stood between him, his hard-on, and the mesmerized waitress who was now staring at the pile of tens and twenties stacked on the table.

"Do you need change?" the waitress mumbled.

"No." Arcona held her coat in front of her like a shield. "This was his first omelet with home fries, and he really enjoyed it. Tell the cook thanks."

"I sure will!" The waitress beamed.

Tyr opened the door, and the cold of the predawn pressed close and trickled down their collars.

Arcona slipped her arms into her coat and shivered. "If this is mild autumn weather, I'm not sure I could live full-time on the East Coast again."

"Trust me, you can get used to anything." Tyr took her hand in his and slipped it into the pocket of his jacket.

She glided her fingers between his, feeling the calluses he'd developed from clutching a shield and sword so long ago and faithfully preserved under enchantment. Would these deeply engrained details of his past change over time and did he have time? "Your hands are so warm. Do you feel the difference from earlier?"

Breathing in the cool salt air, he smiled. "I do."

Arcona fell into rhythm with Tyr's long strides as they walked along the edge of the road toward the bed-and-breakfast.

"I got used to being alone, and that was something I thought I could never endure, but I did." Tyr looked upward at the morning stars. "I've seen a lot of beautiful things in this life, but being a Slayer, I was always detached. There was no heart to anything. It was like watching the world from behind a thick layer of glass. After a while, I just gave up."

"That must have been terrible. I'm sorry."

"*You*." Tyr stressed the word. "The person *you* are now has nothing to be sorry for. You have no idea how good it felt to sit down with you and share a joke and a meal, or even want to roll you in bed and not worry about something horrible happening. I got to where I wouldn't allow myself to go near women. My hunger for blood and desire for release would overwhelm me. It wasn't safe for them, and I knew it was wrong, so I didn't tempt myself with their company. Tonight was the first time since Pompeii that...."

When he didn't finish his thought, she jumped in with her own. "Did you spend all these years without a lover?"

"Why bother? Among all my other problems I couldn't feel love. So the answer is yes."

"You said you tried to get relief."

"That wasn't love." He tensed. "Those were desperate bargains and frustrating transactions, and truth be told, I tried to get release with a few young men, as well. Every attempt ended in rage and disappointment. Nothing worked, until tonight." He pulled her close as he walked. "Can I tell you something?"

"Of course." She squeezed his hand.

"I'm afraid to leave important things unsaid, so I'll just tell you. Even though we were strangers to each other when we first met in Pompeii, my first instinct was to love you. I see now I was right to feel that way. It's odd saying this, because yesterday I would have sworn I hated you."

She glanced up at the sky. "You made a bad first impression in Slayers bar."

Laughter made the corner of his eyes fan. "I know I did. Let me make it up to you." Tyr led her around the back of the inn to the spot where he had concealed his car behind a large dumpster filled with scrap wood. "This isn't the most romantic spot, is it?"

Pulling her hand from his pocket, she rubbed it briskly against her other hand. "Let's turn the heater on and think about where we can go."

"We can check in to a hotel." His voice had a deep, dreamy tone.

"A warm bed sounds good, but the hotel has to be local. I'm still wearing the damn amulet." Grabbing hold of the bronzework, she lifted it to her chin. The thong tangled in her hair and shooting pain shot through her chest. "Ouch!" She immediately let it drop. "What if I can never take it off?"

"After what we've been through, *never* is a meaningless word. We'll talk to Dame Bishop tomorrow. Maybe she can help us."

"What? I don't trust her."

"Dame Bishop is not what you think she is. We need to talk about that, but let's get you warm first." Leaning close, he gently kissed the crown of her head. "I know where we can go." He opened the car door for her and tipped the driver seat forward, clearing the way for her to climb in back. "Welcome to Chez Dacian."

"The backseat?" She scoffed. "I'm not seventeen anymore."

"None of us are. Climb in. We can warm up while we decide what to do next."

"Why do I think I'm playing into one of your long-cherished fantasies?" She scooted past him and clambered into the lushly padded backseat. "Get the heater going."

He reached over the driver seat, pressed his thumb against the yellow button, and started the powerful V-8. The engine turned over with a well-maintained purr.

"You don't have to use that turbo rocket launcher to start the car?" Relief flooded her voice.

"No, that's just for getaways." He turned on the heater.

"Good. I hated the sound of that thing. It's terrifying."

A mock wounded expression tugged at his brows that made him look like a giant puppy. "I love that feature. I designed it myself. I'm sorry you don't appreciate it."

She shook her head. "It was the kidnapping I didn't appreciate."

Fresh, cool air blew into the cab.

"It might take a moment for the heater to kick in." He turned toward her. "Arcona, I need to tell you something. I'm the one who gave Dame Bishop the loan of the amulet and asked her to cast a circle of fate to draw you in."

"I think I already know the answer, but tell me why?"

"I searched, but I couldn't find you on my own. The reason I couldn't find you is so obvious now — I was looking for the wrong Arcona. You've changed so much over the centuries. Desperate to find you, I went to great lengths. Years ago, I approached Dame Bishop and asked her what I would need to do in order to set a soul trap for you and lure you in. She advised I hunt down a significant item from your past life as a Teuton, even a bone from your skeleton. Of course, I never found any bones, but then I heard about an archeological dig in Pompeii in search of a patron. I even bought the land where Lupus Unguis once stood. It's a museum and gift shop now." He laughed but sounded worried. "They sell lots of tiny winged phalluses cast in bronze to tourists. You gotta love the irony."

"How long have you been hunting me?" Her words were breathy.

"I've always been on the lookout for you, but my deal with Dame Bishop was struck twenty years ago."

Oh no. *Here comes another reality meltdown.* Could she handle it? "What? Twenty years ago I was just a little girl taking a Hello Kitty backpack to school."

"Dame Bishop and I made a contract. She agreed to cast an enchantment that guaranteed you would step into her circle at a predestined time in the future."

"Thank God all of this didn't happen when I was a child."

He dismissed her comment with a brusque wave of his hand. "It couldn't have happened then. Dame Bishop assured me your soul would be attracted into the circle at the perfect point in time when you were ready to confront the truth. Unfortunately, no one knew when to expect that predestined moment, only that it would happen eventually. If not this lifetime, the next. Matters couldn't be rushed, so we waited."

"This is pretty hard to believe, but I guess it's no more outlandish than the rest of this stuff. How was all this accomplished?"

"After I met with Dame Bishop, I was on a mission. I went looking for something from Lupus Unguis that would attract your soul, something your soul would recognize. I was hoping for a piece of a hair comb, a bracelet, anything, but when the amulet was unearthed, I knew fate had taken my side of the argument."

"So I was lured here?"

"Gently lured here. Dame Bishop warned me that you would only step into the circle when your soul was ready and that I had to be patient." A nervous smile crossed his lips. "I know all about patience."

"So it was never a sure thing?"

"Your freewill carried you into the circle on All Souls' Day. I saw it as a sign that you knew you were guilty."

Her gaze met his. Compassion radiated from his face. "You don't feel that way now?"

He squeezed her hand. "We've reached an understanding I *never* expected to reach."

Confusion, anger, pity, and relief flooded her thoughts. She rubbed her forehead. "I don't know how I feel about all this."

Dipping his chin, Tyr looked humbled. "Arcona, I stalked you and set a trap. I spent years planning my revenge. I had every intention of carrying us both into the death realm. But you have my word that my heart and mind have been changed. As things stand now, I'd put my miserable existence on the line for you in a flash." He placed his hand on his chest. "I'll even understand if you never want to see me again. Say the word and I'll disappear. You'll never have to be afraid of me. I will never harm you."

The thought of never seeing him again left her desolate.

"Have you forgiven me for what I did to you?" Her throat tensed and her voice became ragged from emotion.

With a featherlight touch, he stroked her cheek. "Completely."

"Then I forgive you. We can be free of the hurt."

His eyes shone with tears. "I can't believe what has happened to us. It's too good. Do I even deserve it?"

"You do." She kissed his mouth. "We do." But what if Tyr was dying? How long did they have? "I guess we just take this one step at a time."

Overwhelmed by emotion, Tyr broke eye contact and nodded his head. "If I got one good day with you, it would make up for an eternity of bad days."

How long did they have? She wanted solid answers in a situation where none were offered. "Make this a good day."

Tyr settled onto the backseat and patted his knee. "Come here."

Sliding across the seat, she straddled his lap, facing him, sitting so close it felt as if they were sharing the same warm breath. Looking into his eyes, she brushed her hands against the sides of his face. "What happens at sunrise?" she whispered.

His eyes glittered. "What do you mean?"

"Am I going to lose you? What happens to Slayers when they die?"

"Sunlight doesn't harm Slayers, if that's what you're worried about. The usual way we die is decapitation, and then our bodies turn to dust. I've seen it happen to others and wished I could stop fighting and simply allow it to happen to me, but it's hard to give in, even if you think you want it. Some part of me always resisted."

"Did Varn ever tell you the secret? How his Strix killed her firstborn?"

"No. The bastard never told me. I'm not sure he ever knew. I suspect it's something intangible between a Strix and her Slayer that can't be easily shared."

"Has *this* ever happened?"

"What is *this*?"

"What we've done. What we're doing. You know, forgiving each other and moving through it?"

He shook his head. "I've never heard of such a thing."

She caressed the gritty stubble on his jaw, allowing her fingertips to linger on the shallow scar on his cheek. "From this moment onward, I want to enjoy all I can with you, without regrets." Slipping the coat from her shoulders, she let it drop to the floor and snuggled close to his chest. "Take your jacket off."

Tyr helped her to tug the jacket from his shoulders and tossed it aside. He slid lower in the seat and gazed at her with a wide-eyed, innocent expression she could hardly believe he was capable of.

She skimmed her hands across his tight black T-shirt. "I'd love to take this off and look at your beautiful chest, but we should keep some clothes on in case someone walks past."

"No one will bother us." He cradled the back of her head and pulled her in to a kiss.

She parted her lips in a soft embrace that showed complete acceptance and trust, gliding the tip of her tongue against his beautiful mouth.

* * * *

Tyr returned Arcona's kiss, taking in the warmth of her natural scent just below the faint hint of green apple soap from the inn. Life had come full circle. Once again, Arcona was in his arms, but this time the darkness and the secrets were gone. Now he knew her heart and she knew his. Neither was perfect, but they were perfect for each other.

The delicate weave of her sweater did little to separate them. When she shifted on his lap, her lush curves swayed beneath. Lifting the hem, he pushed it higher and exposed the soft undercurves of her breasts.

A mischievous gleam shone in her eyes. "I'm warming up real fast."

The sight of her partially undressed on his lap was unbearably enticing. He allowed his hands to explore, feeling her smooth skin beneath his palms. "I think the backseat is turning you on."

"I think you are." Her voice was husky.

He brushed the pads of his thumbs against her breasts, teasing her nipples to peaks. His cock pressed hard against his jeans. "I'm going to have to unzip."

"Good." She made the most beautiful little sounds as he touched her.

He thought the zipper of his jeans might burst. It almost hurt to be so close and yet held apart from her by a tough layer of denim. He wanted her naked in the backseat but knew he couldn't have it. "I wish we were in a soft bed behind a locked door. I'm going crazy thinking about what I want to do to you."

"You should be thinking about what you can do to me in a car." She pulled the amulet aside and allowed it to drop behind her shoulder, where it was out of the way. "Adapt." Reaching for the snap on his pants, she unfastened it. "Improvise." It popped open, slightly parting the zipper.

"And overcome." She rubbed her palm against him before drawing the zipper downward. "What have we here? Boxers or briefs?" She tugged the waist of his jeans lower. The glistening head of his cock thrust upward. "Oh. Commando. I should have guessed."

He lifted his hips so she could pull his jeans farther down his thighs. "Come closer."

"You better believe I'll get closer." She rose to her knees and brushed her breasts against his lips.

He grasped her waist and held her steady as he circled the tip of his tongue around her nipple until the sweater was damp. Using the edges of his teeth, he grazed the delicate fabric and delivered a tiny nip.

Arcona swayed in his hold with lips parted in a rapturous expression. Her hand glided between them as she reached down to unzip her jeans. The metallic click of the zipper teeth parting drove him wild, because he knew luscious curves were almost within reach. He helped tug Arcona's jeans down her hips until they rumpled midway on her thighs.

A pair of black lace panties clung to her hips. He hooked his fingers under the fabric, half toying with the idea of simply shredding them instead of struggling to take them off intact. "What about these?"

"Rip them." A sweet smile lit her lips. "You're not wearing underwear, so why should I?"

He twisted the delicate lace around his fingers and shredded the seams apart with a thread-popping tear. He plucked the lacy bit of fabric from between her thighs and tossed the thrashed garment aside.

She responded with a soft chuckle. "You're the only guy I ever met who could actually rip panties."

"It was nothing," he boasted, but he was surprised by how much effort he'd exerted on something that should have been easy. His fingers smarted from the slicing bite of a few tough threads. Without doubt he was changing, losing strength, but it was worth it to have even a few hours again as a man. "Lie down."

She swung a leg off his lap and arched back against the seat as she carefully wiggled her jeans a little farther down her legs. "I thought we weren't getting undressed."

"We're not, at least not completely. Just take off one pants leg."

Kicking a boot off, she slid one leg free of her jeans. "If I didn't know better, I'd say you'd done this before."

"I haven't, but I'm sure I'll do it again. You look good lying across the backseat."

Taking hold of her legs, he carefully pulled her toward him, placing her ankle over his shoulder. Bending down, he brushed his face between her thighs. Heat rolled off her skin and her inviting warm scent filled his senses. With eyes closed, he committed the luscious moment to memory.

"You feel so good." She rocked her hips against his mouth. Her uninhibited response and soft sounds transformed the backseat into a sacred place. Moist breath and body heat fogged the windows, creating a curtain of privacy inside their own hidden world.

With unrushed adoration, he drank her in loving every second of contact.

Something heavy smashed into the side door. A violent *thunk* rattled the car. In a blur of motion, the car tipped and rose on the driver side as if a forklift had seized, elevated, and prepared to overturn it.

Arcona screamed as the car rolled onto its side.

He toppled onto Arcona. They both slid across the seat and smacked against the passenger side.

She curled into a ball, trembling. "What's going on?"

Tyr strained to straighten an arm and pushed away to avoid crushing her. The car was released with an abrupt drop and crashed to the ground with a hard bounce. He almost bit his tongue and cursed at whatever was out there. He smeared his palm across the steamed window to look.

A shadowy specter appeared at the window and pressed close to the glass. Varn's pale, slashed face peered inside the car. "Aha!" Varn's enraged gaze looked psychotic. He clawed his fingers against the side windows. "Good news!" he shouted. "I'm feeling like myself again, only better!"

The gruesome grin on Varn's face exposed a glimpse of his back molars through the slit in his cheek. His still-incomplete healing left half of his face a jagged slash of scar tissue. "I may not be pretty but I'm built like a fucking tank!"

"Oh my God!" Arcona scrambled to tug her sweater downward and pull up her jeans with terrified urgency.

Tyr lunged toward the driver seat to lock the car but Varn threw the door open first. "Get out of the way, old man." Varn's icy gaze riveted on Arcona. "I want another drink from your little friend." He grasped the door handle and twisted it until the metal snapped.

"Look at that!" Varn's eyes gleamed with pride as he tossed the shattered chrome handle away. "I'm as strong as you ever were. Maybe more…." He glowered at Tyr, and his voice dropped to a threatening rumble. "This showdown has been a long time coming, hasn't it? Let's get it on and get it over with. Climb out of the car, Dacian, and face me, man-to-man."

"Varn, you're not a man!" Tyr shouted. "You're a Slayer. You're missing a heart."

"Boo hoo for me." Varn's face collapsed in a clownishly exaggerated frown that highlighted the horrendous damage done to him. "Now hand the little bitch over. I want another bite of Strix."

Tyr pushed Arcona behind him. "Leave her alone. I won't let you have her."

"You don't have a choice." Varn blocked the way. "My strength has increased. We're finally equals. I'll take her by force if I have to." He motioned for Tyr to move aside. "But this doesn't have to get nasty between you and me, brother. We can share. She'd make an exquisite blood slave. Isn't this what you've always wanted, you and me punishing a Strix and growing stronger from it?" He touched the ridge of gaping scar tissue on his mouth and jaw and thrust his hand forward. "I have more healing to do. I need blood. Hand her over."

"No." Tyr fished around the floor of the car for Arcona's trench coat. He found it and tossed it to her.

Arcona was quick to slide her arms into the coat sleeves.

"Give her to me!" Varn struck the roof of the car with his fist with such force the metal dented. "Stop stalling, brother, unless you want me to rip your limbs off and toss them in the dumpster."

Tyr scanned the construction yard, searching for a weapon he could reach. "Fuck off!"

"What's wrong with you?" Varn glared in disgust. "Why so possessive? Remember when we used to hunt as a team? We always shared the kill like good companions should. Those were good days."

"No, they weren't," Tyr snapped.

Varn's gaze narrowed on Arcona. "She's a Strix reborn. You know how rare she is. Let's make full use of her. Drinking her blood will make us powerful beyond our wildest dreams. We'll almost be gods. Exploit her. Don't be a fool. You're never gonna get another chance like this—ever."

"I know." Tyr shuddered. Only hours earlier, he'd sounded exactly like Varn: vengeful, angry, and selfish. The thought left him nauseated.

Reaching into the car, Varn grabbed at Arcona but she reared away. "I'm not going to waste time with your bullshit." He clawed the air inches from Arcona's face. "Get over here, bitch, and I won't be as hard on you."

"Stop!" Tyr shoved Varn hard, but couldn't budge him. The full extent of his plight became clear. Varn was solid as steel while his own strength had diminished, almost to the point of being a mere human once again.

In a flash, he knew his only hope for Arcona's survival was in hiding that fact from Varn for as long as possible.

"Why are you protecting her?" Varn sneered. "You raved for centuries about how much you hated her. You said no punishment was too severe for a Strix. What's changed? Let's use her for the one thing she's good for—her blood."

Arcona looked into Tyr's eyes. "I'm sorry."

Tyr realized Arcona suspected the true nature of the situation; he was no longer a match for Varn's enhanced strength.

Wanting to spare her worry and fear, he prepared to tell her a soothing little lie. "It's going to be—"

Arcona leaped over Tyr's lap and grabbed Varn's hand. "Take me. I'll cooperate."

Varn snatched Arcona out of the car with lightning speed and clutched her against his chest like a python tightening its death throttle.

"No!" Tyr tried to grab on to Arcona's leg, but she wriggled free and he lost his grip.

"You've made a good choice." Varn smoothed Arcona's tousled hair and leered into her face. "I'm glad you're being reasonable." He locked his arms around her like a vise. "If you're willing to be my blood slave, I'm willing to go easier on you. You're a valuable treasure, one I hope to keep alive as long as possible."

In self-disgust he'd allowed her to slip beyond his protection. His heart shattered. Her brave but foolish actions had been done to spare him. Feeling utter helplessness, he jumped out of the car.

The resolute expression on Arcona's face warned him she meant to go through with this. Fear for her sickened him. With her gaze fixed on his, she silently mouthed the word *Go*. Tyr faintly shook his head.

"What's going on between you?" Varn took a step back, dragging Arcona with him.

"Nothing." Arcona cuddled closer to Varn, as if she craved nearness to such a monster. "Here's something to consider: I would accept you both as masters. I ask only that you protect me from, and not share me with, other Slayers."

"Arcona, no!" Every nerve in Tyr's body screamed.

"See?" Varn grinned. "Smart girl. She's being realistic."

"I've already spent time alone with Tyr." Arcona addressed Varn in the sweetest tone. "Now it's my turn to get to know you better."

"Don't do it, Arcona." In frustration, Tyr dug his fingernails deep into his palms. He ached to punch Varn in the face and grab Arcona back, but he knew in his present weakened state, Varn could crush every bone in his body before he landed a single blow.

"I like your new attitude." Varn's grip across Arcona's throat tightened as if he meant to threaten her with an inescapable choke hold.

Arcona made fleeting eye contact with Tyr. Her gaze darted toward a pile of construction equipment stacked in the back of the inn, and a stacked cord of wood. "Tyr, why don't you leave me alone for a little while with Varn?"

"That's right, Tyr. Leave us alone." Varn imitated Arcona in a high-pitched mocking voice. He hauled her toward the back door of the inn. "I'm going to enjoy every fucking minute of this."

Chapter Fourteen

Arcona hated being so close to Varn. He reeked of menace, and his solid forearm locked securely around her throat reminded her of how powerless she was. He dragged her toward the back stairs of the inn and she took short staggering steps to keep pace.

"You don't have to use force," she muttered.

"I like force." Varn shoved her resisting body up the stairs. He slid a chilly hand beneath Arcona's sweater. "I see Tyr got rid of the bra." A low growl rose from deep in his throat. "I liked my first taste. I want more Strix blood, and this time I don't expect to be interrupted."

He kicked the back door open and roughly flung Arcona inside the dark inn.

She flailed her arms as she struggled to regain her balance.

He glanced around at the unfinished, unfurnished downstairs. "I guess you'll have to just lie on the floor."

"It's too cold." She protested. It was also too close to Tyr. If he heard her suffering, and he would, he'd race inside to rescue her and Varn would rip him limb from limb while she watched in horror. "The upstairs is furnished. There are blankets on the bed."

Varn grunted a displeased sound at the prospect of inconvenience. "So?"

Think of something. Stay alive. Help Tyr. "If I go into shock and die, I'm no further use to you."

"True." Varn hauled Arcona across the downstairs toward the staircase. Taking long strides, he climbed two steps at a time, carrying her at his side like a rag doll.

The toes of her boots bumped against the crest of each step as Varn dragged her up the stairs at surprising speed. She strained to see into the darkness, alert for noise or movement. For Tyr's sake, she hoped he wasn't following.

"I don't know what's wrong with Tyr," Varn mumbled, not caring that she overheard his personal angst. "We've been through so much, and this should be our greatest day. You're not going to ruin things between us, Strix. We're blood brothers in the truest sense. He let me have you first. Think about that. Once we're done with you, he'll come around. He always does."

The inn was silent. She prayed she could survive on her own, but panic set in when they reached the top of the third flight. Once again she would be subjected to Varn's vicious style of feeding.

Varn stopped at the top of the stairs. His nostrils flared as he sniffed the air. "You used the room at the end of the hall, didn't you?"

"Yes." Her voice cracked.

"I knew it. Tyr's stronger, but my senses have always been keener." He stomped down the hall with Arcona half dangling under his arm, muttering unintelligible words. Thrusting the bedroom door open with his boot, he scanned the room.

A few stubborn embers smoldered in the hearth and Varn's damaged face looked even more evil by the faint glow of the fire. The bedcovers were rumpled on the mattress. "Quite a cozy little love nest. What is this?" He leaned over the bed and drew a sharp inhalation. "It smells like rut in here. Man and woman." A look of accusation burned in his eyes. "So did the car, for that matter. How is that possible?" He shoved her aside.

She staggered sideways and almost toppled.

He knelt on the bed and sniffed the covers like a dog. A moment later, he raced to the shower stall and sniffed. "I smell Tyr's scent and male seed, lots of it." He glared at Arcona. "You fucked him, and he came. How did you do that?"

Varn stalked toward her. He reached for her throat, his fingers locking tight, choking off air. "Whatever you did for him, witch, I expect you to do the same for me. I've gone without a real fuck for a thousand years. Touch it." He released her. "What?"

"Put your hand between my legs and touch it," he demanded. Hesitating, she looked around the room for a lamp, a clock, anything she might grab and bash against his arrogant head. "Don't just stand there. Do it!" Varn grabbed her wrist and thrust her hand between his legs. "You broke the curse for him, didn't you?"

She shook her head. "I don't know what you're talking about."

"I think you know exactly what I'm talking about." He clutched at the amulet around her neck and twisted the thong like a garrote. "What sort of magic did you use? Did you use enchanted words or potions? Was blood shared? Tell me! How did you make him come?"

"It just happened." She groaned. Varn squeezed her wrist so tightly her fingertips tingled. She tried to pull away, but couldn't.

"That's why Tyr's acting so strangely. Strix blood with benefits." He leered. "This is an interesting development. I've never seen anything like this. It makes sense. He's getting off with you and doesn't want to share the bounty."

A ragged sigh of disgust crossed his lips. "Do you know how long I've gone without getting properly laid? A thousand fucking years!" His mouth curled into an ugly grimace.

"You're something different aren't you? A new sort of Strix. You can change a Slayer without killing him, can't you?"

Arcona shook her head. "I don't know how to do anything!"

"I think you do." Varn snarled. "That's why Tyr fought to keep you to himself. He figured it out before I did. Greedy bastard. I always shared with him. From now on, witch, you're going to fuck me and only me," he threatened. "And I'm going to come hard and often. Forget about Tyr. After I get what I need from you, years, decades from now, I'd rather snap your neck than share you. Let's see how Tyr feels about that."

"Oh God." His harsh grip left her hands throbbing from lack of blood.

Varn's eyes had a manic gleam. "As your new master, you will submit solely to me. I'm going to start by fucking you while I feed." He picked her up and threw her onto the mattress.

She landed hard on the bed. The breath whistled out of her. Varn pounced and was on top of her in an instant, pinning her to the bed with a firm grip. She tried to fight her way out from beneath him, but he fell against her, heavy as iron.

"Stop struggling. It's useless." He gripped her throat and held her captive. With his free hand, he pushed her sweater above her breasts. "I want some of what he had, and I want it now." The slit in his cheek flapped open as he spoke. He lifted his arm with the heavy silver wrist cuff and flicked the tiny needle-sharp blade open. The shining blade hovered in front of her throat.

"I stake my claim on you. You're my blood slave." Varn's chilling gaze swept over her. "Before I tear off what's left of your clothing and roll you onto your belly, I want to hear you call me master."

Trembling, she looked at Varn's once-handsome face, feeling nothing but revulsion. She parted her lips and hesitated. Everything depended on making him believe she was his so that he wouldn't challenge and destroy Tyr. "You're my mast—"

Swoop, thunk. A blade arced through the air with lethal force. A horrible wet sound bubbled forth. Varn's mouth gaped open in surprise. His severed head tipped forward, rolled off his shoulders, and fell onto the bed, oozing thick blackened blood onto the covers.

Arcona scrambled backward in a frantic attempt to escape Varn's falling body. She slammed into the iron bed frame. Panting in hysteria, she hyperventilated.

"Are you all right, my love?" Tyr stood beside the bed, holding a bloodied ax. "Did he hurt you?"

She shook her head, curled her knees toward her chest, and sobbed. The horrible expression on Varn's face was burned into her mind. Even with her eyes shut, it lingered.

Tyr tossed the ax to the floor and was at her side in an instant, wrapping his arms around her. "It's over," he whispered. "Sweetheart, come away from the bed." He lifted her into his arms and stepped away from Varn's body.

In an instant, she was cradled against Tyr's chest. Snuggling closer, she listened to the reassuring rhythm of his heartbeat. She glanced over her shoulder at Varn's blood-drenched, headless body lying sprawled across the mattress, and nearly retched. "Oh, God, what are we going to do? We have to hide the body."

He stroked her hair. "Watch."

An odd hissing sound rose from the bed. Varn's body sizzled. A faint stream of bluish smoke swirled into the air above him. Within moments, Varn shriveled until he resembled a twisted heap of scorched twigs. Finally, the body crumbled and collapsed into a grayish pile of powder-fine dust.

"He's gone." Arcona trembled in shock. "Turned to ash."

Tyr kissed the top of her head. "That's what happens to Slayers. I've seen it many times. When they die, their bodies show their true age."

They both stared in silence at the silt-like ashes, unable to look away.

His voice had reduced to a raspy husk. "I can't believe Varn allowed me to sneak up on him and take his head. He'd avoided such a disaster for so long."

"He was distracted." Arcona shuddered. "He thought things were going to change for him." The impulse to weep or be sick crept up on her. "You did the right thing. Varn had no intention of sharing; he was going to hurt me. Once he realized he could get away with it, I'm certain he would have killed you."

Tyr lifted the top bedcover off the mattress with care. He carried it to the fireplace and brushed what remained of Varn into the hearth. Even the blood had turned to an inoffensive powdery ash. He frowned as his palm scraped the bedcovers clean. "Varn was a violent man and a vicious Slayer. He'd traveled the world and lived more than a millennium, but learned little. I guess that's how it is for some souls."

Arcona straightened her sweater and crossed her arms over her chest. "Let's get out of here."

Tyr picked up the ax and offered Arcona his free hand.

She grasped his hand and they left the dark room together, feeling their way along the banister. By the time they reached the bottom flight of stairs the broad windows below revealed the first golden thread of sunlight in the east.

They walked out of the inn. A chilly breeze slapped her senses awake.

Tyr tossed the ax beside the woodpile where it belonged. He gazed at the dent in his car's roof and opened the damaged car door. "Damn, Varn," he grumbled.

Arcona climbed in the passenger seat and immediately buckled the safety belt across her chest, vowing to face no more risk or danger.

Tyr started the engine and glanced over at her. "Where to?"

She gripped the amulet in shaky hands. "I'd like to run as far from here as possible, but I can't leave Salem with this thing. I suppose we should go see Dame Bishop."

He nodded. "All right." The engine purred as he pulled onto a paved road strewn with dry leaves. "Do you remember where the shop is?"

"Not really. Don't you know? You went there, too. It's not far from the waterfront, but I swear the shop moved itself around. I walked blocks away from it in one direction, and I looked up only to find it in front of me again. The best I can say is let's head toward the harbor and maybe we'll find it." She paused. "What about Slayers? Do you remember how to get there? Slayers bar was next door to the Silver Moon Scrying Shoppe."

Tyr shook his head. "Slayers wasn't next door. It's not in Salem. That was just an illusion. Slayers exists somewhere where people like me living under enchantment can gather."

"So where is it?"

"I don't know. The old gods like Odin set aside special realms for their eternal warriors. Slayers was Varn's manifestation, so who knows what happened to it after he died. It may have gone to Valhalla with him."

Biting her lip, she gazed at the lightening sky. "Did Varn really go to Valhalla, or somewhere else?"

"I have no idea." Tyr came to an intersection and looked up and down the quaint, old-town streets of Salem's historical district. "I'm not getting any sense of where the shop might be, and that's odd because I usually have a strong sense of place and direction."

She patted his knee. "Maybe that's a good thing, another positive sign you're not a Slayer anymore."

"I hope you're right." He grinned. "Or maybe it just means I'm lost."

Arcona sighed. "How many men does it take to ask for directions?"

Tyr's face went blank.

"Your expression says it all. The correct answer is zero. Men never willingly ask for directions." She laughed.

Tyr's face remained neutral. "I don't get it."

"It's a joke. You know, men never ask for directions, anywhere, anytime."

He looked confused. "How is that a joke? No man wishes to ask directions. It lowers his status in the tribe. Everyone knows this."

"Never mind." She rolled her eyes. "Good grief, you sound just like any other man, Slayer or not."

They methodically drove up and down Salem's tree-lined streets, seeing nothing close to Slayers bar or the Wiccan scrying shop. The sun climbed higher and a pink dawn brightened the horizon.

They turned down a narrow street and found the way blocked by a tank-like armored car with a heraldic shield and lance painted on its big square hood and engine idling.

"Stop!" Arcona raised her palm into the air. "Pull over. That's it. The entrance to the Silver Moon Scrying Shoppe is behind the armored car."

Tyr pulled over to the curb.

Arcona leaped out of the car before the engine even shut off. While wrapping her coat tightly around her, she ran across the street toward the armored car. When she reached the towering door on the driver side, she pounded her palm against the solid steel. "Good morning!" she called out. "Do you work for the transport company sent by the Smithsonian? I have what you're waiting for. I need to speak to you."

The driver behind the thick-paned window glared down at her with a tense expression on his lips.

"Don't spook the driver." Dame Bishop stepped out from behind the hulking vehicle. "They don't like being approached or spoken to. They'll just ignore you."

Arcona stared at Dame Bishop in awe. Without doubt, this was the same woman she'd met yesterday, yet there was a profound difference. Dame Bishop's eyes and flowing silvery hair were the same, but this morning, she appeared smooth-skinned, glowing, and at least twenty years younger than the night before.

"Wait a moment." Arcona faltered on the curb. "Are you Dame Bishop's daughter?"

"Nope," the attractive woman's reply was brisk. "It's me." She looked Arcona over with analytical focus. "I see you survived the night in relatively good condition. I credit my spiced cider for that. You're a bit bruised and disheveled but alive, and that's what counts. I must say I'm impressed with your tenacity. Your situation was one of the diciest I've ever seen. Matters could have gone either way in a heartbeat." She glanced around. "Where's that angry young man? Did the Dacian make it through the ordeal in one piece?"

Tyr leaped from the car, darted across the street, and stood at Arcona's side. He wrapped his arm around her shoulders and pulled her close in a gesture that radiated his intention to be protective of her. His gaze swept toward Dame Bishop with suspicion. "Can she help you?" he whispered near Arcona's ear.

"What a transformation! You look like a new man." Dame Bishop skimmed her gaze over Tyr head to foot and beamed. "I see my spiced cider did its magic again."

Tempted to slap the smug lady, Arcona glared at Dame Bishop instead. "Cider? What are you talking about?"

"The cider you drank in my shop last night carried a powerful regenerative spell. I knew you'd be dealing with a lot within a short period of time. I did suspect you'd be facing excessive blood loss, especially with the Slayers involved." Dame Bishop shrugged. "I hope its other side effects were manageable."

Her apprehension built. "What other side effects?"

"Along with pronounced aphrodisiac properties, rose tears can make people remember their buried thoughts and true feelings. I knew Tyr would drink from your throat. I wanted him to get a dose of my cider through you and remember that he wasn't always angry with you. I wanted him to have a chance to free himself from the rage and isolation of being a Slayer."

"Don't smile when you say it. This wasn't a game!" Arcona was tempted to throttle Dame Bishop's throat. "I know about the plan to lure me in. How do you live with yourself? I was drugged and assaulted by a crazed Viking. I could have been killed!" She clutched the amulet. "What will happen to me? Am I trapped by this thing?"

"Once a Strix, always a Strix," Dame Bishop chanted in a singsong voice. "But a clever witch can learn new tricks. You learned a lot last night, didn't you? Power is never what it looks like on the surface, and that's a hard lesson to absorb." She tapped a dainty gloved fingertip to her lips. "Have you made any recent attempts to remove the amulet?"

"I tried multiple times last night." Arcona tangled her fingers in the amulet's leather thong. "The thing burned me every time. It was horrible."

"Try again," Dame Bishop insisted.

"You don't understand. The pain is searing." Arcona knew she was whining but couldn't help herself. "I don't dare touch it."

"Then let him do it." Dame Bishop motioned toward Tyr. "Do you understand why she did what she did?"

Tyr nodded. "I saw everything."

Dame Bishop leaned closer to Tyr. "Can you let the past go? Don't answer too quickly. It's never as easy as you think."

"Yes," He answered without hesitation. "I'm ready to let it go. I am certain."

"Answer truthfully." Dame Bishop pressed her palms together. "Do you love her? Not a projection of some unattainable ideal or a stranger standing on a balcony. Can you love this woman as she is?"

"I can. I do." The words rolled off Tyr's tongue. "Arcona is my match. She's smart and strong and I always wanted her as my woman. I just forgot."

Arcona glanced at Dame Bishop. "How do you know about the balcony?"

374

"Trade secret." A victorious smile lit Dame Bishop's face. She focused on Tyr. "Set her free. Take the amulet off her."

Tyr reached for the leather thong and lifted it over Arcona's head.

Arcona braced, waiting for the first blazing-hot stab of pain as Tyr raised the amulet off her chest, but he easily slipped it over her head and into his palm without the slightest incident. She almost squealed with delight when nothing happened. "It's off!"

Dame Bishop fished her hand through a tote bag dangling on her elbow and pulled out the amulet's carved wooden box. She opened the box and presented it to Tyr. "Put the amulet inside."

Tyr placed it in the box and coiled the leather thong on top of the broad slab of amber.

Dame Bishop snapped the box shut. "Thank you." She turned and walked toward the back of the armored car and pounded her fist on the door.

The steel doors opened and a guard's hand reached out, took the box from Dame Bishop, and immediately retreated inside the safety of the interior, shut the steel doors, and locked them. A moment later, the boxy vehicle rumbled away from the curb and drove around the corner, leaving only a whiff of diesel in its wake.

Dame Bishop crossed her arms in front of her chest. "I'm glad that little drama's over and the amulet's safely on its way to a secure museum vault where it can rest in peace for a while." She pointed a gloved fingertip at Tyr's heart. "You do know you're dying, don't you? The process has already started."

Tyr looked stricken. "When?"

"Not so eager to die anymore, are you?" Dame Bishop's lips curled at the edges into a sly smile. "Who knows when? One year, perhaps sixty. You'll have to live within the same human limitations and accept the mystery just like everyone else. Giving due credit to Arcona, you're not a Slayer anymore. That's over. You're mortal now, and your days are numbered, so enjoy them and make them meaningful."

Tyr's stood with his mouth agape, looking as if he'd burst if he didn't speak, yet said nothing.

"While you're mulling that over, I'd like to have a private word with Arcona." Dame Bishop turned her back to Tyr and took Arcona by the arm, steering her toward the front of the Silver Moon Scrying Shoppe.

Arcona tensed. "Are we going inside the shop?" She wasn't sure she could stand any more of Dame Bishop's tricks or potions.

"No, actually, I'm closing this shop down."

Arcona was astonished. "But you've been here since 1992. What's changed?"

Dame Bishop shook her head. "Correction. I've been in Salem since 1692, and I'm not going anywhere. Only the shop's location will change. It can only be used once per customer, and we're done with this location. I'll go where I'm needed; I'm not sure where. There are many other realms and realities to choose from." She smiled a rosy, apple-cheeked grin. "But you already know that." She pointed toward the horrible tableau in the window display of a woman with a noose around her neck. "That's me. I'm Bridget Bishop. When the Salem witch trials' alarm bell rang, I was the first witch to hang. I've always been a trendsetter."

She stared. "Holy shit."

"That's old news." Dame Bishop leaned close to Arcona's ear and whispered, "Let's be practical and speak of other more pressing matters. The future's closer than you think. There's a little soul hovering above your left shoulder, waiting for permission to cross over. She says she's willing to wait if you're not ready now. Her name is Malyka, and she wants to be with you and Tyr. Would you like to keep her, or should I ask her to leave? It's not too late."

"Don't send her away!" Arcona snapped. "Tell her she's welcome."

"That part's up to you, and you can do that on your own schedule." Dame Bishop tugged on the large ring of skeleton keys hanging on her belt, slipped a key into the shop's front door, and opened it.

Arcona scoffed. "Wait a moment. Last night I bolted the door from the inside."

"I know. It didn't make a bit of difference to me." Dame Bishop lingered in the doorway and looked into Arcona's eyes. "I have a lot of respect for you. In many ways, we're kindred souls, but you should go. You have a lot to figure out." Her gaze darted toward Tyr, who was waiting patiently a few yards away. "If I were you, I'd consider keeping that man. He's the right man for you." With a serene smile, she slipped inside the shop and closed the door.

The shop door clicked shut in Arcona's stunned face. For a moment, she didn't know what to do with herself. "That's it?"

Tyr approached Arcona, covering the distance between them in several long strides. "What did she say?"

Arcona held out her hand. "Walk with me." She grasped his hand. "I have one last thing I must do."

They strolled a few blocks toward a seaside palisade lined with shops and cafés that were just opening for the day. The early morning light sparkled on the calm harbor.

They stepped aside as a pair of whippet-lean cyclists and an overbundled jogger huffed past.

Tyr wrapped his arm around Arcona's waist and drew her close. "What do you need to do?"

She dug deep into her coat pocket until she felt the smooth piece of amber from Witch Casey's wish bag. Pulling the amber free, she held it in her palm. In the morning light, it glittered a rich russety gold. "I'm supposed to make a wish and return the stone to nature."

He plucked the tiny piece of amber from her palm and held it to the sunlight. "Can I make a wish, too?" Without waiting for her to answer, he mumbled a few foreign words, pressed a soft kiss to the amber, and handed it back to her.

She stopped and looked out on the sea. The water lapped against the mossy rocks below. A few tiny green crabs scuttled away when her shadow fell across the rocks. "This place is peaceful." She held the amber to her lips and thought of all the changes a two-thousand-year-old gladiator would bring to her life. Could they find common ground and get along? Would he be content to live a smaller life as her lover, companion, or maybe more?

"I would." Tyr's hand brushed her shoulder.

She gasped in surprise. "Was I speaking out loud?"

"No." His warm hazel eyes were full of depth in the bright light. "But I can see from the look on your face that you're worried, and you shouldn't be. I want you to know we share the same wish."

Holding the amber in her raised hand, she gestured for him to join her. "Then let's do this together."

He reached for her hand and clasped it. Together, they tossed the amber high into the air and watched as it arced above the water and plunked down into the harbor with a slight splash.

"Now the sea knows our secret, and the sea is forever." She squinted at the sky and saw an airplane's contrail streaking west. "I think that's my missed flight. They'll be wheeling the beverage cart down the aisle in a few minutes." Facing Tyr, she reached her hand inside his leather jacket. His big body was so warm it was almost hot to the touch. "Have you ever been on an airplane?"

His brows shot upward. "I used to dogfight with a machine gun mounted on the front of my biplane in World War I."

She laughed. "I should have guessed."

He grasped her hand. "Why don't I drive us home?"

"Us?"

"I'm not letting you go, Arcona. I'll never settle for anyone else."

"You want to drive us cross-country in a turbojet muscle car?"

"Why not? We can stop wherever we like, take our time, and get to know each other."

"That's a good idea. We should find out if we can even get along." She wrapped her arms around his chest and snuggled inside his open jacket to escape the brisk ocean breeze. "Let's leave right away. I have some calls to make and a lot to decide. Maybe we can find a quiet hotel this afternoon and just crash, make love, take a long bath, and sleep. I can't wait."

Tyr lifted her chin. He kissed Arcona's lips and gazed into her eyes. "I don't need more time to be certain of what I already know." He brushed another soft kiss on her lips.

She drew away. "As soon as my phone recharges, remind me to call my friend Devon and warn her to treat that stone she picked from the wish bag with respect."

Epilogue

West Los Angeles. Two Months later.

Arcona hurried toward the coffeemaker and hit the button. She called into the bedroom. "Tyr, wake up!"

Tyr was stretched across their queen-size bed, taking up the lion's share of the mattress. He'd kicked a long leg free of the covers. The humid air near the beach had rumpled his hair into golden waves.

For safety's sake, they had decided to live in her little home, at least for now. Returning to any of Tyr's other properties and alerting the other Slayers to his whereabouts seemed unwise. For the foreseeable future, she'd just have to imagine what his mahogany library looked like and dream.

She snatched the sheet away and looked at the stunning lines of Tyr's muscular body. "Sleeping beauty, it's time to get up."

Rubbing his eyes, he groaned. "Really? Why so early?"

"If we don't leave soon, we're going to hit traffic."

"I was hoping we could have breakfast together."

"Most days we can, but this is your first day on the job. The department supervisor will want to talk to you about security protocols and a dozen other things. They'll also take a photo for your ID badge, so—"

"So I should comb my hair and not give the camera my Dacian Dagger death stare?"

"Yep. It's not a mug shot or an arena mural. You want to look friendly and sane."

He laughed. "When I interviewed for your department, no one else there looked friendly or sane." He shrugged. "Except for you, dear."

"Good save." Arcona laughed. "I'm making coffee."

He sniffed the air. "Smells great. I need it."

Tyr had developed more than a tolerance of coffee. During the many stops during their slow-paced drive across America, he'd learned to spot the cheerful green mermaid of his favorite coffee franchise and steer toward it. He was now as big an addict as her. She sat on the edge of the bed and grasped his hand. "Are you nervous about going to work?"

The way he immediately turned his attention toward a blank wall betrayed his true feelings.

"There's no need. You're a department asset."

"I feel like a fraud."

She reached for the stack of professionally forged documents — passport, driver's license, social security card, and even numerous academic degrees from foreign universities, waiting to be framed. Tyr had spent thousands of dollars on the highest quality forgeries he could attain, but he was no fake. Throughout the centuries, he'd acquired a great deal of wealth, so money had been no obstacle setting up a paper trail to back them up. A casual online search could easily confirm his new identity: Tyr Dacian, aged thirty-five.

"I'm twenty-eight." He balked. "Not thirty-five."

"Is that what you're worried about? I thought you were regretting taking *Dacian* as your official surname."

His eyes flashed. "Never!"

"For the degrees you claimed to earn and all the things you've done with your life, thirty-five is more believable." She touched his face. "Besides, becoming a human again has put some city-miles on you."

Tyr's nostrils flared. "Is that bad?"

His face had weathered and added a few lines but the effects could have been from the bad sunburn acquired on a hike through the Grand Canyon. She kissed his cheek. "No."

Standing straight, he drew his shoulders back and thrust his chest forward as if he were standing in full armor, sword in hand, before a cheering crowd in the arena. "I'm ready for the research job. I want all my years of experience to mean something and be useful to someone. I don't care about preserving every detail of history's battles, even though I have the most knowledge in those areas. I'd like to teach people how others lived, not how they died. So many small but important things have gotten lost along the way. I think I could do the most good in that department."

In the morning light, he looked so handsome; a blond titan ready to take on academia. Each day with Tyr got better. Just when she thought her heart had reached its limits, she found yet another reason to love him more. "I think you're right." His offered his hand. A beautiful softness lit his eyes from within. "Come here, love. Lie with me."

Shaking her head, she smiled. "We'll be late."

"No, we won't." Rising from the bed, he led her into the bathroom. "This is going to be a quickie in the shower. We'll save water and time. Tell me that's not a great idea."

Twirling her hair into a topknot, she followed. Experience had taught her that arguing with a stubborn Dacian was a complete waste of time. "It's a great idea."

He turned on the faucet. Within moments the water warmed and steamy mist fogged the mirrors. "I'll always think of that first shower with you."

She tugged a well-worn Radiohead T-shirt that doubled as pajamas over her head. Tossing it into a clothes hamper, she stood naked beside him. "I wonder if the bed-and-breakfast we *illegally trespassed* and decapitated a man in has opened for business."

He shrugged. "I just hope they washed the bedding."

"No shit."

Taking hold of her hand, Tyr led her into the shower stall. A cascade of pulsing warm water rained down on them. He cupped the sides of her face and kissed her mouth. His soft lips glided against hers. "I love you," he whispered.

Tangling her fingers in his damp hair, she returned his kiss. "I love you, too." It surprised her how easy it was to say it and mean it.

He pressed her firmly against the wet tiles, steam rising. "I promise I'll take my time with you tonight." His broad hands grasped her ass and lifted her to his hip level with ease. She wrapped her legs around his hips, clutching his shoulders like a life raft.

"That's better." A mischievous grin lit his face. His cock prodded between her thighs. Tyr's solid chest brushed her breasts. Now wet and shiny, her nipples looked larger than usual. She wished they were cuddled in bed where he could suck and gently play with her like he did late at night. With ease, she guided him inside her.

He thrust slowly. She closed her eyes, surrendering to the sensations of his heavy arms holding her up, protecting and adoring her. No man had ever made her feel so safe. All movement was caring but a powerful ferocity lurked beneath. Skin to skin they slid against each other. His gruff breath near her ear and faster motions alerted her he was close to climax. Every muscle tensed as he thrust deep inside her and stilled. "Arcona," he moaned, and it gave her chills every time he cried her name at that crucial moment.

She kissed his mouth, biting gently on his bottom lip. The sexy sound of his ragged breath as he came down always turned her on. "You owe me."

"I'm yours all night. I promise."

Smiling, she knew he meant it.

They stayed pressed to the tiles a few moments longer before the water started to cool. Each quickly soaped and rinsed.

The first out of the shower, Tyr grabbed a towel and strode into the bedroom to dress.

She moved at her own pace, her body still on fire and wanting more. After patting herself dry, she shut the bathroom door and reached for a small box set inconspicuously behind a stack of towels. The slender lilac carton was labeled First to Know.

Quietly she ripped open the top of the box and removed a plastic wand with a tiny window on the tip, sat down on the toilet and peed on it. Shaking it off, she set the wand on the countertop on a tissue and brushed her teeth. The temptation to look was tremendous, but she resisted until enough time had passed.

Only after wrapping herself in a plush bathrobe and combing her hair did she look at the wand. Two distinct purple lines showed clearly in the window. "Yes!" she shouted.

Tyr rapped his knuckles on the bathroom door. "Everything okay?"

Arcona opened the door to a stunning sight. Tyr stood tall and elegant in charcoal gray trousers and a crisp white shirt, looking like an upscale ad for men's cologne. His wavy hair was sleeked away from his face. "You clean up good."

A brilliant smile crinkled the tiny lines around his eyes. "Thanks."

"Guess what. You're going to get two new jobs today."

"Really? Historical research partner, and what's the other job?"

She pulled the plastic wand from behind her back. "Your other new job title is—Dad. You're going to be a father."

"Me?" He fell silent. His smile faded.

Time stretched while she held her breath.

He shook his head. "You're not joking? This is real?"

"No joke." She offered the wand for his inspection. "This is the second positive test in a row."

"Holy Mother Nerthus! This is wonderful." He scooped her into his arms and spun around the bedroom until they were both laughing and dizzy.

Author's Note

I took liberties with the description of Pompeii's amphitheater. The amphitheater was built in approximately 70 BC, almost 150 years before it was partially destroyed by Vesuvius's catastrophic eruption in August of 79 AD. Buried in ash, but otherwise intact, the amphitheater remains the world's oldest standing arena.

Pompeii's amphitheater was constructed in the Greek style, which favored a fairly shallow earthwork dug into the ground. Only a balustrade and a drop of two meters separated the audience from the action below. Viewers seated too near the rim faced grave danger from hurled weapons and wild beasts. Unlike later Roman arenas, Pompeii's arena contained no underworld of dungeons, animal cages, elevators, painted scenery, and even sophisticated hydraulic systems. The amphitheater's only subterranean chamber is a corridor that runs continuously around the ellipse.

This is a work of fiction, and for the sake of drama, I added an underworld to Pompeii's arena to reflect what Roman audiences in 79 AD would have expected in a well-funded gladiatorial show.

Katalina Leon.

Want more sexy paranormal adventure?
Coming Soon
Claimed by Dragons

If you enjoyed *The Strix*, you'll love Devon's crazy adventure in *Claimed by Dragons*. Dame Bishop and Witch Casey are at it again. Devon's wish stone leads her to a forbidden cave on Kilimanjaro and delivers not one but two sexy dragon shifters into her life. But when professional dragon hunters make a move, the new threesome must band together and fight for their lives.

Katalina Leon.

Author's Bio

Katalina Leon is an artist and author who can't commit to a single romance subgenre. Her favorite playgrounds are historical, Sci-fi, contemporary, and most of all paranormal realms. Lately, she has paranormal romance and vampires on the brain. Katalina brings a sense of adventure and a touch of the mystical to romance. She believes there's a daring heroine inside every woman who wants to take a wild ride with a strong worthy hero.

Claimed by Dragons, coming soon, and *Lord Griffin's Prize*, part of *Emerald Isle Enchantment*, available October 2016.

Look for these other titles available now:
Vampire Picnic: Ravenscroft
Wild Cards, Charmed in Vegas book 5
Star Crossed, Boxed Set
MacBrun, Bearly a Nip
Bite of the Moon, Boxed Set
Hoodoo Blue, Sorcery by the Sea book 1
Forsaken Realms, Bounty Hunters United book 1
The Virgin and Her Wolf, 1Night Stand series, Audible, coming soon.
Dark Sky
Uncaged, Black Hills Wolves Book 25, Audible coming soon.
Portrait of a Lone Wolf, Black Hills Wolves book 7, Audible coming soon.
Claimed by Dragons

Lord Griffin's Prize
Emerald Isle Enchantment, Boxed Set

www.ingramcontent.com/pod-product-compliance
Lightning Source LLC
Chambersburg PA
CBHW032130190626
46814CB00005BA/1639